The Wolves of Pilovo

Thomas Coohill

Nature Fiction Publishing
Loudonville, New York
2006

For

Patricia

Joseph

Thomas

Matthew

and all my Russian friends

©2006 Thomas Coohill

All rights reserved. Printed in the United States of America. No part of this book may be used or reproduced in any manner whatsoever without written permission except in the case of brief quotations embodied in critical articles or reviews.

Cover Art By Barbara Fugate
www.barbarafugate.com

Russian Names

At the time of this event, and in a village as small as Pilovo, almost all of the people would have had the same surname. Therefore, they were never used. Even the Christian names would have been very similar or identical. For variety the people would add little descriptive adjectives to the first name. For example, Peter would normally be called by the nickname Pet'ya. Other Peters might be called Pet'ya-dlinnyi (tall), or Pet'ya-kosoi (squint-eyed), or Pet'ya-maloi (junior).

I have chosen to use first names that are more familiar to an English-speaking audience. I have also varied the surnames for easier identification of the characters.

In many places I used the Russian convention for nicknames; Russians usually use the last part of a name, or how the last part is pronounced, for the nickname. Nikolai is Kolai; Alexander is Sasha.

Also, to make it closer to the true pronunciation, I have sometimes slightly changed a name. For example, Alla should really be Alya, and Peter, Petr. I think it makes for an easier read.

Russian villagers almost never used terms of endearment. So you won't see many "Dears" here either. A peasant would express emotion by voice inflection, changing the pronunciation of a name to show affection. That can't be done in writing.

Cast

Families:

Karpov: Ivan, Anna, Misha, little Ivan, and Uncle Pasha
Zobov: Sergi, Manja, Sonya, and Grandma
Pavlovsky: Sasha, Alla, Alexi, Gregor, and Peter
Kovalev: Vlad, Elena, Timor, and Tonya
Buckavev: Fedor, Luba, Dasha, and Natasha

Others:

Pavel Vavilin, Party leader
Romanov, old bachelor
Yuri and Karl, village bachelors
Beatrice, old widow
Yakov, blind man
Stephan Volkov
Nicholas (Kolai) Mendelev, Soviet Army pilot, and various other soldiers

Wolves:

Maala and Tuva, alpha pair
Vaal and Seena
Reina and Vorna
Loka and Kaala
Mogla, Unal, Sana, and Bunta

The Wolves of Pilovo

1

Pilovo, Siberia
Winter, 1927

Sergi called for the vote. That Pasha was guilty was obvious; that was not the question. He had molested the Karpov girl twice, observed the second time by Tonya Kovalev as she hid in the barn. She wondered why Misha had not resisted more; but Misha was in a trance-like state; afraid to deny her uncle; sure that what he was doing was wrong. She hoped it would end and no one would find out; her parents would punish her for this. But Tonya told Sonya, who told Dasha, who told her mother, Luba, and she told Fedor, who told Ivan Karpov, who, in spite of his brother-in-law's protestations, called for a council. Pasha, his hands bound behind him, sweating from the fear of the certain verdict, tried at first to turn the discussion to the scene of an uncle showing tender concern for his upset niece. It didn't work. Pasha had been suspected of this type of thing before; only now was the evidence in hand. The men looked at him with disgust, no pity in their glances. Why had he not married? Why did he not show affection to the widows? Why had he chosen little girls, even his own niece? The men raised their hands.

Pasha, sent outside to stand in the snow, awaited the inevitable sentence. He thought of running away. Perhaps he could find a way out of his bondage, overpower Karl, who was guarding him, and make for the woods. If he beat the messengers to the other villages, he could move on ahead of the story and maybe make it to a city where he could fall into obscurity and start again. Start what? He knew the urge to do the same thing would overcome his intent to keep pure. It always did. It was something beyond his control, beyond his reason, beyond his hope. Maybe he should kill himself, forget the Church's ban on suicide, cleanse his family from the curse of his presence.

The side door slammed open. Sasha motioned to Karl to bring Pasha; the jury waited. Once inside, Pasha was forced to his knees in front of the arc of men filling the back of the room.

Sergi spoke, "You will be punished in the traditional way. Should you live, you will be given a chance to prove to us that you have changed. Should you die, God's punishment will rid you of the torment that would await you in the afterlife. Beg for forgiveness from God; we will show you justice."

Pasha was yanked to his feet and led out the door, his hands still bound behind his back. The whole village, including the children, were watching. Only the men and the mothers would follow the group into the forest. It was enough for the others to know what awaited Pasha. A fair trial by torture, deserved, final in its judgment. The village would be satisfied no matter which way it came out.

The walk was about a third of a mile, but due to the deep snow on the trail and the stumbling Pasha, it took almost twenty minutes. Two men went ahead into the small clearing and sawed a cut in the pine tree four feet above the snow. Sap oozed out from the interior, dripping an inch down the trunk before it froze. The assembly arrived.

Pasha was forced to his knees, his face almost touching the tree. Sergi stepped forward, opened the buttons on the front of Pasha's coat, pulled the coat over Pasha's shoulders and down his back, pinning his arms and exposing his chest. The men pulled back the trunk above the cut by drawing in the rope attached to the lower limbs; the cut opened a few inches. Sergi and Sasha forced Pasha's head forward so that his beard slid into the cut. The men eased off on the rope, the trunk snapped back, pinning the beard. A little blood flowed from Pasha's chin and nose, where the bark had scratched him.

Sasha passed around a pouch of salt, each villager tossing a pinch over their left shoulder. Then they retreated. It was not proper to watch a man in this agony. They would know the outcome when, or if, Pasha returned to the village. That was enough, it was out of their hands. A few of the men wagered on the result.

Once alone, Pasha knew his choices. Without his coat he would freeze to death in half an hour. If he could summon courage and strength, he could pull the beard out of his face and survive. He backed his head away slowly, feeling the tension build on his chin. When he reached the limit of his stretched skin he stopped. Already the pain had started, and not only on his face. His wrists had been tied too tight, and the lack of circulation in his hands made them stiffen and chill. He might not have the half hour he thought.

Girding himself for the pain, Pasha tried to pull harder. It hurt, but did not work; the beard held. He pulled hard again, tears rolling down his cheeks and freezing on his beard. Nothing. With a cry he pulled even harder; it was not possible.

He had to think. Yes, there was only one way to pull the beard from his face. He brought his chin flush with the trunk, held his breath, then quickly jerked his head backward. He almost passed out from the pain, but he felt a few hairs go. This was the way. He waited a bit to catch his courage, put his chin against the tree again and yanked back with all of his might; more hair came out, the blood spilling now as the skin tore from his face.

He had to keep conscious; to keep his will together; to see this through. Already his chest was cold, his fingers numb. He begged God for forgiveness, for another chance, for the courage to do this and live again in the village, for help in changing his ways. He bent forward again, more than half his beard still in the tree. He let loose a guttural moan and jerked back hard. The right side of his face gave way and the beard sprung out, flopping onto the trunk. He was almost free! One more pull and he fell backward, onto his frozen hands. The pain shot up through his arms and back; something had broken.

Pasha rolled to his side. He slid forward, to the tree, pushing with his knees and leaned against the trunk. Through his tears, he could see the remains of his beard hanging in the cut, blood covered and already frozen, pieces of skin among the hairs. He slid his face against the tree and tried to stand, tearing his shirt and face. With great effort he made it. He was erect, leaning on the tree.

The numbness was up to his elbows, his chest was already freezing, his face opened and painful, his neck exposed. He could not fall again if he hoped to make it in time. Slowly, to keep his wits, he turned and started for the village. He kept his legs splayed outward, to give him better balance, and made sure that one foot was secure on the snow before he threw the other one forward. The movement sent warming blood to his extremities, except to his bound hands. Every effort was to keep from falling, to keep moving forward, keep focused on the path to the village. The cold sliced at his neck and face, tearing at his raw chin; his chest was almost brittle, his back starting to numb. Only his legs kept functioning, propelling him down the path toward the warmth and safety of the village. He knew how long it had taken to get up the path, he would have to be quicker going down.

As he moved through the snow, he kept up a steady prayer for help. Part of him wanted to give up, to drop to the snow and let the frost lull him to sleep, to end the agony. Maybe that would be better. But still he tried, seeing his breath waft into the air, showing him that he was still alive. He pushed on.

Pasha kept his head down to shield his neck and to make sure he stayed on the path. He tried not to slip, to keep to the snow covered part, to avoid the places the villagers had pounded down before. That part was slick, trouble. Sometimes he strayed too close to the trees, sometimes too close to the uncovered ice. Still he stumbled on.

Pasha raised his head, he had gone almost a quarter of a mile, more than halfway home. As he looked in the distance, he saw movement to his right. He turned, as best he could, and saw the wolves, four of them, watching. They didn't respond to Pasha's frightened stare, but kept their jaws open, tongues partly out, steamed breath pulsing from their mouths. Each wolf's glare focused on the wounded man, observing him like a curiosity, as if he could not be approached for a smell or a lick.

"My God, they will eat me! Not this!" Pasha started to call to the village, but noticed that the wolves were not moving toward him; they stayed off the path in the forest. Pasha was afraid that if he called he would excite them and they would attack. Besides, in his weakened state, would his call be heard in the village?

The sting of the wind on his neck reminded him that he had no choice. He must chance enticing the wolves by walking as fast as he could, to do otherwise would mean the certainty of a cold death.

The wolves kept up with Pasha as he moved; watching, not attacking, keeping to the woods; parallel to the path of the man; not getting closer; escorting Pasha towards the village. They bounded in small snow puffed arcs, then stopped to keep pace with the human. No wolf uttered a sound, the forest only echoed the thud of Pasha's stilted steps and the faint murmur of paws as they landed in the soft snow. The wolves disappeared at times into the trees, but, always, reappeared no further off than before.

Pasha tried to go faster, feeling the cold driving deeper into his flesh. His left foot went out for the next step and sunk into the snow. He did not see the tree root, buried near his toe. He moved his right foot, came forward on his left, and jammed his left toes against the root. He pitched face first into the snow, a muffled cry coming from his frozen lips.

The wolves stopped, no more than thirty yards away. They waited for him to move again.

Pasha tried to gauge his situation. Dying from the frost, wolves nearby, strength gone. He rolled toward the path. No, he must roll toward the tree for leverage to get up again. His legs were failing him, weak, ineffective as his energy ebbed away. He again thought to call to the villagers, but he knew they would be inside, waiting to see if he would return. They would not, could not, help him.

He lay less than 200 yards from safety; from the warmth of a fireplace; from relief from the cold; from the wonder of his family if he made it. Twenty minutes had passed and his hands were frozen hard, his progress stopped. He knew he would die. He could not raise himself; his legs seemed severed from his body. Maybe this was better; maybe this was right. He wouldn't have to live in shame: God would forgive him. The cold began to feel good, cutting off his pain. The forest seemed peaceful. He forgot about the wolves. He made a last effort to turn over and face upwards. He didn't want to die with his face in the snow.

Pasha blinked at the bright light coming through the trees. Filtered by his tears, it gave a soft glow to the needles of the fir trees and the branches of the birch. He laughed at his problem, saw in his misery the end to his suffering. Maybe this was as it was ordained to be; maybe this was his destiny; maybe his suffering would save him.

"Please God, forgive me," he murmured. "I was not always a bad man. I know I was wrong. Let me come to you."

The wolves looked for any movement from the man lying near them. He seemed to be dying, his short breaths coming slower now. Then he fell asleep without breathing, his frozen face staring upward. The lead wolf jerked his head backwards, the signal for retreat. The others followed him toward the pack.

The frozen body, lying in the trees, would be seen by the villagers later in the day when they went back up the trail. Sasha thought, "He almost made it; may he rest in peace."

No one noticed the wolf tracks further off in the forest.

2

Friday, December 16th

Flying low over the vast terrain of Siberia, one sees forest unending. In winter, the glare from the snow blanches out the white of the birches that fill the lesostep region in the middle latitudes of the western part of "The Sleeping Land." The glint of a forest lake, the light from a twisting river, draws the eye away from the green cover and to the open cuts that run in straight lines from the water sources into the woods. At the intersections of some cuts, or at the ends of others, a small opening would show the hand of man. Nestled in one such opening was the village of Pilovo.

Sasha Pavlovsky hurried toward the village, to arrive home before twilight. He had walked to the cabin of Oleg, the forest man, bringing him cakes and bees wax to help in the winter ahead. He cursed softly at himself for allowing the old man's tales to keep him so late. The temperature was dropping with the dying sun and tree shadows covered the path. A quarter of a mile from the houses, Sasha saw the slim figure of what he thought was Dimitry's dog pass across the path and into the trees. As he went by this spot he called, "Penji, Penji," to the dog, but it did not come.

When Sasha came to the turn near the place where the path headed down to the village, he saw the dog again. This time the animal stayed in the path and turned towards the man. Sasha started to call the name again but stopped. This wasn't Penji, the ears were too short, the raised hair too long, the teeth in the curled black mouth too large.

Sasha stopped and stared. Unal, the speckled wolf, faced the man, began a low growl, raised her tail, fixed her pale brown eyes on the human, and set herself to spring.

Sasha looked to each side to see if a stick was handy, all the stones were buried in the snow. He saw a short piece of branch and moved cautiously toward it, bending slightly to pick it up with his right hand. The wolf's eyes followed him. With the weapon secure in his grasp, Sasha began a slow turn to his left, keeping the stick thrust outward, toward the wolf. Unal turned with him.

Now off the trail and in the trees, Sasha kept moving ahead and left, trying to circle the wolf and get between it and the village. The animal backed down the trail never taking its gaze from the man.

Sasha had the twin problem of keeping the wolf at bay and trying to step backwards through the forest without taking his eyes of the animal. He waved the stick and shouted, "Go away! Go away!"

The wolf made a short run at the man, testing his weakness. Sasha darted to his left, caught a small rock with his foot, and stumbled backward, losing sight of the wolf as he fell in the snow. The wolf now ran straight at him, bounding the few remaining yards. When she was about eight feet away, she sprang.

Sasha recovered from the fall and was just getting up again when the wolf hit him in the chest. The force of the blow drove both of them against a tree, the wolf trying to bite Sasha's neck. Sasha braced his left forearm against the animal's throat, and tried to beat the wolf with the stick, but the short little blows on her back had no effect. He shoved his forearm harder against the wolf's neck, forcing her head up and back. Slowly, to control the wolf, he brought his right hand up and above his face, positioning the stick across the wolf's mouth. The wolf snapped her jaws open and closed, attempting to bite, as Sasha maneuvered the stick into position. When the jaws opened again, he thrust the stick in sideways, forcing it to the back of the jaw, the wolf's lips straddling it on either side.

Unal champed down on the stick, breaking it in half. Sasha's hand, holding half of the stick, slid down the side of the wolf's head, ripping her ear. Now his right hand was pushing the wolf's head to the left, away from his face, but the strength of the wolf's neck forced it back. For seconds man and wolf looked directly at each other. Sasha knew he could not hold the wolf's head for long, so he dropped the stick and grabbed at the neck of the wolf with his right hand, fighting to keep her from biting his face. The strength of the animal and the awkwardness of his hold on its neck was almost beyond his strength. The she-wolf thrust again, breaking Sasha's hold and pinning him against the tree. Her head and neck drove past the frightened man, who now grabbed the back of the wolf's neck and held tightly as he hugged her to his body.

Both arms locked around the back of the wolf's neck, Sasha felt, at first, relief. His muscles no longer ached and the hold he had on the wolf seemed more natural and easier to maintain. For a moment neither moved. Then the wolf began to twist and squirm, trying to break the man's hold. Sasha hugged the wolf tighter. The wolf bucked and tried to get her back legs set into Sasha's stomach, but he slid his right arm down around her back hindquarters and held tight. Now the wolf was flat against the man, their bodies as one, their heads side by side, giving the wolf no place to attack.

Unal was already weakening. It had been two weeks since her last meal and her strength was almost gone. The only reason she was near the village of the humans was to find easy prey, but this man was too strong for her. She moved her jaw to the right, trying to bite the man's face, but it was no use, her head was being held too far back over the man's shoulder.

Sasha felt the wolf's mouth at the side of his neck. He knew if he could hold her like this she would be unable to bite him, but he also knew they couldn't stay in this position forever.

Only one solution seemed possible. Sasha pushed away from the tree with his back, holding tight to the wolf. The animal bucked again to break the hold but couldn't. Sasha took a few steps forward. He compensated for the weight of the wolf by leaning backward a little as he walked, trying to achieve a balance so he wouldn't fall. Gradually he found a pace that allowed him to imprison the wolf in his hold yet go forward. He was now back on the trail, headed for the village.

The wolf's breath panted in Sasha's ear, the smell of rancid teeth reaching his nose, drops of saliva dripping down his neck, underneath his collar. Her breathing was heavy but slow, her legs splayed around Sasha's trunk. Here was a 195 pound man, stumbling down the trail with a 90 pound wolf in his arms, neither knowing what would come next.

Unal relaxed for a moment. She needed to regroup her strength to fight this man, or at least to get away. But Sasha didn't loosen his grip, he had to hold the wolf tight and hope he could walk all the way to the village.

At this time of day, and in this cold, no one was outside when Sasha came down the trail. He headed for Dimitry's home, knowing that the blacksmith would have an axe inside. When he reached the door, he banged against it with his forearms, never letting his head move from it's position locked with the wolf.

Dimitry's wife opened the door. "My God! A wolf! Dimitry, come, come!"

Penji barked, and backed further away in the room, frightened of the wolf smell.

"Hold the dog!" shouted Dimitry, as he grabbed his axe and ran to the door.

The two men talked over the wolf, planning how to kill it, Penji yelping in the background. Dimitry's wife took the hot poker from the fire and held it in front of her. Unal yelped.

Sasha stepped back a few paces so that Dimitry could get outside, close the door and have room to swing his axe.

"Now," Dimitry shouted.

Sasha let go of the wolf and jumped backwards. Unal, startled, hit the ground and bounded off to the left. Dimitry brought his axe down in a wild swing, missing the wolf and pinning the axe in the ground through the snow and ice. He wrestled to pull it out, but the wolf was gone, out of the village, into the woods.

Sasha limped back and rested against the door.

"Next time you bring me food, kill it first," said Dimitry.

Sasha was exhausted, his weak smile belying his pent up fear. He followed Dimitry into the house, waiting to catch his breath before he answered their questions.

3

Canus Lupus

Maala sat down on his haunches, straightened his powerful neck, threw back his grey head, and throated a plaintive howl up into the cold sky. Tuva, at his side, scanned the distance, looking for signs of other packs. They had chosen the top of the hill, raising themselves above the surrounding trees, allowing the cry to carry over the taiga.

Two miles away, Vaal, the black wolf, heard the call. He wondered if he should answer. This sounded like a large male, even larger than he. Should he ignore this and continue as he was? No, these were bad times, his pack needed help, just as this wolf's cry showed he needed help.

Vaal yelped a local call to his pack mates. When they assembled, he began the whining sounds that transformed the dominant command of his call into the signal for discussion. He asked the hungry pack for reasons to question the distant call they had heard. The pack remained silent, sensing they had no other option but to reply to the howl that had come to them through the trees.

"We will answer," Vaal said. He then raised his head and returned Maala's call in a series of stacatto replies.

"Yes, we are coming," they said. "We are coming."

Maala continued to call, keeping a steady rate of two howls per minute for almost one hour. Between calls, he listened as other packs joined in the response, the woods chorusing their replies, the taiga alive with the sounds. Packs assembled, their leaders instructing them by sounds and gestures to follow. Each alpha male led the way through the deep snow, making a path for the others, the followers stepping into his pawprints, each as large as a curled human hand, as they moved single file through the forest. An inexperienced tracker would have thought that a lone wolf had made the trail, so exact was the order of the pack. From above, an eagle saw the lines of wolves moving over the terrain, radiating inward toward the spot where Maala waited. She followed, hoping for the remains of a meal.

Vaal's pack, the closest, arrived first. He saw, as he suspected from the call, that Maala was a magnificent male, over six feet long, weighing 165 pounds. He had all the markings of an alpha male; the multicolored fur that would glow grey in the moonlight; the black piping around the eyes, eyebrows, ears, nose and rimming the jaws, that would emphasize his gestures as he ordered the pack to act. His mouth was fringed in white, to highlight the black piping; the tan backing covering much of the fur behind his head also accented the darker stripes of blackened fur that ridged his back and extended along his tail. The dark fur of his guard hairs straddled his spine, cradling his barrel chest. His soft undercoat was full, to ward off the frost. He would be the largest wolf sighted that year in all of Russia.

Vaal sensed that he would have to submit to Maala, but protocol required that he try to assert his dominance. He growled, curled back his lips, bared his teeth at Maala, snapping quick bites in the air to show his ferocity. Maala raised himself to his full height and barked a reply.

"Brother, we are all in trouble. I will lead, you will help."

They circled in a display, each making darting moves toward the other, the packs awaiting the outcome. Maala feigned a retreat, then rushed Vaal, catching him at the side of the neck and tossing him into the snow. They exchanged mild bites, Maala straddling the fallen Vaal. Suddenly Vaal went limp, laid on his back, and licked the underside of Maala's mouth.

Maala twitched his left ear forward and squinted his yellow-green eyes at the rest of Vaal's pack. None of them dared question this signal; they accepted his right of dominance. He bared his forty-two teeth by retracting his snout into a snarl, the display being more of an attempt to deter aggression than to express his obvious strength. He had no reason to kill or maim any of this pack if they followed him. He needed their help to find prey.

It was the same with each of the other packs as they arrived. Maala would subjugate the alpha male, restating the fact that he would lead the growing assemblage. This first night would see the pack increase to fifty-eight members, each knowing that many of them would be dead before spring unless they could find a new source of game. The alpha males formed a large circle, touching noses and wagging tales, a show of togetherness.

Maala stood apart on a little hillock, facing the packs.

"Welcome my brothers. We have only seen each other when we compete for the same game. I know you are all good hunters, as are we. But even a good hunter grows desperate when there is no quarry. The elk have moved too far north, the deer are scant, the boars stay in their burrows, and the rabbits hide and wait for the spring. Even the mice huddle against the cold and remain inside. How long can we live on berries and nuts?"

He paused; only the alpha males and females would respond.

"We are starving," said Vaal. "Our bones are bared on our chests and our legs grow weak even in a short run. The pups die after they are born, their mother's milk dry. We have to regain our strength before we become too sick to pursue our prey. We cannot wait."

Other pack members joined in with stories of failed hunts, diseased prey, cold so bitter that each breath stung. A keen observer could read the signals as the wolves communicated. The tails assuming various positions; up, down, straight back, bent down in mid-tail; the combinations signifying intent. The observer would also see the variety of body moves; facial expressions; movements of the eyes, ears and nose; positioning of the head; slight hunching of the shoulders and the neck; changes in the position of the legs and in the manner in which each wolf stood erect or groveled near the ground.

They asked Maala what he planned to do.

"I called you for a reason. You know of tales of winters like this, when our ancestors shivered and died. You know that sometimes they survived these times. We may be able to survive also," spoke Maala

Seena, Vaal's mate, rose, shook the snow off her pelt, and called to Maala, "How will we do this? Have you not seen your pack grow thin? Do you think the game will return? The days are turning colder, we have many months to wait for the thaw."

Maala barked. "I am not a fool. I would not have called for you if I did not have a plan. You would not have been summoned if I could carry out this plan with just my own pack. The legends tell us that when we are starving we put aside our loyalty to separate packs and form a Great Hannal. In a hannal we must forget our differences and track and kill together. When the crisis passes the hannal will break and we become one with our pack mates again. We can no longer rely on the game we catch, we have to adapt. Some of you already know that easy prey exist near the places where humans live. Dogs, horses, goats, sometimes sheep. These animals are slow, weak, not used to battle. They fight confused; they whine; they are cowards. They are no match for a lone wolf, and helpless when confronted with a pack."

"Why do you need us?", asked Reina, his pack assembled around him.

"Because of their masters. Humans protect their animals, they have weapons, they are cunning."

Vorna, Reina's female, spoke next. "How do we avoid these humans? They will not let us take their stock. They will kill us if we try."

"Not if we confuse them," replied Maala. "A hannal, such as this, can attack from all sides, can frighten the humans for awhile, can keep them at bay until we are well fed."

Maala pointed out the strengths and weaknesses of the humans, and how the wolves could benefit from human faults. He reminded them of the poor sense of smell that humans seemed to have; how they could be followed at close range as long as they had no sight line to the wolves; how they could not run far or for long in their thick winter pelts; how they panicked when they had no weapons; how weak they were compared to an animal that has to kill to survive. But he also told them of human power, to beware of human toughness, their cooperation in hunts, their relentless pursuit of game, their obsession with revenge, their weapons.

He told them how he watched the humans in the nearby village injure and then desert one of their own, leaving him to die in the cold.

"How do you know these things," asked Seena.

"When I was young my father told me of the great wolf Demja. At a time when wolves all over this land were dying of starvation, he formed a hannal and attacked the villages of the Kurins."

"I know that story," said Reina. "Demja and his hannal were followed and killed by the humans."

"Yes," said Maala. "But we can learn from their mistakes and survive."

"What mistakes?" asked Loka.

Demja's pack killed humans. Humans will fight to defend their animals and kill us if they can, but they will track us forever if we kill even one of them. They are not like us, they do not call off the hunt when it is going bad, they continue, even if they may die themselves. And there are many of them, an endless number that keep coming until they finish the prey. They will never rest until we are dead and they are satisfied. So we will not attack them. Once we have our fill of their animals, we will leave this place and these humans, and find other animals in other villages to feed us later."

The wolves wondered if Maala were right. Could they take the human's stock and not feel their wrath? What other alternative did they have?

Vaal spoke, "I am with Maala. Better to try this than to die slowly at the hands of winter."

The reluctant alphas signed agreement.

4

Saturday Morning, December 17th

"You're no better than barbarians," snapped Pavel Vavilin. "A mock trial and a cruel execution of a man based only on the testimony of a little girl."

"Pasha was guilty," said Sergi. "If you were part of the village you would know. We understand each other, we know how to handle our affairs."

"Who would choose to be like you?" Pavel shouted. "You continue as you are, locked in the past like dead men! Can't you see that the Revolution changed us? Pasha should have had a fair trial and, if found guilty, a humane punishment."

"Humane?" Cried Sergi. "You call the wars humane? How many died to create your State? How many will you kill to preserve it?"

"You talk like an fool, Zubov," replied Pavel. "Now that the Whites have been defeated we can cease the killings. Now is the time to reap the fruit of our ordeal."

"And what will you substitute for our councils?" asked Sergi.

"Rules! And fair judgments for all as the State orders. No quick opinions from those caught up in the heat of the thing. A chance to redeem oneself," said Pavel.

"Pasha was judged by God," said Sergi. "Can the State improve on that?"

Pavel knew it was useless. Sergi was the village leader and the people looked to him for guidance. And, to tell the truth, Pavel Vavilin cared little about the life and people of Pilovo, the village he had been assigned to by the Party. Born in Moscow, Pavel had no interest in rural communities, and even less in Siberia. In 1924, he had been sent to this small village as part of the plan to convert the peasants to the new Soviet system. There were no clear guidelines on how best to accomplish this, and many villagers had little interest in complying. He had only convinced a few to join the Party, and they did it more out of compliance than conviction. With little power, and less influence, his job seemed meaningless. He became despondent. Why had he not been assigned to at least a town, or someplace less remote than this village?

Pavel was of medium height with a thin oblong face. His cheeks were drawn in, causing his mouth to thrust forward in a continual pout. He had sharp features below narrow eyes, and looked somewhat like a young Lenin, a comparison he liked to evoke. Always a fine dresser, not that it would count for much in a backward village, Pavel kept himself spotless, from the top of his short hair and trim beard, down to his filed and cleaned fingernails. He looked more like a banker than a "people's worker" and a veteran of the wars. He had to report to the Party leaders only once every season.

But Pavel knew better than to complain. If he wanted to get out of Pilovo he must earn a new posting. He walked away from Sergi to his small hut and leaned back against the outside wall, abandoning himself to reverie, trying to forget his troubles. But Pilovo was the here and now.

"Party Leader Vavilin," shouted Karl, coming, as he always did, to curry Pavel's favor. "How are you this fine day?"

"What's so fine about today or any other day in this God forsaken place?" Pavel said, blowing breath into his cupped gloves to help ward off the freezing temperature.

"God? Who is that?" teased Karl.

"Don't bother me, Karl," sneered Pavel. "I have little time for your jokes or your pandering. Tell me how to get these villagers to accept the Party, then you can be my friend."

"Oh, that's simple. Give them something. Show them that the Party will make their life better. That is the way to the peasant heart."

Pavel looked away. He was in no mood for Karl or any other of these country folk. Just look at this place, he thought, it hasn't changed since the last century - the houses painted in garish colors, useless ornate eaves cluttering up the window frames – a waste of time when they could have been doing something useful for themselves or for others. Their devotion to the village church, their reliance on God to provide. What they needed was a good dose of the world outside this forest. Then they would know that power protects, that in numbers there is strength, that when it matters, a man must belong to something.

But no! Here the people made the monotony of their life their solace. Spending their time making trinkets and colorful clothes. How boring it was.

"How can I change them when they are content in their ignorance and misery?" Pavel mused. "My God, they suit their surroundings!"

He went back inside his hut, mostly to get out of the cold, but also to cut off the conversation with Karl. The days were already very short, and the depression that always seeped into his mind when the days waned was starting to gnaw at him again.

By now, the start of the winter of 1927, people were already prepared for the bleak weather. The harvest had been bad this fall, due to the late spring, and the heavy summer rains that rotted the crops in the field. Food would be scare and what was in the larders now did not portend a festive season. But the villagers approached this problem with the stoic shrugs and dismissals that they always made to see it through to the next summer. Too compliant to complain. At least in the cities you could place the blame on others: the farmers had failed, the trucks were delivering things late, the Party planning was wrong. But peasants blamed themselves for their misfortune, and looked to God for solace.

"Well, let God feed them this winter," mused Pavel. "Maybe He'll send manna from heaven," he sneered, thinking it would disappear into the snow.

On his way home, Karl passed Manja Zubov. "My palm itches. What does it mean?" he called.

"Right hand you get money; left hand you give it," she said.

Timor Kovalev was 18 and almost as tall as his father. The family began to allow him the chores usually reserved for adults, and he reveled in his new responsibilities. He was chosen to drive to Pulni to buy provisions for both the Kovalevs and the Zubovs and also for a few items for other villagers, including a present for his mother's birthday. It would be the last trip before the heavy snows set in and the roads became unpassable.

He harnessed the horse to the sleigh in the barn, hefting the big collar over its head, and securing the reins through the openings at the sides. He knew he had to tighten it properly to prevent any undue strain on the horse's neck and shoulders. He opened the barn doors and trotted the horse to the path. It was 8:30 am and the sun was just rising in the trees. Timor wanted to drive the sleigh now, in a hurry to be an adult with an adult's mission. He was dressed in his long coat, fur hat, and warmest gloves. The drive to Pulni would take about two hours. Then he would need at least three more hours to pick up everything on his list and give the shopman the bowls and furs his parents used for barter. He was to leave for home before 1:30 pm to avoid darkness. This was more than the other boys his age had done; what a story he would have to tell tomorrow. In his excitement he started off, and left the barn doors open.

Timor took the main trail toward Pulni, keeping to a steady trot, not tiring the horse. The sky was overcast, and Timor could see the horse's breath coming in bursts as her powerful legs pounded the ground. The sleigh bells tinkled as the cab slid along the rutted frozen track. The village dissolved slowly behind him as the sleigh entered the woods. He reached Pulni at 10:30 am.

The excitement of being in a town without his parents kept Timor from minding his time. He saw a beautiful red sash that would look fine on Sonja Zubov and asked the storekeeper the price.

"One and a half rubles," was the reply.

Timor asked if there was a way he could work for the sash.

"You can have it if you chop six cords of wood," said the shopkeeper.

"Can I do some now and some when I come again in eight weeks?"

"You're a Kovalev, so your word is good. But I want at least two cords today," said the man.

Timor went behind the shop and started chopping the long birch trunks into one meter lengths. Then he split these into four pieces each. He finished the two cords by 2:30 pm.

"It will be dark before you get home," said the shopkeeper. "Do you want to stay here tonight?"

"No, I must get home," said Timor, mindful of what his father would say if he was late with his mother's gift.

"Well, be careful," said the man.

Timor loaded the sleigh and rode out of Pulni. He was thankful that the day wasn't too cold; or was he just so excited that he was warming up his own clothes? He kept his attention forward of the horse, looking for obstacles that may have fallen across the path during the day. He was surprised at the amount of work this was. Holding the reins tight, but not too tight. Keeping the horse's head up but not jerking the reins too hard. Watching ahead. Making sure everything was all right. It was not like when his father was driving. Then it was all so casual, so easy, so rote, that the trip was almost boring. This wasn't boring. This was more like work!

He was two-thirds of the way home when the sun set. The dark forest was frightening, even to Timor, and the horse sensed it too. In less than an hour they would be home and safe

Timor saw the shape before he heard the sound. A little forward of the sleigh and to his left, he noticed the alternate shadow in the trees as it seemed to connect the trunks then disappear, connect them again and disappear, like a dotted line on a chart. Was he imagining it? No, there was more than one of these. Then came the first howl, followed by a few whines. Wolves!

Timor tried to count the wolf cries. Six, eight, maybe more. They were clearly visible to his left and maybe some to his right. He looked behind the sleigh and saw three wolves coming along the path toward him, their backs lifting and falling as they ran. His turn jerked the reins, pulling the horse's head to the left, which pitched the sleigh off the trail, almost into the trees.

"Watch out!" Peter thought. "Stay alert and keep the sleigh straight!"

The wolves were loping in long strides as they gathered closer to the sleigh. Peter tried to keep the horse going in the right direction, but she was laboring to get out of the harness. The big yoke flopped left and right as she tossed her head. Peter tried to go faster, but the terrified horse had all she could do to keep running. The wolves, now nearing the opening at the footstep of the sleigh, seemed confident that their prey was in range.

Ahead, the trail entered a large clearing where the trail to Pilovo intersected it. Quickly, Peter realized he could not slow down for this turn, but had to try and take it at near full speed. He headed the horse to the left toward the rutted track, pulled her head to the right, and turned the sleigh in a wide arc. The runners bounced in and out of the ruts as the sleigh bounded out of the path to make the turn. This threw up enough snow and ice to back the wolves off a bit and allow the turn to be finished without an attack on either the sleigh or the horse. Peter had to increase his speed or the wolves would be in the carriage and on the horse. He whipped the horse to spur her on.

She dug into the trail and started to gallop faster. The wolves fell behind. "If we can keep this pace, then maybe we can beat them home," thought Peter. He was torn between whipping her again, to make her go even faster, or trying to concentrate on making it home before she collapsed. He kept the steady pace.

The wolves kept up their pursuit. They could sense that the horse was tiring and knew they could run at this pace longer than she could. They again divided, three off to the left, two to the right, and three behind. They were gaining slowly.

Timor saw that the wolves were fresher than his horse. She was laboring heavily, wheezing with every step, and running flat out. He prayed she would make it to the village.

But the wolves knew to attack before the village. About two miles out they began. One wolf made a leap into the carriage, snarling and biting at Timor, trying to stop the sleigh so that the pack could attack the horse. But Timor kicked at his neck, catching the beast in the throat and hurling it out the front of the carriage. The left runner bounced over the wolf's body, almost overturning the sled.

Another wolf went for the horse. He bounded into the rigging and clawed his way onto the horse's back. He tried to bite into her neck; Timor lashed him with the whip. The end caught the wolf across the eyes, and he fell backward. Timor whipped furiously at the tormented animal as it stumbled off the horse and under the sleigh. The horse was veering wildly.

Timor again pulled the horse to the center of the path and whipped her to a gallop. The village was less than a mile ahead.

The wolves kept coming, their prey in view. They tried again to mount the horse and get into the wagon, but Timor kept them away with his whip. The horse was confused, hearing the cracking of the whip from all sides, not knowing which way to turn. Timor grasped the reins tighter.

"Keep going straight, girl, only a little while to the house."

The sleigh flew toward the village, the sleigh bells rung wildly as the reins slapped at the horse's back. Timor worried how he could stop and jump off the sleigh when he got to the house without being savaged by the wolves. As he turned into the final path toward his home, he saw the barn doors he had left open, and headed straight for them. The horse bolted through the open doors and reared to a stop, her head hitting the top crossbeam as the sleigh crashed into her haunches.

Timor vaulted off the sleigh and raced to the doors. He closed them both and slid the bar through the handles. Safe!

The wolves halted when they saw the lights from the houses. Maala had told them not to enter the nests of the men. They were tired from the chase and upset at missing the horse. A few more chases like this would test the last of their strength.

Timor's mother ran in through the side door. She saw her son and the frightened horse, and knew immediately they had been chased.

"Wolves," said Elena.

"Yes, mother," said Timor. "Where is father's rifle?"

"It's in the cupboard near the kitchen door, but it's not loaded. I don't know where your father keeps the shells. He's over at the Zubov's."

Timor ran to the doors and peeked out. No wolves. He waited several minutes. Nothing.

"We told you to come back before it got dark. Are you crazy to risk your life?" Elena shouted. "Why don't you listen to us? You think you are an adult? No grown man travels through the woods at night!"

Timor almost wished he had been bitten, then it would be all sympathy, not a lecture.

"I'm going to the Zubov's," he said.

"Haven't you had enough trouble for one day?" Elena asked.

"No mother, the wolves are gone, they didn't come into the village. I need to find father and see if we should follow them with the rifle."

"Please," she said. "Let them be. Night is their time, not ours."

"I'll go and ask father."

Vlad listened to his son, slowly shaking his head as the boy talked.

"I let you go alone because I thought you were smart, but you are not. Do you want to ruin your mother's party? You know how she gets."

Timor was sorry, but he was more interested in tracking the wolves.

"Not now," said Vlad. "We will never find them in the dark. Besides, it was your fault they chased you. Never go into the woods at night. You could have lost your life, the horse, everything."

Timor knew it was useless to argue. He had made a mistake, survived it, and had to accept the blame. But the story he would tell tomorrow!

5

Sunday, December 18th
The Feast of Saint Elena

It started from Manja's lips, whispers into the ear of Luba, and spread into every house, even the Pavlovsky's.

"Who's saying this," said Alla. "It's so unfair."

Sasha said, "Let it be. If you ignore a rumor it goes away."

"I hope Alexi hasn't heard, teenage boys are so sensitive."

"He knows it not true," said Sasha.

"He just needs time to pick a girl, he shouldn't be hurried," said Alla.

Some believed it. Wasn't the boy slight, with feminine features? Didn't he avoid the village girls?"

"Not a real man," said Manja.

"But he's so nice,: said Luba.

"More proof. A young man his age is arrogant, full of himself, like Timor," said Manja.

"Oh, I hope you're wrong," said Luba. Still, she told Elena, and she told Anna...

To Timor's disappointment, no one made much of his story. The adults and the older teenagers thought that Timor was impetuous and foolish and the wolves were just behaving by instinct. And, no one wanted to take away from his mother's saint's day by gossiping over a sleigh ride.

The villagers were all in or near the church, waiting for the priest to arrive. Father Mishka only visited once a month. The other holy days were handled by Ivan Karpov. Everyone was trying to put their arguments behind them, especially before father arrived.

"No more," said Sergi. "You tell Vavilin yourself, I am no go-between."

"It's your job," Ivan said. "You have to protect the village, and the Church is part of it. I don't want that Moscovite telling us when or if we can have service."

"So what? Pavel speaks but he doesn't act," said Sergi.

"Look at him over there, watching us. Who knows what he tells his comrades?" Ivan said. "These atheists will be the death of us."

"Stop exaggerating. He's harmless for now."

"What about later?"

"Later's later," said Sergi. "We have enough troubles to last us through this winter. I don't need any more headaches from you."

And Ivan had headaches enough himself. Anna was hiding at home, still bearing the disgrace of what her brother Pasha had done, and Misha was confused, avoiding her parents.

In fact, it looked like it was going to be an odd winter for everyone. First there was the wolf that attacked Sasha, so close to the village. Then there was Timor's harrowing sleigh ride, which only added to the stories Oleg had told Sasha of seeing so many wolves in the forest. And Romanov was talking again about the lack of game and the bitter cold and how it reminded him of 1897, a "wolf winter" when the starving animals entered villages. But no wolf had ever entered Pilovo, as far as anyone could remember, and people just had to be a little more careful. They shouldn't be in the woods at night, or travel alone, and they must watch out for each other and their animals.

Even the children knew that wolves shunned man, and with good reason. People had more to worry about from some crazed bear wandering in for food, or from hungry rodents eating their grain supply. Or from the cold!

The villagers filed into St. Stephan's. Anna Karpov came late, staying in back, avoiding everyone. When mass ended she hurried home alone.

Unal, the lone female, still starving and weak, saw the goat seemingly lost in the forest away from the village. She circled to the goat's left, cutting off the path of retreat, and began a slow lope toward the prey. She stopped when the goat raised her head and look at her.

The goat brayed and stepped back. He looked aside for other wolves and saw that this one was alone. But that didn't calm his shaking legs or ease his fear. He ran deeper into the woods.

The running excited Unal. Now the prey would not fight, just show his haunches and let her attack. She would be on him in a few seconds.

Unal ran toward the goat near the birch tree at her right. She heard the sound, like the snapping of a giant tree limb, before she felt the pain. In her rush she had missed seeing the trap.

The pain ran up from her leg and back from her snout. The trap caught her just above the paw and while closing, had torn the right side of her snout, snapping off two teeth and a part of her lower lip and fur. She dropped immediately, pulled down by the force of the trap and her own momentum. She lay for a minute, trying to overcome the pain.

Her breathing was heavy, mostly from the wound on her snout, but even though she pulled, the trap held her leg. She hopped about, dragging the heavy trap with her until it reached the end of its tether. The goat stood motionless, watching the wolf and wondering what to do next. Unal showed her bloody teeth to the prey. She knew she had to free herself from the trap and forget about the goat.

Unal had been warned since as far as she could remember about the snares of the humans.

"Never run without looking," said her father."The forest is full of troubles."

And now she was caught in one of them. She was not with any pack, simply following the trails that she hopped would lead her to the hannal that she had heard called as the wolf cries relayed Maala's message though the woods. She had to reach it to survive, her bones already bare on her cheat, her pups already dead, her mate killed by a boar they had tried to attack. She knew that only the strongest wolf could forage alone and never during such a bitter cold.

"I must free myself, save my energy to find the hannal," she thought.

She tried to push the left side of her nose into the jaws of the trap. They did not move. She clawed at them with her hind paws.

Unal forgot the pain in her mouth, and started to gnaw at her trapped leg above the forepaw. The pain of her own teeth biting into her flesh was worse than that from the trap. But she knew this was the way, it had to be done. She started chewing on the leg, tearing away the fur and muscle until she reached the joint. She bit and pulled at the tendons that connected the joint, they were tough, but she had pulled them off prey before. Her teeth latched onto the elastic and she pulled again. The tendons slipped from her jaw and snapped back to the bone. She almost passed out from the hurt. But Unal kept at it, chewing at the bones until the strands separated. Finally she had them weakened and they gave way with the next pull. Now her foreleg was hanging from her thigh, limp and bloody. She set here teeth around the bone and pulled hard. The leg snapped apart, freeing her.

Unal stopped to push her bleeding leg into the snow. Her quick breaths reviving her as the cold shut off the pain. She waited until the blood crusted and froze before she began to search again for the hannal. Maybe food was there.

Her three legged gait caused little pain but slowed her progress to no more then a hobble. She knew the hannal would be somewhere ahead, waiting for the packs to assemble. She mustn't stop, that was the weak way; she needed to push on, listen for the sounds, trust her nose. Just when she thought she could go no further, her legs trembling from fatigue, her heart pumping wildly, Unal looked up and saw Tuva. This was the alpha female, erect, tail high, staring at Unal with her almond shaped amber eyes. Tuva's outer coat, firm and white, framed her neck, her fangs protruded over the bottom lip of her closed mouth. Unal kept her mouth open, exposing her teeth, showing her submission. Unal guessed Tuva to be five years old and more powerful than any she wolf she had seen. A quick fear entered her mind, "Would this wolf kill me?"

Tuva watched Unal approach and prepared for a lunge at the intruder. Why was she coming on? Did she not smell the scents, see the markings, know that this was our territory? But then Tuva saw the limp.

Tuva trotted toward the lone female. "Stop! Come no further. This is the pack of Maala. You have no pack, you are not wanted here."

"I need help," said Unal. "I was caught in a human's snare."

"Do you not know that I could kill you? Should kill you! We do not accept loners."

But Tuva was saying what she had no intention of doing. These times were unusual and required unusual response. She saw Unal's subservient tail tucked between her legs, her front leg bent almost in a posture bow. Tuva said, "Follow me to the hannal."

The other wolves were surprised to see Tuva leading an injured wolf into the pack. What would Maala say?

Maala turned to watch them approach, Tuva at a slow walk, Unal trying to keep up. Tuva stopped and let Unal approach alone.

Unal stood still while Maala sniffed her groin and then covered her snout with his teeth, showing affection but not acceptance. He backed away and asked, "How did you lose your leg?"

Unal explained. Maala said, "You show great courage, first to free yourself from the snare, and then to approach us alone."

Unal dropped to the snow. She kept the prone gesture as she told Maala about her attack on the man. Maala listened carefully. Unal said she would have killed the human if she had not been so weak, and even then, she was able to escape when the humans attacked her.

Maala spoke, "But we are preparing for a great hunt and have many hungry members to feed. You cannot help us.

You are injured, a burden. We will not kill you, nor will we drive you away. You must feed yourself."

Unal knew the meaning. She limped off and nested in the snow, nearby but separate from the pack. Some game would pass her way, some remains from the hannal, or she would die. This was better than death in the human trap, or freezing alone.

"Come," shouted Sergi. "It's over here!"

Sasha and Yuri moved through the snow to the base of the tree.

"See, the trap closed on his front paw and part of his snout. See the white fur and the tooth."

"It was a female, the droppings show," said Yuri.

"Look at the coloring. This was the wolf that attacked me, she must have chewed off her leg to get away, the blood trail should lead us to her," said Sasha.

"Why follow? This one won't last long. And even if she survives this, the winter will get her. The pack won't waste their energy trying to save a wolf that can't hunt," said Yuri.

"Yes, of course, but I thought she might be some meat, I have tried wolf stew and it isn't that bad," said Sasha.

"For the pigs maybe or the dogs," laughed Yuri.

"The dogs won't eat it. They must feel the kinship or be afraid of retaliation," said Sergi.

The Pavlovskys were getting ready for Elena's party.

"Today you should talk to Vlad," said Alla. "Stop him from being such a burden to Elena."

"Why would he listen to me?" Asked Sergi.

"Well, promise me you'll try."

"I'll think about it."

Manja Zubov was complaining to Sergi, "Those Pavlovskys have everything. Did you see the new sink Sasha made? And look at their woodpile."

"They have three boys to help, Manja," said Sergi. "Besides, they offered us some wood."

"Oh, sure, help the needy. We don't even have new window glass like the Buckavevs."

"We have enough," Sergi answered. "I can't do anymore."

The party was in the Zubov's house since the Kovalev's hut was too small. Father Mishka could not attend; he had another service in the next village. For Anna it would be the first time, after the disgrace of Pasha, that she would have to talk to people. It was hard to tell who would have it worse, Anna or her husband. Ivan, being the church deacon, was expected to mold his family into an example of Christian life, and Anna, the village beauty, knew the delight she took in this was wrong. Perhaps this was why God had punished them so. Also, Anna felt, she might have to explain what Pasha did. Ivan said no.

"People will understand, probably before we do. Things like this happen in families; we are no different."

"But how can I face them?" Anna replied. "It was my brother; he lived with us; I failed to protect my daughter."

"So did I! Let it rest; we have little choice; it will be forgotten soon; these things just take a little time."

"No, I can't go to Elena's party."

"Don't do that to us," said Ivan. "We have to get our life back to normal. It will be hard the first time we go out, but that would be true whether we do it today or next month, and the healing won't start until we start living a normal life."

"But it's only been four days."

"Four days, four months, it's the same; besides, Misha will watch us to see how we behave. If we make more of this, she will be slower in putting it behind her. Do it for her."

And it was true, Misha was watching her parents for clues to the importance of what had occurred. She knew they blamed her for not stopping it sooner; did they think she led Uncle Pasha on? Little had been spoken between her and her parents, and she thought this meant disapproval. What it really meant was pain. Neither Anna nor Ivan could bear to discuss this with the girl, and they tried to keep little Ivan as far in the dark as possible. In fact, all the adult villagers refrained from talking about this to the children, and the children were left to conjure up the meaning of it themselves.

But it had to begin to end sometime, and today was as good a start as any. They left for the party.

6

Monday, December 19th

The little dog Pushkin was out for a romp in the fields. Now two and grown to 20 pounds, she ran up and down the meadow, under the watchful eye of Maala, crouched in the forest outside of the village. He was testing the former alpha males as lieutenants, seeing how they would obey him, yet still control their old pack mates. He saw the dog approaching. "Do you see the dog? He is our cousin," said Vorna."

"No!" shouted Vaal. "He is a slave to humans. He takes his food from their hand! He would not survive a week in the forest."

Tuva sneered. "Dog lives for humans. See how he waits for their commands; see how he fetches. He warns man of our coming. He will even give his life to save them. He yearns for man's approval for even his smallest deed. He is bred to please, look at the varieties. None of us differ that much, the grey wolf and the black are the same. Dog wastes his time napping. He has no life of his own."

Reina, "We can kill him without any remorse. He disgraces the species. Man whips him, kicks him, neuters him, and still he licks man's face. The dog would not flee, not take his freedom, even if it were offered to him. He is lost forever as a servant to the species that rules him."

Pushkin sniffed at the base of the tree, trying to pick up the scent she had found. It was very strong, canine, maybe a new dog. But the scent was everywhere, not just here. Strong and mixed. A pack of dogs? The smell led her deeper into the woods.

"Pushkin–Pushkin!" a human called. "Come back, girl."

"The bitch's master is nearby," said Vaal.

"But she is wandering into the woods. He will not see her," said Vorna.

Pushkin stiffened a bit. The smell overpowering now and not reassuring. How many animals were there?

Maala spoke again. "You are right, take this bitch. She is not much, but a little is better than nothing. We can't let her invade our territory and escape."

The pack trotted toward the dog, flanking her on both sides, between her and the village. Once encircled, Pushkin saw the trouble for the first time. These big, wild dogs were not like the ones in the village; they bared their teeth at her.

Pushkin started a frantic bark trying to alert her master.

The man walked toward the woods, his axe in hand. When he heard the bark of a wolf and the yelp of Pushkin, he started running.

Maala let Tuva take the kill. She went straight at Pushkin, biting her back just below the forelegs. She raised the little dog in the air and shook her, breaking her spine, then threw the body at Maala's feet.

Pushkin lay there paralyzed, offering no resistance. She was helpless as the pack tore at her flesh. She died confused.

The man saw the wolves ahead and shouted, "Back, back! Get away."

Maala whined. "Let's go! It is the human! Leave the dog, she is mostly eaten anyway."

The man burst into the little clearing. He saw the torn remains of Pushkin littering the forest floor. The last wolves were leaving at the back of the clearing. He hurled his axe at them. They left the half eaten dog and retreated into the forest.

Reina spoke next. "Why did we run away? There are many of us and only one human."

"Because we want their animals, not them. We have to keep to our plan," said Maala.

"But you saw how these humans treat each other. They left one of their own to die in the woods, tearing off his pelt and sticking him to a tree," whined Vaal.

"And he was weak and needed help, but they let him wander alone and die," said Tuva.

"Why they did this I don't know, but we were right to avoid that man. Maybe it was a trick to see if we were near the village," replied Maala.

"It was not a trick," said Vaal. "This human was cut off from his pack, and you said he was sick."

"Maybe the cold is killing them too and they had to let this weak one die," Maala ended.

Maala and the alpha males and females stopped their trot and gathered again further off in the woods, half a mile from the village.

Maala barked a command. "We must be careful now that the humans know we are here. They will be more wary and will protect their animals. We will try small attacks at first to test them. We may be able to get many of their animals this way. Don't risk attacking the humans, we can have our fill without having to fight them. I know this is the way."

It was Reina who spoke next. "Suppose they attack us? Do we still cower and run away?"

"I did not say we will cower!" Maala barked. "We protect our kind if we have to, but we never take the strong prey, the weak are ours."

Yuri carried the few remains of Pushkin back to the house, then went to see Sergi.

"Come and look at what has happened to Pushkin," he sobbed.

Sergi, seeing what was left of the dog, said one word. "Wolves."

"Yes, of course. And close to the village."

"They do that sometime. I'm sorry about Pushkin. Soma is in heat; you can have her best pup."

"For what, wolf food?"

"Now Yuri, I know you're upset, but these things happen. Those wolves are far away by now."

"God, I hope not. I'm going to track them and kill them all."

"Let me go with you."

Sergi let Yuri lead the way into the forest. He wanted him to get this over with. Maybe a few miles of tracking, and then home.

Yuri was the villages' best woodsman. He was rugged and hearty, and today he was wearing boots made the old way, from birch bark lined and stuffed with grass. He hadn't thought to change to his more practical rubber boots, since he had to hurry to have any hope of tracking these wolves. Besides, the grass kept his feet warm.

Yuri and Sergi came to the little opening where Pushkin had been killed.

"Look, it's like I said, all these tracks! There must have been dozens of them," said Yuri

Sergi was a little surprised. "Yes, it was a large pack. It seems they have moved west."

"We can go back and get blankets and sleep on the trail tonight. Tomorrow we will find them."

"Now, Yuri, you know we can't be out in this cold. Let's go back and plan what we want to do in the morning."

The next morning, the exhausted Yuri slept late. Sergi came over before noon and talked to him.

"It's senseless to try to follow a wolf in the forest. They could be 20 miles away by now."

"Shouldn't we at least try?," pleaded Yuri.

"Better that we wrap Pushkin up and put her outside. We will bury her in the spring, when the ground is soft."

"Why do they attack helpless things?"

"Because they're killers."

7

Tuesday, December 20th

"To hell with the Czar, to hell with the Premier, to hell with the Party, to hell with the Church, and to hell with you!" Romanov was consistent.

Romanov was thought a bit of a fool by the rest of the village. He claimed descendence from the Romanovs of St. Petersburg and tried to flaunt his "royalty" in their faces. No one believed him. Which true Romanov would be spending most of his adult life in Pilovo? He had come here at the turn of the century, when he was 37, alone, with no evident background. Everyone wanted to know his history, but no one believed anything he said. They called him "Mayor" to mock his supposed blue blood and, to their surprise, he liked it.

"But just come to the meetings once or twice a month. A few Wednesday won't kill you," pleaded Ivan.

"I go to church every Sunday, that's enough! God is reasonable, heaven is perfect, once you're there it doesn't matter how high your place. Besides, I don't want a high place, just let me in."

"But you must see that it's not enough. You have to want God in your heart."

"God has heaven. What does he want with my heart?"

"If you would just do some more, maybe teach the children on Sunday. They love your stories."

"The trouble with you Christians is you never get enough! At least the Muslims leave us alone. But no, you people bother us over and over. You say He's the God of peace? Then give me peace. Get out!"

One of the larger homes in Pilovo belonged to the Pavlovskys. Alexander (Sasha) was a tall man, powerfully built yet gentle, with a mild disposition. Though a bit of a dreamer, he worked hard. His wife Alla, short and pretty, was vigorous, calculating, and always kept after Sasha to do more. She wanted the best for their children and worked at it. People looked up to them, although some of the men resented Sasha's industriousness, and most of the women thought Alla was too pushy.

Alla was preparing kidney stew for dinner. She had gotten a little goat's blood and would use it to flavor the broth. The peas had been the one good crop she had that summer; the potatoes had rotted in the damp August fields; mushrooms were plenty due to the moisture; pine nuts and berries were in scant supply. How they would survive this winter with so little food was a worry she postponed until later.

With both hands he lifted the heavy cast iron pot from the stove. Her forefinger slipped off the pot holder and she burned it on the hot handle.

"Saint Peter be with me, I'll kiss a fool," she shouted.

"What's that?", asked Sasha.

"Nothing, I just was talking to myself."

"Any answers?", said Sasha.

She ladled out a portion for Sasha, who could never wait until dinner.

"Go clean that tar off your hands first," she said.

Sasha went to the pail near the back door and worked to remove the tar. He had just finished treating some wood and sealing off the cracks in the oat bucket. He returned and sat down in the chair nearest the stove and began spooning the soup into his mouth, warming his other hand on the bowl.

"It's good, but needs more blood," he complained.

"And where will I get that? You go bleed a goat in this weather."

Sasha and Alla had three sons. This was a great pride for them, but it would have been nice for Alla to have some female help in the kitchen and someone to train and talk to. Little Sasha (Alexi) was the oldest, and like many first sons, he was watched more carefully when he was young, more was expected from him, and he was his parent's joy. He favored his mother's side of the family, medium height, fine featured, slight build, quick tempered. He hated that he had a pretty face, almost cute, with dark curly hair, not old enough to realize the attraction that held for women. That didn't help him with his brothers, both of whom showed signs of growing past him in the next few years. But Alexi knew his place as the first child and so did his siblings.

Peter was the youngest and in many ways the most spoiled, if any of the Pavlovsky children could be considered spoiled. He was his mother's favorite, although she would have never known or admitted it. He was at that awkward age when his parts were growing independently of each other. He had his father's sandy hair and large nose and his mother's small mouth and gapped teeth. Alexi and Peter came closer as they got older; Alexi often looking after his younger brother. This was especially true when Gregor and Peter fought. Gregor, being in the middle, was close to neither of his two siblings, and was, in a sense, neglected by his parents. It seemed that Alexi was getting to do all the things an older son could, while Peter was getting the favors reserved for the youngest. There was nothing much for Gregor and, though a good son, he resented it. Gregor naturally became the quiet one in the family. He was not morose, but he lived more in his own world than the others, and no one seemed to mind. He preferred those chores that needed only one son and ignored his brothers.

This arrangement seemed to work well for everyone.

Thus it was no surprise that Gregor volunteered to chop the wood for the family. It was a one man job, certainly good work for a 16 year old, and he could be alone in the forest for long periods. Gregor had the build of a laborer; large hands and feet, a broad back, a thick neck. He was already handsome in a rugged way, and when he began to notice girls they would respond. But that was for later. For now, Gregor liked the forest, he liked the solitude, and he liked the work of chopping birches to prepare them for the drag to the village where he would cut them into logs for the fire. Since this winter was so cold, he had a lot of chopping to do. He didn't mind this because he could see his muscles developing, and he reveled in it. He even wondered if he would grow bigger than his father, whom he resembled. But he knew for certain that in a few years he would be stronger than Alexi and perhaps thrash him, just once, to let him know it. While Gregor didn't live for that, he did enjoy thinking about it, although he suspected that he would never carry it through out of respect for his parents. It was a nice thought while he worked.

Alla hoped for a daughter-in-law in the near future. Alexi hadn't courted any of the village girls, but he was certainly straining himself to get to know someone else very well.

Alla lectured him on the proper choice. "The Pavolvskys are a respected family, you can't marry just anyone. Sonya Zubov is fine, but I don't want to hear about the Lutev girl or that Olga Shmenev. Their families are low class. You must marry at your station."

"But, mother, Sonya is Timor's girl, and, besides, I am not interested in any of the others."

"So, who interests you?" Snapped Alla. "You be careful."

Alla was dying to know Alexi's thoughts. In the summer he had walked, several times, to the village of Baykiv, 15 miles away, to see Karin Morozov, a girl Alla had only met once, but who seemed nice and was from a good family. Maybe this was the one for Alexi? Then the rumors would stop.

The thought of another woman in her home thrilled Alla. It would take a few years after his marriage for Alexi to build a house for his bride and during that time Alla and she would run the Pavlovsky home. To have someone to talk to; to make meals together; to help run the loom and stitch the clothing; to laugh when the men did something stupid; to hear the gossip from another village. These were things Alla could hope for when the boys brought their girls home.

Both Alla's and Sasha's parents had died within the last six years. Alla especially missed her father, who had been a comfort to her and Sasha, and a source of that wisdom that comes with age. He had a quieting influence on them all. Even though Alla knew the villagers envied her, she felt a loss they did not have. She tried not to covet those families that had girls; those that had three generations under the same roof; those that had grandchildren; those that knew the fullness of community with their kinsmen. She would have much of that in a few years.

Sasha would kid her, "What woman could want more than to have four men taking care of her and doing all the chores she wanted?"

"You'll see," said Alla. "When our daughter-in-laws come you'll be giddy with delight; the most contented man in the village.

"And if you don't stop teasing me about this," she continued. "I'll make sure they only listen to me and leave you and the boys to your work."

After lunch, the boys got ready for their chores. The day was cold but clear. No snow was on the horizon, a good day to chop wood. Gregor threw his wool coat on over his tunic, put on his sheepskin-lined mittens, and his fur hat.

"I'm going to get some wood."

"Good, but don't stay out too long. It's cold again today," Alla said. "And look out for the Bukavev's goat and the Luskey's dog. I don't like what happened to Pushkin. Maybe the wolves are still around."

"Don't worry mother; if I see them I will bring them home with me when I finish." He was not about to walk back early just for some strays.

Gregor left through the side door near the woodshed, turned right into the shed and picked out the axe and the harness he would need to pull the logs. He never used the sled when it was this cold, since the trunks slid on the ice as well as the sled did.

He walked to the end of the village and up the northwest trail a quarter of a mile into the birches. The only sounds were the woodpeckers and the nutcrackers busy keeping themselves full for the winter; the snow silenced everything else. He would go off the trail about 30 yards and begin his work. On this clear a day someone in the village could hear the faint sound of chopping from this distance, but it was not likely anyone would be out in the cold for long, and even if so, he would have his hat on so tightly it would muffle the sound. Gregor hiked into a small clearing that he had hacked out himself just this year. He liked to take big swings with the axe, and he could do it here without hitting another tree. They could heat their home from the trees surrounding this one clearing for at least three years.

Gregor selected a sturdy birch about 14 inches in diameter and began to chop at its base. He kept a slow but steady pace so he would not tire quickly. He wanted to chop for about two hours. As always, the first birch was down in 20 minutes. He then began to pare off the small side branches so that it would pull easily through the trail. When he was finished he found a similar sized birch and began again. It was going to be a fine day.

It was early afternoon and Gregor had not yet returned.

"I hope he isn't wearing himself out up there," said Alla.

Sasha shook his head. "He's a young man, he won't wear out. He just wants to do more."

"Well, God knows we need it. One big blizzard and we would use all of the wood in the pile. The bigger the better."

Gregor had just finished his third tree and was looking for a suitable one with which to end the day. Then he would ferry them back to the house one or two at a time. That would still give him plenty of light to finish chopping two of the trees into logs. Not a bad day's work.

Reina was hunched down in the trees about twenty yards from the human. Three of his eastern pack mates were with him, all males.

"Look at this human; he is alone; why must we live on dogs and goats? Why not take some humans," asked Reina?

"But Maala says no; he does not want to test the humans. Besides, this one is young and strong; can we kill him?" Loka asked.

"The four of us can. He is only one, and humans run slowly in the forest snow. They need great effort to move their limbs. I have heard that they panic easily."

"Let's go! Why wait?" said another.

"Because we are wrong to do this without Maala's permission. Do you want to face his anger?" asked Loka.

"Maala is the one who is wrong! Did he not tell of the great Demja? He attacked humans. We can do this: Maala will see the wisdom of it," snorted Reina.

"I think we should listen to Maala," whined Loka.

"Then crawl back to the hannal and eat mice," said Reina.

Reina growled to the others, "Maala will be proud of us when he sees we have succeeded. Then we can eat animals or humans when we wish. Now, let the human turn away from us and begin his work. We can get closer and be on him before he can run."

Gregor found the last tree for the day. It was at the northwest corner of the clearing no more than 15 yards from the opening to the path home. He raised his axe and began to hack at the base; the axe was beginning to get heavy.

"Now," barked Reina. "Take him!"

Gregor heard a rustle of snow and ice off to his right. He put down his axe and turned to see what was causing it. The first wolf was just a few yards away and heading straight for him. He could make out two or three more wolves behind this one. As he reached down for the axe, the wolf crashed into his right shoulder. But Gregor's movement caused the wolf to tumble to the right, only a piece of coat in its mouth. Gregor raised his axe and caught the second wolf in mid-air, driving the blade through Loka's mid-section and gutting the animal before it landed. The third wolf stopped just out of reach of the axe.

"Never stop!" Reina said. "Surprise and speed are our friends."

Gregor was encircled now by three wolves. They looked at him curiously as he stumbled about, trying to keep the axe between each of them and him. The wolves made darting moves to close in, but Gregor parried each move with his blade.

"All at once when I whine," said Reina.

Gregor backed near a large birch. This gave him some protection from behind and also a balance point to face his attackers. He kept moving the axe in an arc to keep the wolves at bay. As he jockeyed for position near the tree he stumbled down onto one knee.

Reina whined. The wolves attacked.

By the time Gregor righted himself one wolf was already at his legs. He swung the axe down at the back of the animal, splitting it's spine. A second wolf latched onto his left arm and pulled him down, away from the tree. Reina went straight for the neck, jerking Gregor backwards with his momentum. It was Reina's first taste of human blood, too sweet. But it was there, meat to be had, and he was hungry. The wolf with Gregor's arm in its mouth yanked him along the ground. Gregor tried to keep them from his face, but Reina had a hold on his neck, his teeth already sunk into tissue. Blood gushed onto his clothing. He lifted his right arm to swipe at the wolves, but he was failing. Panic set in, then quiet.

Sasha asked, "Where is the boy?"

"Alexi, Peter, go up to the clearing and see if your brother is all right. He may have cut himself again with the axe. You know how hard he works. He never took this long before. Go help him."

Peter and Alexi bundled themselves up and went to look for their brother.

"I thought this was one job Gregor could do by himself. But no! We have to go help him even with this," said Alexi.

"Maybe he found a girlfriend," laughed Peter.

"Not Gregor! More likely he found himself!"

The brothers tumbled and shoved each other on their way to the clearing.

Alexi found the set of tracks leading into the clearing.

"Gregor must be in there, but I hear no chopping. Either he's resting or he's fallen asleep."

"He wouldn't fall asleep out here; he'd freeze before nightfall. I think he's in trouble," said Peter.

Peter ran ahead, and reached the clearing before Alexi. Immediately he saw the remains of his brother sprawled out on the snow near the base of a tree. He ran towards the body, calling behind to Alexi.

"Hurry! Gregor is bleeding!"

The two brothers looked down at what was left of Gregor. Part of his neck was torn off, and he had bled to death from the wound. But there was more. Most of the muscles around the limbs were torn away or gone. His belly was opened and gutted.

"We have to return to the village!" Alexi shouted. "We need help. Look at this wolf. Gregor almost cut him in two, but there were others. They may still be nearby."

"Yes," cried Peter. "We have to warn the village and get help. Then we can track and kill the wolves that did this."

Reina was down in the snow not 40 yards from the boys.

"We attack again; it must be finished. Come."

By now four more wolves had joined the pack; along with the two survivors they made for the brothers as they headed for the trail back to the village. Peter heard them first and turned; they were only a few yards away.

"Alexi! Wolves! Help!"

Alexi spun in his tracks and faced the animals. He called to Peter.

"Get back to back with me. We will face them together!"

"Maybe they will leave if we stare them down."

The two boys stood with their backs pressed to each other. They tried to stare at the wolves, but this just convinced the animals that this prey must be taken. The wolves circled at a distance of ten feet.

"Watch," said Reina. "They may have weapons like the last one."

After a few minutes the wolves came to understand that the boys were defenseless. Reina barked again, and they dove in for the attack. This time Reina went straight for Alexi's leg; he knew now that humans were helpless when they were down. Just like elk. The boys had a wolf at each leg, biting into their hamstrings, and one at their body trying for the throat. Alexi pressed his body toward the wolf at his chest, as he had heard his father did. The wolf's head was next to his, touching his cheek. Neither could do much damage as long as Alexi was standing. The wolf tried to get his forelegs over Alexi's shoulders, but Alexi took that opportunity to grab the legs and spread them with his arms. He stumbled and fell onto the wolf, splaying the animal's legs and tearing them aside with a series of cracks. One of the upper ribs of the wolf pierced it's heart. But Alexi was down and fighting off the other two.

Peter had one wolf by the throat but was not strong enough to strangle it. He fell over backwards, three wolves at his body. In desperation he tried to punch at the wolf, but his arm went down its throat. The animal pulled back, choking on Peter's arm. Peter rammed it down further. The wolf twisted in his fury, and he lifted Peter back onto his feet. His arm was now at the back of the wolf's throat. The other wolves pulled at the muscles in his legs. He stumbled again and felt his body go numb. He turned to Alexi for help but Alexi was on his back, his body torn open, the starving wolves tearing chunks of flesh.

8

Tuesday, late afternoon

It was an hour before Sasha began to worry again about the boys.

"They really should be back by now, it's getting dark, they know not to be out this late. I hope they're not fooling around, especially with Gregor. You know how mad he gets if they tease him," said Sasha.

"Maybe they stopped off at Romanov's place. It's on the way, and they love his old tales of the revolution when he was in St. Petersburg," answered Alla.

"Petrograd! You know how the government hates the old names. Remember, Petrograd, Petrograd, Petrograd!"

"It's St. Petersburg, you old fool. No matter what they call it now. Doesn't Peter the Great deserve to have his memory kept?"

"Yes! That's why we say Petrograd. We can't use church names anymore."

"Call it what you wish. It was St. Petersburg when I was born and it will be St. Petersburg when I die."

"Fine, but keep it to yourself, we don't need trouble," said Sasha.

"Who's to give trouble? Comrade Vavilin? No one else cares for the new names. If they want changes, they can send a doctor here. Now that would make me a true communist!"

Another 15 minutes went by and Sasha now felt the trouble in his heart. The boys were smarter than this; they wouldn't make their father wait. He put on his coat and went to see if Sergi heard anything.

"How would I know?" said Sergi. "Who's outside in this weather?"

"Do you think we should go look for them?"

"Yes, of course, let's get a few others. We will need some luchinas to light the way and a sled in case one of them is injured."

Some men brought out the birch to make the torches Sergi wanted. Within ten minutes a party of eight was heading up the trail to the clearing. It was getting colder; the smoke from the torches rose into the waning sunlight. The luchinas burned slowly, with an intense glow. There was some joking about what the boys were up to, but the older men had a sense that there was trouble and were morose.

The men climbed up the path straining to hear something. It was silent. They came to the place where Gregor usually went for wood. When they entered the clearing Sasha let out with a wail that was heard back in the village. Alla now knew.

"I heard a man cry out; I hope your boys are not hurt," said Manja.

Alla knew not to follow. She hoped that Manja was wrong and that the cry was of joy. But she knew that Sasha would chastise the boys if they were not hurt when he saw them, not act pleased.

Reina watched as the pack grew from six to more than 40. All the wolves were curious about the killing of the three humans and emboldened by the success of Reina and the others.

All except Maala.

"Why have you done this? Do you not remember what I said? Do you realize what course we are now on? You kill one human and the others will follow and keep after us until they kill us all! Did you not listen to my story of Demja? His mistake was to kill humans They will fight for their animals but they will kill for their kind."

Reina saw what was coming. Maala lunged at him, clamping his teeth into the back of Reina's spine. Maala jerked his great head back until the spine almost broke. Then he let go. Reina fell, almost lifeless, to the forest floor, whimpering and yelping.

Maala stopped his attack, "If you disobey me again I will kill you. We cannot do as each choses, we must work as a hannal; and obey the hannal rules; my rules! You have placed us in jeopardy. I hope for our sake that we have not already gone too far."

Maala knew what had begun and what the end might be.

"Now we have no choice; we must continue. Killing just one human is enough to excite their packs. We will kill these others and the rest will become afraid for a while, not pursue us. By then we will be far away and safe. Maybe." Maala finished.

Maala now led the hannal again; none would cross him twice.

"Listen," said Reina, regaining some of his confidence. "It is not difficult if you are careful. The first human had a weapon and that was a problem, but the last two only killed one of us."

"What of these new humans? They carry fire," Vaal asked.

"Yes," answered Maala. "We must be careful. Let them turn and head away. We will attack from behind."

Sasha was on his knees next to the bodies of Peter and Alexi. Blood was everywhere; the boys mutilated almost beyond recognition. Wolf prints surrounded them. Sergi had discovered the body of Gregor and wanted with all his heart to shield it from Sasha.

"Send someone back for our weapons," sobbed Sasha. "The wolves are near, I sense it, we can find them now."

"No, we must return to the village and prepare a proper search tomorrow. We need more men; besides, it's getting dark and the wolf knows it," said Sergi. "Let's collect the boys on the sled and bring them home."

"We'll kill all those wolves or, by God, we'll die trying," said Dimitry.

The torn bodies of the Pavlovsky boys were loaded onto the sled. The rescue party turned for the village. Maala and the others were ready.

"Now, their backs are to us."

The wolves attacked just as the men were walking single file on the path to the village. The charge came from the rear and the sides and concentrated on the last four men in the file. The torches these men carried fell to the ground and went out. This encouraged the wolves, who tore into the humans. Again, there were too many wolves for the men.

Dimitry the blacksmith, and his oldest son, were taken first. Dimitry was powerful, but he spent too much of his effort defending little Dimitry, and that was enough to allow the wolves to latch onto his legs and tear open his haunches. He managed to break the front leg of one wolf, but that meant nothing to the pack.

Boris and Pulgi were also taken as they hurried to join the men in front. The wolves moved so fast in the snow that the men had little time to shout to their comrades for help, and less time to ward off the bites and rushes of the animals that now surrounded them.

The attack was over in a few minutes; the wolves had leveled their prey and turned their attention to the remaining men.

The men in the front of the line wheeled and faced the wolves, their torches between the animals and themselves.

"Keep the torches in their faces and back down to the trail," screamed Sergi.

The women in the houses nearest the clearing heard the sounds coming from the woods and came out and huddled together. More men from the village grabbed axes and pikes and ran up the path.

The men nearest the wolves, swept their torches left and right in an arc, managing to keep the wolves at bay. They stayed in a tight bundle, encouraging each other as they slowly stepped backwards toward the village.

"Watch the fire!" Maala shouted. "These humans are dangerous. Try to get around and attack from the side."

The four men in the back of the file were dead or dying, the work of almost 20 wolves. They had to be abandoned as Sasha and the others tried to get back to the houses. The men coming up the trail reinforced the rescuers. Alla saw the group backing toward the village.

"The men are in trouble, get more torches and heat some water," she said.

Some of the women ran up the trail, torches high above their heads.

"Back, back," cried Maala. "Much fire."

The line of men watched the wolves retreat, then backed into the village.

"We'll meet in the church," said Ivan.

The men spread throughout the village, telling everyone to come to the church. Many of the villagers were out of their houses, trying to see what the commotion was about. Now they knew.

The wolves tore the remaining meat from the dead men and retreated into the forest.

When most of the villagers were in the church, Sasha spoke; his voice trembling as he tried to control himself.

"My boys are dead; they were attacked and killed by wolves. We saw many wolves ourselves. They were vicious, they attacked us too. The torches saved us, but even then the wolves were persistent and kept just out of range of the fire. They even attacked us as we were retreating to the village. They killed Dimitry and little Dimitry, Boris, and Pulgi. Their torches fell useless into the snow."

"I have never heard of wolves attacking men with torches," said Ivan. "They must have been rabid."

"No, no. Let me speak," said Sasha, trying again to stand, his legs weak from the effort. "I think these wolves are different. They are hungry like us, and they seem determined to eat anything they can get. They even ate the flesh from my boys."

"How many are there?"

"The 30 we saw and probably a lot more. I have never seen such a large pack. They must be banding together," said Sergi.

"My father told me of such things. In his time a band of over 40 wolves attacked a caravan near Irkust. They had to be driven off with rifles. They killed nine men, and they were not afraid of humans," said Karl.

"It's the winter! The cold, the lack of food. Wolves only group together when they are forced to. They know that to attack us means they have to cooperate. They have used up their normal food sources and want to try us next," said Yuri.

"Let's be calm," said Sergi. "We have to plan how to kill these wolves, then the danger will pass."

"Calm! Have you lost a husband?" said Manja. "Have you lost three sons, like Alla? You stay calm. I say we attack the wolves now!"

"With what? The new government has taken away most of our rifles; we have little ammunition for the guns that remain. Most of our weapons are old and some are rusted. Maybe we can kill some of the wolves, but what of the others? Maybe the wolves are still massing in this area. Maybe there are hundreds," Ivan said.

The meeting was frantic. The village had never faced such a problem.

"Let's send men to Pulni to get help. They can go by day with a few guns. The wolves may not attack if shots are fired," said Karl.

Others chimed in, "Forget Pulni. Before you get there the wolves will be far away."

"Sure. Let's let the wolves leave first! Who wants to meet up with them on the road to Pulni?"

"Wait, wait, we have to be reasonable. We have loved ones to bury. We have to grieve. We need time to plan. If we go off half-cocked we won't accomplish anything."

"Sure, talk about it."

"I don't mean that, I want them all dead to. But if we act in haste we will get nothing done. We first have to scout out the direction the wolves have taken, then see how many men we need to track them. We will get them, no doubt, but only if we do it right," finished Sergi.

Vlad Kovalev spoke, "Don't include me in your plans. I will take care of my own family without your help. I'm not in the mood to risk my life for any of you. You behave like frightened children, panicking at the first sign of trouble. Go ahead, talk your problems over, just leave me out of them." He left the gathering and headed home.

The village did nothing. The majority thought the wolves would retreat after having seen so much fire on the trail. Someone even suggested that the forest be set afire, but the snow and the cold would limit that or it might turn toward the village. With no consensus, the villagers decided to stay at home, watch out for their families, and, if possible, each other, and hope the wolves would leave.

Vaal led the remaining pack back into the forest. Maala followed from the rear. He wanted to keep a look-out in case any humans came after them. They had already lost three of their own and were being careful not to lose anymore. But they had killed seven humans and that had been a little meat for some of them.

Later, when the hannal was sitting down for the night, Vaal said, "It was easy. The humans are slow and frightened. We can do this

"Yes, I know," said Maala. "They are not as hard to kill as a bear and slower then elk. They are almost defenseless without their weapons. But you see they have fire?"

9

Wednesday, December 21st

Alla slid from under her blanket, slid her covered feet into her slippers, and walked across the cold floor. She had slept little, and though she was still tired, she couldn't stay in bed. She went to the grating and lit the fire.

Sasha felt her go. He wanted to stay in bed forever, forget yesterday, change what happened. He stared at the whitewashed ceiling, trying to think of something to do or say that would comfort her.

"Don't get up, I'll bring you your tea in bed," said Alla.

"No, I'm not sleepy. How are you doing?"

"Numb. I don't feel a thing. I can hardly do this. I have to concentrate and tell myself how to prepare the tea. It's as if I have forgotten everything."

"Forget the tea."

"No, no, I have to do something."

Sasha sat up.

"We have to have a service for the boys," he said.

"How? Father Mishka is away and won't be back for another two weeks."

"Yes, I know, but Ivan can do a little blessing until Father returns."

"They can't be buried until spring," sobbed Alla.

"We will put their best clothes on them and wrap them in canvas. Then we can lay their bodies near the shed, under the little roof. At least it will be some sort of ceremony."

"Oh God, Sasha, this is so hard!"

"Try not to question it Alla. It's God's will."

"No, it isn't!"

Sasha went over and held his wife. He didn't think God cared either. They sat at the table, morose, lost in their despondence.

"No daughters-in-law," said Alla softly.

"And no grandchildren," she continued. "Nothing, no one to be with us; to comfort us in our old age; to continue our line; to remember us."

"I know," responded Sasha. "We are truly alone. When we die it is over, as if we had never lived."

"Did we want too much?" Alla sobbed.

"Now we will be forgotten as soon as they throw the earth over us," said Sasha, with a vacant stare. "Why bother going on? Whom can we share life with; who can we give our love to? Who?"

"I don't want to go on," cried Alla. "It would be better to die now, without having to watch the two of us shrivel up and blow away with the last wind. Tell me I'm wrong Sasha! Tell me it will be all right!"

"I can't," wept Sasha, laying his head on his forearms.

Natasha and Dasha Bukavev were playing in the bedroom they shared with their parents. Both girls were still in their bedclothes, warm stockings tight around their legs, fur slippers on their feet.

Luba called to them. "Girls, stop that noise and get dressed."

"One minute, Mama," shouted Natasha, just as Dasha hurled a pillow at her face.

Luba Bukavev was a kind woman, loud-mouthed but cheerful, with a voice that the villagers said "could call sheep from hell!" She was fat, squat and contented, having given up the worry of beauty years ago.

"Don't try to fool me," said Luba. "I can hear your fighting. Do I have to come out of the kitchen and take my broom to you?"

"No, no, Mama, we are getting ready now," replied Natasha, and cuffed Luba to shut her up.

Fedor, Luba's husband, was wiry and squint-eyed, like his Mongolian ancestors. In contrast to his looks, he was the village joker. There was the day of the fall cabbage festival, when all the women prepared their best cabbage dishes for the noon contest. Everyone ate their fill. Later in the day the villagers heard loud hollow sounds coming from the outhouses as the people passed the gases from the cabbage feast. Fedor had connected birch tubes to the back of the privies, just below the seats. Some thought it funny, most thought it rude. Fedor didn't care.

Fedor entered the house by the side door. "No sign of that goat. I looked everywhere, she's gone."

"Did she go into the woods?" Luba asked.

"Hard to tell with the snow last night; no tracks. Besides, she usually doesn't stray that far."

"I'm going over to help Alla, see to the girls," said Luba.

Luba went to Alla's house to help with the preparation of the clothing for the boys funeral. Although Alla was expected to choose everything, she would need someone to guide her through the ritual.

Alla went to the boys' bedroom and began to lay out their clothing. For Alexi she choose a black tunic, a gown of pale white with deep green bordering, his favorite red leggings and his finest boots. Each item had a special feel for her; except for the boots, she had made them herself.

"That's fine," comforted Luba. "Now let's see what we have for Gregor."

It was difficult for both woman to imagine how the clothing would fit on the torn and partly eaten bodies of the boys. But the women would help Alla through that, hiding those wounds they could, filling the holes here and there. Ivan had already rearranged the boys faces to remove the frightened stares and open mouths.

Alla continued. For Gregor she choose the leather vest he wore so proudly on the first day that Sasha had let him hunt with the rifle. Luba took it from Alla's hands and laid it on the bed. Alla added Gregor's pine bark boots that he had made himself, with Yuri's help, and his tan gown with the orange trim.

Peter was the hardest. Although she tried not to favor any of her children, Alla couldn't help her feelings for Peter. He was her youngest; he resembled Sasha so much; he hadn't begun to feel that distance from his mother that all teenagers find for a time. Her baby.

Luba sensed Alla's hesitation. "Let me pick out Peter's clothes."

"No, Luba, I have to do it," said Alla, her voice almost inaudible. "He was my baby; my little one."

Alla took the grey gown she had made him when Peter was twelve. It would be a little small, but could be made to fit. In her mind she could see Peter jumping on the bed; the gown lifting and falling as he rose and fell; the blue piping setting off his blue eyes.

She then chose his fur slippers and brown vest, and rolled his fur hat and tied it together, just like Peter did when he took it with him on a day when the weather might turn bad. They would place the hat next to the body. She added the thin red sash that he wore on Sundays, and the small relic from the cloth of Saint Peter of Russia, that he always carried in his pocket.

Almost in a faint, she backed over to the chair and sat down.

"Let me take these to the church," said Luba. "You stay here with Sasha. Someone will be over to get you before the service starts."

As she left the house, Luba turned to Sasha. "Take care of her; I'm afraid this is too much for anyone to bear."

"I'll try," answered the dazed man.

St. Stephan's was full. Nothing like these killings had ever occurred in Pilovo. Each person went over to the families that had suffered a loss and gave the best condolences they could. No one felt much like repeating the normal platitudes. This was beyond that.

It was most disheartening to see the Pavlovskys huddled together, no longer a family but a couple. If they could be stricken with such a catastrophe, who was safe?

When Elena hugged Alla she felt as if she had an old rag doll in her arms. How could her friend survive this?

Ivan moved to the front of the church, just on the parishioners' side of the altar screen. The seven bodies were laid in a row, taking up the whole width of the church.

"Our boys, our men, who hurt no one, were taken from us by the power of the devil. You all have seen the devil! He walks on four legs, has sharp teeth, kills for his own pleasure, eats our dead. He lives in the forest and watches us," said Ivan.

The four families in mourning stood in the front, almost touching the bodies. The rest of the villagers stood behind them.

"Let us not forget who did this. He should be hunted and killed. He must be cleansed from Russia! We cannot live with him."

Ivan turned to the grieving families, "Don't harden your hearts against God. There is a reason for this. We can't always tell the reason, but God's Will will prevail. Don't question it. Let your grief come out at the devil. He lives in our land. We must fight him when we can."

Alla heard little of what Ivan was saying. She seemed to be in a transient state, neither awake nor asleep. The condolences from the people went by her ears unheard. Her grip on Sasha's arm was so intense that his muscles cramped. He said nothing.

Stephan Volkov, standing at the very back of the church, was despondent. More than anyone he hated the wolf. For years now the villagers, had shunned him, in some cases even feared him, and called him the Wolfman. Stephan had a mirror, he saw what they saw. His face turning deep red around the jowls and over the nose, the highlighting of the eyes, the color and shadowing causing his nose to appear more like a snout. At least he could hide some of the color changes on his body, but not his face!

He had gone to Moscow, the longest journey of his life, to see the doctors. They told him he had a disease called

Lupus, explaining to him that the color changes were due to his skin reacting with things like the sun. That explained why it was worse in the summer. So Stephan kept out of the sun as much as possible. That helped some.

But even in the winter his face would at times change. Sometimes it really did happen at full moon. He would awake the next day and the streaks would be across his cheekbones and down to his neck. Were the doctors right? Or were the old tales true? Had Stephan been bitten by a she-wolf in heat? Did his mother touch a she-wolf's lair when she was carrying him? Had a male wolf impregnated his mother while she slept? The signs were there.

Stephan was 31 and single. His native town had rejected him, the last village had stoned him. Where could he go? Pilovo was his final stop; no other place would accept him. Even in Moscow the people crossed themselves when they saw him.

So it was natural that he lived at the edge of town, closest to the forest. Not to be with wolves! But to be away from humans. Only Ivan, the Pavlovskys, and Father Mishka had any sympathy for him, and Stephan wasn't sure that they didn't have to grit their teeth to do it.

The worst were the children. They taunted him mercilessly, howling and turning their fur hats into wolf ears as they circled and called him names. Their parents usually stopped them, but they couldn't be there all the time. Stephan had to bear it. He longed to be normal.

Some of the men were no better. Vlad Kovalev, small and mean, openly ridiculed the young man. He even tried to get the other villagers to expel Stephan, or at least make him live in the forest with the rest of the animals. He was relentless in his hatred towards the poor boy.

"Hey wolfboy!" he would shout. "Go catch me a rabbit for dinner."

Stephan endured it all; what else could he do? He wondered if he should end his life. But then the church would not bury him, not even on the ground of the cemetery named after his patron saint.

He was trapped in a world he hated.

When the service, such as it was, was over, a little procession formed at the back of the church. Many of the people, as they filed past, placed small remembrances by the bodies of the dead: a piece of candy, a picture of a saint, something that linked them to each of their former friends. These would be buried with the bodies. Ivan lead the people away, first toward Alla's house. Sasha and Alla walked behind, and then the other villagers. Even Pavel followed, far in the rear.

They came to the shed. The boys' bodies, on three wooden slabs, were placed in a rack hastily built by Yuri. Little Ivan held the bowl of holy water, the handle of the aspergill pointing toward his father. Ivan let the head fill, then sprinkled each body with holy water as it was slid into place. It froze. He waved the censur over each corpse, covering them with incense. A last prayer was said, and the procession wandered off in the direction of the other houses that had lost a family member, and so on.

When all the bodies were put in their places, the people went to Alla's house. Vlad Kovalev came late, having missed the service as usual. He didn't go to church; he felt no need; that was for the unthinking, the foolish mystics. Elena had arrived earlier with some food; she was a devout Christian, always praying for Vlad to change, to mellow, to stop hating so much. He was her "cross to bear."

The women had food and drink ready for the gathering. Manja played her concertina, Yakov his lute. The music, the drinking, being together, all this was consoling. Sad songs were sung, the men hanging their heads when they finished. The children ran about, almost oblivious to what was going on. But they heralded the fact that time would put this behind everyone. Even Alla smiled for a moment as they frolicked unheeded.

Five hours later the last visitor left Sasha's home. Many were drunk, and they had eaten all the cakes and stews, except for the food that was prepared for the Pavlovskys to eat tomorrow and the next day.

Alla closed the door and shuttered and covered the windows. She held tight to Sasha and they wept.

Seena licked the pup, her tongue sliding skin in rolls along its back. She nudged it closer to her dry teat, hoping the action would start a flow.

"The pup is dead," said Vaal.

"No, not yet. She is just weak," said Seena.

Only two of the litter showed any movement, and that just a nervous shudder.

"Come, Seena. The hannal is moving," said Vaal.

"You go, I must stay with my pups."

Vaal went to Tuva, who trotted back to the young mother.

"You must come," she said.

Seena looked up and said, "They are my first. Please, let me stay, maybe one will live."

"Your milk is dry. You'll have no more until next year."

"If I leave they all die," said Seena.

"Pups die. It is the way. You have to think of the pack, the hannal."

Tuva pushed her snout under Seena's head, lifting the frightened female. Seena knew. She raised onto her legs, looked down at the moribund pups, then at Vaal, standing near the trail.

Seena moved slowly, trying not to look back, leaving her whelps to the cold.

Vaal came alongside, and sheparded his mate back to the hannal.

Tuva watched, the dead and dying pups to weak to call for their mother.

"Another year, another year," thought Tuva.

Maala was trying to plan, the events of yesterday filling his mind. He wanted to make sure that all the wolves got to eat. He was still uncertain about the humans.

"Are there enough animals and people for all of us to eat our fill?" he whined.

Tuva nodded. "Yes, we will have enough food for a month. Then we can take another village."

"But I have to be sure," mused Maala.

Kaala, the mate of the dead Loka, spoke next. "I am not afraid of humans. Send me and a few others to the town. We will show you how easy it is to take them."

"All right," said Maala."Take Bunta and Sana with you, but wait until tomorrow. The men are quiet now. They will have forgotten what happened yesterday, and their guard will be down. But don't take risks."

"Tomorrow we go," said Kaala."When we come back you will see, we will have eaten as we wished."

10

Wednesday evening

Shocked, the villagers had almost forgotten about the wolves. They made some preparations on the previous night, but the funeral service for the Pavlovsky boys had diverted their attention for most of the morning. The dour wake and drunkenness left them limp for the rest of the day. It wasn't until evening that any of them began to worry.

"Monday I saw a hat on the bed in Alla's house," said Manja. "She should pay attention. No wonder Gregor was killed."

"Don't talk about superstitions now," said Sergi.

"Superstitions! Do bad things not come in threes? Are not all three Pavlovsky boys dead?"

"Sasha and Alla need our help," said Sergi. "Let's calm down."

"What if the wolves come back?" Manja asked.

"We just have to be careful when we go into the forest. We should go in groups with weapons and torches," said Sergi.

Karl spoke. "They're gone. That's how they work, kill a little here, kill a little there, then move on."

"I'm not so sure," mused Sergi. "But they do seem to have gone."

"Yes, yes," said Karl. "That's how they do it. We haven't heard a thing for over a day. It's already night and still no problems. They've left all right."

Sergi wondered. "Should we pursue them?"

"Why, you'll never catch up to them now," said Karl.

"Maybe we should warn the other villages?," asked Elena.

In his mocking way Vlad answered, "Do you want to travel through the forest to do that?"

"I'm not afraid."

"Neither was Gregor."

The others looked at him. It wasn't proper to name the recent dead.

Sergi broke the silence, "Besides, we don't know what direction they took. Which village should we warn?"

"It can wait. Let's collect ourselves and heal our wounded. We can attend to the wolves later if they ever return," said Ivan.

Sergi summed it up. "Let it be for now. If they were in the area we would have heard from them today. They would have taken some of the dogs or such. They must have left. We can send a party to the other villages on the weekend. That's soon enough. We probably put a good scare into them with our torches."

They decided to wait a few days to let everyone calm down before they thought again about ways to make themselves safer from wolves this winter. After all, what could be worse than what had already happened?

Yuri shook his head, thinking, "Why don't we at least try to track the wolves? Are we afraid?"

He walked slowly back to his hut, coming around to the side near the forest. Back near the tree line he saw his bee hives. He went over to see if the frost had damaged them yet. Yuri's honey was the best in the village. He would feed various types of berries to the bees to flavor the honey differently. This year it was blackberries. He loved summer, when he could watch the bees at work making honey for him.

He thought of those days, then he raised his head and hurled curses to the trees.

"I will get even. I will get even." He cried. "No wolf will be safe from now on."

Then he lowered his arms and walked away dejectedly, back to his hut.

The village of Pilovo was small even by Siberian standards. Twenty-six homes were clustered around a central well that was frozen for most of the year. In the winter there was plenty of snow to melt for water. The wooden houses had thatched roofs except for those few villagers who could afford wood. The church was all wood and could accommodate all the villagers when the priest visited once a month. There were several barns belonging to the prominent families but these were shared when needed. The roads into town from the north and the south were wide enough for two sleds and passed the well and the church. The side roads were merely paths that led to the forest, the other houses, the barns, and wherever the men kept their tools and horses. There was no central stable.

The Zobovs had the finest house in the village. It was the only one with two stories; ground floor for the animals, upper one for the family. Although this was a sign of their prominence, it was not without its problems. In the summer they were above the dampness of the thaw and the mud that came with it, but the smell of the animals was strongest then, and it rose into the house with each breath. In the winter the floor of the upper story was warmed by the heat rising from the animals, but if a cold wind found the cracks in the lower walls, the upper floor got colder than those houses that were set on the ground. Manja made thick rugs to cover the walls and floors, but still, in a bad winter, the cold persisted. It was cold now.

Still is was nice to be able to go downstairs for some milk, to hear the lulling sounds of the sleeping animals below, to let the stairs rub the dirt off their boots as they ascended, to be different from the others. Besides, Sergi's grandfather had built this home, and he and Manja were privileged to share it with his mother.

Sonya Zubov threw on her scarf and started for the back door. Manja called to her. "Put on your coat and hat. It's freezing out there."

"But Mother, I am just going for milk. I'll be back in a moment."

Before Manja could reply, Sonja was out the door, down the steps, through the barn, and headed for the little shed that had the wooden milk containers nestled next to the wall. She lifted the lid of one container and pulled hard on the stick that was frozen into the top of the milk. Lifting out a chunk of frozen milk, she set it on top of the wooden lid and pecked at it with the small axe she carried. When she had chopped off about two quarts, she returned the bulk of the milk to the container, collected the frozen pieces into the bucket she carried, and replaced the lid. She hurried to bring the milk into the house. Mother had been right, it was too cold to be out with just a scarf over her clothes.

Once inside the house, Sonya brought the bucket near the fireplace. She set it down close enough to the fire to allow it to melt, and watched it periodically to make sure it did not overheat and curdle.

Manja was at the small cabinet table near the oven. She had taken fresh bread out of the oven and was letting it cool before she sliced it for the family dinner. Stew was simmering on the stove.

The small mirror on the wall opposite the window gave Manja brief glimpses of the mole near the end of her nose, as she hurried back and forth in the kitchen. When she was young, the small flat black dot was almost as pretty as a beauty mark, but, over the years, it had grown and raised and now tiny black hairs were beginning to sprout from its top. She heard tales of doctors in the cities who could remove moles and leave a smooth spot behind, like new skin. How she would love that! But when would she ever get to Moscow, and how could she pay the doctor? Besides, God punishes the vain.

Sergi came in from the woodshed hauling logs for the fire. The shed was connected to the back of the first floor so that one could enter it without having to brave the cold outside. Sergi was middle-aged, growing a stomach that flopped over the leather belt around his waist. This was his seventh year as village leader and it was enough. Who needed the extra aggravation, the focus for complaints over petty things, the ear for all gossip? And he saw how it had changed Manja. Now she was in everybody's business, opinions about everything, half thinking she was the village queen. Pilovo had made it through the Red and White wars, mainly because it was bypassed by both armies. But now the new rulers wanted to change everything. Well, let someone else do that!

Sergi thought the best thing was to spend more time with his family. After all, Sonya was a wonderful daughter, tall and straight, with flowing blond hair and a quiet manner that caused even the contented men to look at her longer than they should have. She was now of marrying age, and that festival would be a lot of work for both of her parents. "Yes," thought Sergi, "it is time to end my leadership of the village, after the marriage this summer." Then he would help with the new couple's house, make them some furniture, get to know his new son-in-law, and let others worry about the village.

Manja disagreed. She liked being the leader's wife, and hoped Sergi would forget about resigning after the wedding.

Karl and Yakov walked together to the Zubovs, Karl slightly ahead as he let the blind Yakov hold onto his arm. Manja often had the bachelors in for a meal, wanting to hear what they had heard. Sergi let the men in and offered them a drink.

Grandma Zubov was shouting at Sonya. "Get those shoes off the table! You know that means a fight."

"Sorry Grandmother," said Sonya, who picked up the shoes and ran a cloth over the table top.

The table was prepared and Manja, Sergi, Sonja, and the two men sat down. Grandma Zubov stayed in the corner near her bed, her babushka wrapped tightly around her head. She always ate alone when they had company. That way she could avoid the conversations that became more irrelevant to her as she got older. The young people didn't appreciate her advice anyway. A stack of birch bark bowls were in front of Sergi. Like all the utensils made from birch, they were light, pretty, and long lasting. Manja had a special skill for steaming the bark, and her vessels were sought after by the other villagers. She had prepared extra bark this fall and was using it to make gifts for Christmas – a barrel for the Pavlovskys, some tuesas for the Bukavevs to store their cheese and berries, a trunk for Sonja for her hope chest. Now they seemed so petty after the trouble the village faced. She had even made some tuesas for herself to put more salt and nuts away for the winter, and to allow her to increase the families supply of water and milk. Her vessels lasted for years and kept the mice and mold away, but she wasn't thinking so far ahead anymore.

Sergi ladled the warm milk into the bowls and passed them around. Sonja soaked some of her bread, in little pieces, in her bowl.

"God bless this food," started Sergi. "Thank you, Lord for this bounty and for all the gifts which we receive from you."

"Amen," replied the others.

"We toast the Pavlovsky boys, and Demitry and his son and Pulgi and Boris, may they rest in peace."

Manja and Sonya set the table again. Five fresh bowls were placed in front of Sergi, and he ladled the beet soup into each. With bachelors you always had to give a full helping. They never knew when their next good meal would come.

Sonja brought Grandma a bowl of soup directly from the stove before the others were served.

Yakov slid his right hand over to feel for the spoon, which dropped to the floor.

Grandma Zubov blessed herself. "Now we will have a female visitor," she murmured.

Yakov cradled the bowl in his left hand and raised it near his mouth. Sonya brought him a new spoon and he began to ladle the hot broth in.

"Manja, you make the best borscht."

"Sure I do and the most, too."

Karl laughed, "Yakov is a flatterer. I say your borscht is the best but I mean it."

"Why don't you both eat more and talk less?" said Sergi. "I eat better when we have company, too."

Sonya said little. Russian children knew when to speak and when to stay quiet. And she wanted to hear more about the wolf attack.

"Tell me more about what you saw," asked Yakov.

Karl started. "Well, it was horrible. We went into the clearing and saw those boys all torn apart by the wolves. Sasha couldn't bear it. We had to gather the remains and bring them home."

Sergi agreed. "But then the wolves came back. That's not normal. Why did they not run from us as usual?"

"I don't know. Maybe they were very hungry. They seemed determined not to let us go."

Yakov put his bowl down. "How could they attack so many men? Weren't the torches enough to protect you?"

"They came at us from the rear, grabbing the men in back."

"Yes, they would have grabbed all of us if the torches had gone out."

"It was strange. I think they know better now," said Sergi.

"Why? You only killed three wolves. They killed seven of you," said Manja.

"Why are we trying to guess the mind of an animal? They were hungry. They killed some of us. They ate, and they left. It's as simple as that," said Karl.

Grandma spoke. "Why didn't the wolves eat all of the flesh from the bodies if they were so hungry?"

"Who knows? Maybe they always do that, and besides, our torches drove them away."

Sonya saw Manja move her eyes, so she got up and went to the stove. The stew Manja had made was ready to serve. The potatoes had sunk to the bottom, and the cabbage was wilted. The little bit of veal was braised and would be tasty. She stirred the pot to bring the contents back up. Then she picked it up by the wooden handle and placed it on the trivet in front of Sergi.

Sergi talked as he parcelled out the stew.

"Sonya, more bread. And get Yakov a new spoon, his has some dirt from the stove on it."

"Yes, Father."

This part of the meal ended the conversation for a while. Everyone was hungry, and Manja really was the best cook in the village. Karl and Yakov were on their second helping when Fedor came in.

"I'm sorry to interrupt your dinner, but, Karl, you are needed at the Karpov's. They want you to nail a window shut with one of those beams you have in your shed."

"Well, tell them to wait. I'll be over after I eat. They won't be attacked before then."

"It's not a joke," frowned Fedor.

"I know, but it's not an emergency either. You go help them, and I'll get there shortly. I won't miss any of Manja's dinner."

Fedor left.

"Some people overreact to everything."

"Sure, Karl, but they are afraid."

"Well, so am I. A little. But let's be reasonable. Wolves won't come into the village."

"No, they won't. But we better prepare anyway to keep our spirits up."

"My spirits are ready for dessert! What will that be, Manja, some of your apple cakes?"

"Not hard to guess after this year. Old apples are all I have."

"Your pastry will make them young again."

"And you, old and fat."

Romanov was sitting in the center of the circle of children. It had become something of a tradition for him to tell stories to them on Wednesday evenings and the parents hoped that this night it would get the children's minds elsewhere.

"Once, in a village like this, two children decided to run away from home. They took some biscuits and dried meat, wrapped them in a cloth, and headed out to the forest. The boy had to walk slower because the girl could not keep up. She was younger. When they got to the trees they turned to look at their house one last time, then they kept on."

"Mr. Mayor, did they say goodbye to their parents?" little Tonya Kovalev asked.

"Of course not," said Romanov. "They were running away."

He continued, "So they walked all day, deeper and deeper into the forest, further from the village with every step. They were heading for the river that ran south, hoping to catch a boat there and get far away. But this first night they had to sleep in the woods."

Dasha wondered, "Did they bring any bedclothes?"

"No, they slept in the same cloths they wore."

"But wouldn't they get all stinky?"

"Yes, but that's part of the fun of running away. Now be still or I won't get to the good part."

The other children looked at each other, with glances that read, "Be quiet, I want to hear the rest."

Romanov, "They made a little clear area around the base of a fir tree, swept away the cones and pebbles and filled the holes with dirt; it was comfortable enough. Then they sat down to eat the meat and biscuits, wishing they had brought something to drink. But they didn't complain, they knew they were having fun.

"It was summer, so the sun stayed up a long time, and the boy and girl talked and talked. They laughed thinking about what their parents would say; how the other children would envy them; how grown up they had become in just one day. When the sun went down, they could hear the rabbits heading home to their burrows, the birds settling down on the branches, the night sounds beginning to start.

"Then they heard something else. Piercing the darkness came a course howl that cut into both of them – it was a wolf. The howl kept repeating, filling the woods with an eerie sound. The children backed closer to the tree, hoping the wolf would not see them. They waited for hours, hearing him come closer, then go away, hearing him hunting, then hearing nothing. They were not sleepy."

"Did they have a gun?" Misha asked.

"Of course not, they were too small to fire a gun. Use your brains."

"Couldn't they run home?" Natasha said.

"No, it was too far, and too dark. Besides, who can outrun a wolf? Now keep quiet so I can get on with this.

"The boy saw the wolf first, its great head sliding between two bushes to the right of where they lay. It sniffed the air, looked around, fixed on the two children and grinned. Then it came into the clearing and stood in front of them. To their surprise it spoke."

"Little girl and boy, where do you come from?"

"Almost too nervous to reply, the boy said, 'From the village, we are running away.'"

"Oh yes, it is good to run away, I can help you. I know the forest; I can take you where you want to go; you will be safe with me."

"But we want to be alone, to go our own way. That's why we left the village."

"No, no, that's too dangerous. You won't last long out here. This is the place for animals, you need my help."

"The boy thought that perhaps the wolf was right. They didn't know the forest, they hadn't even found the river, but the wolf would know. And the wolf seemed so nice, not like those stories they had heard in the village. Maybe their parents had lied to them?"

"Yes, we will follow you. Please take us to the river."

"The river? Oh yes, I can take you there. I will go slow so you can follow."

"So they followed the wolf further into the woods, walking all night. When day broke they were beside a hill, near a great forest, one where the trees were tallest and the ground dark. The wolf stopped."

"You need rest; we will stop here. Sleep awhile and I will see if I can find you some food."

"It didn't take long for the children to fall asleep, they were so tired. They slept for a long time, and when they awoke it was late afternoon. At first they thought it was night, since everything was so dark, but when they rubbed their eyes they realized they were in a cave, and they were not alone.

"A different wolf came to them." So you are the little children that came this morning. Welcome," said the female wolf.

"Then the children saw the others. Six more wolves of different sizes. The littlest wolves were shouting, "We are hungry now mamma, let us eat."

"In a minute," the she-wolf replied. "Your father is coming back soon."

"The children were hungry, too, and hoped that the father wolf would bring things that they could eat, and show them a stream to drink from.

"When the father wolf returned, he assembled the family at the entrance to the cave. They spoke to each other in whispers, glancing at the children as they talked. Then they turned to them, saying,

"Come, children, it is time we ate."

"The boy and girl stood up and walked toward the entrance. The little wolves ran at them, biting into their cloths. It didn't hurt much, this play, but the children asked the mother wolf to call it off.

"Children," she barked. "Leave them to us, you will get yours later." The boy and girl were puzzled by this. Where was the food?

The mother wolf trotted over. "It is so nice of you to come," she said, then bit hard into the little girl. Before he could run, the father had the little boy down, under his belly, ready to be eaten.

"The children called for their parents. They didn't come. They called for their friends. They didn't come. They screamed, but no people could hear them. They were so far away, so alone, so free. They never had to return to the village."

The children were frozen silent. They had heard wolf stories before, but this one was worse. They thought of their friends the Pavlovsky boys, and little Dimitry. They got up and started leaving.

Romanov watched them go. He wanted to scare them tonight, make them wary, keep them from listening to the nonsense their parents were saying about the wolves leaving. He had no children of his own, and, though he would never tell them, he loved these ones.

Later in the evening, Beatrice, the old widow, was arguing with Yuri. "Leave me alone, I don't need your help, go help others if that's what you want to do, but don't worry about me."

"But we do worry. You have no one. Let me just sleep over a few nights until we are sure there is no danger," said Yuri.

"What danger? Don't you know I've been chased by wolves twice, and they never got me? My husband was no fool. He knew not to show fear to an animal. They smell it."

"I know you can usually take care of yourself, but this may be different."

"Things haven't changed much in my lifetime; I don't expect they will before I die, and I want to be on my own. You can start throwing dirt on me once I start accepting favors."

"All right, but I'll come over and check later."

"Yes, yes, just go now, find something useful to do."

Yuri left, shaking his head. He couldn't understand old people, but it had been a quiet day. Maybe Beatrice was right, and the peril was over. Who was to say; she certainly had seen more in her life than Yuri expected to in his. A few of the men were gathering at Sergi's for some wine and talk. He'd ask them about leaving Beatrice alone.

Beatrice was mumbling to herself, "They think I'm so feeble. When I was a girl we had no rubber boots, no motors to help with the work, no trips to the towns. We did for ourselves and we did well. I don't want any smelly man lying around snoring, expecting breakfast. When I stop doing things for myself they can take me away. Who wants to live depending on others? Have they no pride?"

On his way home from Beatrice's, Yuri stopped at the Zobov's. Once inside, he pulled Sergi aside. "I was in the woods before the attack. There were many wolf tracks, more then the ones we saw in the clearing. Did you notice?"

"No, but so what? Wolves often come close to the village, but then they move on."

"I know, but this was different. The tracks were grouped. They were there for some time."

"But they're gone now, eh?" Sergi said.

11

Thursday, December 22nd

In a small village, in winter, privacy was almost impossible, especially for teenagers. Parents knew that very young children could not get into serious trouble, but teenagers were a different matter. Give them a chance and their hormones would rule them. Keep them busy, work them hard, watch them so they were never alone, and you may keep them from having bastards.

Sonya Zubov and Timor Kovalev could not control their urge to be together. They knew that the summer would bring the weather to provide the festival for their marriage. But summer was six months away. Maybe a little play could keep them from the frustration that gnawed at their very bones. Timor had pulled back a few times squirting his seed on Sonya's belly. That was fine for him but Sonya had to pretend to be satisfied when her desire not only peaked but was panting in its want for completion. She hoped to hold out till June so she could give him the virginity all men wanted. She wanted her parents to be proud when the first baby came a year later. She wanted the villagers to see them as a couple, not as wanton lovers that couldn't wait. And – she worried that a pregnancy might drive Timor away. She had been told repeatedly that men were fickle and would promise even marriage to get at her unique possession. But she had urges too.

Sjholkov's barn became their meeting place. He had neglected it in his later years, but it was still useful for the storage of hay and implements. Any animal could kick it down in a moment, so none were stabled there. People visited the barn occasionally to recover some tool or load a wagon with hay, but the old door gave plenty of warning when someone was entering and ample time to scrunch down in the upper loft and hide. In fact, it was fun to hide together when someone was just a few feet below and didn't know anyone was there and in flagrante. So Sonja usually found a way to accept Timor's proposals to meet, always with the warning that he not go too far.

The cold often provided additional cover. Who wished to go out, even to the barn, on a bitter cold day? Chores could wait until the wind stopped, or the day cleared, or the cold spell snapped. Manja should have known that Sonya seemed too eager to work on these days. Where was the reluctance and the laziness that usually characterized her response to her mother's incessant demand for chores? But work done was work done even if Sonya seemed to take a long time in doing it.

Today Sonya wrapped herself in her warmest shawl, covered her head and twirled it around her neck one and one half times. She slipped a kulich into the bottom of her left sleeve – something sweet to give to Timor when they were done. Sonya picked up the basket and went to search for the awl and hammer that father said was somewhere in the barn. This could easily take an hour and she didn't need that with Timor's speed. But maybe she could slow him down this time, get him to notice her needs, keep the moment longer, make him appreciate her wants for a while. The stories of the forest wolves worried her some, but they wouldn't come right into the village in the daylight nor would they attack a human when the village was awake and alert.

Timor Kovalev told his mother, "I am going out to find the stone Sjholkov leaves around to use. Our knives could use some sharpening."

His mother didn't respond. She was glad to see him go, even on as flimsy an excuse as this, instead of having him sulk around the house like a caged bear. He was as moody as all the Kovalevs.

Sonja was already in the barn when he arrived.

"I'm up here."

"Why did you climb up so fast?"

"Well, you know, those wolves."

Timor chided her for bringing up that subject. "Who are you, Goldilocks?"

"Those were bears," she reminded him.

"In Russia they would be wolves!"

But it was hopeless, she wanted to be with him, needed to be with him, and would risk the shame of discovery to be with him. His shame would be less, but he was risking the wrath of both fathers.

Thursday morning was calm throughout the village. It appeared that the wolves had really gone. None were even heard. The villagers spent the time getting the cabins ready for the hard days ahead. Wood had to be moved closer to the homes. Guns, the few that they had, were cleaned, the bullets kept at hand. The men had met in the morning to count the amount of fire power they had: six rifles, two shotguns, and a pistol; 37 bullets for the rifles, 28 shells for the shotguns, and 21 bullets for the pistol. That was all! If every bullet killed, that would mean 86 dead wolves. But they knew that at best one in five would kill, so maybe 17 wolves could be eliminated. If the wolves attacked they would have to use pitchforks and pikes. But that seemed unlikely now.

No wolves were seen. Perhaps they had left. Wolves did that; they were unpredictable. They had probably moved on.

The barn was quiet, except for the creaking of the old wood and the sounds of some titmice burrowing through the hay. The soft hay dampened every footfall, every movement. Even the rustling of the hay when they moved seemed to be a natural sound caused by the wind that blew through the cracks in the boards. They were blissfully alone, private, enraptured with each other and their togetherness. Sonya hollowed out a nest in the hay so that they were surrounded by its warmth and out of view if someone should come in. Timor was above her, his knees on either side of her hips, bent over as he undid her tunic and began to unbutton her over-blouse. His haste slowed him down as did the catches she had sewn into the tunic to make it harder for him. She laughed quietly as he fumbled with hurry, enjoying the moment, savoring the hold she had over his feelings.

After what seemed like hours he had her naked from the waist up, her young breasts pouting up at him. They seemed wider, flattened by her supine position. Sonya sat up and started on Timor's tunic, slapping his hand when he tried to help. Soon they were embracing, feeling the warmth of their desire, in each others arms. Timor started to kiss Sonya, but it was Sonya who did the real kissing. She was eager today and felt it was his turn to stop them before they went too far. But Timor was already removing Sonya's long skirt and tugging at her under linens. Before he finished he was up on his feet, removing his shirt. There, strapped around his waist was the sash he had bought her in Pulni. She let out a quick gasp and unwound it, holding the fabric up in the light, the ribbons flowing through her hands.

"It's beautiful, Timor," she said, placing it over her breasts. "When did you get it?"

"Never mind," he replied. "Just tell me if you like it."

"Of course I like it, silly. I like everything you give me. But how could you afford this?"

"Don't ask, maybe I'll tell you later."

Timor stretched and took off more of his clothes. Sonya was excited watching him undress. He was no longer a boy, but a well muscled man, ready for independence and for the responsibilities it entailed. His hard body was worth looking at itself, but there would be time for that later when they were finished and lying together in the hay. Timor began pulling down his trousers.

Sonya laughed again, this time at his rampant penis so rigid that he had to fight it to take his trousers off. She thought it funny that the very part of him that so wanted her would try to prevent him from exposing it. She wanted to look at it, touch it, feel its length, examine its details. The round head with its circular jowls, the underside with its crossroads, the length with its throbbing veins. She could look at it for hours. She wanted him to stroke it for her but knew that was her job and that Timor would not admit that he did that when she was not available. But he was too much in a rush, so he flung off his underwear and laid her down on her back and smothered her with kisses as he bucked between her thighs.

She kept saying. "Easy, easy, I don't want you to come."

Sonya managed to slow Timor's rhythm to a level that kept him aroused but unfinished, and started on her own path to orgasm. She had taken a few steps down this road before, but Timor was always done before she got very far. Today it would be different. Sonya held his hips and told him to stop. "Kiss me some more. I want to wait."

Timor kissed her and allowed her to hold him still. He felt, and for the first time, that he wished to remain on the brink and revel in that feeling of precum that always preceded his explosion. If he could hold that back he might enjoy this even more. Her moans were deeper now and he was beside himself trying to stay on the edge but not fall over. This was the best time.

Sonya was getting closer to a feeling that she had never had but knew was coming. If she could hold Timor off for a few more minutes, she would enter a new level of fulfillment that was known only to women. She wanted that, forgot all thought of disgrace, family, pregnancy; they could be worried about later. She was not at that time that gave children, she could chance it now. She guided Timor into the best mounting position. It surprised her that she knew what this was, but all of her instincts were pouring through her body down to her pelvis. She knew what to do and she ached to do it. Timor rose up on his hands and began to penetrate her slowly. She looked at him with eyes that seemed like pools of desire; unfocused, wide, imploring, older. She loved loving him.

Sonya tried to stop Timor's grunting, "Easy, easy, wait for me." Her own moaning was carrying her away with its rhythm. The lovers were sweating, pumping, sliding over each other, reaching for a new climax. They did not hear the creak of the wall plank as Kaala entered the barn. Kaala heard them, however.

Timor was on the brink of coming. Sonya was grinding her hips to match him. She could feel her orgasm approaching.

"Please wait, I'm almost there. Wait I want to come!"

"Hurry, hurry, I can't hold off much longer. I won't be able to stop, hurry."

Sonya threw her head back as her peak approached. She looked up glassy-eyed to watch Timor's muscular pumping. This would be the time.

Kaala had found the ladder and was now in the loft. She saw the two humans and wondered why they were ignoring her. Usually their senses were keen enough to know when danger was this close. But these two were different, they were oblivious to her. Cautiously, Kaala approached Timor from behind. She saw the humping movement of the man's back. This was her chance.

Kaala sprung, sunk her teeth into the side of Timor's neck and jerked his head upward. Her powerful hind legs dug into his back. Timor gurgled a loud wail, blood poured from his mouth and neck. Sonya thought she was hallucinating. Was this the way a lover looked through the rush of orgasm? Then she saw the hair of the wolf over Timor's shoulder. She tried to scream but nothing came out. She tried to move but couldn't. She tried to help Timor but her arms were frozen in position. Kaala's claws were over Timor's shoulders. She flexed her powerful back legs and gutted Timor from behind. Timor's body rolled to the left, the blood gushing in spurts. Kaala snapped her head back and forth, tearing the boy in chunks. Timor went limp, his neck severed, his blank eyes rolled into his head. Kaala savaged his side, tore large pieces from his buttocks, his thighs.

Sonya rose slowly, trancelike, backing away from the wolf and the remains of her lover. The kulich fell from her hand onto the loft floor. Kaala looked up and turned from the boy, baring her teeth at Sonya. Frightened, Sonya saw the pitchfork and reached for it with her left hand. Kaala knew about humans and their weapons and circled to Sonya's right. She waited until the girl appeared to stumble and sprung at her neck. Sonya tumbled backwards but kept the fork between her and the wolf. She braced it on the planking, anchoring it with both hands. Kaala came down on to her in a great leap but the fork caught the wolf in the chest. The blades penetrated through her back and cradled her spine. She yelped in agony and slashed at Sonya's breasts. Sonya saw her flesh flying away as Kaala died, impaled on the fork.

Sonya lay there, the wolf's blood dripping onto her naked body.

Bunta and Sana were already in the barn and climbing up the hay bales into the loft when they heard Kaala's death call. Sonya saw both of them coming at her. She pulled at the fork to yank it out of Kaala but it was stuck. She planted her left foot on the wolf's chest and pulled harder. It was still stuck when Sana began her leap but Sonya marshalled all of her remaining strength and pulled the fork clear.

The sweeping motion of the fork caught Sana in the left eye and drove her past the girl as she tore at her right shoulder with her paw. Sonya spun to the right from the wolf's momentum, Bunta bit into her side.

"No, no," screamed Sonya. She reeled from the blow. Bunta and the girl fell off the loft onto the barn floor. Sonya staggered to her feet, her torn side gushing blood. This time Bunta went for the neck and brought the girl down. Sonya hardly resisted, the wolf severed her throat. She gasped, trying to get air into her lungs, hearing it pass out from her neck. Dimly she saw Sana coming down on her too. She tried again to scream but only a low gurgling came from her mouth. Life oozed from her, the pain subsided.

12

Thursday afternoon

"So we go," said Reina. "We are all hungry. Some of the hannal haven't eaten in weeks."

"Be patient," said Maala. "If we attack it will be in evening. Humans are weak in the dark, they do not see well. We already know they are prey in the daylight, nighttime will only be better."

"But we took those two humans with ease," whined Sana.

"Yes, but the female killed Kaala, and you're half-blinded."

"So what? Since when do we stop the hunt when one of us dies?" asked Reina.

"We have to mourn our dead," Maala answered.

"Maala's right," said Tuva. "We can attack the village tonight. They will be less wary then. If we go in darkness, we can be in the village before they see us."

"They see us better when daylight hits the snow," said Vaal.

"I know," growled Maala. "Stupid attacks will cost us our lives. We rest now."

The pack matted on the forest floor, licked their legs and necks and waited for the moon to rise. The plan was to attack the village animals first, then see if the humans came out of their lairs. All of them should eat that night. If they ate at will, they could return to the forest full. This was the solution to their problems.

"Where is that girl?"

Sergi stopped his carving, "She's a good girl Manja. I'm sure she's off doing what she said. Give her some time, what's the hurry on a day like this?"

"Well, I need her to help start supper."

"Okay, Okay, I'll go check. Where did she go, to the old barn?"

"I think so. She went to find those tools of yours."

Sergi put on his parka and boots and left for the barn. He walked slowly, thinking about the Pavlovsky boys. How can Alla and Sasha continue? When will it all hit them?

The barn door was open. Even Sonya knew she should close it when she was through. But teenagers were teenagers and all in all she was a good daughter.

Sergi looked into the barn. At first he saw nothing, but he sensed something was in there. Stepping over the sill, he entered the barn. There was a bundle on the barn floor mixed in among some hay that had fallen from the loft. He went over to see.

Manja saw Sergi running home. She opened the door for him.

"What's the matter?"

"It's..it's...she's dead...she's dead!"

Manja fell back into the chair.

"My daughter, my daughter! God has cursed this village!"

Sergi clutched Manja to his chest, looking over her shoulder at Grandma Zubov.

"Wolves?" Grandma asked.

"Yes, they're back."

"Take me to her," said Manja.

"No, you can't see this. I will do it."

"Take me, she's my only daughter."

Sergi went for Fedor and Ivan. Their wives and Grandma Zubov came as well. Ivan went in first. He brought holy water and sprinkled the body. Manja collapsed when she saw her young girl shredded.

Grandma Zubov shook her head. "It is the work of Satan. He lives here. He is doing these things."

Luba held Manja and turned her away from the body. The men began to place Sonya on the canvas they brought.

Luba saw blood stains near the back of the barn. They were coming from the loft.

"Wait! Fedor, look back there."

They scanned the blood trail, seeing that it came from above.

"You go up Fedor, see what's there."

Fedor climbed the ladder slowly. He no more wanted to go into the loft than anyone else, but someone had to. He saw the wolf first. Kaala lay open on the hay, her chest split wide and her entrails spilling over onto the loft floor.

"There is a dead wolf up here...and wait...my God it's Timor. He's naked too and his neck is torn apart."

"Saint Peter help us!", pleaded Anna. "No more please."

Ivan spoke first. "I will go and tell the Kovalevs."

"Tell everyone, and soon. The wolves are back."

Everyone but Yuri. He had been at the edge of the woods, not far from the barn, when the wolves fled. One wolf made off quickly into the forest, but the other one, bleeding from one eye, appeared disoriented. She almost stumbled into Yuri's path.

At first the man tried to run toward the village, but Sana was in his path. He then tried to circle the wolf, but Sana, sensing danger, kept him at bay. Neither wanted trouble.

Sana, convinced that she must wound or frighten this prey, began a slow advance toward Yuri. She kept the right side of her face, the good eye, toward the man, making sure that he didn't shift position and put her at a disadvantage. The man was backing away.

Finally she charged, catching Yuri in the side. They fell into the snow, the man on top. The strength of the wolf caused him to buck and jump as she twisted under his weight. He was almost riding her, one hand tearing at her ear, the other latched onto her neck.

The wolf dropped on her front legs, hurling Yuri over her head; his left hand grasped at the left side of her face, scratching the wounded eye. The wolf cried out, a wail that stopped Bunta in her tracks.

Yuri hurried to his feet, his right hand searching his pocket for his knife. The wolf came at him again, but this time he was ready. He plunged the blade into the side of the animal, twisting the handle as he went. It slid in parallel to the ribs, causing pain, but little damage. The wolf pitched back, the knife still in her side.

Now Yuri was on the village side of the forest. He began to back away again, this time toward safety. He knew enough about wolves not to show her his back or to excite her further by running away. But Sana was too hurt to follow. Then Bunta arrived, saw her wounded packmate and ran into position between her and the man.

As Yuri kept backing away, Bunta stayed in position.

Again, neither man nor wolf wanted a fight. Yuri was now out of the woods and closer to the barn; he kept going, reaching the safety of the shed near the barn, stumbling inside and collapsing from the effort. He would need time to recover and head for home. The wolves retreated into the forest, Bunta sheparding the limping Sana, leading her home to the pack.

Vasja Luskey saw Reisa hurrying home.

"What's happened?" he asked.

"It's Sonya and Timor, they have been killed in the barn."

"More wolves?"

"Yes, right in the village," she answered.

Peter and Maria were in the kitchen listening.

"We have to get the house ready, they may come back," said Vasja.

"Yes, yes. Children! You're not to leave the house unless I say so."

"Yes, mother."

Vasya looked through the curtain. All he could see was the Zobov house, then the barn, and, no more than thirty yards further, the woods. He turned toward Reisa, who was still lecturing the children.

"We start now, while it is still light. The door comes first, then I'll bring in more wood and my axe."

"And I'll get the potatoes and peas from storage, and bring in more milk."

The children looked at each other.

13

Thursday evening

After supper, the howl of a dog was heard. It was Penji, Dimitry's dog, wailing in the silver light.

"You hear that?" said Romanov.

"The dog misses his master," said Ivan.

"If you believe that you're a fool."

The realization of what happened to Sonya and Timor settled on the village. Was no one safe? How had wolves come into town unseen, killed two of the children, and escaped unnoticed. Were they ghosts?

The old barn was a bit away from any of the houses. Between the hay and the walls and the fact that no one was outside, it was possible that the cries for help from the teenagers had gone unheard. If so, who was safe?

There was no discussion now. Everyone knew that they had to make their homes safe until the wolves left for good. Even Sergi now knew that these animals were different.

"I can't imagine what has gotten into them. Don't they know we will kill all of them once we get the chance?"

Manja murmured. "Will we get the chance?"
"Of course we will. If there's a God in heaven."
"If, if."

Pavel Vavilin went to see the Buckavevs. He would have to report these deaths and wanted a clear description from a family that had not suffered a loss. Fedor was one of the few that treated Pavel with civility, his pleasant nature overcoming his mistrust. They sat and talked.

Vlad Kovalev alternated between cursing the wolves and screaming about how Timor had disobeyed his parents and disgraced them with the Zubov girl.

"Do none of the young listen anymore!" he shouted at Elena.

She didn't answer. Elena knew Vlad could not understand her agony or forgive their son. For the first time she let herself think about how evil Vlad was. Had he no sense of decency, no care for her sorrow? The Zubovs had lost their only child, a wonderful daughter, the Kovalev's future daughter-in-law, and they lost her in a way they would never had suspected. How long had she and Timor been meeting this way? Couldn't they at least have waited until the summer? Had the wolves brought God's judgment to them? She sent Tonya over to the Zubov's, partially to ease Manja's mind, she doted so much on the little girl, but also because there was no need for a nine year old to hear all this.

And now another funeral tomorrow. When will it all stop?

Stephan Volkov stayed in his house all day. He heard about Timor and Sonya from Yuri who visited the young man wondering why he was not out talking to the others. When he entered Stephan's hut, he knew why; the signs were back. Yuri promised not to tell anyone and left Stephan to himself, asking him to come to his house if he had trouble, knowing he wouldn't come.

When Stephan awoke that morning, he saw the streaks in the mirror. In the early light his reflection was lupine, his eyes and nose accented, his forehead colored as if covered with hair. Even his teeth seemed larger, rimmed by the dark red marks around his lips.

"Why now!" Stephan thought. "Why am I turning into a wolf when they are killing our people?"

He knew better than to show himself to the others. How could they understand this now? Besides, maybe they were right, maybe the wolves were calling to him as a brother, maybe his changes were a signal, maybe he was a werewolf.

Confused, Stephan stayed alone. Sometimes the signs left in a few days; maybe by then he would be normal again. Unless the wolves came back.

After dinner Sasha and others heard the first cry of a watchdog. In agony the animal yelped and whined. They knew it was wolves.

"I'm going out to kill them," said Sasha.

"No," cried Alla. "We have suffered enough. Let the others do it."

The scene was the same in every home. Who could summon the courage to go out at night and attack the wolves? They wouldn't enter the houses, but they would attack a man if he came to them.

The whole evening the village lay paralyzed. One by one the dogs were picked off by the wolves. Their horrid whines could be heard by everyone as the wolves tore into them. Some of the dogs attacked, even though they were frightened by the size and numbers of the pack, but they could hardly match the strength and ferocity of their wild cousins. Even the largest, used to having his way with the other dogs, fell easily. The wolves showed no remorse, they killed each dog in turn, tearing into its flesh while it was still alive. Other dogs cowered and tried to show submission; the wolves ignored this and killed them too. The wailing howls and barks went unheeded. The wolves ate at leisure.

The children were especially despondent, hearing their animals crying for help. What was wrong with their father; hadn't he always protected them and the animals? Why was he staying inside like a coward? What was going on? It was doubly hard on the teenage boys. How could their parents keep them from fighting; from going out to save what was theirs? Why was this different; who were these wolves to come in and kill their livestock without being killed themselves? The few shots coming from the houses were a feeble response to such a great danger. Hadn't they trained the animals to obey them; didn't they owe them their protection?

The wolves came closer to the huts, realizing that the humans would not stop them. Now it was the horses' turn. There were only nine horses in the village, but that would be a good meal for many wolves.

The villagers watched from the windows, as the wolves closed in. Several wolves were shot by those who had guns. Those without guns kept their windows shuttered. No horse was safe, even those in the barns. The noise from the frightened animals filled almost every home. First the wolves broke through the flimsy doors, panicking the horses. Then they fanned out in groups of six or so, each sensing that a horse kill would be like an elk. When they had one backed into a corner, wild eyed and lathering, they sent in the first wolf to attack the nose. With a wolf on his head, the horse bucked and kicked; the wolves tried to stay away from the horses' powerful hooves. The wolf latched onto the horse's face bit down harder on the nose, causing the animal great pain. The weight of the wolf was too great for the horse to keep from falling to the ground. As it lowered its head to try and shake the wolf off, the rest of the pack came in. The next wolf went for the neck, blood gushed out and weaken the animal. The remaining pack went for the legs, and brought the horse down. Once down, the horse knew he would lose; a few furtive kicks did nothing; he succumbed, killed in his stall. The bellowing and moaning rang throughout the houses. Some horses inflicted terrible kicks to the wolves; that didn't stop them. Some horses ran out of the barns; they didn't get far. The wolves were too many; they savaged one horse after another. Their cries filled the village. Everyone thought that by now these wolves must have had their fill of flesh. They would go now and leave them alone.

Mogla and Quarta, wolves from the northern pack, sniffed at the broad door that shuttered the lower part of the Zubov house.

"Goat, I smell goat; and horse; strong smells, many animals," said Quarta.

"How do we get into this place?" asked Mogla.

Quarta wondered. The house was well protected, no openings, no windows, heavy doors, no obvious entry. By now seven more wolves had joined them. They sensed a feast waited inside.

The animals inside the house smelled the wolves also. They knew what this meant. The goats bayed and pulled at their tethers. The horses paced in their stalls, whinnying and bucking in fear. Wolves! Could they run away? The mare kicked at the front of her stall, frightening the goats even more. By now the whole barn was in a state of panic, chickens flying everywhere, the noise building upon itself. Confused, wanting to get out, the mare kicked at the back of her stall, once, twice, three times. The last kick splintered two boards, which rotated about the nails hammered into their tops. She kicked again. A piece of the back of the stall gave way, not enough for her to back through, but enough for the wolves to see an opening. They headed for it.

Upstairs. the Zobovs knew what was happening. Sergi loaded his rifle, trying to keep Manja and Grandma calm among the commotion.

"How will you shoot them?," asked Manja. "You can't go out there, they will attack you."

"I'll open the barn door a crack and fire point blank at them, that might chase them away."

"Be careful, they are everywhere."

Sergi unlatched the door on the upper stairway and started down the steps. The panic of the animals had raised a haze of dust and the confusion left no clear path to the door. He shouted for calm; knowing that was impossible; he had to chase the wolves away for that. At the bottom of the stairs he saw the real problem.

Staring at him, no more than fifteen feet away, was a wolf. Both man and animal stayed still as the chaos raged around them. Both were surprised to see the other. Sergi backed toward the steps, aimed his rifle at the wolf. The wolf came forward, keeping the distance between them constant. Things seemed to be happening slowly; it was almost as if this wolf and Sergi were in a different time, tense but measured, not the agitated time of the animals in the barn. Nether seemed to want to change it.

Sergi saw several other wolves, heading for the animals. He could only fire at one before they would turn on him. He backed up the steps, one at a time, feeling for the next level with his heels, hoping not to trip. The wolf kept coming.

Sergi paused at the landing on the top of the stairs; he kept his right hand on the rifle and turned so that his left hand could feel for the lever. He didn't call for his family; he wanted no part of this for them. The handle slipped into his palm, just as the wolf began to ascend. Sergi moved backward, opened the latch and pushed the door open into the house. The wolf mounted the first few steps.

Once Sergi knew he would be safe in the house, he fired down the steps. The bullet missed to the left, and embedded in the wood near the base of the wall. Sergi jumped back into the house, and closed the door. The wolf vaulted to the landing, pawing at the entrance.

"Everyone back," shouted Sergi. "The wolves are in the barn, attacking the stock. Manja, push the table over here."

Sergi reloaded his rifle as his wife shoved the table against the door.

"Now pile heavy things on it; we must not let them in."

Manja and Grandma and little Tonya Kovalev put pots, bricks, anything they could find on the table. The door was secure.

"What about the horses, the goats?" asked Manja.

"I don't know," Sergi answered. "We have only one way down to the barn, and the wolves will get us on the stairs."

"Can you shoot them from the trap door?"

"Yes, maybe that would work."

They hurried to the pantry and rolled back the rug. Sergi hefted the trap door handle, and raised the floor up. He latched it on the hook with the rope. Now he could see below. Animals and wolves filled his view. He aimed at a wolf that was straddling one of the goats and fired. The wolf turned to her side, stumbled off the goat, dropped to one leg and pawed at the air with the other. Sergi loaded again and aimed at another wolf who was biting the mare. He missed, hitting the mare in the haunch. The mare rose on her hind legs, kicked her hooves in the air, and fell forward onto the wolf. Segri heard a bone break, he hoped it was a wolf's.

Two wolves had already dragged a goat back through the hole in the wall and out into the snow. One horse was already dead. The chickens were in the ceiling, away from the fray. Sergi fired again, at the wolves eating the horse. They stopped.

Mogla said, "Wait, the fire stick is here. We leave."

The wolves began to retreat. Sergi fired again, hitting a wolf in the foreleg; he reloaded again, but by now the wolves had slipped back through the opening and into the snow. Sergi left the hatch and headed for the door.

"Not yet," Manja said. "Don't chase them, wait until they leave and we can go downstairs and see to the animals."

Sergi turned to Manja, "They will not go far unless we chase them." He pulled back the heavy table, unlatched the door, and started down the steps.

"Be careful," cried Manja. "We need you here, not running through the village after wolves."

Sergi descended slowly, scanning the barn for any stray wolves. He inched toward the breach in the wall, near the frightened, wounded, wild-eyed mare. The wolves were outside, eating the goat. Sergi raised his rifle.

Quarta saw the man and howled. The mare bucked again, her right hind leg hitting Sergi in his side. He fell through the opening, not eight feet from the wolves.

"He has the firestick," barked Mogla. "Watch."

Sergi was confused. The wolves were not coming to him, they seemed to sense his weapon. Did they know that he had only one shot? They could take him before he reloaded. But they weren't retreating either. He took a chance, firing directly at the nearest wolf. The bullet caught the animal just below the neck, on the top of the left foreleg. She rolled to her left, then got up and began to limp backward. The others backed off too.

Sergi watched, gauging the movement of the pack, wanting to reload, afraid that any movement would stop the wolves from retreating. It took him a full minute to put a new shell in the chamber. He shot again. Now the wolves went into full retreat, making the forest edge in seconds. Sergi backed into the barn again, calling upstairs to Manja, "Come down, I need help."

Manja was already on the landing, ready to defend Sergi if the wolves attacked again. She told Grandma and Tonya to stay at the door, just in case, and went down to her husband. They braced the hole shut, things were safe for a while. They turned to the animals; they had work to do; the wolves were gone.

And so it seemed. After the last of the other horses were killed the wolves retreated to the woods, dragging some of the dead dogs with them. Calm came to the village. It was 10 pm.

Maala and the others massed again in the forest, about 600 yards from the village. The size of the hannal had grown to nearly 100 as the scent of food permeated to nearby packs. Just seeing well-fed brothers made the new arrivals expectant. The newcomers shared in the remains of the dogs dragged back by the others.

Vaal spoke first. "These animals were easy, but how does it feel to kill a human? Are they easy, too? How do they taste?"

"They taste sweet. I don't like it," said Reina.

Maala spoke, "They are not easy. We lost four brothers to kill eight humans. Sana is injured too, and some others were hit with the fire from the sticks. They know how to use fire. They have noise sticks that can kill from far away! We have to be careful."

Sana spoke next. "I will be fine and ready to attack the humans again. Even in their lairs they are helpless. Kaala died, but we killed two humans easily."

"And most of them do not protect their dogs or their horses. They must be weak," said Reina.

"Maybe, but we should be sure. We can send a small pack tomorrow to see if they can be attacked in their nests. There are many of them. Enough to feed us all," said Vaal.

"No. We can't give the humans time to prepare, we have to go back now. Once you have killed one human you must kill them all. That was the mistake Demja made with the Kurins. He left some of them alive. We can't chance that.

Besides, some of the hannal have not eaten yet. Tonight all of them will eat and eat again," said Maala.

"Once all the humans are gone we will feed on the rest of their animals at will," he continued. "They have goats and sheep and more dogs. We will be full for weeks."

The moon rose full into the night air, silhouetting the birches, outlining the houses. It was just above the tree line and the comparison made it look huge in the snow laden sky. Large gaps between the few clouds allowed moonbeams to penetrate down to the snow; reflections lighted the fields and the paths, giving the village a cold phosphorescent glow. The sight lines from the houses to the woods were clear and sharp and the villagers, each in their own house, kept at least one family member at a window, looking for wolves.

Before midnight the whole hannal moved again toward the village. The wolves glistened like silver streaks in the moonlight, gliding with their graceful gate over their darker reflections on the snow. They came in six columns of about fifteen each, downwind, even though they knew humans had little sense of smell. The columns were spread out over a front of 70 yards coming into the village from the southwest. They trotted to the forest edge and stopped. They had not been sighted.

"Now we start," said Maala. "Head straight for the small huts near us. Remember to keep up the attack; confuse the humans; do no let them have time to help each other."

Stephan, his home being so close to the village edge, was the first to see the wolves approaching. He knew they would attack the villagers next. He wanted to stop them; to call to them; to make them leave. But again, maybe the people were right? Maybe he was an animal, more wolf than man?

Stephan opened his door and walked toward the pack heading for his side of the village. The streaks on his faced turned grey in the moonlight. He was frightened yet curious. If they accepted him it would answer the question that had nagged him his whole life. Which was he, man or wolf? He kept the backs of his hands toward the wolves, to minimize threat, just as he would to a fierce dog.

Maala stopped. The man came forward.

"This man holds his arms out and his hands open. No weapons?"

"He is still human," whined Tuva.

"But why doesn't he run? Why doesn't he fear us?"

"It's a trick! He is dangerous."

"No, he wants something."

"Watch. He is getting closer."

Stephan walked into the pack, softly chanting, "God be with me, God be with me."

The wolves had not retreated, that would be cowardice. They waited for Stephan to come to them. Here was something they had not expected, and a small fear nestled in their minds. They sniffed his clothes, his hands, human smells.

Stephan began to relax, he wasn't being threatened by these animals, they seemed to accept him. Could he be one of them?

Tuva growled. She wanted to pull this man down, or at least scare him away, to make him run as prey always ran when the pack came near. But she watched Maala for a lead.

Maala wondered if they should attack; what prey could be easier? But the smell of fear had left this man, he was different, to be avoided.

"Leave him alone, go around him to the human nests," said Maala.

The wolves parted, not wanting to touch this one. They left Stephan behind, confused at their lack of response.

Stephan ran around the wolves and fronted them again.

"Kill me, spare the village, I am not one of you. You are evil, kill me, please."

Tuva asked, "What should we do Maala? This human should be taken."

"No! Follow me to the huts, leave this human alone."

The wolves parted again, leaving the desperate man behind. Stephan shouted to the villagers, "They are coming, kill them, they are coming!"

Some people in the houses saw what had happened. So Stephan really was a wolf! See how the wolves had accepted him. Was he telling them things about the village? Why wasn't he hurt?

Vlad Kovalev had seen enough; he knew the village was cursed with Stephan; he had tried to run him off several times; make him live elsewhere, the forest, the next village, anywhere but Pilovo.

"I told the others he was a bad omen. Why didn't they listen to me?"

"Please, Vlad," pleaded Elena. "Leave him alone."

"What! So he can help his comrads?"

He opened his window, leveled his rifle, put Stephan in his sights, and fired. Stephan caught the bullet in his chest and dropped backward. He turned toward the Kovalev house, a puzzled look on his face.

"You fools! I'm a man! Save your bullets for them."

Maala was puzzled also. This was queer behavior for humans. What were they to expect next?

Stephan fell in the snow, bleeding from the chest. He wanted to die, to be relieved. He would know the answer in a short while. He prayed to Saint Stephan for forgiveness; for being what he was; for his despair. The pain from the wound subsided; Stephan felt a calm he had not felt in life; he knew he was going to a place of love, a place of understanding; he knew he would be accepted.

The packs now began to run straight for the homes.

The first wolves to reach a hut found the door bolted shut. It was the home of the Kovalev's. Vlad saw the wolves coming for the door and ran to buttress the frame with his body while Elena brought chairs and the large bed to wedge against the frame. Elena carried as much as she could to add to the weight behind the door. The wolves scratched at the foundation, but it was too hard to penetrate. The head of a wolf broke through part of the pantry window, but Elena took her frying pan and stuck it into the opening; the wolf backed away. The hut held; the wolves retreated.

It was too bad that the Karpovs did not do the same. They believed that the peril had passed and, disregarding the advice of the others, did not have their door secured. The door rattled as three wolves pushed at it. Ivan ran to block the door, but the wolves kept pounding until the latch gave way. They shoved the door in, over the fallen body of Ivan, saw Anna and made for her. She shrieked and fell offering no resistance at all.

Misha crawled up onto the top of the oven, the warm bricks holding the body of the trembling girl. A wolf approached cautiously, aware of the heat and the danger. He pushed his snout into the pile of boots and clothing near Misha. Misha looked wide-eyed at the animal.

"Please, please, go away," she begged.

The wolf cocked his head to one side, wondering if prey could be this easy. He latched onto Misha's dress and slowly pulled her off the oven and down to the floor. Misha covered her head and cried. The wolf took his first bite from her shoulder.

Ivan got up from under the fallen door and ran out to get help. He got a few yards away before the wolves brought him down from behind. His screams alerted the rest of the village.

"The wolves are back! They are in Karpov's house! Bolt your doors!" shouted others.

Little Ivan was cornered. He knew the rest of his family were dead or dying; he had no one to help him, but still he fought when the wolves closed in on him.

A third group of wolves assaulted the home of Beatrice. Old and alone, she had let the house fall into disrepair. The villagers helped her when they could, but still her home was vulnerable. Yuri had planned to sleep near her house to protect her, but he was at the church with a few of the men, planning a possible defense for the village.

Her door was easy to open. She kept it that way because she was too weak to open a tight door. All she had was a loose latch and a roll of old clothing she kept at the bottom to keep out the drafts. She hadn't taken any of the precautions she promised she would.

"I have lived through worse than this," she said, to anyone who asked.

The first wolf came in, throwing his heavy body at the front door, breaking through when the latch gave way. He stopped when he saw Beatrice, snarled to show her his teeth, then went for her. He bit into her neck forcing her back into the fireplace. He backed off as the sparks shot up around them. Beatrice sat up, bleeding from the wound. She grabbed an andiron and poked at the wolf. The other wolves stood by.

"Come on you devil! I'll skewer you like a rabbit!"

The flames licked at her shawl. She knew she had to get away from the fire. The wolves were wary and gave her some distance. She waved the iron at them.

"So now you are afraid! Good, I've lived longer than you have. You won't get me. Go away, get out, go away."

The black wolf made a lunge at her legs, but the old woman moved, found her strength, and jabbed him with the iron. Now she was to the side of the fireplace, her shawl in flames. She couldn't stop to tear it off and still keep the wolves away, so she reached down and grabbed the shovel. She scooped up a shovel full of embers and threw them at the wolves. They split into a semicircle before the crazed human. By now the flames were all around her. Choking on the fumes, she stumbled forward, throwing another batch of hot embers at them. They whined in fright.

"So – you don't like that, do you? Fire is my friend. You may kill me, but by all that's holy, I'll kill you too."

The embers caught the blankets near Beatrice's bed setting the curtains on fire. Soon the whole cottage was burning. The wolves looked for a way out, but Beatrice moved toward the door, sprinkling embers at them as she tried to escape. The black wolf lunged at her again and caught her in the calf. She went down, now engulfed in fire. But, when she fell, her body jolted the door closed, and the wolves saw no way out. The flaming woman cackled once she realized what she had done.

"I die, but you devils die with me," she laughed. "God be my solace," she murmured as the smoke started closing her throat.

Some of the villagers watched from their windows, one eye on the burning cottage, one on the wolves that were attacking everywhere. It was too late to help Beatrice. Their shame did not conquer their fear and they stayed inside. Beatrice hardly screamed at all but the wolves howled terribly. The fire ran up their fur, into their eyes, they stumbled, confused and trapped. The hut burst into flame, an inferno, the walls caved in, the roof collapsed, a burning pyre of wood and flesh.

The other wolves turned away. They needed other prey.

The Luskeys were prepared for the wolves. Vasja and Peter had bolstered the front door with heavy logs from the woodpile. The wolves threw themselves at their door, but it held. Still the family was terrified. Sana ran around to the side of the house, up onto a wagon and saw the outlines of the family through the mica window. She was not sure about this barrier, she had no experience with it, but it looked flimsy to her so she ran straight at it. Reisa turned screaming as Sana vaulted though the window, landing near the bed. Sana stopped. The Luskeys were rooted in place except for Vasja, who picked up a log and got between the wolf and his family. For thirty long seconds it was a standoff; then two other wolves followed Sana through the window. They advanced slowly. Vasja told Peter to try to get to the kitchen to get knives. As Peter moved to his left, the wolves advanced further.

"Now," said Sana.

The three of them attacked Vasja, and drove him to the floor. He braced the log above his face to ward them off. Peter jumped onto one wolf while Reisa made it to the kitchen. She grabbed two knives, ran back into the room, and started slashing at the wolf on top of her husband. Little Maria cried in the corner. The fight was raging all over the small room. Peter was in the clutches of a wolf, his arm almost bitten off. Sana spun around and bit Reisa and Vaal knocked her down. Vasja tried to get up, but Sana turned on him again, this time at his face.

Peter was losing blood, dragged by the wolf, who released his bite then clamped down higher on his arm. Peter tore at the wolf's eyes, but his attempt was feeble. The wolf was killing him slowly. Reisa was savaged from behind by Vaal. He had the back of her head in his mouth, tearing at the skin as she wailed and stumbled. Vasja was immobile as Sana released his face and bit through his neck. The wolves started to tear off the clothes of the humans to get at the meat on their limbs. They jerked large pieces off, and raised their necks to swallow them whole. This was the first real meal for some of them in months.

When the wolves were done, they noticed Maria in the corner. Vaal trotted up to the screaming girl. He looked at her a bit puzzled; then dove into her shoulder and began eating again.

The feast continued.

14

Blind Yakov could only hear the wolves. He was making his way home from the Karpov's when the wolves attacked. He needed a steady pace to keep his bearings. Now his problem now was to run to safety, but in which direction?

He heard the wolves coming closer and began to trot. He was headed for the opening near the town square, no safety there.

Romanov saw Yakov flailing the air as he ran. He picked up his pike and ran into the center of the village. Two wolves chased Yakov; Romanov chased them.

Yakov stopped when he reached the steps of St. Stephan's. One wolf had his coat in its mouth trying to pull him down. The men in the church were looking out the side windows and did not see Yakov or the wolves in front.

Romanov arrived in time to bury his pike in the back of the other wolf. It yelped and fell. He jerked the pike out and faced the first wolf who had released his hold on Yakov's coat.

"Get up the steps and enter the church, Yakov," Romanov shouted.

"Yes, Mayor, God bless you," sobbed Yakov, as he stumbled toward the church door.

Romanov faced the wolf.

"Come, come, get your dinner," he teased.

The wolf was frightened by this man. But four other wolves had run over in the excitement. The man was doomed.

Romanov decided to take one more wolf with him. He waited until the small grey made a lunge at his legs and shoved the pike into its mouth. The wolf raised up and twisted, blood spurting from her mouth. Romanov pushed the pike in deeper.

Some of the villagers witnessed the whole scene, the rescue of Yakov, the killing of one wolf and the skewering of another by the old man.

Turning from his window, Sasha Pavlovsky said to Alla, "Maybe he does have better blood than the rest of us. I am going out to help him."

"No, no, please Sasha, we have suffered enough. I need you now, you're all I've got. Romanov is as good as dead, stay with me. Please, please!" he begged.

The other wolves latched onto Romanov's arms, extended to hold the pike. A scuffle began. It was no match. They had him under them before he could resist further. No cry came from his dying body. The wolves left him, better to eat this one later.

Fedor watched the wolves come toward his house. Luba and his two daughters were hiding in the wood pile. The first wolf lunged at the door, but it held. Fedor went to check the window. He had hardly gotten there when Bunta hurled through, shattering the glass. Fedor fell backward, hitting his head on the flagstones near the oven. Blearily he reached up and grabbed the hot poker from the stove, whipping Bunta across the face with it.

"Watch for the man," she whined. "He has a stick."

The three wolves who followed Bunta into the house now scanned the home for others. Seena saw little Dasha move near the woodpile and trotted into the shed after her.

"Here are the others," she barked.

Luba shoved the girls behind her. She threw wood at the wolves who spread out and began their attack at once.

Seena went for Dasha, bit into the girl's side, lifted her off the ground, and shook her in the air. Luba screamed. Bunta turned toward the woman. Snarling, she set herself into a striking pose, ready to pounce.

Luba sobbed. "Oh dear God, not this...!"

The wolf leaned toward the terrified woman, sensing she would offer no resistance. Luba scampered up the woodpile; the logs slid out from under her feet, tumbling over the earthen floor. Bunta backed off.

Luba's hands kept windmilling backward as she grabbed at the wood. The pile fell with a crash onto the ground, Luba in the middle.

Bunta cocked her head to the left. Was this prey really so easy? She stepped over the fallen logs and placed her front paws on Luba's belly. Luba screamed.

Bunta reached down with her snout and pulled at the shawl covering the woman. It unraveled in a long string, some of it wrapping around Bunta's neck. She tried to shake it off but it stayed.

Bunta ignored the cloth and turned toward the exposed neck. She could see the veins popping and moving as the prey quivered and gulped. She bit just below the larynx.

Luba felt the wolf savaging her neck, opening a large wound. Curiously she felt no pain. It was as if she were watching the animal attack someone else, or even less, that she was being attacked without feeling anything. Time slowed. Luba tried to call to Fedor but couldn't.

Bunta jerked her neck upwards. A large piece of Luba's neck split off. Blood gushed out of the opening onto the woodpile.

Luba could see her flesh hanging from Bunta's teeth. Was this what death was like? Was it really this painless? Could she recover?

Fedor reached the shed just as Unga was killing Natasha. He picked up a blood-soaked log to hit the wolf. But he saw that Natasha was already dying. There was nothing he could do, so he turned and raced out of the hut. He was leaving his family behind, but they were all dead. No one could blame him, could they? He managed to avoid any of the other wolves. They seemed too busy with their other kills.

He hid in the barn loft.

Maala thought, "This is easier than it should be."

He heard tales from other wolves about the strength and ferocity of men. These humans were not so. Could they all be like this? Were those tales only exaggerations from a few cowards?

Tuva came to his side. "You were right, they are weak in the dark. Even their fire is of little help to them."

"So it seems," replied Maala. "Tonight we all eat. Then there are other villages, other people."

Sana joined them. "The human meat has little taste, but it is still enough. We can kill some of these tonight and the rest tomorrow."

"Yes, it's like having a flock of sheep in a pen. They stay here, and we eat them when we want."

They trotted to the center of town to rest.

It was the same in most of the village. A few wolves were killed by the guns, but most of their attacks had been successful. Fear was rampant, even in the homes that remained untouched.

Sasha said, "We are trapped. If one of us tried to leave we would be at their mercy. Maybe they will tire and leave us if they can't get in the rest of the homes."

Alla answered, "We stay here. We can live for weeks indoors. How long can a wolf wait, one day, three days?"

"I don't know, some of us can hold out, but you've seen what the wolves can do. They have no fear of crashing into the homes. They throw themselves at the doors and windows. Just a few of the houses can survive that. But you're right, tonight we have to stay here. There are no other choices," finished Sasha.

When the rest of the wolves were full and tired and could fight no more, they gathered near the well to sleep.

Before they did, Maala stood and started a long howl. Soon the other alphas joined in and then the rest of the hannal. The chorus howl filled the village and pierced into the houses. Sometimes 50 wolves were howling at once, in a cadence frightening yet beautiful. The sound was louder than any party, any church choir, anything the village had ever heard. It echoed off the church walls, off the tree lines, down the well where it reverberated off the ice surface and exited back up again, mixing in low groans and coarse hollow cries, carrying over the open paths. It seemed to surround everything and everyone, penetrating each home, pulsing in loudness and pitch. It lasted over an hour.

The villagers were more frightened now than ever. The victory song of the wolves stood their neck hairs on edge. It was unworldly, striking a deep fear in the minds of the people. Something from their past had returned, something primal, something so evil they were helpless to stop it.

When the wolves finished howling, they lay down, each in a tight bundle, legs tucked under the belly, tail wrapped over the face for warmth. Many would sleep deeper than they had in months, fed, content.

The men in the church were trapped for the night, but so were those in the houses. All were paralyzed by terror.

Some wolves went back into the empty houses they had savaged for a night's rest. Most of the villagers stayed awake. It was three days before Christmas.

The young wolves clustered about Mogla, hoping to hear him speak of the old times.

"Why do we fear men; why do we hate them," asked a yearling?

Mogla began, "Back in a time when even the forests were young," he said, sitting on his haunches in the middle of the circle, "man lived with the other animals in the woods."

The younger wolves clustered to the inside of the circle, hearing the story for the first time, before the repetition would change it to memory.

"All animals have their ways, each separate, but part of the world of the forest. Humans were hunters like us, and we fought for some of the same prey, but always with the rules we obey when another pack takes a kill. Never did we fight each other."

Mogla was the oldest male in the pack, still able to hunt, but also responsible for telling, over and over, the myths he had learned, so that they would stay in the minds of the wolves. He continued,"The humans were cunning, they knew their strengths, they knew their weaknesses, they knew when to hunt and when to stop. They banded in families and worked as a pack to bring down their prey. They even left some food uneaten for the latter days. They were survivors.

"Then they began to change. Their females no longer hunted but stayed in their nests and tended the young, never leaving them alone. Their males made fierce weapons, so they could kill any animal they wished. They built traps to catch the deer, the beaver, even the boar. They pulled fish out of the river with sticks. Some of their forest ways grew weak, they ran slower, they could not smell far, they hunted only in the light. Even so, their new cunning made them the rulers of the woods.

"But, they changed so much that one day they left the forest to live in the clearings. They became odd, killing trees and building nests that they kept for many years; staying in one spot; hunting in one place. They even caught some of the other animals and kept them near their lairs, only to kill them when they were hungry. No animal could trust them again.

"They took some of us and turned us into dogs, lapping at their feet, coming to their call. They stole milk from their cattle, eggs from their birds, pelts from their sheep. They even made their own fire to burn their kills before they ate them. They were not animals anymore."

Mogla twisted his neck, stretched his forelegs, and went on. "Once, one of their fires burned their own lairs and they hurried to leave that place for another. In their flight, they left one of their young behind. This young one cried out for his parents, but they were too far away to hear. He survived but was alone for a long time and began to starve. Kela, the great she-wolf, saw the young human and took pity on it. She carried it to her pack and suckled it as her own. Maoliki, her male, questioned this.

"Why do you keep one of them," he asked? "They left him to die, the way of all animals. It must not be changed.'

"But I am still rich in milk from the pups, I have enough for this little one," she answered.

Maoliki spoke again. "You are changing the way of the wild. That is trouble."

"Trouble from one as small as this? Will he not know I am his mother when he grows?" Kela asked.

"So she kept the human and reared it as her own, as part of that year's litter, teaching it to hunt like a wolf, eat like a wolf, learn the way of the pack and his duty to Maoliki.

"But, one day, the pack was seen by some humans who were following the same game. They noticed the young white one, running on two legs, as they do, among the yearlings. They told other humans.

"Their story was hardly believed among the men, but they listened to the pleadings of their females, and went to see if it was true.

When they came upon Maoliki's pack, they saw the human one and wondered, "Is this a real human or just a white wolf?"'

"They attacked the pack with their weapons, killing some, driving the rest of the pack away, cutting the young one out from the others. The young one fought against the men, biting and clawing, but the humans were careful not to harm it. They carried it away with them to their lairs.

"At first, the young one tried to run away, and the humans had to keep him in a pen, like their other animals. But, slowly, he learned their ways, and became like them.

"Now the humans knew that, for the first time, they had a hunter who could help them attack us. You see, he grew until he was as large as the biggest human, yet part of him was still wolf. He saw further, smelled better, ran faster, than the other men. He became their greatest hunter and led them to the lairs of the packs. He knew when we would run; when we would fight; how we could be confused and killed.

"On one hunt, the young one came upon his former pack, surrounding an elk kill. He stopped and wondered what he should do. But, the other humans barked their sounds at him, telling him he must not pity any animal. So, the men attacked, driving the pack away from the kill. But that was not enough. They tracked the pack through the forest until they had them backed between the black mountain and the wild water. The wolves had no choice but to run at the humans and try to break through back to the woods. But the men's weapons were too much, they began to stab the wolves with their sticks, and shoot them with their arrows. Even so the wolves fought on, lead by Maoliki.

"The young one was running in among the wolves, calling to his kind to keep the wolves confused. He came to a small hill, jumped to its top and signalled for the men to follow. But Maoliki saw him too and began to attack.

"Kela whined to Maoliki to leave the young one be. Maoliki barked back, "You see what he is doing; you see what he has become. I must kill him to save the pack."

"So, Maoliki came to the hill and bared his teeth at the young one. Stop this! I will let you run away, back to your kind, this once. But you are never to attack us again!"

"But the young one did not run away, he stood there confused, until the men shouted, 'You must kill the wolf or he will kill you.'

"The young one shifted his stick, pointing it at Maoliki, poised to throw it should Maoliki come forward. Against the pleadings of Kela, Maoliki attacked, hoping that the young one would flee.

"But the young one stayed, and when Maoliki leapt at him, he buried his stick into Maoliki's side.

"The pack leader howled to the sky, the stick pierced his heart. He looked at the young one, then closed his jaws and he died. Kela saw the death of her partner and attacked the young one herself.

"The young one cried, 'Please mother, not you! I am sorry I killed Maoliki, but I won't fight against you!'

"Kela stopped, wondering what she should do. A human saw the wolf standing still, and hurled his stick at her. It caught the she-wolf in the neck, blood spurted everywhere.

"The young human ran down from the hill and placed his mother's head in his paws. Kela looked at him, unable to speak. She died as the young one tried to pull the stick from her throat.

"Then the young one rose above his mother and howled a great wolf cry into the air. The humans rushed to him, holding his legs and trying to calm him. He kicked and fought, but they carried him back to their clearing. His bond with us now broken.

"By the next season he would forget his wolf friends. He would hunt us again as the leader of their pack. He alone would cause much of the slaughter that visited all wolves for many years. He became human.

"So, when you look through the trees and see man, you must beware! No human, even one who has eaten with us, can be trusted. They do not obey the rules of the forest. They have little fear when they are together, they do with us as they wish, they kill without eating. They are not like other animals. Fear them."

Mogla watched. The young wolves kept silent, knowing they would carry the tale on.

Then one spoke, "Why do we fight them now?"

"We are starving," said Mogla. "Only then do we take the chance."

15

Friday morning, December 23rd
Iennisseik Army Air Base

Sergeant Nicholas (Kolai) Mendelev was preparing for his first solo flight. He was especially proud of his new position as a Soviet pilot in the new Air Corps. His tailored new flying suit fit perfectly on his 5'9" frame, leaving room in the trousers for comfort while sitting in a cramped cockpit seat. Kolai kept his hair short and his round face well shaven, making him look even younger than his 31 years. Except for his decision to leave his village, this was the most important day of his life. The Vauzen BBC was parked near the main hanger, its nose pointed toward the runway. It was 10:40 am when squadron leader Major Kostenich led him to the craft placed outside the doors on the tarmac.

"You will have little trouble, the wind is mild, the skies clear, and the forecast is steady for a few hours. Just remember to complete the flight plan I have laid out for you and no more. Don't stray from your course and don't become so engrossed in your freedom that you try to extend it. First solo flying can be euphoric, but fuel is costly. Besides, you don't want any mistakes. You'll be in the air often now and will have many chances to prove yourself. Today is only to show that you can fly on your own. Be back in time since the weather is expected to change later. Try anything extra and you will not become a captain, Sergeant Mendelev."

Kolai was exhilarated but at the same time tense and nervous. He knew he could do this and yearned to be alone in the sky, but he was apprehensive about relying on his new skills alone. Kostenich had warned him of this and told him how he didn't eat before his first solo because he didn't want anything to soil his flight suit. Kolai had eaten, more to calm his stomach than any sense of hunger, but now he regretted it. He wanted to complete this and start his Christmas leave, going to Moscow for the first time.

The Vauzen cockpit was open when Kolai stepped onto the wing. He lifted his leg over the sill, planted his right foot on the cabin floor, brought his body into the cockpit, and settled into the tight seat. He checked his gauges, especially the fuel, which was full. New pilots always got a full tank, even when supply was short, in case they encountered trouble. Kolai pulled his helmet onto his head, tugged at the chin straps to cinch them down for a tight fit. Then he brought his goggles forward and adjusted them on his nose, hoping to keep them clear of fog from his breath or from sweat, should the sun hit the cockpit at the right angle. He made sure all his buttons were fastened, his gloves tight on his hands, and his pants inside his boots. He studied the flight plan for the last time. East to Kiren, northeast to Erda, then southwest back to base. All straight vectors. With a sigh he waved that he was ready.

The mechanic spun the propeller; after three tries it caught in a whirl of snow and oil vapors. He revved the engine, checked the gauges again, and released the wheel brakes. Skidding slightly to the left, he proceeded toward the runway. A left turn into the wind and he opened the throttle, picking up speed as he taxied down the pavement. He could see the red flags at the end of the runway. He pulled back the throttle and began to accelerate smoothly, straightening out his path. The speedometer read 30-50-80 miles per hour. The wings lifted when he hit 90, and he was airborne. His nervous handling caused the wings to dip and wobble, but he soon controlled that and flew directly west into the wind. Major Kostenich smiled as he watched Mendelev drift off and up over the field. He was a good student and would make a fine pilot. The new Soviet Union would rely on men like him.

Kolai rose to 1000 feet, then banked into a long U turn, coming back over the runway, waving to Kostenich on the ground as he sped past. Then he began his ascent. The poplar trees became match sticks as he went up; the pines green blurs; the small lakes pie plates; and finally the earth a map, just like it was drawn on the flight plan.

He leveled off at 4000 feet and headed east southeast, toward Kiren, just the other side of the Urals.

Kolai marked his map with his checkpoints when he cleared the Urals. He waited until he was over Kiren and then turned northeast on a heading that would bring him to Elda. He saw a few people coming outdoors on the cold day probably to view the unaccustomed sight of an airplane. He circled the town twice for their enjoyment and returned to course. The trip was going well: all the instruments were functioning, the cabin was reasonably warm, visibility 20 miles, a perfect day for a new pilot. Kolai noted again the sameness of the landscape from the air. Heavy forests full of birch, laden with snow, white earth glaring with ice as he looked east, frozen lakes, small villages, no more than clearings in the forest, trails radiating outward. The time to Elda should be about 35 minutes, maybe a little less with this light tail wind. He ran through Kostenich's instructions – attend to your gauges – check visibility – watch the weather – look for trouble ahead – reference your ground points.

For the first time Kolai enjoyed checking the ground points. When he was with Kostenich, it was always a test, and usually a small correction, making him often hesitate before saying something he already knew. Now he was his own judge, steering his flight, making his circuit. For some reason this made him hungry, and he reached back for the satchel of food that he had stowed behind the seat, enough for a few days should he fail to return home. As he fumbled to open its contents the wings tipped to the left, and he had to steer back on course. "Wait - you'll be back at base in an hour or so," he thought.

Kolai rounded Elda at 12:10 pm and vectored southeast to return to base. That 143 miles would complete his circuit. Visibility held but the temperature here at the Siberian border had dropped. Like all pilots he had a hidden fear of crashing in Siberia. It was foolish to think that a few miles had put him into the forbidding environment he knew so well. Few Russians had lived in Siberia before the time of Ivan the Terrible, and few wanted to now. It was a cold, bleak, hard life. Who could prefer that to the more cultured ways west of the mountains? Kolai knew that when he left his village and Alla behind. He needed something more, to be his own man not a peasant. Still, the birch trees were beautiful, their white and black bark etching the snow. One could become mesmerized with the Siberian landscape, at once foreboding, alluring, mysterious, and threatening.

It was the sameness that bothered Kolai. Without maps or a compass a man would be disoriented here, wandering forever until the cold, always the cold, ended his journey.

Kolai was surprised that he harbored these old thoughts, his former feelings. He was a modern aviator, an officer in the new Soviet Army, not some ignorant woodsman from a fairy tale. If he got in trouble, he could radio his base for help. If he was downed, he had three days' rations to reach some village using his maps and compass. If downed and injured – well that was different. But why dwell on that? Why had the mere crossing of the Siberian border, nothing to an aircraft, started him thinking of a crash? Just get back over the Urals and head home!

Kolai tried to concentrate on the return to base –some hot tea – the luncheon celebration of his first solo – the cognac and vodka – a night to let go and savor the day. He banked further right and set his course southwest, 90 miles to home. For the first time the sun was out, mostly above him, occasionally coming into the cockpit from the right. He thought of wedging some paper into the windscreen as a glare shield, but this was forbidden by the rules, even though many pilots did it. In his enthusiasm, he might forget to remove it before he landed. He wanted no demerits on this flight.

"Stick to the rules," Kostenich said. "No changes, get home on time."

A small headwind was coming over the right wing. In his excitement Kolai had not recalculated his course to account for it. He was now 64 miles from base, but 12 miles southeast of his intended vector. He quickly made the correction and angled back toward his true course. He could not find his ground points, which was no surprise due to the course change, but they should come in view in the next ten minutes or so. Visibility was still clear enough to see a small village up ahead in an opening in the forest. The tree line angled away from the village on the east and the west, and then an almost naked north-south corridor was barren for a few miles. Kolai checked his map – "My God, it's Pilovo!" He didn't realize how close he was to his birthplace, where he was raised, what he had left. It looked so different from the sky, so foreign. But still…his parents were buried there, did Alla marry, did anyone think of him? He surprised himself with these emotions.

It was 12:39 pm.

He descended to 800 feet to make sure of this new bearing and roared over the village from the northeast. Yes it was Pilovo, seven miles off his course. As he rose again Kolai saw a picture of the village flash back into his consciousness. A few dozen homes, some without any chimney smoke, people darting among the cabins, none of them even looking up to see the plane. How many flights had these villagers seen to be so blasé about him? It was an insult for Kolai to realize that even his own people could ignore his achievement. As he rose to bank away his mind's eye reran the scene he had just seen. Dark people, running fast, oblong (perhaps bent over?), what was this, some new winter festival? Curious, Kolai decided to make another pass over the village. Surely people would wave this time. He banked right and came down to 200 feet, straight north-south, a clear view into the village. This time the people could not help but notice him.

As he approached the village the dark figures were still running both into and out of the homes. What was going on? One mile out and the figures assumed the oblong shape again. Were they running this fast on their hands and knees? A half mile and it was clear – these were not people, they were animals – wolves! Wolves in his village? Wolves in houses? Where were the people? When over the village he noticed some figures not moving. He swung back for a closer look and saw the red stains around the people lying in the snow.

"My God - they are dead! Three – five – at least eight bodies lying spread out on the snow, red blood, torn limbs.....! No – no, the wolves are in the town, they are killing my villagers – they are in the houses – why aren't they being stopped?"

16

Friday afternoon

Sergi was the first to hear the faint buzzing of the Vuazen engine. He ran to the window but could not locate the source; others picked it up and wondered if it was coming from the sky. Manja, at the window that faced east, was the first to see the plane fly over the village. She had heard of such machines but had never seen one. How to signal it? No one would go outside and risk being spotted by the wolves. The buzzing subsided. Arguments ensued in many homes. "We should have signaled that airship – but now it's gone!" Then the sound started again. Everyone knew this was their only chance to get help.

 Fedor returned to his hut that morning and found his family dead; he knew they would be. Luba, who had never harmed anyone, lay with her neck open, her stockings ripped off and her legs eaten. Fedor could see the bones, white against the red stain. Dasha was gone, dragged away. Natasha, or what remained of the girl, was near the fireplace, her hand open upward as if waving, parts of her legs and torso strewn over the room. Fedor dropped to his knees and cried. He had failed to protect them; he was disgraced, less than a man. It would have been better if he had fought the wolves to the death. When he heard the plane's engine, he knew he had to choose. He grabbed his wife's red and green shawl, several of her bright red scarves, wrapped himself in the gay colors, clutched the scarves in his right hand, and headed toward the window.

He opened the window and waved the scarves in the air, in the hope that the pilot might see them if he passed again. He heard the wolves yelping and snarling at the plane as it passed overhead and disappeared to the north. He waited. Yes, the sound was coming back for a third run, this time from the north. He had to try to redeem his cowardice. He climbed out onto the snow, hollering and waving the scarves. He could see the plane clearly – was the pilot looking at him?

"My God, he must look!" Fedor waved and ran, waved and ran.

Kolai saw a hand jutting out from the window waving a red scarf. Was someone alive and afraid to come out? But then the figure crawled through the window and started to run toward the plane.

Mogla saw the brightly colored man first. He turned to attack, confused by the waving and the red colors. What was this human up to? Was it one of their tricks?

Fedor saw Mogla move toward him and began to retreat to the door. Reina blocked his path. More wolves circled him. Fedor waved the scarves in their faces hoping to scare them away. They snarled but kept their distance.

Kolai saw the figure of what he thought was a woman waving frantically, surrounded by wolves. Kolai couldn't tell her that he already had seen her and knew the trouble. Wolves dragged the woman down, but she still waved the scarves at the plane.

No aid came from the villagers, whose frozen stares behind their windows told their grief and helplessness. They saw Fedor rise and stumble twice, striking at the wolves with his arms, fighting to stay alive. It was useless. Fedor had no weapon and the effort to fight when so bundled up in clothes weakened him quickly. He fell to his knees, tried to protect his head, dying as the wolves bit into his trunk and limbs.

Sasha saw the pilot dip his wings – had they signaled for help and been seen? Surely help must come, but when?

"Help us – help us!" screamed Fedor.

Kolai passed over a fourth time and dipped his wings again. Would his people know that was a signal? That he had seen them, that he would get help, that they must hold on?

"Stay inside – I am Kolai - I will come back – I will bring help - hang on!"

Fedor grinned, thought of now joining his family, and felt his life slip away.

It was 12:53 pm.

17

Kolai pulled the throttle back to maximum; this was not the time to stay within his instructions to keep the engine below 6200 rpm, he must push the limits. The Vauzen surged forward into the headwind and reached 210 mph. Base was now only 24 minutes away. His radio was almost useless because of the bank of rain clouds ahead. Where had they come from so fast? They were too high to climb over and too wide to skirt. Besides, he had no time to waste; his people needed help now. Why had the weather turned bad so quickly? Why weren't the wolves being shot by the villagers?

He nosed the plane directly toward base into dark, grey clouds. The moisture buildup blocked his vision, Kolai was flying blind, hoping his instruments would tell him if he got too close to the mountains. The excess weight of the hail caused the wings to shudder under the driving force of the revved up engine. Kolai was caught between the need to hurry and the possibility of crashing if he continued to push the craft to its limit. He also had to stay high enough to clear the mountain. How many extra minutes could he add to insure that he got to base and start a rescue? Otherwise the village was doomed.

He eased up slightly, bringing the engine down to 5600 rpm. His time to base now 22 minutes. Kolai was in a dreamlike trance. He couldn't see anything but grey and black, it was even hard to tell that he was moving, time and position seemed suspended. Only the drone of the engine seemed real. Finally the Vauzen broke clear of the cloud bank, and Kolai could see the outline of the base nine miles ahead. Kolai's radio cleared.

"This is Mendelev, flight 21, nine miles out, immediate landing requested, no fly by, emergency in Pilovo, prepare rescue party."

"This is control; runway clear, land at will."

It was 1:22 pm.

Kolai braked the aircraft to a full stop, opened the cockpit and shouted to the groundsman.

"Get Colonel Federov; we have to hurry!"

He climbed out onto the wing, jumped down to the tarmac, and ran toward the center. The officers were already assembling when he burst into the room.

"Wolves are attacking the village of Pilovo; they are in the houses, dead bodies are on the ground; people are still alive; they need help."

Then he told of Fedor's attempt to signal him as he was being pulled apart by the wolves. His legs weakened so he sat down, drained from the adrenaline rush of the last 40 minutes; he was almost faint.

"We have to get to Pilovo now."

"Pilovo" asked Federov? "Where is that?"

"Just off my course, not far from here. It's where I am from."

"Your village," said Federov?

"Yes, long ago, please I'll explain later."

"How many wolves did you see there?" Federov asked.

"I don't know, maybe 60, maybe more."

"60?"

"Yes, at least."

"Is the village approachable by air?" Kostenich asked.

"There is a narrow north-south corridor where our planes could land."

"How far?"

"Maybe 25 minutes with this tailwind if we fly directly to it."

"What about the storm that passed here?" Federov asked.

"Yes, it's approaching there, but I flew through it. If we get there ahead of it, we would have clear conditions for landing. It may pass a little north of the town, so we could come in from the south if it holds."

Sergeant Buckov, the base weatherman, entered the room.

"That hail is now a line of rapidly building thunderheads just east of here. Maybe the mountains will break them up before they reach Pilovo. The best course would be to fly around them from the south and then up to Pilovo. The squall line is 80 miles wide. A southeast vector and then north to the village could put you there in about 55 minutes. If you can land, you can help them. You can't risk flying into those clouds and not getting there at all. I hope the storm slows down. If the clouds reach Pilovo first, then I don't know how you will land."

"But we must try. Full tanks," ordered Federov.

"Major Kostenich, take four planes, four men each, extra rifles, extra ammunition, follow the course Sergeant Mendelev described to Pilovo, land and kill the wolves. Also bring food and water, and medical supplies."

"Sir, we can be off in 25 minutes."

"Make it sooner!"

"Mendelev! Rest, have a meal, you and I will follow them when the weather clears."

"Sir, I want to go first, I know the village, it's off our standard charts, but I can find it even in the storm."

"You're in no condition to pilot a plane in these circumstances around a thunderstorm. Remember you have just one solo under your belt."

"Then as a passenger? Let me go, please?"

"All right, do it, rest on board."

At 1:50 pm the four rescue planes lifted off from Kirov base and headed east toward the edge of the building cloud heads. The weather was worsening; the clouds had picked up additional moisture and were now almost black. Upper level turbulence was mixing the layers, throwing a menacing view of the storm ahead. They would have to avoid these clouds to stay airborne.

Colonel Federov watched from the control tower as the planes lifted into the clouds. The view of his planes against the backdrop of the thick clouds disturbed him a great deal. He would love to recall them, but this emergency had to be handled. Like all Russians he was brought up on tales of wolves attacking people. But wolves in the houses? That was alarming. Now it was a race between the clouds and the planes to Pilovo.

Sergeant Buckov was doubtful; his Slavic pessimism told him the worst always happened. Besides, he placed the clouds' velocity at 18 mph southeast and, allowing for maximum air speed, the planes would reach Pilovo just as the clouds approached. Only a change in weather would help. Could they land before visibility was shut down? They could fly by instruments, but landing was another matter, and there was no tarmac in the woods. Were the paths wide; were there hidden rocks and tree stumps; what if—? They needed some luck, and Buckov knew that most luck was bad. He went to Federov with his worries.

"Colonel, we must assume that the planes might not make it."

"Why are you so doubtful?"

"It's the weather, sir. They might not be able to land."

"So what do you suggest?"

"Send some trucks, they won't have to navigate around this storm. A direct approach through the storm could put the trucks in the village less than one hour after the planes. The trucks should make it; besides, they can carry more medicine, supplies and men."

"Get 20 men and two trucks and take the two wolfhounds with you."

Buckov returned in ten minutes with his plan.

"Colonel Federov, if they take the paved road northeast for 20 miles, this cutaway for 12, drive directly over Lake Kalma, and approach Pilovo from the south, they can be there in less than an hour and a half. That's assuming there are no obstacles to trucks south of Pilovo."

"Then get them underway. If the planes fail they should be at the village just after sunset but before it's too dark. I've told Major Kostenich that they should not risk landing unless they can see the town. Dead pilots won't help those villagers."

"Yes, sir, I will get the trucks off right away."

Federov told Buckov to radio ahead to the planes, telling them of the truck convoy.

Buckov returned. "Sir, we can't signal the planes, it's the storm."

"I understand, but I hope the planes don't take desperate chances. If they can't land the trucks will handle this. Pray the weather holds."

Colonel Federov slumped in his chair. Surely this two-pronged rescue will work. It was as much as he could do.

The trucks left at 2:38 pm.

18

Friday afternoon

Sergi knew the worst was the wait. Some hope is crueler than none. The wolves would not stop, but keep attacking until everyone was dead. How long would that be? Hours? A day? Several days? Not likely.

Fedor's dead body lay twisted in the snow. The wolves ignored it. Maala had an uneasy feeling about the courage of this human. Were there others like him? The humans had been cowed, much to the wolves' liking. Was this one demented or brave? No others ventured out.

Sergi and his family, their home so close to the Bukavev's, looked out from their barricaded windows at the dead Fedor. The body had to be left there to freeze. Everyone had to try to survive until the army plane returned with help, if it returned at all. Sergi wondered how far away the Army base was, several hours? Then another hour to prepare a rescue team, a hour to get back? How could they be back before sundown? He figured a dozen soldiers could dispatch the wolves, maybe more if they wanted to surround them and prevent any man-eaters from escaping into the forest to kill again. But they had to get here before dark.

Sergi wanted them all killed. Any grudging respect he had for wolves was gone. They were wanton killers: children, the old, no one was safe. They should be destroyed. He knew that he would shoot every wolf he saw from now on. They were all man-eaters. In his head he could see the wolves being shot repeatedly. The bullets spurting out of their backs as they fell. He delighted in this. Kill them – kill all the wolves of Russia – rid us of the beast! Kill – kill – kill!

Meanwhile, he had to take action. "I'm going out there."

"No, Sergi. Fedor is dead, you can't help him now," said Manja.

"I won't leave him there for them to come back and eat again. He tried to help us all. The man is a Christian, we need something to bury."

Before she could stop him, Sergi was out the door and heading for the body of Fedor. No wolf saw him. When he reached the dead man, he looked down at the strange expression on Fedor's face; calm, even perhaps a grin; what was he thinking when he died? Sergi started to pull on Fedor's arm, hoping to drag him back to his house; the arm came off. Segri knelt down and reached under the man with both arms, laying the loose arm on top. He pushed down hard on his legs, lifting what remained of Fedor and turning for the house. Now Maala saw him.

"Another human," he said, and began to trot towards him.

But Sergi was already near the Bukavev door, and inside before the wolves could get close. He lay the body down and immediately barricaded the door; then he saw the broken window, and barricaded that too. He picked Fedor up again, lying the dead man on the bed, his loose arm still on his chest. He found a blanket and covered the body. Then he waited until the wolves had gone again and sprinted home. At least it was something.

From the cabin windows the villagers shouted and signalled to one another that they should wait and hope that a rescue party would come. The day was clear; the pilot had seen Fedor; they would be saved. It was essential not to take any more risks, not to lose another person on this day. The airplanes could be back before nightfall. The wolves were doomed. No slip-ups now, no drop in vigilance, keep your guard up, survive a few more hours, no celebration yet, just make it to evening and things will get better. Sasha poured an extra cognac for him and Alla from their one bottle. The end of their ordeal may be near.

"Let's be prudent, we know the army will save us."

Pavel wondered otherwise. Sure it seemed that the plane had seen them and understood their plight, but how long would it take for a rescue party to form and get here? Would they send planes, trucks, men on skis? Who knows? And why were the villagers so cowed, so disorganized, so ineffective in their attempts to save themselves?

But was it really any business of his? No one sought his counsel, or would listen if he gave it. They thought of him as nobody, if they thought of him at all. It was at times like these that Pavel most wanted to leave Pilovo. In fact, he would leave now if he thought he could make it to town. But that seemed impossible; there really were wolves all over the forest, and a man alone would have little chance of making it. No, he would have to sit it out too. God, how he longed for comrades to work with, to join in the effort, to take control of their fate, to fight!

Pavel had given his fall report last month. It was the same as always; no problems, little progress, little hope for change.

His superior asked, "Can't you try harder? Why don't I see evidence that the villagers are accepting you? You are there for a purpose, not a rest. I want some progress in the next report."

"Alright," thought Pavel. "I'll give you progress next time." Who would check on it anyway? Except for him, none of them had never been to Pilovo and would never go. "He'll get the report he wants."

Why the bother? Pavel didn't want to harm these people, he wanted to leave them. They seemed happy in their ways, like dumb animals who knew no better, had never seen a concert, never a ballet. They would be so frightened in a city that they would never return. Damn them! He just wanted relief from the boredom; a change; any change. And now this.

Yes, he would wait like the others. Why was he even worried about them; they surely weren't concerned about his welfare? No one had even thought to talk to him about any of this. Was he invisible; did they think he didn't care if children were killed; was this not proof that Christians were no better than anyone else? What kind of people were they?

Pavel remembered when he was in the army, four years ago. There was a purpose then, to defeat the Whites, to free the worker, to help the peasant. Men woke up every day with a purpose; shape the country in a new mold; make Russia great; share everything; keep a goal in mind. Was it just this posting that cut him off from all that, or had the Revolution already died?

Inaction was the worst thing; Pavel could hardly bear it. Alone, he would sometimes shout at the walls, "Give me something to do!"

19

Friday 2:15 pm

The four planes kept the squall line to their left and headed southeast. The thunderheads continued to build as the upswell from the frosted ground pumped moisture into the air. Major Kostenich signalled: "Stay well to the south of the cloudbank, we have to avoid the squall line before we cut north. Follow me and stay in touch in case visibility falls."

Kolai felt relieved. The hot tea and sugar cookies had brought his nerves under control, and the noodle and cabbage soup, lukewarm as it was, revived him. He searched the north for a break in the squall line. Eighty miles out Kostenich began a slow northern turn to front the clouds. He could see a corridor of clearer air east of his position and immediately south of the clouds. It may be possible to burst into this gap and land near Pilovo if the clouds would just slow a bit. His speedometer was at 180 mph – 23 minutes to Pilovo. The other three planes raced single file behind him, slicing down the corridor, lightning flashing in the clouds to their left.

"Hold course – Pilovo is dead ahead – right before the clouds – we will land as soon as possible."

Fifteen miles from the village the squall line turned ahead of the planes and began to engulf the town.

"Fly directly into the clouds – stay low – look for openings to land. We are less than six minutes to the village – land in any clearing and march directly to the village – stay together – rifles ready – form groups if you see others – the larger the group the better for us."

Mendelev was wiping the inside glass in the cockpit, but still he saw little. The hail and snow had begun and visibility was gone, even at ground level. Should they call off the landing? "No!" he thought. "We are too close to call it off, we must chance it. A few hours could mean death to any villagers who are still alive."

The six minutes were up. Kostenich lowered the nose of the Sikorsky, and headed down. He ordered his three passengers to look for trees. At 90 feet they saw trees in all directions.

"Up - up! We are in the forest. We missed the corridor!"

Major Kostenich nosed the plane up, buffeting into the wind. He knew that the air patterns would not be in his favor, not this close to the ground, not this close to the trees. As he tried to guess where to aim the plane, the right wing caught the top of a fir, rotating the whole craft to the right, and back down toward the ground. Before he could respond, the fuselage crashed into the top of a large pine, nose first, pointing downward.

The force of the plane sheared off the higher branches of the tree, as the main body of the airship plunged down the trunk. At each level, the limbs crashed into the small plane, slowing it down further. The soldiers in the back were already unconscious, as was Kostenich. His head had hit the control panel when the plane caught the top of the tree. Only Kolai saw the mad rush of the branches popping in and out of view as they continued down.

The fuselage finally wedged into the fork of a lower limb with a thud that shook the whole cabin. It stopped ten feet above the forest floor.

It was 2:47 pm.

Sergeant Kirev kept the lead truck at 45 mph as they came toward the end of the cleared road. It was now 3:04 pm. He saw the cutaway in the forest angling off to the east. It was unimproved, rutted, prone to uneven and dangerous changes in the surface. It was a mess. Though it was narrow, it could take a truck of this size. Kirev slowed to 20 mph to ensure that the trucks did not hit any danger too hard or have unnecessary flats. Lose an axle or a wheel and the path would be blocked.

As agonizingly slow as this was, it was better than getting bogged down in the forest. Colonel Federov impressed upon him the importance of reaching the village. "Speed is secondary to arrival." Both trucks bumped and slid over the path, bottoming out frequently and jolting the men. It was frustratingly slow but steady.

"Easy - easy, a few more minutes won't hurt. We can still get to the village before sundown with enough daylight to see the wolves," whispered Kirev, to no one in particular.

Kirev knew something about the forest. He had been raised just west of the Urals, not far from the Siberian border, in a village only a little bigger than Pilovo. He knew the strengths and weaknesses of village people, how they could survive the hardest of times, yet fail if a new situation confronted them. Although he loved his people, he felt they lacked education and imagination. That was why, like Kolai, he had left for the city when he was still a young man.

At first, his family almost shunned him; was he too good for them; why didn't he come back and care for his parents? But Kirev found a life for himself in the army, a place for training, a place to grow, a steady career. And when he did visit home last year they were impressed with his uniform and the figure he cut. He brought with him some canned food from the commissary, a real help for a bad season. He looked like a man in command, someone his parents could be proud of. He stayed two days.

Now he had to help some other village, filled with people much like his own, or so he imagined. Not ignorant, just limited; deserving of his concern, his aid. He would get through to them; he would bring what they needed. Oh the pilots would get there first, but the trucks would bring the supplies, the medicine and food to place the village back to where it had been. The villagers would know what that meant.

He pushed on, always remembering that the goal was not to break down, but to arrive. A truck was not an airplane, it was sure and steady.

They cleared the cutaway at 3:31 pm. The frozen lake lay ahead. Kirev signaled the following truck to stop. He left his vehicle and went back to talk to the other driver.

"The lake is two miles across. We have to aim for the break in the trees here (he pointed to the map). You stay close enough to see my back lights but give yourself enough space to stop if we stop. If we stop you steer a little to our right, I don't want you slamming into my ass. Don't assume you have good traction. Visibility is getting worse but we may still be able to see the break. Then it's only a mile or two of trail until we break clear of the forest just south of the village. We will stop again there. Then turn due north for about three miles and we should be in Pilovo. Don't lose us. We have to stay together. If I get too far ahead, beep your horn. We will stop next at the eastern shore of the lake."

Sergeant Semenov was the first pilot to touch down. He had lost Major Kostenich in the storm, and headed down just south of the village. He tried to keep his plane in the corridor as it skidded along the ice. He saw a rock outcropping ahead and turned to avoid it. This maneuver caused his right ski to break lose, and the post dug into the ice causing the plane to spin out of control. It spiralled toward the village sliding on the ice until it hit the well in the center of town. Here it broke in two, the passenger cabin planning ahead, the tail off to the left of the well.

Sergeant Kyagova knew that the two planes ahead of him were in trouble. It was impossible to see in this storm. He lost the lead plane but knew the six minutes were up. He felt he had found the corridor, but he had to stay clear of this storm. At thirty feet, visibility was still poor, so he raised up, aborted his landing, and brought his plane off to the east of where he had last seen Major Kostenich's craft.

Banking east, Kyagova looked for an opening to land, but the whole region was now blanketed in hail and snow. "Does anyone see a clearing?"

"No, sir. We are in the thick of the storm."

Just then the plane sprang upward, slammed to the left, and fell again. They had hit a pocket in the cloud. The radio tore out of the console and smashed against the seat.

"We have to clear this squall. We'll do no one any good if we crash."

"Sir, those people in the village have little time. Some of our men may be in need of help on the ground. We must try to land."

"Where? I cannot risk our lives in a futile attempt to land here."

"But sir, they—"

"No! We cannot risk it."

Kyagova banked into a U turn, heading south to clear the storm line. Better to land south of his target and taxi as far as he could, then they could walk to the village. Three miles south of Pilovo, the corridor came into clear view. He was just south of the storm and began a new descent. He was able to set the skis down softly as he lowered his craft onto the frozen snow. The plane slid forward at 85 mph, the braking minimal, the flaps frozen. He could do nothing but hold on and steer straight in the hope that they would stop. As the Vuazen careened down the path no one could see anything. The snow, even more than the hail, whited out the view; the plane's propeller swirled it around them, made it impossible to even hope to see. Then it happened. The left ski caught a snow-covered boulder and lifted the left side of the plane briefly into the air. The right wing dug into the ice, the fuselage rotating down and to the right, exploding as it hit the ground. Sergeant Kyagova and his men were drenched in fuel as the wing came apart. They opened the cockpit to escape but were engulfed in fire. In the back the two privates choked on the burning fuel and lost consciousness as they fought to get over their burning colleagues in the front. The Vauzen skidded to a halt, burning out of control.

Sergeant Moskalenko followed the tail of Kyagova's plane as far as he could to about one minute short of touchdown. He too was now three miles south of the village. He landed in a clear space in the corridor. His wing flaps were not as frozen, and he was able to brake faster as he slid toward the village. Then he saw an explosion and a fire ahead. Moskalenko raised his left flaps, banking sharply to the left to avoid the flames. As the plane skidded sideways, he fought to straighten out the fuselage so he could turn right again. He slowly evened it out in the blinding hail, and began a right turn back into the corridor. Immediately, he saw trees at the front of the plane and aimed for a small path, but the trees sheared off both wings and the fuselage skidded deep into the woods. A large fir tree loomed ahead, and the cockpit slammed into it. The men jolted forward in the cabin; Moskalenko was unconscious and so was his co-pilot. The two privates in the back crawled over them, injured and bleeding, and fell onto the snow. They were dazed, trying to get their bearings.

Sasha saw the first plane briefly as it cleared the trees, banked east, and disappeared. Had he heard a muffled thud; was that the sound of the plane trying to gain altitude? Why hadn't it landed? The storm had just started; they had better land soon or it would get worse.

Then he heard the sound of a crash south of the village. What was happening? To his amazement, he saw the fuselage of a plane careen into town and split apart at the well. When the crew cabin stopped it was within 30 yards of his house. He could clearly see movement as the crew attempted to leave. But the wolves saw it too.

To Sasha's horror the wolves attacked the plane and began to maul the soldiers. But at least the crew fought back. Several shots were fired and a few wolves were hit. Five animals were already at the cockpit tearing at two of the men. One man seemed to have a dead wolf attached to his neck, both fell onto the snow. Sergeant Semenov was being dragged from the wing, alive but unconscious as two wolves worked to sever his head from his body. No one moved from the huts.

The rest of the village watched as the crew near the well tried to pry themselves out of the twisted cockpit. Sergeant Semenov tumbled out onto the ice, bleeding from a broken collarbone. The soldier in the front was unconscious from a blow to the head. One private in the back screamed when his splintered leg gave way as he tried to rise from his seat. Private Gonshevsky leapt aside from the plane cabin, his rifle cocked and ready. The wolves, confused, began a slow lope toward the new humans. Gonshevsky leveled his barrel and shot at the lead wolf, missing to the left, the snow leaping up from the bullet. The wolves stopped and cocked their heads. They proceeded more slowly. Sergeant Semenov stumbled back toward the cockpit to get a rifle but was taken down by Vaal from behind. He bit into the soldier's collarbone, dislodging it from its cradle. Semenov fainted.

The solder in the cockpit managed to load his rifle and aim it by resting the muzzle on the seat back. He fired at Sana and hit her in the haunches. Bunta leapt over Vaal into the cockpit and started to savage the man, but the soldier jammed his rifle under her chin and fired, lifting off the back of Bunta's head. He then slumped back into the seat, his face torn, and his neck bleeding from Bunta's attack.

Gonshevsky reloaded and shot again as a wolf came straight at him. It tumbled dead at his feet. Quarta leapt at him from behind, knocked him down and bit into his neck. Gonshevsky removed his bayonet, twisted his arm over his shoulder, and hacked at Quarta, severing her jugular. They tumbled together as the other wolves closed in.

20

Friday 3:05 pm

Sasha turned from the window and looked at his wife.

"Now no one will come in time. The rescuers are dead. Either they crashed or the wolves got them. With this weather, no other planes will be able to come for days. How can we fight these wolves? How much time do we have left? We can't wait for them to pick us off one or two at a time. They are already in some of the houses. We have to do something to kill them!"

Sasha decided to rally the other men into the barn, using the women as messengers. At least they could comfort one another. But how to do this without being set upon by the wolves?

As Sasha was putting on his coat, Alla pleaded, "Don't go out there. You won't make it. The wolves will see you and attack. Please, stay with me, I have no one else."

"Don't worry, Alla, I will be cautious. If they come for me I will hurry back here. Watch."

Sasha dashed from his house over to Sergi's, avoiding, as much as possible, any lines of sight that the wolves might have to him. Manja, looking out a window, saw him coming and hollered to Sergi to open the door and let him in.

Sasha entered the Zubov house. "We need a diversion to get the wolves away so we can meet in the barn."

Sergi asked, "Why? What can we do there?"

"I don't know, but we have to do something. First we need to get everyone together; maybe we can decide upon a plan to defend ourselves, or maybe even to attack. But for now, here is my idea. Vasili is fast and a good climber. If he ran to the tall pine near the church and climbed up, the wolves might follow him, surround the tree, and be distracted."

"You're asking a lot from him."

"But all of us we will be in on anything we decide to do. He needs to spend about half an hour in the tree; by then we will be assembled in the barn. Maybe we can come up with a way to save us. We have to try!"

"Yes, Sasha, you're right. This hiding in our homes is not going to work. The wolves sense our fear and it encourages them."

"All right, you're with me, I will go to Vasili and ask him to help," said Sasha.

Sasha left from the shed attached to Sergi's house. This gave him a short run to Vasili's home. Vasili also saw him coming and was ready at the door. A few wolves looked up but did nothing, since the man was already entering a hut.

"Are you crazy? How did you know I would see you and come to the door? We are barricaded in here against the wolves."

"We have to take chances. You saw the rescue team die. You know we can't make it another night. Half the village will be eaten by morning."

"But what can we do?"

"Vasili, all of us have to do something. I am here to ask you to distract the wolves so we can assemble the rest of the men in the barn."

"And how can I do that?"

"Well, you dress warmly, run past the well to the big pine near the church, the wolves will follow."

"What?!!!"

"Hear me out. You can climb the tree before any of them get to you. You are our best runner and best climber. Give us one half hour of diversion, to get all the others into the barn, and we will be ready to come and get you back."

"And what if you're not ready?"

"We have to trust each other or we will all die. Do this for your family and mine."

"Sasha, I know you're a good man, but this is too much to ask."

"Please, Vasili, it will work, I know it. If it fails I will come to the tree to rescue you myself, no matter what. The wolves are curious but they seem lethargic today, they saw me outside and didn't attack. Their bellies must be full; maybe they are waiting for the night, who knows? Let's surprise them before it gets dark. Besides, you are too fast for them over this short distance. You will have surprise on your side."

"Okay, Sasha, but you take care of my family if I don't come back."

"We're all one family now."

Vasili opened his front door, his wife ready to barricade it as soon as he was outside. He began a slow walk toward the church, hoping not to alert any of the wolves. When he was 40 yards from the church, Reina spotted him.

"A human is out. See, near the road."

Vasili started to run. Five wolves immediately took up the chase. As Vasili neared the tree, he could sense the wolves close behind and gaining. Sasha was wrong, they weren't lethargic. He knew he had only one chance to keep away from them. With a final spurt, he vaulted up the trunk, using his boots to grip the bark as his momentum carried him up a few feet, he was hoping to catch the lowest bough and swing further up from there. His first foothold was firm, and he scrambled up about eight feet. Then he began to lose his grip on the bark and slip, even as his feet kept trying to get a firm hold. Just when he began to feel he could run no higher, he stretched his arms overhead, reached high, and gripped the lowest bough. With a jerk he pulled himself up and away from the wolves.

"Christ-Jesus, that was close," he thought. Then he shimmied out a little on the branch and took off one glove, loosed his red bandana, slid it off his neck, and waved it high. The other wolves began to gather at the base of the tree. Some were excited by the chase and tried to scamper up the trunk to Vasili. The bough was too high. Vasili kept at it, waving the enticing scarf, keeping the wolves interested. Sasha, back home, watched for this signal.

"Okay, now we move! Alla, go to each house you can and tell the men to assemble in the barn. Have them bring everything they think might be if use, all their weapons, guns, pikes, pitchforks, and tell Yuri to bring his bow and arrows. Tell the others to bring kindling for a fire; wolves hate fire. Have the women who don't need to protect any children come also. Let them help you get others. Watch for the wolves. If they come for you, hide in the nearest house."

Alla began her rounds, making sure to stay out of view of the wolves. She stopped at the home of the Zubov's and told them to help. Little Tonya Kovalev was there, having spent the night, afraid to go home with the wolves outside. Now, unnoticed by the Zubovs, she slipped out the door and ran to tell her parents.

Maala spotted the girl first. He and Tuva had not joined in the hunt for the man at the tree. Vaal saw her also.

"A little one,"whined Vaal. "Easy to catch."

"Let's go," said Maala.

The three wolves raced across the village, directly toward the girl. Tonya saw them coming and swerved to avoid their path. Vaal caught her first, biting at her heel and tumbling her into the snow. Tonya jumped up and circled to her left, back toward Karl's hut. Tuva charged and bit her in the arm, then backed away. The wolves could play with this one. Maala tore at her leg then also retreated.

They let her run again, but she ran slower, her torn right leg dragging along the crust of the snow. The wolves trotted behind. They were in no hurry, their prey was cornered, they had already tasted its blood. Besides, they were no longer hungry. Tonya glanced, terrified, at the locked doors and shuttered windows of Karl's house. She beat on the door, crying for help.

Karl began to put on his coat. Then he stopped.

"I can't risk my life for this girl," he thought. "If I open the door the wolves will take me too. She is as good as dead already. The village will need me to survive and help the others later.'

"I'm sorry little Tonja," he whispered through the door.

Karl watched at his window as Tonya backed away. She saw Karl's eyes; she knew he wouldn't help. She didn't expect this. She headed instead for the woodpile leaning against the back shed. The stacking had left a small triangular shaped tubular opening near the bottom just large enough for a nine year old. She plunged headlong into the tunnel, stabbing her right arm ahead and trailing the left one so that her rotated shoulders could squeeze into the tube. She wriggled to the middle, about three feet from the opening, and was stopped as the passage narrowed.

Maala arrived first. He jammed his head and forelegs into the tube until his mouth was at Tonya's legs. Her left leg slammed at his nose, making him retreat. Tuva replaced him. She turned her face to deflect the jabbing foot and bit down hard on Tonya's crippled leg. The girl screamed in the iced tube, the sound reverberating in the confinement. Tuva pulled harder, bending her strong hind legs, and digging her forenails into the ice. Slowly she dragged the screaming girl out of the tube. Tonya tried to grip the slippery walls, felt the frozen splinters tear at her hands and hips, but she couldn't stop sliding out with the wolf. For a moment the light dazed her eyes. She was exposed now, Tuva at her feet, Maala and Vaal at her head. She looked up just as some saliva dripped from Vaal onto her face. She raised her arms to keep the wolves away from her head. Maala clamped his strong jaw onto her forearm and yanked his head left and right. It was hopeless, she was too weak, the teeth were too many, the pain too great. She passed into unconsciousness.

The wolves kept eating.

Karl watched the poor girl being dragged out from the woodpile onto the ice. He blessed himself, embarrassed that he was turning to religion in his peril, and prayed for the soul of the girl. He did nothing else.

Sasha and Sergi slipped out of their houses and headed for the barn. Once inside they began to secure all the barn openings except for the small door to the left of the main doors. People arrived bringing pikes, knives, even tongs from the fireplaces. Yuri came with pieces of wood and matches for the fire, more knives, two pokers, a bow with a few arrows, and a rusty scimitar. Soon most of the village men and boys were there, plus most of the older teenage girls, and some of the women. Alla kept all of the children in her house for protection.

To everyone's surprise, Pavel Vavilin entered the barn. Who had asked him to come? But Pavel was as frightened as they were and wanted to know what was going on. He was certainly going to be asked about this later.

Sasha was the first to speak after everyone had assembled in the barn.

"These wolves have us at their mercy," he began. "We stay cowered in our houses while they rest for the next attack. You saw the soldiers fail to get to us. We have to save ourselves, at least try something. Let's not pretend that some of us won't die. But let's try to save the rest."

"How can we fight them without weapons?" Vlad asked. He had yet to hear of what had happened to Tonja.

Karl entered the barn, looked for Vlad and pulled him into the corner.

"Vlad," he whispered. "I'm sorry, there was nothing I could do."

Vlad, "About what?"

"Please forgive me," started Karl. "I saw the wolves take Tonja."

Vlad backed away. Tonja dead? His girl dead? How?

Karl explained.

Vlad's wail cut-off the talk among the villagers. Everyone turned toward him. Wild eyed, he bumped against the barn wall, his fingers feeling the wood behind him as he moved crab-like towards the door. No one tried to stop him or even talk to him. They were as stunned as he was, now hearing the news of Tonya's death for the first time.

Vlad fumbled to release the catch on the small door and fell backwards through the opening, cradling his shotgun in his hand. He righted himself and walked trance-like, away from the barn. Elena, who just now realized what had happened, ran after him.

Yuri began to go also, but Sergi stopped him and revolted the door.

"Let them get home again," he said. "They need time to grieve; they will be no help to us here today."

Elena caught up with Vlad. She struggled to control her own emotions so that she could help her husband.

"Let us go to the house," she implored.

"No!" Vlad shouted. "We will find our daughter first. They killed our only son and now our little one. Once we have the body of our daughter in a safe place, I will kill as many of them as I can, and I'll do it right now! I won't wait anymore!"

They arrived at Karl's and began to search around the outside of the hut. When they rounded the left side they saw Tonja; or what was left of Tonja. She was almost unrecognizable except for her clothing. Pieces of flesh were strewn about the reddened snow. They stopped to look at the remains of their daughter, Elena bending down to clutch the fabric she had made for her; Vlad too stunned to move.

Seena saw them first. "More humans," she barked. She wasted no time, attacking from behind the woodpile, mauling Elena. Vlad was jolted out of his trance; he picked up a piece of pointed wood and dove for Seena, missing her as she spun to his right.

Maala, Tuva, and Vaal moved in. The man was easy prey; his efforts to shield himself uncoordinated and ineffective. Vlad flailed at the wolves, but they ran under his arms and bit into his clothing, dragging him toward the woodpile. Vlad tumbled against the pile; Maala bit through his collarbone, pinning the man down. Vlad kept trying to hit the wolves with the wood, but it was useless; he was down, they were in control. The last thing he heard was Elena screaming.

The people in the barn could hear what was happening to the Kovalev's. How could they hope to defeat these animals? And if the wolves killed the adults, who would protect the children sequestered in the houses?

Surprisingly, Pavel spoke, and, for the first time, he was listened to. "You have to come to your senses. Are you not smarter than them? Are you cowards? You must act; no one can save you but yourselves. I was in the army. Those planes couldn't signal back to base in this storm, and even if they could, the next flights would have to wait out the night and the weather. They won't arrive in time to save us. And I know something about wolves. At night I've seen them scavenge dead soldiers on the battlefield, tearing off their flesh. They are tenacious, they even come back after you've shot at them, and now that they know they have us cornered, they will attack relentlessly."

"Who are you to speak, Vavilin?" challenged Sergi. "Your kind took away many of our weapons; you limit our ammunition; you tell us you will keep us safe. What safety have you given?"

Pavel looked straight at Sergi. "I promise you nothing, but I know what cooperation can do. We have to act together, according to a plan. If you try to do this independently the wolves will pick you off one by one."

"I agree," shouted Sasha. "If Vavilin has a good plan I will follow it. I don't care whose it is."

Pavel smiled. "No more hiding. We take the initiative. Better to die fighting than holed up like frightened rabbits. We have some weapons, some ammunition, if we use them carefully we can start to turn this battle, put the wolf on the defensive, let him know we are dangerous too."

Both men and women started offering suggestions to anyone who would listen. They talked of what they had seen the wolves do; of stories they had heard from others in the past; of ways to attack. They felt the disgust of the inactive; the shame of the coward. The mood swung to action, to going after their tormentors. No one pushed his idea just to win the argument; the best ideas were agreed upon.

Pavel stood near the loft listening, cajoling, melding the thoughts of those trying to help. Then he mounted a hay bale and summarized the plan. "We will attract the wolves to the barn, get them inside, on our turf. Acting together we can kill as many of the wolves as possible, make them retreat to the forest. Then someone has to go to get help."

In all about forty villagers had come into the barn, against the eighty or so remaining wolves. They listened to the rest of Pavel's plan. It might work. What choice did they have?

Vasili waited in the tree.

Kolai awoke to find himself stuck to the window. His open head wounds had oozed blood, matting his hair, which froze and stuck to the inside of the pane. Part of his upper face on the right side was stuck also. The knapsack in his lap was covered with spilled blood; it had cushioned his body from hitting the front of the cockpit. He was conscious but stunned.

Slowly, he pulled at the frozen hair, breaking it off from the window pane; some of the glass came off with it. When he was free, he tried to look about the cabin at the others. Major Kostenich looked dead; Kolai reached across, took off his gloves, and felt for a pulse under the man's jacket; nothing. The others were the same. Then he worked at opening the hinges that attached the cockpit to the cabin. That took awhile, but he finally freed the frame and pushed it away from him. It fell to the ground, the sound of breaking glass telling Kolai he might be further above the snow then he thought.

He looked down to the base of the tree. He would have to jump. With great effort, Kolai managed to get out of the cockpit, one leg on the branch, the other on the remains of the wing. He tried to revive the men in back. It was hopeless; one had a broken neck, the other was dead from the collision.

Kolai tried to think of what to do. He reached into the cabin and pulled out the two rifles he could see that weren't wedged under a body. Then he found a box of shells and pulled that out by the hemp rope. He dropped the rifles and the box onto the snow, slid down so that he was hanging by his hands from the limb, and dropped to the forest floor. He stumbled and fell; righted himself; assessed the situation.

He must be north of the village, he thought, but not far away. Kolai slung the rifles over his right shoulder, lifted the box of ammunition with his left hand, and began walking in what he thought was the direction of the village.

The walk took twenty five minutes, but ahead, Kolai could see the first familiar houses; he also saw wolves in the distance. He kept his line of sight so that the wolves could not see him coming toward the huts. He aimed for the house nearest his path, keeping it between him and the wolves. It was the home of the Pavlovsky's.

Alla heard the pounding at the back of the shed. She told the children she was minding to stay where they were and ran to the back of the house. Yes, it was a man, a soldier, trying to get in. Quickly, Alla moved the furniture away and opened the door. Kolai stumbled inside, almost fainting from the effort. Alla helped him into the living room.

"Who are you, where are the others?" Alla asked.

"I don't know," Kolai replied. "Have no other soldiers come?"

"Just some in a airplane that crashed near the well. The wolves killed them."

"My God, and anyone else?"

"No, just you."

Kolai asked for something to drink, to get his senses. Alla brought over some cognac and poured him a glass. It cleared his head.

She offered a wet cloth to wipe his face, then realized, "My God – Kolai, it's you!"

Still dazed, he mumbled, "Alla?"

"Yes, Kolai, yes."

"My God, my God," sobbed Alla.

"You must be married by now?"

"Yes, to Sasha."

"You married Sasha?"

"Oh, Kolai, you left, I was confused. I think I did the right thing."

"Of course," he said, coming to his senses.

"Where is Sasha now," he croaked?

"Sasha is with the other men in the barn, they are making a plan to fight the wolves."

"How far is the barn," he asked, putting things behind him?

"Just over there. Come to the window, I will show you."

Kolai looked over to the barn. He could run to it before the wolves got to him. He had to find out what was happening.

"Open the front door and let me run over to the barn."

"Yes, yes, the men need to see you," replied Alla. "Tell them who you are."

Kolai almost fell as he left the house, he was still not right from the crash. He managed to slip and slide toward the barn, trying to reach it before the wolves saw him. But a wolf near the Luskey house saw the running man and attacked.

Kolai stopped in his tracks. This wolf could cut off his approach to the barn, he had to be killed. Kolai opened his jacket and fumbled for his pistol. His fingers were almost frozen, but he managed to get the gun out and cock it. The wolf came straight toward him, slowly cutting the distance between them. Neither hungry nor tired, the wolf seemed confidant that this man was his.

Kolai had been raised to shoot, he knew of animals and their ways. But the wolf stopped when he raised his arm and pointed his pistol at him. Kolai kept the gun leveled at the wolf, then tried to circle to his right, hoping to get closer to the barn without causing the wolf to attack. He would shoot when he knew he could get to safety; he didn't want to draw any other wolves toward him.

The wolf moved sideways, to keep his body between the barn and Kolai, wondering if he should call for his brothers.

Kolai saw that he could not get around the wolf; he also knew that exposed as he was he was more vulnerable the longer he stayed out. He had to act. He waited until the wolf was close to him; it had not rushed him as he thought it would. But he knew enough to realize that it was now within the distance where it could spring on him with one bound. He pointed the pistol in front of his face, locked his arm in as straight a position as he could, aimed carefully, and fired. The wolf dropped immediately, the bullet pierced its brain. Kolai ran on to the barn door.

Inside the barn, the sound of the shot stopped all talk. Who was outside? Sasha went to the loft opening, pulled it back, and looked down. "Open the door," he shouted.

Sergi got the barn door open and watched Kolai fall through onto the floor. Then Kolai got up and leaned against the inside of the wall.

The sight of this single soldier did not raise the hopes of anyone. Here was a wounded man, blood caked over his hair and face, exhausted, barely able to stand, hardly the rescue party they had hoped for. But he did have two rifles and a pistol in his hand, a box of ammunition, and he was from the army. That was something.

"I'm Kolai," he said.

"Mendelev," they asked?

"Yes, where are the other soldiers?"

Sasha explained to him what they had seen. Four soldiers dead, at least two planes crashed, if the explosion from the south was a plane. Nothing else.

"There were four planes," said Kolai. "The men in my plane are all dead but for me. That leaves one plane unaccounted for."

"It may have flown away," said Sasha. "We could hear planes, but we couldn't see them in this storm. Maybe it couldn't land."

"But you don't know," continued Kolai. "I may be the only survivor."

"Can you help us with our plan?" Pavel asked. "We need someone who knows how to plan an attack."

Kolai nodded, dropped his weapons and went to plan with the men. He was home.

21

Kirev kept a steady pace across the frozen lake. The storm obscured the far shore, but if they headed east by northeast they should reach the break in the trees. Visibility had deteriorated rapidly but they pushed ahead. Traction was fading as the first hail hardened the surface. Ahead, snow blanketed the eastern part of the lake. They moved into the hail, and could see no more than 40 feet. Kirev slowed to 10 mph wanting to make sure he could stop when they reached the eastern shore of the lake. In three minutes he spotted the grey outline of the trees and began pumping his brakes. Nansky saw his tail lights blink on and off. He turned his wheels slightly to the right and began to pump as well. The first contact locked the left brake shoe within the wheel and it froze in position. He could feel the play in the brake pedal. With his left rear wheel locked the truck began to skid sideways toward the bank. Nansky pressed down harder on the pedal, and the shoe broke loose. The truck slid around on the ice and crashed backward into the bank, up the gentle slope, and caught a small boulder with its right rear wheel. The tire blew when the rim bent under the force and the truck bounced to a halt.

Kirev saw Nansky's truck off to his right as it slammed into the bank. He brought his truck to a full stop just shy of the shore, got out and trotted to where Nansky had stopped.

"Are you okay?"

"No one is hurt, but my rear wheel is bent."

"Can you drive like that?"

"No, the wheel is lost."

"We could put your men in our truck, but then we would have only one vehicle and if that breaks down, nothing to get us to Pilovo. Better that you have the men change the wheel. We still haven't seen the break in the trees. It's not here, so we have to go search for it. We'll come back and tell you where it is once we've found it."

"Fine, fine. We should be ready to go again by then."

"I hope so."

Nansky ordered four men to get the spare out and change the wheel. They had to dig a hole to anchor the jack in the snow and block the other wheels so the truck didn't slide back down the slope onto the lake. Changing the frozen wheel was not easy. First they had to loosen the jammed nuts, wrestle the spare wheel onto the lugs, and with frozen fingers, start the nuts turning back on the lugs. The ice had to be cleared off the well to let them position the spare.

Meanwhile Kirev drove slowly northward along the lake shore, as close as he dared, to find the opening in the trees. He allowed two miles to do this. Private Krinsk watched carefully from the right side of the cab, window down, blocking the snow with a canvas as he searched the shore. He yelled at Kirev to slow down so that he could be sure not to miss anything. Slowly they searched, one mile, a mile and a half, two miles, nothing.

"There's nothing here Sergeant, just trees. We should have seen it by now if it's this way."

"I'll turn back south, but look again some more over my arms. I'll sit back to let you see."

The truck did a U turn and retraced its path back down the lake.

"Still nothing, Sergeant, unless we're too far from the trees to see it."

After a few minutes they passed Nansky's truck and kept going south. One half mile, one mile....."

"Wait!"

"What?"

"I think I see a clearing in the trees."

Kirev stopped the truck.

"We have to be sure. Take two men and go out and check."

Krinsk and two soldiers jumped from the truck and trotted and slid to the shore. Yes! Fifty feet to the left was an opening. Krinsk sent one man back to tell Kirev, then he walked into the path to make sure it didn't dead-end. After 70 yards he knew it was the path. Yes, this was the break shown on the map. He ran back to the truck to tell Kirev.

Krinsk shouted over the engine noise, "Sir, the break is here. I walked into it. It's wide enough for our truck, and I think it goes on for awhile."

"Good. Wait here, I'll go get Nansky and his truck. Stay visible and flag us down when we return, this stuff is getting worse."

It was now 3:54 pm. The sun would go down at 4:03 pm; darkness would be total at 4:28 pm. At least the moon would be full tonight. They still had a chance to reach Pilovo before night set in.

Kirev and Nansky, now without brakes, eased their trucks up the slope and into the opening. They knew from the map that after less than two miles this path should intersect the north-south corridor, about three miles south of Pilovo. Progress was achingly slow. The road was terrible, not fit for a cart, much less a truck. The trucks lurched from one side to the other; the trees tore at the sides in the narrow spots; the traction was poor. Kirev thought of the villagers waiting, waiting, as he slowly approached them. How many more would die if they were 20 minutes late? How many if they broke down? How many if they didn't make it?

Ahead, in the middle of the path, the outline of something brown appeared, piled up in the snow. Kirev slowed, not wanting to lose what little momentum he had on the ice, and rolled down the window. He stuck his head out far enough to see clearly, but kept a steady hand on the wheel. It was a reindeer, nearly dead, partly gutted, blocking the path. He stopped the truck and signalled to Nansky to stop also.

"Krinsk," he said. "Take three men and move the deer away. Be quick about it."

Krinsk opened his door, dropped to the ground, and went back to choose three helpers. They walked to the deer, a large female, about 250 pounds, and started pulling it to the right of the path.

Then the forest erupted in sound.

The roar so frightened the men that two of them fell onto the snow. Krinsk turned to the left, in time to see the bear leap into the path, stopping just short of the deer. The bear raised on his hind legs, pawed the air, and roared again. No one moved.

Kirev shouted, "Load your rifles. Shoot the thing."

They aimed, backed away slowly, hoping the bear wouldn't move.

But the bear dropped into a crouch, sniffed the air, and charged, right for Krinsk. He caught the private in the chest with his front paw, knocking him to the right, off the path.

Krinsk saw blood spurting from his vest, through the hole the bear had torn in his ribs. He pressed his hand down to stop the flow, and felt, even through the clothing, the pulsing of his heart as it pumped the blood out of his body. He lay there and bled.

Nansky was already out of his truck and opening the back tailgate to loose the two wolfhounds. They bounded out, turned toward the front of the truck, and ran at the bear.

The bear dropped the second soldier he had gripped in his arms and faced the dogs. They didn't hesitate, but went straight at the bear, one vaulting toward the head, the other at its legs. The bear swung his right paw and caught the first dog in mid-air, ripping open its trunk. His swipe disemboweled it as he tossed it over his left shoulder. Then he reached down and grabbed the other dog with both paws. The hound had already bitten into the bear's stomach, and held fast as the bear raised the dogs hindquarters up to his head. He jerked the dog back and forth, trying to dislodge it, but the dog's bite held. Another roar filled the path as the bear tore at the dog, ripping off one leg and mauling its back. The dog was dying, but still his jaws locked onto the bear's belly. The bear roared again.

By now, two of the men from Nansky's truck had loaded their rifles and aimed at the bear. Seeing that both dogs were gone, they fired, one bullet hitting the bear above the eyes, skidding along its thick skull, and exiting at the top of head. The other shot missed to the left. Several more men started shooting, hitting the bear three more times. The bear dropped down, the dog's front quarters still in its stomach, and charged. The men scattered, trying to reload as they ran.

Nansky ran for his truck, the bear close behind, passing Kirev's truck in its charge. Nansky slammed the driver's door shut, just as the bear came up to the running board. Nansky tried to slide under the wheel and over the gear shift to get to the right side of the cabin, but the bear smashed the window and latched onto his shoulder. Nansky screamed as the bear dragged him from the truck, tearing open the door as he moved. Kirev and the soldiers saw Nansky in the bear's grasp. They leveled their rifles.

"Don't shoot until he releases him," shouted Kirev. "Make sure he's clear of the bear."

"Bullshit," thought one man. "He'll be dead by then." So he fired, right into the bear's ear.

Another roar shook the air. The bear dropped Nansky and stumbled toward the men. They all fired, pieces of blood soaked fur flying as the bear fell. They reloaded and fired again.

"Enough," said Kirev, walking over to the mangled body of his comrade. Nansky's shoulder was torn from his body, his face and chest raked open with wounds, his upper lip gone.

"Hold on," said Kirev. "We will stop the bleeding."

Which was all they could do. Nansky died before they lifted him into the truck. His body, and that of Krinsk, were placed inside, the wounded soldier next to them. The remains of the dogs were left behind, the convoy continued on.

They bounded ahead, Kirev focused again on his mission. Get to Pilovo.

At 4:04 pm the tree shadows on both sides disappeared. They were clear of the path. They turned left and headed up the corridor for the village.

Kirev stopped his truck and got out to talk to the other driver.

"Okay, we head due north. I think we can go a little faster here, maybe 25. We should be in Pilovo just before darkness."

"Maybe the planes are already there. They may have beat the storm. If they landed the wolves may already be under control. What do you think?"

"I am an army man. I think nothing. No matter what, we have to get to the village as soon as we can. I hope you're right but, who knows?"

Kirev slipped the truck into gear and headed up the corridor. He held it at a steady speed. Things seemed to be going better now. The pilots would probably have tea ready for them when they arrived.

22

Private Zhuravkin surveyed the scene around him. Kyagova's plane still burning; Moskalenko and his aide unconscious. Only he and Terentskaya were able to continue.

"Are you all right, Terentskaya?"

"Yes, comrade. I can function. Where are we?"

"I think south of the village, maybe two or three miles. We have to see if Boren and Sergeant Moskalenko are still alive."

Zhuravkin went back to the cockpit to check on Moskalenko. He pushed the body back slowly from the controls and massaged the head. Moskalenko blinked twice, opened his eyes, moaned and began to see again.

Terentskaya tried to revive Boren, but he was in a deep faint and, though alive, remained unconscious. Terentskaya took two blankets from the rear of the cockpit and wrapped Boren's legs and chest. Perhaps he would awaken soon.

Zhuravkin, "Sergeant, we have crashed but we are all alive. Can you understand me?"

"Yes. Where are we?"

"I think we are close to the village. It must be just north of here. We landed in the storm. Sergeant Kyagova's plane was ahead of us. It exploded and is burning. I think they are all dead. You saved us by turning off into the forest."

"We have to go help our comrades."

"Sir, it's too late to help them. We saw no one moving there. The fuel exploded. No one can be alive."

"My God, help me out of here. We have to judge our situation. Where are the other two planes?"

Zhuravkin unbuckled Moskalenko from his harness and helped him out of the cockpit and onto the ice. Moskalenko removed his gloves and rubbed his face and eyes.

"How is Boren?"

"Still unconscious, sir."

"We can leave him here and return later to help him. Remove the rifles and ammunition. Let's see if any of Kyagova's crew is alive."

The three soldiers walked through the trees toward the smoldering plane, past the sheared off wings of their own craft, and out into the opening. Kyagova's plane was still in flames but burning lower now. Between the flames they could see the blackened figures of the crew, none of them moving. They walked around the plane and headed north.

Terentskaya thought that he had heard shots coming from that direction earlier. Had the other two planes landed safely? Were they already shooting the wolves?

And why only a few shots? There were supposed to be at least 60 wolves. They followed the path, hoping to reach either the village or the downed plane.

Still blinded by the swirling snow, they were further from the village than they thought. The walk through the corridor would take some time.

23

Friday 4:05 pm

Pavel climbed up on the hay and addressed the group again.

"We have only one chance. The sun is setting. We cannot survive another night of wolf attacks, and, except for the Sergeant here, our rescuers are either dead or gone. No one else can reach us in this storm. We must kill the wolves ourselves. Those who survive have to take the women and children and head south for Pulni in the daylight. Some of you should make it.

"The plan is this. We build a large pile of kindling near the south wall of the barn. Four of us go out and entice the wolves in here. The rest of you stay in the loft. Once all the wolves are in the barn we barricade the door. Wolves become cowed when they are confined. They will be confused and slink around with their tails down before they decide to attack.

"Once the door is closed, Yuri will shoot a flaming arrow into the kindling. The flames will further confuse them. Then we attack. Try to keep them between you and the flames. If you are attacked kill that wolf, even if you are dying. If each of us kills one wolf most of them will be dead.

"We have 15 minutes before the whole barn catches fire. We must be finished by then. When the walls collapse, you will have to find your own way out. Since you believe in God, this is the time to make your peace with Him."

Pavel, Sergi, Sasha, and Yuri opened the small door and trotted outside to the edge of the barn. Kolai was in the loft, his rifle pointed outside the window, ready to kill any wolves if one of the men should slip when they were hurrying back to the barn. Most of the wolves were still near the church, yelping at Vasili in the tree. Yuri lifted his head and howled loudly. He wanted revenge for Pushkin. Reina was the first to turn.

He whined to the others, "A human is here, wait, more of them let's bring them down."

Maala heard the cry too. "Our brothers have found something."

The wolves began to gather again and ran toward the barn.

Three of the men held their ground as the wolves formed into a pack and started running towards them. Sergi ran back to the barn door and climbed up above the sill on the inside, ready to drop and lock the door once the wolves were inside. Then Pavel ran inside to the back of the barn near the unlit bonfire and tied the heavy rope beneath his armpits. The men in the loft took up the slack over the pulley.

Yuri was the last to run. He watched the wolves close in as he backed towards the door. He hoped his timing was right, slow enough to keep them coming, fast enough to find safety. He prayed he wouldn't slip on the ice.

Reina rounded the barn just as Yuri bolted through the doorway. She was the first wolf inside. Yuri clambered up the ladder to the loft. Vaal and Tuva followed quickly in pursuit. Reina attempted the ladder but was driven back by a pitchfork poking at his nose. The wolves whirled towards Pavel suspended on the top of the kindling for the bonfire. Tuva and Vaal almost reached him, but the men at the top yanked Pavel up into the loft. He swung back onto the loft floor and removed the rope.

"So far it's working."

By now over 20 wolves had entered the barn. Reina was confused. The humans were here, their smell was everywhere, but they were above them out of reach. The walls surrounded them; the sky was gone; the forest gone; the ice gone; this was not their place; this was not their world; they were not made for this. This was man's place.

Sergi watched as more wolves filed in. From a crack above the door, he could see some stragglers; so could Kolai, waiting to fire again once most of the wolves were inside.

Sergi slammed the door shut and drove the wooden plank through the slots they had just nailed to the inside of the door and down into the hole they had hacked out of the barn floor. The door was now secure. No man or wolf could escape without removing the plank.

For a long minute everything was silent. The humans watched as the wolves moved on the ground, trying to leap from the bales to the loft. But the people had taken care of that, no bales were high enough or close enough. Some animals had their tails down, some cowered near the walls. No human moved.

"We are in a bad place," said Reina.

"The humans have tricked us. We either kill them now or be killed ourselves," said Tuva.

Vaal, "No we must get out of here, we can kill the humans later. This place is evil. It is man's place. We are not safe here."

"We can't get out," snapped Maala. "We must fight now."

Pavel signaled to Yuri who lit the end of his arrow and shot it into the straw at the base of the bonfire. The fire caught instantly, and the flames shot up the stack.

"Fire, man's companion," shouted Maala. "We must leave!"

The strongest men dropped to the floor near the doors. Yuri now shot his arrows at the wolves; Sasha speared them with a pike; the women and boys hurled stones, pots, anything down on them; the wolves backed nearer the fire.

"No, attack the humans," shouted Maala. "We are trapped. We must fight to get out."

Reina led a charge, vaulting at Karl, who took one step backward, dropped to one knee and braced his pitchfork to catch Reina in the air. As Reina fell, his right paw grazed the fork as it entered his chest below the collarbone. The blades split into his cavity, impaling his heart as they tore into his flesh. He died as he landed on Karl. Karl turned and threw Reina off him, pulling out the fork. Sana hit him from behind trying to bite his neck but Karl rolled toward the door. He whirled and slashed at Sana catching her by the neck and causing her to jerk sideways. The days of waiting were over – no more cowardly inaction – the day of the wolf was ending – man was on the attack!

Those men who had guns fired carefully into the wolves. They had to be sure that none of the villagers were behind or close to the wolf they were shooting at. The sound of the shots frightened the wolves even further. Maybe 20 were killed by the bullets.

Kolai perched up in the loft window knew that all the wolves had not entered the barn. He alternated his firing, sometimes shooting at a wolf in the barn, other times shooting at the wolves who were outside. After he hit two of the outside wolves, the rest of the pack retreated to the northeast corner of the village.

Throughout the barn the battle continued. Knives, pokers, pikes, anything was used to skewer the wolves. Yuri sliced off a wolf's head with the scimitar; four women dropped onto the floor and took flaming branches from the fire, waving them at the frightened animals. Everyone was caught up in the melee. Manja saw a wolf topple her husband. She jumped from the loft, her kitchen knife in hand, onto the wolf's back. She drove the knife repeatedly into the wolf, killing it as it mauled Sergi. No one held back. It was them or the wolves. No one ran – to where? It was their time to kill.

Sergi knew they must finish off all these wolves, since many remained outside. When the barn burned down they would have to kill those also.

The wolves had their victories, too. Maala and Vaal had killed two of the women, and Tuva had torn a man apart. But the contest seemed lost to them. They wanted to leave, but they couldn't get away. They were cornered and had to fight on.

"Don't be afraid," barked Maala. We can still beat these humans. Remember how we cowed them last night."

But the rifles had an effect. Kolai was a skilled sharpshooter, his bullets had a telling impact. He was careful to fire only when a wolf was in the path of the shot; he killed seven wolves himself.

By now the flames were raging out of control. Fire was everywhere. Wolves and people could hardly see each other in the smoke. Each person had to fight the wolf attacking him; he couldn't see to help anyone else. The same was true for the animals. They bit what was closest to them; no cooperation was possible in this hunt. Kolai put down his rifle and jumped to the barn floor, using his pistol at close range.

The fire blew out the roof, it licked over the eaves, and the barn walls caved in. Flaming pieces of wood and straw flew in all directions. A timber fell onto one man pinning him and Seena to the floor. They both died in the heat. Everyone kept stabbing at any wolf nearby. In the confusion some wolves limped off through the openings in the fallen walls and made it to the safety of the forest.

But the humans were not stopping now. They ran after them, there was no thought of turning back now. It was kill now or lose forever.

Vasili dropped from the tree and joined them.

Even the wolves outside the barn, those who had retreated, were confused when they saw it collapse. They too were wondering what to do, when Maala bellowed, "Take to the forest. Stay with me."

24

Friday, sunset

Vaal huddled with the remaining wolves at the forest edge.

"The humans tricked us. Reina was wrong to lead us into the barn. We have lost, we must retreat into the forest, and hope that these men do not hunt us down."

Sana, "Let us leave now before they kill us."

"No. We can't retreat at the first defeat. The darkness is here. It is our time again," said Maala.

Seena, "What of the noise sticks? How many are there?"

Maala, "The noise sticks are not effective at close range, they are too long and take time to fire. If we come in quickly they won't see us until we are so close that they can't point them at us. We must attack now before they lose their fear of us."

Sana, injured and bleeding, said, "My pack will not go. We are leaving this place full of the smell of our dead brothers."

Maala, "Then go! Slink back into the forest! Allow man to defeat you. We will attack from the front. Head first for the humans with the noise sticks. Kill them and the rest will be at our mercy."

Vaal brought the pack behind the village west of the barn, to avoid the flames. They saw the villagers running from the burning barn toward St. Stephan's.

Kirev saw a shape ahead as the trucks pushed forward in the snow. It was 4:11 pm, the sun had set and with the storm the darkness was increasing rapidly. At closer view the shape was a smoldering airplane, crashed and burning. Kirev dropped three men off to see to survivors and continued on. A few hundred yards ahead he saw three figures stumbling northward, obviously near exhaustion. He stopped to find out why they were here.

"What is happening?"

"We don't know; the village is ahead somewhere."

Kirev told the men to get aboard and pushed on.

After two miles they began to think that they saw the village huts. Then with a roar a barn wall collapsed and flames leapt into the dusk. Silhouetted in the flames were running wolves and – yes! – men chasing them!

Kirev headed the trucks straight for the burning barn. They stopped between the barn and the church. The soldiers dropped from the trucks, saw both wolves and men coming toward them.

"Fire at the wolves!" Kirev ordered.

In the initial confusion shots were fired in several directions and both wolves and men were hit.

"Stop! Line up in a row and only fire if you see a clear background behind the wolf. Watch for men in the distance. We have time now. Take them down one by one."

The firing ceased as the men regrouped.

"Yes, we have to systematically kill them. See to any wounded," shouted Kirev.

Pavel and Kolai raced towards him.

"Who is in command here?" Kolai asked.

"Well, Sergeant Moskalenko is, but he's injured from the crash. So, yes, I guess I'm in command."

"No, I am," said Kolai. "Get your men ready."

Pavel explained, "The children are in the house over there." He pointed. "Most of the rest of us are outside. We have killed many of the wolves, but there may be a dozen or two left."

Kolai started talking rapidly, "Collect the men. We need order to finish this job. Are there any pilots here besides you, Sergeant? Piloff, take a squad of men and see to the barn. The rest stay with me."

The wolves again retreated close to the woods.

Maala spoke first, "This is our chance. There are more men with more noise sticks. We attack at once. Otherwise they will pursue us with the noise-sticks and kill us in the forest."

It was 4:28 pm.

The village was alive with people and solders hurrying about. First they collected all the children and herded them over to where the soldiers were forming.

"Let's get the young ones to a safe place near here where we can guard them," shouted Kolai. "The house they are in is too far away."

Kirev moved the women and children to the three sturdiest houses closest to the well. He ringed these with ten men all facing the woods. The descending blackness enveloped them. The men gathered straw and birch and made torches to help the soldiers see the wolves, should they come toward them. They drove the torches into the ice outside the perimeter of the line of solders. Meanwhile, Kolai spoke to Sasha.

"We have 21 soldiers here. How many of our people know how to use a rifle? We can use the rest to move the ammunition and man the pitchforks should they be needed."

"Do you think the wolves will come back? The fire and your rifles should have frightened them away," asked Sasha.

"How would I know? We must be ready in either case 'till morning. Then we can assess the damage and continue from there."

"Okay, I'll tell the men."

Kolai wondered how these trucks had come. Why didn't the pilots know of this; it could have saved lives. But, no matter now, the village would be safe, he could ask his questions later.

Kirev was looking sideways at the well when the first wolves attacked the ring of soldiers. Their dark shapes were invisible

163

until they passed the flickering glow of the torches. They bounded the 20 feet between the torches and the soldiers in a second, jumping some of the men as they tried to aim. In the commotion a few wolves were shot, but the rest ran in among the men.

"My God, they attack at will, what kind of wolves are these," said Kirev?

It was impossible to keep order. Wolves were in front of, behind, next to, everywhere. The reloading of the rifles was slow; some of the village men ran away to the houses. The determination of the pack was overwhelming. Shots rang out; most missed.

As soon as one group of wolves were driven off another seemed to replace them. Ears laid back, teeth bared, they charged the men before they could be seen.

Because of the dark there seemed to be more wolves than there really were. A wolf would attack one man, fall aside, bite into his neighbor, tear at the legs of another. The flickering light from the torches made their fangs appear to move in a staccato series of motions. Their eyes glowed yellow and green.

"We need more men," shouted Kolai.

"I'll go get them," said Kirev.

Kirev came back with the other soldiers from the burned barn.

"The barn is empty. We don't need to station anyone there."

He had these men form a line 40 feet from the houses, where they could reload and shoot without hitting each other.

"First kill the wolves that are not close to the men. Attack with your bayonets if you run out of bullets. Get an angle on your target. Watch for men in the line of fire," said Kolai.

Tuva saw that even these men could be cornered. She asked Maala.

"Can we kill them, too?"

"I think so. They have many weapons, but they act confused. We have to keep up our attack, don't give them time to prepare."

Instinctively the wolves knew that the attack must be relentless. The humans moved like wounded animals; the time to finish them was now. They raced back to the village center and, without stopping, into the midst of the men. They fell on the humans with a fury that would finish any prey.

No wolf was idle; each had a man to attack. They would fight with one, break off if they were losing, and attack another. If one of their brothers was in trouble, they would go to his aid. These men did not fight well if more than one wolf attacked, but, a soldier had time to reload when left alone, and then they were on the attack again.

The carnage continued for over an hour. The soldiers killed wolves, but more replaced them. The wolves killed a few men but were becoming disorganized and disoriented as the bullets felled their comrades. Because of the darkness no one, neither man nor animal, knew who was winning.

Tuva came at the men from the side near the houses. She trotted to a place just outside the light of the torches and set a line on a soldier who was aiming at Maala. She came in fast and low, snow rising from her paws. When she was within eight feet of Kirov she sprung into the air, opening her jaws as she rose.

Kolai saw her. He spun and aimed. The wolf was between him and Kirev; he had no choice but to fire.

The bullet hit Tuva just below the breast bone, turning her to the left, past Kirev. She rotated in the air, seeing men, black sky, and then snow. She landed on her belly; barely felt the pain; her right leg shattered on impact; blood oozed from her mouth. Breathing heavily, she tried to lift herself on her good leg, but stumbled nose-first into the ground, her hind legs trying to grip the ice before she fell again. It was no use; she heaved up one final time and fell splayed on the ice. Her tongue lolled out the side of her mouth. She thought of Maala and the pack, of the forest and the game, of the days spent running. Her eyes turned upward and then stopped in a frozen stare.

Maala finished with the man he was attacking, turned and saw Tuva down on the ice. He knew from the way she was sprawled out that she was dead. But right now he had to go on, with what little fight he had left in him.

Vaal had just killed a soldier; he looked for his next prey.

Kolai was loading his rifle when Vaal made for his side; he brought the gun up too late to shoot, but the stock caught the wolf under the chin and turned him off into the snow. Man and wolf had time to recover, each looked at the other, neither knew what to expect. Vaal righted himself and attacked again. This time Kolai was ready; he aimed at Vaal's head and fired. The bullet caught Vaal just below the left eye and tunnelled through to his brain. Vaal saw a second of flashing light and then tumbled away on his back. His legs pawed the air briefly and then he rolled over on his side. Kolai reloaded.

Then the men heard a shot coming from the trees. A wolf fell. After a few seconds another shot rang out. It was Oleg, the mountain man, the first time he had been near the village in years. His shots confused the wolves, they seemed to be surrounded by the fire-sticks. Oleg shot again and another wolf fell. Now the men saw the flash from Oleg's gun coming from high in a tree. He had climbed up in the commotion and was safe to fire at will. The wolves spun in circles, wondering where to attack.

The she-wolf Seena leapt at Kirev. He braced, then ran his bayonet into her underside, cutting the rib cage. The blade stopped in her heart. Kirev flipped her body over his shoulder and she slid off the rifle.

The courage of the wolves was not enough. The men were too many; their noise-sticks too many; the wolves too few.

Even so, just when it seemed that the men had the wolves under control, a new group would attack from a different direction.

Few of the solders had experience killing animals with rifles. Some had fought in the recent wars, but killing men was different. Here there were no lines of battle; no set movements; no organized forays. The only thing certain was chaos. But the steady firing was having its toll. The wolves were losing. No matter how gallant, they could not win against these new men. Now the smell of wolf's blood filled the air.

"Stay alert. There can't be too many more," hollered Kolai. "Keep your rifles loaded. We have to make sure that no wolves stay in the village."

The men had to make certain that each shot was at a wolf and not in a direction that might hit a house or some of the villagers who were running to and fro helping the solders reload and replacing the torches.

It was like fighting in a dream; little light to see by; an enemy that obeyed no rules; a balance between action and restraint.

But the steady firing of the rifles had its effect. The wolves were less bold, looking more like prey than predator. Only their courage kept them in the fight.

Then a wolf cry pierced the air. Even the men stopped to listen. The same wolf howled again; it was Unal. She had caught up with the hannal, and, from her spot on the small hill near Sergi's house, she could see all the men and all the wolves. She called. "Brothers, they are too many!"

Maala yelped a reply, "Listen to her. Come back to the woods."

It was 5:35 pm. The commotion stopped.

"Hold your fire," shouted Kirev.

The smoldering barn, the dead wolves, the dead men, all the debris and exhaustion, left the soldiers and the villagers spent. But the threat seemed to have passed. The wolves were gone, or so it seemed. It was time to regroup and assess the damage.

Kirev and Kolai positioned a few men along the perimeter between the church and the houses nearest the forest. Once again, fresh torches were rammed into the snow.

"Watch for them to return," said Kolai. "Fire at will if you see a wolf; call if you need help."

Kolai turned to view the bodies lying bleeding on the ground. Two medics were busy trying to bandage the wounded and get others to help haul them inside the homes. A fragile peace seemed to fill the air; maybe there was time for relief.

Maala limped into the blackness of the forest with the remaining wolves.

"We have lost most of the hannal. The men with weapons have won for now. The fire was too much. We need to rest and decide what to do later."

He scanned the remains of his own pack. Where were the others? Had the humans really killed so many? Tuva and Vaal were gone; where were Seena and Vorna? Reina? Bunta? Could they be dead? Had all the packs been defeated?

He waited as the rest of the hannal filed in. Many of them limped or bled or were wounded. None seemed ready to fight on. They dropped in the snow near Maala, hoping he would tell them how to continue. Would they attack the men again, or had the men won? Was Maala right when he said the men would track and kill them if they took one human life? Would they attack a different village or would they try to survive without the animals of man?

Maala knew the answers but now was not the time to give them. The wolves were still in danger; most of the alphas were dead, killed when they led their packs in charges. He was alone; Tuva dead, their offspring slaughtered. He knew the few alphas still alive would form new packs from the remains of the hannal. He didn't know if the hannal should remain together. All of his plans were colored by his defeat. For now he had to lead the hannal to safety.

"Come, my brothers," gasped Maala. "We have to leave. The others will join us when they can."

He knew enough about men to realize that they had to trot all night to get a safe distance away. But they were well fed, and, though tired and injured, they were strong and knew how to pace themselves. They vanished into the forest.

25

Saturday, December 24th

Saturday morning revealed the true nature of the situation.

Dead wolves were everywhere. The soldiers counted 63. Blood trails led into the forest. Surely some of these wounded wolves would die also.

And it proved to be true. The squad of men sent to test the forest trails to see where the wolves had retreated found dead wolves lying in the snow.

But the village scene was not much better. In addition to the nine people already dead before Friday's attack, there were losses in every quarter. Little Tonya and her family, all of Fedor's family, Beatrice, the Karpovs, the Luskeys, Romanov, six of the village children, three women and six men in the barn, four between the houses, and more. In all, the village had lost 44 people.

The soldiers' losses were also significant. There were the four men in Kyagova's plane, four in the other two planes, and five that night.

That wolves could kill so many was unbelievable.

Pavel spoke first, "I have seen it so I believe it. When I write this up, there will be many wagging heads in Moscow."

"Yes," said Kolai. "I never believed those old tales my grandparents told me, right here in this village, when I was a boy."

"Well, we know better now," they all thought.

Although despondent, the villagers knew they had to clean up the town and keep busy. The funeral tomorrow would be so large that the soldiers would have to help them get ready for it.

A funeral on Christmas Day?

Yes, and then they knew they should take some time to celebrate, even though they didn't want to.

"I know how they feel," murmured Alla. "I felt the same. But we have to go on. We always have."

"We Russians seem to collect the problems of the world. First the famine, then the wars, then the comet, then the civil war, and now this," Manja said.

"But the Bible says the Jews were made to suffer for a purpose," mused Sasha. "Maybe this has a purpose also?"

"There is no purpose. Evil exists in its own right. It strikes where it can. If you believe in God you must also believe in the devil. When this is over, we will see things like it again. We were put on this earth to suffer and suffer we will," said Manja.

Maala raised his neck, threw back his grey head and howled. The pack assembled again and headed east.

Kolai thought he heard a howl coming from the north. He must have been mistaken. His nerves were playing tricks on him.

Alla and Sasha knew they should take control of the pain the village would now feel. They had been through the beginnings of despair for the last few days and although they would need a long time to recover, they could at least help their neighbors. But they also knew that the village would never return to normal. Too much had happened; too many had suffered too great a loss.

Pilovo would become a story, passing into the realm of Russian legends. In its repetition it would change. The wolves would become devils, the people fools. How could they have left themselves so unprotected? Men would tell the story as if it could never have happened to them; not to smart people who protected their families.

No, Pilovo would be a lesson; the villagers of Pilovo an example. There would be no heroes; all of them, people and wolves, would be victims of the telling. People who left Pilovo would never mention it as their former home. If they did, they would be looked at with the glance that the knowing reserve for the stupid; the people who should be avoided.

Pavel would report otherwise.

26

Sunday, Christmas Day

Sergi, wounded himself in the barn, knew that the villagers could stand only a brief sermon. They were here to pray over their dead, without even a priest to console them. The bodies were laid out in the front of the church in as organized a pile as could be arranged within the limited space. The sheets and sacking that covered the dead had been taken from the meager supply of the homes. Sasha had walked to Oleg's hut and asked him to come to the service. Oleg said no.

Sergi started. "I have no words to explain what we have been through. Our daughter is dead; our grief is endless; we cannot ask you for solace when you have so much pain yourselves.

"When we are this confused we should pray. Prayer is a comfort itself; now it must also be a consolation. Don't question God's ways; He gave us free will and He guides our daily lives; He does not always intervene to protect us in our troubles, our suffering shapes us for our reward. When we see St. Peter, he will know what our trials have been; he will weigh those against our sins; he will see a people forged from a cruel earth, who had horrors thrust upon them and lived through the torment."

The women moved in an ellipse around the front of the church, each shaking birch ash on the bodies. Sasha followed, sprinkling holy water on the covered faces of the corpses. They sang the hymn of the dead, asking God to deliver their loved ones from evil and place them at His side.

"Oh, Lord we are not worthy to ask you to take our dearly departed brothers into your Kingdom, but speak but the Word and their souls shall be healed," they chanted.

The church was crowded with villagers and the soldiers who stood with their backs to the far walls. They were more stunned than grief-stricken; more confused than sorrowful; overwhelmed but not broken. Pavel stayed in the back corner, wishing the parishioners well, praying to no one.

The sight of the children was especially poignant. The older ones knew what had happened and faced the loss better than most of the adults. They felt that the adults would make things right again and explain to them the reason for this catastrophe. The younger children were mostly bewildered, neither knowing nor feeling the weight of what was to come.

Sergi lit the incense burner and began to move slowly toward the back of the church. A few soldiers went out the door and stood at the steps to allow the parishioners to part and leave a path for Sergi and the beginning of the procession.

The altar women followed Sergi, and, after them, the men carrying the bodies. It took fifteen men three trips to carry all the corpses out. They were loaded onto sleighs and carts, except for the soldiers, who would be taken back in the trucks.

When everyone was outside the church, Sergi began the slow walk to the village edge where the hay barn had been. The long procession followed the corpses, Pavel trailing at the back. The frozen bodies were placed as carefully as could be managed onto a platform the men had erected to hold all of the dead until spring.

One body was missing.

27

Monday, December 26th
The Feast of Saint Stephan

Sasha volunteered to conduct the day's service. The church was full again, but only with parishioners and the few soldiers who had remained when the trucks left that morning. They would return to base when the trucks came back in a week. They stayed to help the village recover and to shoot any wolves that might return.

"Today is the feast of St. Stephan," began Sasha. "He was a martyr for the Faith; he suffered for his religion; died for his beliefs.

"But St. Stephan was killed by strangers; those who hated his people; those who mocked his God.

"Stephan Volkov was one of us. He came to Pilovo to escape the taunts and the hatred of those who mocked him. He stayed, not because we were any better than any other village in our scorn, but because he knew it would be the same wherever he went. We were his last hope, and we failed.

"Stephan was killed by one of us. Even those wolves we all hate don't kill their own kind. Are we less than them? Yesterday we begged God for mercy and relief from our troubles, for consolation from our despair, for hope for our future. Today we beg him for forgiveness.

"How can we close our grief when we closed our hearts to Stephan? What have we learned from our disgrace? What have we taught our children? How can we ask for solace when we gave none?

"Let us resolve to change, to throw away our prejudices, to accept those who are different from us, and to see in all God's children that essence that is human, beautiful, godlike.

"When we leave this church today, let it be with a healed heart, a soul ready to see the good in others. What is past, is past; what is tomorrow, is ours to change."

Sergi, Sasha, Karl, and Yuri lifted the body of Stephan off the wooden plank and carried it shoulder high through the assembly. Everyone reached to touch the young man they had scorned for so long. With each touch, they uttered a silent prayer for him and one for themselves.

Outside the church the procession turned into the graveyard. The soldiers, with great effort, had hacked out a shallow grave near the side of the church. Stephan's body was lowered into the ground, the women threw dried flowers over the silk cloth they had stitched together for his shroud. Every child was led by the body as it lay in peace.

In the spring a marker would announce;
"Here Lies Stephan Volkov,
Child of the Saint Whose Name He Bore,
May He Forgive His Village,
and Rest In Peace."

Epilogue

Wednesday, January 6th, 1928
Feast of the Epiphany

Alla was coming out of St. Stephan's when she heard the faint buzz. She knew immediately who it was. She had just finished getting the church ready for the Epiphany ceremony, arranging the cloths and altar pieces, placing aside the few gifts. Sasha would conduct the small service.

The sound came from the south as the plane approached the town. The pilot caught sight of the village and eased the Vausen down onto the road about two 200 yards from the well. It was his first landing without a tarmac. He was careful to stay in the middle of the opening. The Vauzen bumped a little as the skis hit the ground, but the snow cover was mostly blown away and the ice smoothed the surface. He braked cautiously to avoid spinning and reduced his speed as he taxied to the center of the village.

The noise had spread quickly through the village. Manja and the others ran to get the children. No one wanted to miss this day.

The pilot cut the engine and raised the cockpit window. By then a small crowd had assembled around the plane. Kolai swung his left leg over the sill and dropped onto the wing. He was back in Pilovo.

The villagers began the hymn "Faith of Our Fathers," assuming the separate parts in harmony, as they had been trained, the cadence rising. The words wafted through the cold air, "In time of peril, standing there."

Kolai was touched. He had asked Colonel Federov to let him go back. Federov needed little excuse, even though the rules forbade it. The Pilovo story was widely known throughout the air corps, and Kolai's name with it.

Alla was the first to approach him. Kolai jumped to the ground to greet her. Before he could think of anything to say, Alla was hugging him and crying. The other villagers closed in. Sasha offered his hand and gestured for Kolai to take Alla's. For several minutes no one spoke. Here was the plane, the pilot, and all the villagers, out celebrating the salvation of Pilovo.

Kolai told them, "I'm sorry I didn't get to you sooner; the weather was too bad."

"You saw us, you brought our rescuers. We owe our lives to you, brother," said Sasha.

"Maybe if I had been faster more would be alive."

Alla answered, "We are here today because of you. Come, we have to celebrate."

Appendix 1

Wolves

When Nature fashioned the predators of the earth, she designed one that was strong, agile, resourceful, and cunning. The wolf.

There are two wolves in the mind of man: wolf, the ruthless predator; wolf, the manlike hunter. The lone wolf and the pack mate. The killer of his livestock and the cousin to his dog. The cold-eyed wanton murderer and the intelligent competitor for game. Those who live closest to the wolf see him as a god, a spirit, a myth maker. They respect his place; they rarely kill him; they never eat his flesh; they learn from his ways; they talk of him as Kaliki, the Spirit of Provider. He has a parallel existence to them. He cares for his family, hunts to survive, is in harmony with nature, and helps maintain the balance in which man lives. He is brother. "Oh, Kaliki, The Watcher!" man cries. "Help us learn from your ways. Keep us sustained."

Those who know wolf as an enemy see him differently. Wolf is a killer; he kills for pleasure; he kills when he is not hungry; he hunts alone; he is the devil; he kills man. This man fears wolf: he hunts him to extinction; he tells tales to his children of wolf and his vicious ways; he sees in wolf the evil of the world and vows to eliminate it. Still the wolf, who preceded man by more than ten million years, survives.

The Russian grey wolf is among the largest left on earth. A male can be over six feet long and weigh up to 165 pounds. The female is smaller but equally as adept at killing prey. The wolf has long legs for traveling quickly in the snow. He can run at 35 miles per hour for several miles. One bound can exceed 16 feet. Forty-two teeth are anchored in a jaw that can crush bone. His canines are over two inches long and can tear through the four inch thick hide and coat of a moose. The wolf can smell odors that are 100 times too faint for the human nose. He can hear another wolf howl six miles away. The howl is the call for assembly.

Pack size varies from two to almost 40. Packs are larger in the winter when the food is scarcer and the cooperation of many is needed to kill the few available prey. The pack is dominated by an alpha male and an alpha female. If the female doesn't produce good litters for the alpha male she will be replaced. Such a loss of face is involved that the displaced alpha female may kill the new alpha female in retaliation, but the alpha male will just choose another female. The pack must grow to survive. The next level of males (beta) is subservient to the alpha but may challenge him for dominance on occasion. If a beta male defeats an alpha male, he becomes the new alpha male.

Wolves usually pair for life, if the alpha male chooses the mate of a beta male, the beta male may attack and try to injure him. But usually, most fights are mere displays, the baring of teeth being more of an attempt to deter aggression and to express strength rather than a real signal to kill or maim. Except on rare occasions, wolves do not kill their own, and will mourn the death of a pack mate for weeks, avoiding play and acting morose.

The grey wolf, which is really multicolored, looks more tan in summer. In twilight, or at night, or in winter, he is truly grey. His face is grey, tan, and black with a little white. His eyes, eyebrows, ears, nose, and mouth are ringed in black to emphasize the gestures he uses in communication. He can signal his intent with the movement of an ear or the squinting of his yellow-green eye. The white coloring around his mouth accents the black piping that rims his jaws. His changes in expression are distinct. Tan backing covers the fur behind his ears, darker stripes of blackened fur ridge his back and extend down along the tail. This is especially true of the dominant members of the pack who do much of the communication. All have vertical blackened fringes of hair running down their sides. All are white under the chin. Coloring is a useful identification for the pack members. Some grey wolves are almost black, a few white, and some creamy white. In winter, the grey wolf grows a thick coat that is almost bear-like in appearance.

Communication is important to the wolf. Besides his facial expressions, the posture of a wolf indicates his intent. If a wolf approaches with his head and tail down, he is acknowledging his inferiority. Head up, ears laid back, and tail held high signals attack. The tail position, up, down, straight back, bent down in mid-tail, and all the combinations, give the wolf dozens of ways to state his message. If he lies down he is content. If he cowers he is frightened. If he curls his lips back and retracts his nose into a snarl, that signals danger to any opponent. If he throws his head back and howls, he is calling for his kind. The howl of a wolf will unnerve a man.

The wolf can speak. He whines for conversation, growls for aggression, barks to signal an attack, and even squeaks when surprised. When calling for assembly, he can howl two times a minute, as the cacophony of the pack joins him. Other wolves know his intention immediately. They watch the alpha male for their signal to act.

And act they can. The charge of a full grown wolf can level a deer. Often a wolf will knock down prey with his forepaws so he can attack the head and neck more easily. He can latch onto the nose of a moose with his teeth and swing back and forth as the moose jerks his head. When the moose falls, the other wolves close in. Just two wolves can topple a moose. An adult wolf can kill prey ten times its size.

If several wolves bring down prey, they stand back and let the alpha male eat first. Sometimes he will let the more mature pups eat with him since they need more food to grow. A male will eat about 20 pounds of meat at one kill and needs about four pounds a day to stay healthy. If necessary he can fast for weeks. The youngest pups have to eat more regularly, usually swallowing regurgitated food from their mother. The betas eat next, and, if any food is left, the lowly omegas. Only the hardiest survive in times of want. A wolf gulps his food down with little chewing. This means that he will pass much of the food value through his system without processing it. He will have to eat again.

And eat he will. Moose, deer, beaver, boar, elk, sheep, cattle, reindeer, horse, pig, dog, cat, bird, rabbit, and even mice. Wolves hunt best in packs. They will stalk and then surround a prey, cutting off the routes of escape. The hunted animal is better off standing his ground than running away. Running excites the pack and makes it bolder. Eye to eye contact disquiets the wolf, and he will look aside. Even with all his skills, the wolf is only successful in about ten percent of his attempts to kill. When natural prey is gone, he will feed on whatever he can get, usually berries and nuts, or animals he normally avoids.

Wolves shun man, especially avoiding adults. They know that humans may be weak alone but can form packs that will follow wolves until they are all killed. Nowhere is this knowledge more crucial to wolf survival than in Russia. Russians think that the wolf kills for pleasure and that he even eats dead humans. He is the killer of their livestock. He especially likes to prey on children. The Russians want to exterminate the wolf, just like he has been exterminated in Western Europe. The government's generous bounties for dead wolves can be as high as the equivalent of three months' pay. There is no limit on the number of wolves a hunter is allowed to kill.

Wolf has reason to retaliate.

Appendix 2

Siberia

When the earth was formed, all the land was together; one large piece floating in the southern ocean. But the forces inside the developing planet tore at the fabric of the crust and fractured the whole into parts. These pieces began to move independently and journey over the waters. Some went westward to create the great continents of Asia and Australia; some formed the predecessors of the Americas. One of the great plates of land crashed into the new Asian continent and threw up the Himalayas; in the western Americas the Pacific plate slid under the continental mass and repeatedly shook the region with quakes.

After the Eurasian plate slowed and settled in the region of the northern pole, the earth cooled. This cooling brought the advance of enormous glaciers southward toward the temperate zones. One series of glaciers was especially thick, heavy, and wide, covering a large area of what is now Russia. When the earth entered its next warming cycle these glaciers began a slow retreat, grinding the land beneath them into a barren, flat, and featureless terrain. This place was so wide, so level, so far north, so lacking in mountains, that there was nothing to stop the arctic winds which rushed unhindered over its surface. Only the hardiest plants survived. When the wind blew, it bent the trees and raised the dust of summer. In winter it blew the snow.

The depth of the snow cover in the steppe region of this flat terrain is more than two feet during the six months of severe winter. Snow is thus the dominant element of the landscape, even when it is not falling. The cold is intense, the wind bitter, and the land unforgiving. Few will venture into its realm. This is Siberia.

Siberia is isolated from any ocean, except the Arctic Sea in the north which is frozen most of the year. Because it lacks a large body of water to moderate the temperatures, Siberia has hot summers and brutal winters. Temperatures often stay at −40°F for weeks in winter; a very cold day is −80°F . Hot summer days can exceed 90°F.

Siberia, The Sleeping Land, is 3000 miles across, essentially all of northern Asia. One of its regions consists of a broad band running east to west in the central latitudes. It is the wooded steppe zone, the lesostep. Here the belt of the swampy taiga begins to disappear, leaving behind the wooded conifer forests and their needle-like leaves. Moving further south into the lesostep, the coniferous trees disappear except for the pine, and grasslands begin to cover the horizon. On the northern side of these grasslands the birch tree, with its pealing bark and small leaves, predominates. Siberia has more birch than any other place on earth, so the forest scene remains unchanged as the seasons pass. The white of the birch is everywhere.

The animals of Siberia have thick pelts to help them weather the cold winters. The brown bear, wolf, elk, reindeer, boar, lynx, polecat, ermine, sable, and the smaller squirrels and chipmunks, all prosper during the summer months, and forage as best they can through the winter. But few people choose to live in such a fierce climate, a place where they can die if exposed even to the normal elements. The hardy Mongolian peoples that did penetrate into this place consisted mostly of small tribes that maintained sparse but stable populations. It wasn't until after the time of Ivan The Terrible that Cossacks and other Russians were forced to move east of the Urals and begin to populate the Siberian steppes. Even German and Greek communities sprung up, filled with those who had little hope in their own countries and were willing to scrape out an existence in this hard land. By nature these people were loners and did not choose to remain in contact with their neighboring villages. Each village thus became an isolated community of hardy but bleak souls who kept to themselves and had as their only goal to make it through to the next year.

Appendix 3

Russian Politics, Culture, and Religion of the Period

At the time of the wolf incident, 1927, a village like Pilovo would have been largely unaffected by the events that were sweeping the new Soviet Union. The beginnings of change would have started in Siberian towns, but not in remote villages. That does not mean that the peasants were unaware of what had occurred in St. Petersburg and elsewhere; they just would not have felt the brunt of the wave of communism that was to engulf the whole nation.

But the Revolution of 1917 initiated the changes that would modify Siberia forever. The concept of the worker and worldwide communism was foreign to a Siberian native. They cared little for what was happening in the towns and cities, and thought that these changes would come to them slowly, if at all. The Revolution handed the land over to the peasants, but this had little effect on the Siberian villagers because they were already self-contained. During the Civil Wars of 1918-25, the Cossack (White) and Red Armies fought to control Siberia. The landscape was overrun with marauding soldiers who cared little for the backward peasants of the villages.

Tens of thousands died as war, famine, and disease swept over the land. In 1927, Stalin began a push to force the remaining peasants into collective farming, hoping to break the peasant's hold on the food supply of the whole country. But although he wanted the peasant's food, he had nothing to offer in return. The struggle between the peasants and the government went on for the next six years until all the land was collectivized. Now even the new farm machinery was owned by the government. During those years the local Party authorities often overdid things in their push to reform the peasants. By the mid-1920s, each village had a Party Leader who watched over the shoulder of the village head and reported to the central committee in the closest city. He only advised. All mistakes were attributed to the head. In some villages the Party Leader, usually resented, was ignored; in others, he had complete power. He was often foreign to the village people and rarely liked. Eventually the Party would win control over the villages, but it was a near thing that the peasants did not revolt during this time.

Nowhere was this feeling of insurrection more prevalent than among the independent farmers of Siberia. Siberian village life had remained almost unchanged for centuries. The transitions of 1927-1933 turned Siberia into a vassal of the state. Stalin's first five year plan, in 1928, had no effect in Pilovo; by the next cycle it would dominate the life of everyone.

In an environment as bleak as Siberia, the people often turn to bright colors and ornate designs to break-up the monotony of their surroundings. The men spent days carving the exterior moldings around the windows and doors of even the simplest hut. These would be painted in bright blues or reds or oranges, usually different from their neighbors and rimming every opening in the house. The eaves of the roofs are likewise adorned. Inside, the bright colors persist. The fireplace/stove is of white tiles, often interspersed with gay greens, reds and blues. This area is central to the home. Boots are placed along a shelf on top of the fireplace to dry. In the winter, children sleep on the bricks over the top of the oven to keep warm. The small stove on one side also heats the kitchen. The fireplace on the other side of the tiles keeps the main room warm in winter. The woodshed was attached to the kitchen so that one did not have to go outside to fetch fuel.

The largest room usually had a couch that doubled as a bed, and a single bed in the corner. In the upper corner of this room was a little altar that contained the family icons, open and facing the room. These could be a triptych of Peter, Jesus, and Paul, a medley of saints, or scenes from the Bible. Candles were burned here on feast days or to commemorate the dead. War memorabilia, if the man had any, were in a glass case over his bed. Photographs or drawings of loved ones were everywhere. Those that had a relic from a saint displayed it in a prominent place on the dresser.

Peasants who lived in thatched huts usually painted the outer walls white or mustard color. Their roofs were steeper than those of the wooden homes to insure that the snow did not accumulate and collapse them. The freezing winters kept the thatch free of pests. The huts in a village were arranged in a pattern that allowed for a few walks and alleys. Otherwise, they were close together so that people could get from one hut to another quickly in the cold. The whole layout of homes was centered around the village church. The village well was in a small plaza in front of the church. The main road ran past the church and, if the village had one, the official's office.

There was little to do in a small village except make sure the harvest was good, that the children were taught the rudiments, and that the traditions were respected. New "traditions" were of no interest to the peasants. "Let the cities have the power and the wars; we will keep the living and the dead."

Siberians wore clothing made mostly from animals; hose of soft reindeer skin, moccasins with hair on the outside to provide a grip on snow, pullover parkas fur-lined with hare or squirrel skin, hats of thick fur, and gloves of sheepskin turned inside out to cover the fingers in wool. The woven cloth was mostly of nettle or hemp, fringed with wool, and rich in embroidery with glass beads, tin ornaments, and colorful dyed fabric. Weaving was a well-practiced art, even used for book covers. Felt was used for a variety of purposes. Even the poorest peasant had bright clothes to wear.

The women were most gaily adorned. A long gown of woven hemp, usually white or yellow, was covered with a tunic of green, blue or deep red. All of these were heavily embroidered. Belts of gold or sashes of red cinched the tunics at the waist. Red or silver piping ran along the borders of the outfits. A kerchief was usually worn, even indoors, often knotted behind the neck with a clasp. A shawl of pretty lace or silk was used on festive occasions, linen or wool for every day. Leather boots in black or brown were for parties and feast days, woven straw slippers, tied to the ankles, were worn indoors. If the floor was warm, the women went barefoot. For weddings and family celebrations the women outdid themselves, wearing see-through linen shawls, ornate caps, richly decorated sleeves and bodices, tassels of gold. Even the young girls were ablaze in reds and silvers.

The men were more subdued. A white gown with a few colors at the neck and sleeves, a vest of brown or black, a dark tunic, usually of one color, and a fur or felt hat. Leggings were more colorful, red and black and yellow. Shoes or boots were almost always black. A sash, if worn, was thinner and less striking than the ones that circled the women's waists.

Blankets, baby clothes, and tablecloths added color to the inside of the house. They were as brightly adorned as the women's clothing. This added a sense of gaiety to the home, especially if some of the walls were painted white. Colorful borders of garden scenes circled the windows and doors; a bower of green and blue leaves, with bright acorns or flowers. Even the stoves were so ringed. Only if the family was very poor did they leave the inner walls as plain logs. But even then they made sure that some corner of the hut had color to break up the monotony of a winter spent mostly indoors.

The Russian Orthodox Church was a powerful force in society. The Russian people were devout and clung to the old ways of Christianity. Both peasant and noble had been reared to respect and honor the Church. It has been argued that the influence of the Church in political matters was part of the reason for Lenin and his followers to overturn the government. The communists worked to discredit the Church and break its hold on the minds and hearts of the people. This was more successful in the cities than it was it the country. Many churches were closed, but Russian children still studied religion; not as a faith, but as a cultural inheritance. The preservation of the magnificent churches in the Kremlin itself attests to the communist regard for the Church as an institution to be handled carefully.

In the small villages the Church would hold sway into the 1930s. The peasants were reluctant to give up that unit which brought them together and helped explain the misery and hardness of their lives. Icons and relics were everywhere. Older people never gave in to the Party; they held their beliefs until they died. Since the Party had little to do with the schooling of rural people until after 1930, Pilovo would still have been a very Christian place.

Russian church holidays are a bit different than those of the west. Christmas is celebrated, but is not as important as Easter. New Year's is not January 1, but, rather, the feast of the Epiphany on January 6. In Pilovo the priest would only be able to visit twice a month, as he rotated through the other villages, therefore, the village men and women provided some of the services of the clergy in his absence. The feast of Saint Stephan, December 26, was also important. Stephan was a martyr who had been stoned by the Romans. On that holy day, Russian people would enter a friend's home and throw nuts on the floor to signify this martyr's ordeal. Every Russian knew his saint's feast day and revered it. Peasants would often remark about a person's characteristics as they related to their patron saint. To a quizzing son a mother might say, "Thomas the Doubter, I named you right!"

DIRTY DEALS
A Devil Kings MC Story

NICOLE JAMES

DIRTY DEALS
A Devil Kings MC Story

NICOLE JAMES

Published by Nicole James
Copyright 2020 Nicole James
All Rights Reserved
Cover Art by Lori Jackson
Cover Photography copyright
By Wander Aguiar
Cover Model: Roddy Hanson
Editing by CookieLynn Publishing

CHAPTER ONE

Ashlynn Fox—

I step out of the hotel's limo onto the tarmac at one of McCarran's aviation hangars. It's where anyone flying private into Las Vegas arrives. I'm here to meet the jet of my biggest whale—that's what we call a high roller, big-stakes gambler here in Sin City.

Carter Maxwell has been known to gamble millions in a weekend. The elite penthouse he's being given complimentary by the hotel casino is so exclusive and so secret not even the biggest rock stars and movie stars can stay there. It's reserved only for our biggest gamblers, and they won't even open it for anyone gambling less than two million.

When you're a high roller, one person largely arranges your Vegas experience—your devoted casino host. That's me, though my official title is luxury concierge.

I watch as the jet taxis up and stops. The sleek lines of the Gulfstream glint in the setting sun. I double-check the tail number to make sure this is the right plane. Not that I need to; I've met his plane enough times to recognize it. But in my line of work I can't afford mistakes, so I double-check *everything*.

I run my hand across the back of my neck, under the collar of my vest. Even though its sleeveless, the thick suit fabric is heavy. I tug at the matching pinstripe skirt that comes to just above my knees.

Even in April, the temperature in Vegas can get warm, and it's currently hovering around eighty. I resist the urge to fan myself with the copy of today's Wall Street Journal I hold in my hand—the one Carter always requires upon landing. I'm sure the news is already hours old, but I'm only too happy to fulfill all his proclivities, and this by far is the easiest.

Thankfully, the door to the jet soon opens, and the stairs drop. Several crewmembers step out to secure things as Mr. Maxwell emerges with his latest girlfriend—one his wife knows nothing about.

He's asked me to make sure she is well entertained with exclusive shopping in the best boutiques while he's at the private tables. The hotel will be comping much of her spending, if not all. That's how important Carter Maxwell is to the Del Sol, the Strip's elite new resort and casino.

My sole responsibility is to ensure that visiting big shots have the best possible experience and thus spend the most possible money at our casino.

Carter Maxwell is such a prize whale, that hosts from all the major casinos compete for the right to manage his itinerary. I won out. I did that by stealing him from a competing casino host and ensuring his first stay in our hotel was epic. I arranged a racecar experience, a private helicopter to the Grand Canyon, and even provided expensive welcome gifts like a Rolex and a twenty thousand dollar painting of an artist I discovered he liked. It worked, and ever since he's been exclusively playing at the Del Sol Hotel and Casino. Now we have a rapport I've worked hard to build.

He strides to me, and I smile brightly, extending my hand. "Mr. Maxwell, I hope your trip was smooth."

He returns my smile with a megawatt one of his own, taking my hand. "Lovely, Ashlynn. You remember Christine."

I smile at the woman who's barely older than I am. She's blonde and thin, with a smile that doesn't reach her bored eyes. I'm not surprised by his taste; he's always run toward leggy blondes, which leaves me out, as my long glossy hair is unfortunately a rich brown, as are my dark eyes. A girl can dream, though, and this man is almost worth bleaching my hair a Marilyn Monroe platinum.

Carter Maxwell is one of the wealthiest men in Denver, and he's got the good looks that rarely come with money like his. He's tall and blond with just a touch of gray at the temples. Thus he can attract and keep lookers like Christine.

I shake her hand. "Christine, you look beautiful. I've arranged some exclusive time in all the best shops and your own private shopper to escort you."

"I'm sure she'll love that. Won't you, my dear?" he asks, and she smiles up at him, turning into a different person.

She purrs like a cat as she strokes his cheek. "I'll be sure to pick up some outfits for your enjoyment as well."

I grit my teeth against the urge to vomit at her fakeness, and wave my hand toward the limo. "Shall we?"

Once we're loaded and on our way, I hand Carter his requested paper. "I've got you in our lavish Skye Penthouse with private pool, spa, sauna and steam room. I've arranged for a private butler and massage therapist for the duration of your stay. You'll find a bottle of Cristal, two bottles of the rare wine from the Rothschild estate you love, and also the Louis XIII cognac you requested."

"Wonderful, Ashlynn. You always take such good care of me, dear."

I smile. "Well, this trip I've got a special surprise for you. I managed to get you ringside seats to the McGregor fight on Saturday."

"I was planning to leave on Thursday."

"Yes, Mr. Maxwell, I just hoped I'd be able to persuade you to extend your stay a few days." It's a ploy I couldn't resist using this time. It's not often a big event like this occurs just beyond the guest's stay.

He runs a hand down his jaw, considering, but I know I've got him.

"We'll see how the next few days go," he says with an eye on Christine.

That's my cue to keep her happy, so he can keep playing. I take the hint and turn to her.

"I've arranged one of our luxury private cabanas for you. It's yours all week, should you choose to leave the penthouse and view the scenery at the pool." I wink at her, and she smiles at my meaning.

Carter laughs. "Just as long as you don't bring any of them back to the penthouse, my dear, have all the fun you desire."

If that's not giving your girl the green light, I don't know what is.

I smile. I've got this in the bag.

Two hours later, I'm seating Carter at a table in one of our private high limit rooms. It's opulent and accommodating with lavish foods catered in, as well as stand-by butlers ready to deliver the attending gamblers' every need.

I pat Carter's shoulder and wish him luck. He has my number and can call for anything that can't be taken care of by the staff.

I've arranged for a handsome escort to accompany Christine to dinner and show her the town. He's one I use regularly to keep the girlfriends occupied, and he does a damn fine job. I've never had any complaints. With that taken care of, my requirements should be complete for the evening.

I exit the high limit room and head toward the casino. There are a few other gamers I've been keeping my eyes on. One in particular is what we call new money. He's developing quite the gambling addiction as his wealth grows each year. I've been giving him increasingly good perks with every visit. My bet is he'll be one of my best whales in a year or two.

As my heels click across the marble floors of the exquisite lobby, I run into John, one of the managers of the hotel.

"Miss Fox, may I speak with you a moment?"

Damn it. I smile brightly. "Yes, sir? What can I do for you?"

"Is Mr. Maxwell all settled?"

"Yes, sir. His line of credit is four million and can be increased if necessary."

"Excellent. I was wondering if you'd be able to fulfill a special request for one of our entertainers."

The hotel often has elite performers, and there's a special concierge to take care of them.

"Can't Ken do it?"

"Not this time. He's too busy with the prima dona currently in residence."

Miss Serena Snow has a two-month run she's in the middle of fulfilling.

"Okay, what do you need?"

"You know Axle Crow?"

"Of course." Everyone in this town knows of Axle Crow. Half the country knows of him. He's one of the biggest country acts since Garth.

"He's staying at Peerless Tower, in the penthouse. He's hosting a private poker party, and he's requested a hostess. You know, just to make sure everyone is well taken care of."

"But, sir, that's off-site."

"Yes, but he's an important act, one we don't want going over to another hotel for his future Vegas residencies."

"I see. But tonight?"

"I'll make sure Evan takes care of anything Mr. Maxwell might need."

"Are you sure?"

"I've already made the arrangements. Ciara's is doing the catering."

Ciara's is our exclusive five-star on-site restaurant.

"If you're sure."

"Go change into something suitable, and I'll have Devon waiting in the limousine to drive you over."

"Yes, sir."

"You're an excellent asset to our hotel, Ashlynn. I'm sure Mr. Crow will be most appreciative."

That's code for a big tip. I'm not so sure, though. I've seen celebrities leave exorbitant tips as well as crappy tips. With Axle Crow, I think the odds are fifty-fifty. So this could be a good night for me or a complete waste of my time.

But if it keeps John happy, that's incentive enough, as long as he remembers all these favors I've been piling up. Someday I'll cash them in.

An hour later I'm stepping out of the limo dressed in a short, sparkly cocktail dress. I glance up at the building. It's thirty-four floors and each one is a single residence.

I take the elevator to the very top, using the private code I've been given. I step into the small entry and ring the bell to the elaborate carved doors. They swing open, and a butler escorts me in. There's a small hall table with a document and pen resting on it.

"Miss Fox, please read and sign this."

I've seen enough non-disclosure agreements to know one. It's pretty standard fare anytime I'm dealing with a celebrity. I scribble my name, barely glancing at the thing.

DIRTY DEALS

"I'm Thomas, Miss Fox. I'll be here all evening should you need anything." He's an older man with thinning hair and a sweet face.

"Thank you, Thomas."

He leads me in. The place is exquisite, with polished travertine floors and high ceilings, expensive artwork and muted lighting. I walk down the short hall that leads to a living room. Floor-to-ceiling windows frame the amazing skyline of the lights of the strip.

The penthouse is fabulous with top of the line everything. There's a terrace out a set of sliding panels with a pool and fire feature. Everything is ultra-modern.

I'm greeted by the head of Ciara's catering, a man named Ryan.

"Ashlynn, glad you're here," he whispers. "This is a complete shit-show."

I follow him into the kitchen where his staff is working. "What's wrong?"

"I was told there'd be a dozen players and their guests. I brought enough for twenty-four."

"And? Is there not enough?"

"Ashlynn, the butler says there are only three people playing tonight. Axle was called away or something, and everyone else cancelled."

"Three people? And they're still playing?"

He nods, arching his brow, then hisses low. "One of them is that Ricardo fellow."

Oh shit. That Ricardo fellow being Ricardo Leona. He's purported to be connected to a major crime family. You can tell me all day long that the mob is gone from Las Vegas, but I've run into enough of his type to be skeptical.

"Who are the other two?" I ask.

He shrugs and leans closer. "They're brothers, but they look mob related, too."

What the hell is Axle Crow doing with mobsters? Maybe that's where he's been getting the money to gamble. I've seen the darker side of human nature, and nothing surprises me anymore.

A man steps into the kitchen. He's in his thirties and dressed in a suit. "Are you the girl from the Del Sol?"

I extend my hand. "Ashlynn Fox."

He ignores it and glances over at Ryan. "You can pack up most of this. We'll only need three entrees and appetizers."

Ryan's livid gaze cuts to me, then he storms off, slamming tray covers.

"It seems things have changed. Perhaps I could be of service another night," I say, trying to smooth things over and hoping to make a quick exit.

"Not at all. We still need a hostess. The remaining guests will be playing as scheduled. Understand?"

Nope. Not at all. And I really don't want to be in a room with mobsters. Of course, I can't say any of that. "Yes, sir, I see."

"This way, please. I'll get you set up, and then I have to get Axle to the airport. He's waiting downstairs in the car."

"And you are?"

"Simon Reed. Mr. Crow's manager."

I'm led through the living room, down a hall to another large room where the poker table has been set up. There's a dealer, but I don't recognize him. I'm sure he's not from our casino. Three gentlemen are already getting set to take their seats.

Apparently I'm here to serve drinks and wait on their every need.

John's going to owe me big time for this favor.

CHAPTER TWO

Ashlynn—

It's been a long night.

Catering has packed up and left. The dealer has departed, and it's just the butler and me with the three guests. The game has broken up finally with Mr. Ricardo Leona being the big winner. This game was played with cash, which is a strange thing to observe. I'm used to the games at the Del Sol all being played with chips. Here, stacks of bills were put in the center of the table. I found it hard to tear my eyes from that much money.

The butler gestures for me to follow him out, and we walk to the living room. He pulls an envelope from his pocket. "Mr. Crow wanted me to convey his gratitude for tonight and give you this as a token of his appreciation. He sees it as a personal favor. Of course you're discretion regarding tonight's players is expected."

"Of course," I say, taking the envelope. "Thank you. Please tell Mr. Crow it was my pleasure."

"And this one is from Mr. Leona."

I take it, feeling something odd inside. It better not be a hotel room key card. "Okay. Thanks."

"I'll show you out."

"I just need to use the restroom, if I may."

"Of course, Miss Fox. It's there." He gestures to a door in the hall leading out. "You can see yourself out, then?"

"Yes. Thank you."

I grab my shoulder bag and walk to the restroom as he heads toward the gaming room.

The hall bath is large and as luxurious as I've ever seen. There's a small velvet tufted bench in front of a makeup mirror. I sit and remove my heels, rubbing my aching feet. I take a pair of black flats from my bag and slip them on, shoving my heels inside. I wash my hands and splash water on my cheeks.

I lean to the mirror, studying the dark circles under my eyes, then check my watch. It's almost five am. In a half hour the sun will rise.

I glance at the envelopes I'd lain on the counter. I rip open the one from Axle. It's ten one hundred dollar bills. I tuck it in my bag and look at the second envelope from Ricardo Leona. I tear it open. Rather than money, it's a gaming chip from the Del Sol. My eyes widen at the value. I've seen one before, but only a select few ever play with them. It's our gold chip worth one hundred thousand dollars.

My jaw drops.

Angry voices jolt me from my numbed stare. I turn to look at the closed door, straining to hear. It's garbled. I crack the door, turn off the light and peer out. I know the importance of the non-disclosure I was asked to sign when I arrived. Anything I overhear I can't tell anyone. That doesn't keep my curiosity from getting the best of me.

They're arguing about the game. Someone is calling another a cheater. Oh crap. I've seen this type of behavior before, and it never ends well.

I can only see part of the room. Ricardo Leona is yelling at one of the other two men. There's a loud bang, and Leona clasps his chest, staggering back.

I cover my mouth, my eyes huge. A second later, I hear Thomas say, "No, no, please."

An arm raises, and the hand holds a gun. There's another blast. I cover my mouth with both hands, tears filling my eyes. I try so hard not to make a sound. My whole body shakes.

I hear murmurs, something about moving the bodies. Both men come into view. The brothers were introduced to me as the Rialtos, Nick and Luca.

"He's dead."

"So what?"

"What the fuck, Nick. You kill a man over a hundred grand?"

"I'd kill a man over a hundred bucks if he cheated me. Besides, I don't like the way he treated Carmella."

"Gonna kill every man who screws over our sister? And the butler? What'd he do?"

"He saw us."

"Lotta people saw us."

"They didn't see us pull the trigger. Might have been a robbery gone bad or one of Axle's crazed stalkers."

"Come on, help me clean our prints from the place. Grabs some towels from the kitchen."

"Think he's got cameras in here?"

The voices retreat into the other room. Now's my chance. I slowly and silently open the door and tip-toe out. I open the door leading to the vestibule with the elevators. As I'm closing it, I see one of the brothers. He looks up, spots me, and starts running toward me. Adrenaline floods my system, and my fight-or-flight instinct kicks in. I hit the elevator button, and the doors slide open. I jump inside and beat on the button to close the doors and hit the first floor button. As the doors slide slowly shut, Nick bursts through the door to the penthouse, his gun raised. I hear it fire, and a shot comes through the top of the door. I shriek at the loud blast in the enclosed space, covering my ears. Time seems to move slowly as I stare up at the numbers, and they begin to descend. Thank God the elevator keeps descending.

There are only two of these in this building, and I know that one always returns to the first floor. This one is reserved for the penthouse, and when not in use, always returns to the penthouse level. It's one of the perks.

I silently try to calculate how much time I'll have before that second elevator reaches the 34th floor and comes back down. Thankfully, I'd called the hotel earlier and had them send Devon with the limo. If I've got any luck at all tonight, he'll be parked at the curb.

I've got thirty floors to figure out what I'm going to do if he's not.

I also have time to think about going to the police. I witnessed a double murder. I don't know about Ricardo Leona, but I know poor Thomas didn't deserve that. I grieve for the man whom I only just met. I'm sure he had a family who loved him. A family who will never see him again. It's not fair, and I can't make it right for them.

And as horrible as it is, I have to think of saving myself, because I've just moved to the top of the Rialto's hit list. And I'm the only one who can save me. There's just one way to do that—run and don't stop until I'm as far away as I can get from Las Vegas.

I watch the numbers flash above the door. My heart pounds in my chest, and the moment those doors open I'm ready to bolt. *Four, three, two, one.* The doors open, and I'm off like a racehorse, charging from the gate. I dash through the lobby and out the glass doors. The sky has that early dawn light that glows on the horizon in the east.

Devon is parked at the curb, dozing in the driver's seat, Motown blaring from the stereo. I grab the door handle, but it's locked. I beat on the window, and he jerks awake and unlocks the doors. I jump in.

The glass divider slides down. "You okay, Miss Fox?"

"Go! Go! Go!" I scream.

He looks at me curiously, but quickly starts the vehicle and hits the gas.

"Don't stop, Devon. Don't stop for anything until you get to the hotel."

"What's happening, Miss Fox? Did someone hurt you?" His concerned eyes meet mine in the rearview mirror.

I shake my head, tears finally streaming down my face. "Just drive."

My mind is frantic as I look out the rear window. We turn the corner, and the front of the building disappears, no one emerging from the door.

I sink back into the seat, but my relief is short lived. They know where I work, and they will come find me. They'll never let me live to testify against them. Not men like them.

I've got a bag packed in my closet. I always keep it there; in my life, things always go sideways, whether it's a relationship or a job. Something always happens, and I'm out the door. I haven't truly felt safe until the Del Sol. I live out of one of the hotel rooms. If that doesn't scream temporary, I don't know what does.

I quickly take stock of my situation.

I've got a good bit of savings in the bank, the thousand dollars in cash that Axle gave me, and that casino chip from Ricardo Leona, now a dead man.

I can cash it in and disappear. I take a breath and think it through. I'll send a valet up to grab my bag while I cash in. I glance up at Devon.

"I need a favor."

His eyes meet mine in the rearview. "Anything, honey."

"Have one of the valets bring my car around to the loading dock." I pass my key fob and room card to him. "Could you go to my room and bring my bag down? It's packed and in the back of my closet. Room 852."

He takes them. "You in trouble, Ashlynn?"

It's the first time he's ever used my first name. He's a big man and intimidating to most people, but to me he's always been a teddy bear.

"I saw something I shouldn't have, Devon."

"You need to leave town?"

I nod.

"Someone gonna come looking for you?"

"Probably."

"They come around, who should I be lookin' for?"

"The Rialto brothers. Ever heard of them?"

He shakes his head. "I'll Google them. I see 'em, I'll run 'em down."

I smile, my eyes glazing over. "Thank you, Devon."

"You gonna tell Mr. Perillo about this?"

Marty Perillo is the hotel's head of security. "No. I just need to leave."

"You want to go to the police?"

"They can't protect me, Devon. Not from these men."

"I'll miss you, Ashlynn."

A tear slides down my face. "I'll miss you, too, Devon. More than you know."

"I'll pass the word. Anyone sees them, we'll hold 'em up, cut their tires if we have to."

"Thank you," I whisper, my voice cracking.

We pull up at the hotel, and I jump out, disappearing through the crowd that even at this hour is still out.

I dash into the casino and go straight to the cashier. I flash my casino identification and pass over my chip. The woman's eyes flash briefly, but she takes my identification and completes the transaction, asking how I'd like my winnings. I say cash, and she doesn't even blink. She stacks up ten stacks of hundred dollar bills, each containing ten thousand dollars, counting it out as I tap my foot. I sign for it and put it in my bag.

"Miss Fox, would you like security to walk you out?"

"Yes, please."

A moment later, two security guards appear. I know one of them.

"Miss Fox, it's good to see you."

"Hi, Tony. Could you… um, escort me to the loading docks? My car is there."

He nods, not batting an eye at the request. "Of course, ma'am."

Five minutes later we're through the huge building and at the loading dock. Devon stands next to my yellow Porsche 918 Cayman Gt4, my baby.

I run to him and hug him. "Thank you, Devon."

He squeezes me back. He and I have spent a lot of time together driving to the airport to meet private jets. He feels as close to family as I have in this town, and I know that sounds odd, but it's an odd town.

"Your bag's in the trunk."

"Thank you for everything."

"You got my number. Call me if you get into trouble."

I nod, knowing I'll never call him.

He reads me like a book and tilts his head. "Honey, at least text me you're okay when you land someplace tonight."

That I can do. "Okay. I promise."

I slip in the leather seat and buckle my seatbelt. I tear off out the back of the hotel, disappearing down back streets through town, heading toward the interstate. I veer up the on ramp and settle into a comfortable speed in the eastbound center lane. I'm ten miles out into the desert before I can finally breathe easy, my tense muscles relaxing.

Only then do I glance over at the leather shoulder tote on the passenger seat, ten stacks of bills weighing it down.

How did my life get so crazy?

CHAPTER THREE

Ashlynn—

Bang.

I jump in my seat, my tattered nerves on edge. What the hell was that? It sounded like something hit my car. I tighten my grip on the steering wheel and look in my rearview mirror. I don't see anything in the road. It's getting late in the evening, and the light is starting to fade. Soon it will be completely dark. I'm on I-20 just past Atlanta. I glance down at my dashboard to my tire monitoring system. It shows the pressure on the left rear tire is dropping.

Damn it. I must have hit a nail or something. Luckily it wasn't a front tire or I'd have a hell of a time steering. There's a sign for an exit coming up. If I can make it there, maybe I can get to a gas station.

I watch the tire pressure rapidly drop until it goes to one pound of pressure.

I limp to the side of the long off ramp and stop. It's not worth damaging the rim, not on a car like this.

The surrounding area is wooded, and the ramp is so long and curved I can't see what's at the end.

I'd hoped to get a little farther before stopping again for another night. I'd driven past a bunch of hotels. Damn it, I should have stopped.

I bang my hand on the steering wheel.

I've been on the road for days now, and no matter how

fabulous this car is I'm tired of being in it.

It's been a long journey. I only made it as far as Winslow, Arizona the first day before I was too tired to go any farther. I got an out of the way motel and paid cash. Maybe I'm paranoid, but I'm afraid they'll track my credit cards.

I texted Devon that first night and told him I was safe. He called me back and told me that indeed the two Rialto brothers had been nosing around the casino. He told them I'd taken a client on a helicopter tour of the Grand Canyon, and the two men had raced off.

God bless him, Devon has been my savior. He warned me to get all my contact numbers off my phone, and then dump it and get a burner phone, thinking they may find a way to track it.

He had me panicking more than I was already, but I followed his advice and made a quick run to pick one up. I also got some duct tape and taped my old phone to the back of the cab of a long-haul trucker parked at the motel whom I overheard telling the clerk was headed to LA.

I was afraid to ask Devon if there'd been any news of a murder at Peerless Tower. I don't want to involve him any further than he already is. If they try to pin this on me, he might be seen as an accomplice after the fact.

I can't worry about that now. I've worried about it all the way from Arizona.

I climb from my car and stare down at my flat tire. Now I have bigger problems.

I squat down to see if I can find the damage, but I can't. Not that it would matter. I already know I'll have to call a tow truck.

The rumble of a motorcycle draws my eyes to a single headlight coming down the ramp. I stand, brightly lit from the headlamp. This morning I'd put on an easy little sundress that was packed away in my bag. It's comfortable to travel in. Now I'm regretting it. I feel too exposed with my bare arms and legs and sandaled feet.

The motorcycle pulls to the shoulder behind me. I can tell by the unmistakable engine sound that it's a Harley. I pop my trunk and dig under my suitcase for the tire iron I keep there. Not because I have any hopes of changing a tire; this model doesn't even come with a spare. No, I carry it for protection. Devon always told me I should carry a gun, just a small one, for protection, that I'm too vulnerable with clients. I never worried or gave it a second thought. I was almost always in the hotel with security around, and anytime I traveled I had Devon with me. He's a big man who intimidates a lot of people, and I was never afraid before.

But now I'm rethinking everything, and I wish I'd taken him up on his offer when he'd told me he'd take me gun shopping. He'd grinned so big when he'd said it, joking that he knew I couldn't turn down shopping.

Now I stand on the darkening road with nothing but this tire iron to protect myself. I grip it tighter.

The man dismounts, and his body is outlined in silhouette as he steps into the blinding headlight. He's tall and fit with long legs, narrow hips, and broad shoulders that roll with his gait. He could easily overpower me and jerk the weapon from my hand, but maybe if I can get in one good swing, I can knock him out.

I retreat as he comes closer.

"Hey, doll. You broke down?" he asks. His voice is deep and somehow soothing, but I'm not trusting that ooey-gooey feeling.

I lift my weapon. "Stay back."

His hands go up, and he stops. "Whoa, whoa. No need for that, darlin'. I'm not gonna hurt you."

I stay where I'm at, the weapon still raised.

His eyes take in the tire, and he jerks his chin toward it. "Just thought you might need some help."

"I've got it," I say.

His eyes drop to the back of my car. "Nevada plates. Car like this, you must be from Vegas."

And just like that he already knows way more about me than I want him to. I keep my mouth shut, not bothering to deny it.

He peers into the open trunk. "You don't even have a spare in this thing, do you?"

I don't know why, but I don't want to admit it to him. "I've called a tow truck. They'll be here any minute."

He shakes his silhouetted head. "Doubt it, babe." He jerks his thumb over his shoulder. "There's a six car pile up back there. I just made it around it. Every spare tow company's gonna be sending their equipment there. You could be here hours."

Perhaps that's why no other car has come down the ramp. If he's telling the truth, there might not be any cars for a long time.

My eyes shift around at the woods. Damn it. I'm going to have to trust him long enough to get off this desolate ramp.

I still can't see his face, so I side step around until my back is to his bike and he's facing the headlight.

Oh *my God*. He's drop-dead gorgeous. Dirty blond hair is slicked back in a short ponytail and the prettiest damn eyes stare back at me. I can't tell if they're blue or green, but they're hypnotizing. A close beard perfectly frames his mouth and runs along his jaw. I've never been much for facial hair, but this one's changing my mind. On him, it works; boy, does it work.

"Name's Rusty. What's yours?"

"Ashlynn." I see no need to give a fake name. I'll never see this guy again.

"Ashlynn," he tries the name out. "Pretty."

My eyes drop to his clothing. He's got on a leather vest with patches on it. He turns to look at my car, and I can see the back of his vest. It says Devil Kings on the top and Georgia on the bottom. A little square says MC.

Great.

"Where's the rest of your gang?" I ask. I look over my shoulder, half expecting them to roll up.

He squats by my tire, examining it, but looks up at me and gives me a megawatt smile, his teeth white and straight. "Just me, Ashlynn."

He continues his study of the tire, running a hand over the treads.

"Here it is. Picked up a nail." He stands and takes out his phone. A moment later he's grunting into it. "Get a can of tire inflator and get your ass over here. I'm on the eastbound ramp off 120 at Stonecrest. Yeah, but there's a big wreck, so take route 278 to Lithonia Industrial and come up the ramp the wrong way. Dumb fuck, I know that shit won't work for a bike. It's not for me. Hurry your ass up, Prospect." He shoves the phone in his pocket and looks at me. "Shouldn't be too long."

I stare at him. Now there's another one coming.

He strolls around my vehicle. "Nice. Bet it handles like a dream." He peers inside. "Five speed?"

"Six."

He whistles. "Not many women I know can drive a manual transmission."

"I must be special." I quirk a brow, and there's that grin again. My stomach does a little flip at the sight of it.

"What sold you on it?"

"I rode in one once." I'm not about to tell him it was with a client.

His eyes sweep over me. "You must travel in some fast circles."

I lift my chin, not willing to divulge anything more.

"Babe, relax. Swear to God, I'm not here to rape or kill you. And although this is one hell of a sweet ride, I'm not gonna jack your car." He makes an x over his chest. "Cross my heart."

I suppose if he'd been after any of those things, he'd be done and gone by now. I lower the tire iron. "You always stop to help damsels in distress, then?" I can't help the sarcastic tone from creeping into my voice.

He chuckles. "Fuck no. Only when they look like you."

"And how do I look?" He's pissing me off again.

"Like a Playboy centerfold. Stacked and racked."

"Don't be vulgar."

"You asked."

I can tell he's enjoying taunting me, but I've been around enough men to know when one is interested.

"Where you headed, Ashlynn?"

I swallow and look away.

He leans against the side of my baby and folds his arms. "We got nothin' but time. Might as well get to know each other."

I want to tell him to get his ass off my car, but since he's the only help in sight I refrain. I should keep my mouth shut entirely, but this is the first human conversation I've had in days. "Not sure. Just kind of playing it by ear."

His head drops to the side. "You don't look like a play-it-by-ear kind of girl."

"I don't?"

"Nope. You look like the kind who's got her whole life planned out to a T."

I'm *so* that girl. I plan everything, prepare for every eventuality. It's scary the way he knows that. Is it the car? My clothes? "Kind of."

There's that chuckle again. His chest shakes with it. "Kind of?"

"Okay, fine. It's true. I usually plan everything. This trip sort of came up out of the blue."

"Vacation?" He glances at the trunk with the one carry-on sized bag that takes up every inch of the tiny compartment. "I'd figure you for more of a three bag minimum traveler. Guess there's no room, though."

"Are you saying I'm high-maintenance?"

"Judging by the car, I'd say yes, but…" He cocks his head to the side, studying me. "You've got that easy kind of beauty. The kind that doesn't take much effort to pull off."

I think that's the sweetest compliment I've ever received. I blink. "Thank you."

"Just stating a fact."

I roll my eyes. The guy's gotta ruin it.

It's quiet for a minute, with nothing but the sound of crickets.

I step a little closer, and now I can read the patches on the front of his vest. I nod to them. "So, you're the President?"

"I am."

I don't even know what questions to ask, but I'm very curious.

The sound of a motorcycle carries through the night air, and a minute later there's a headlight coming up the ramp in the wrong direction. It pulls to the shoulder in front of my car.

The new guy comes over with the requested can, and his president takes it from his hand, shaking it. He squats and attaches the short hose to my tire valve. The tire lifts somewhat and he nods to the prospect. "Check the dash. Should be a tire inflation monitor system. Tell me where this one's at."

I glance up at the other guy. His vest is different with less patches. He's young and appears eager to please. The kid slips in my seat. "You're down three pounds."

His president stands.

"The rim's off the ground, but I'd be careful with it. Drive it a couple miles to allow the tire pressure to increase and the sealant to spread evenly. You should stop and air it up the rest of the way. This is only a quick fix, hundred miles at the most. You'll need to have the tire repaired as soon as possible."

I move to lean inside the passenger side door and dig through my bag to pull out a bill to give him for his trouble. I yank one out of the taped stack and glance up to see eyes on me through the driver side. Crap, I shouldn't have done this.

I slam the door and move around holding the hundred-dollar bill out. "For your trouble. Thank you."

He glances down at the bill. His eyes shift back to the car, then me. He slowly reaches out to take it.

"No problem."

He slides the bill between his fingers, noting its crispness. "You just rob a bank?"

"Of course not."

"You always carry stacks of cash?"

Oh shit, shit, shit. Somehow the money has changed the current in the air. I move quickly to the driver side and slip in, shutting the door and hitting the lock. I fire the car up and it purrs to life. Then I speed off, my heart pounding as I glance in the rearview mirror to see if they're following me.

They're not. The men just stand where I left them, staring after me. The ramp is long and curved. I finally get to the end and go through the light. I see a lodging sign for two motels, then a food and gas sign. I bite my lip, my eyes checking the rearview. That biker saw the money, and the last thing I want is for him to roll up at the gas station and decide to rob me. I head for the hotels. I'll be safer in a room. I can always have someone come and tow the car. Maybe if I'm lucky, there'll be a Porsche dealer close by. I know at the very least there's got to be one in Atlanta.

That biker made no move to chase me down, and I'm sure he could have caught me if he'd wanted it badly enough. Him seeing the money has me rattled. It was a stupid move… digging in the bag. If only he hadn't dipped his head to look at what I was doing. God, I'm such an idiot. I've got to be more careful.

CHAPTER FOUR

Rusty—

I stand at the gun counter of the local sporting goods store, wishing I were anywhere else. Reno dragged me in here with him to get a birthday present for his ol' lady, Kara. I had no idea he meant a pistol. He's got a little Sig Sauer P238 in his hand, pink camo, no less.

"She's left-handed," he tells the sales guy.

"No problem. We can order her the external thumb safety conversion kit."

Reno nods. "I'll need that."

"It's a good little gun. Light weight, no recoil, and the slide's easy," the guy says.

"She'll love it," I agree, grinning. "All chicks want a gun."

"Don't be a dick. I want her to be safe," he snaps.

I can't help giving him hell. Butterfly's kept him on his toes for months. The boy is head-over-heels lovesick. I can't help feeling a little jealous.

The clerk moves off to order the conversion kit, and another clerk waits on someone farther down the long glass case that extends about twenty feet across the back wall of the store.

"What can I help you with, ma'am?"

I'm leaning on the glass with an elbow, facing Reno, my back to them, when I hear the woman respond.

"I'm looking for a small handgun, please."

I recognize the voice straight off. It's the beauty I encountered on the side of the road last week. I straighten, my head swiveling to look over my shoulder. It's her, all right. My first thought is I can't believe my luck. My second is, what the hell is she doing in here? I abandon Reno and walk closer so I can overhear the conversation but hang back near a display, pretending a sudden interest in duck calls. The old man waiting on her shows her the features and benefits of a small Ruger.

She tries it in her hand. With hardly more consideration than she'd take picking out a pack of gum, she hands it back. "I'll take one. Can you put it in a case for me?"

"Ma'am, I'm sorry, but there's a waiting period. You won't be able to take it with you today. I'll need to fill out some paperwork first, and you'll have to come back to pick it up."

"Oh." Her body deflates at the news, and she swallows. "I see. All right."

The old man moves off to get the necessary forms, and I move in.

Almost immediately she feels my presence, and her head jerks up. Her eyes widen. "Oh, it's you."

"How are you?"

"Fine, and you?"

I frown. She seems nervous. I lift my chin at the Ruger sitting in the glass case. "Please tell me I'm not the reason you're buying that gun, darlin'."

"I, um, no of course not."

I cock my head to the side. "Thought you were just passin' through. You're still in town?"

"Obviously." She averts her eyes.

"Babe, do I make you that nervous?"

Her eyes return to me, then look over my shoulder and widen.

I glance back. *Reno.* He's giving her the once over, and I'm sure he's connecting the dots since I did tell him about her. "Scram," I growl.

He smiles and ambles off toward the door.

Ashlynn follows him with her eyes, and then looks at me. "You seem to turn up everywhere I am."

I chuckle. "Sometimes I get lucky."

The clerk returns with her paperwork. I stand silently while she fills it out and notice she scribbles a local address down. I've already got it memorized. I step back when the clerk looks at me. "Can I help you, sir?"

"Nope. Got all I need." I wander outside and find Reno sitting at our bikes in one of the rows. I glance around for that unmistakable yellow sports car and spot it two rows over.

"So, that's the chick?" Reno asks.

"And there's her car. Wait here."

"Sure, take your time. It's only eighty-five degrees out here."

"Fuck off. I just stood in that store for an hour waitin' on you to pick out a pink camo pistol."

"True." He grins.

I amble over to her car. When I do, several customers are checking the vehicle out. When they see me, they take off.

I glance at the tire; it looks brand new, but there's a fine sheen of dust on it, red Georgia clay, which tells me the address she gave must be in the country or at least must have a dirt drive.

I fold my arms and lean against the car. I can't wait to hear this story.

I don't have to wait long. She slows as she sees me, and then beeps the lock on her door.

"So, you live here now?" I ask.

"That's really none of your business."

"Babe, I'm not a bad guy."

"You're vest suggests otherwise."

"The MC thing… that's a deal-breaker for you?"

"Deal-breaker? Oh, no, no, no." She shakes a finger back and forth. "There won't be any deals, so don't get any ideas where you and I are concerned."

I grin. "Ashlynn, I've already got all kinds of ideas where you and I are concerned."

"Rusty, was it? I really don't have time for this."

I clutch at my heart. "Oww, she barely remembers my name. That hurts."

"You think you're pretty memorable, do you?"

"Most women think I am."

"I'm not most women."

"Yeah, I definitely get that. Normally I wouldn't waste my time on a chick who is so *definitely* not interested, but…"

"But?"

"You're not just a challenge, you're a mystery. One I want to figure out."

She huffs, one hand on her doorframe, and looks back at me. "Look, you're an attractive man. Maybe in another time, another life, I'd be very interested, but right now it's just not in the cards." She climbs in the seat, and I squat down between her and the open door.

"How long you stickin' around?"

"None of your business."

"Okay, I get the tough-girl act, I do. But answer me one question."

"Fine. And then you'll let me go?"

"I'll let you *leave*." Not sure I'll ever let her go.

"Okay, what is it?"

"Tell me the truth… You know how to fire a gun?"

DIRTY DEALS

"How hard can it be?"

"You get in a stressful, life or death moment, you want to know what you're doing, Ashlynn. I'd hate to see something happen to you because you forgot to take the safety off."

She bites her lip, and my eyes drop to her mouth. I can feel my dick getting hard just from that gesture.

"Okay, you have a point. Do you know of a gun club or somewhere I can get a lesson?"

I grin. "Yeah, I know of a club where you can get a lesson. Mine."

She frowns. "You mean your motorcycle club? Uh, no. No way."

"Okay. How about your place? You got a lot of dust on this car. You live out in the country?"

"Sort of."

"Can you see your neighbor?"

"One of them through the trees, another down the road."

"Tell you what. When you're license comes through and you pick up your gun, give me a call and I'll give you a lesson. We can do it at your house."

"But what about the neighbors?"

"They aren't gonna call the cops. This is Georgia, doll."

"And what do you want in exchange for this lesson? I'm sure this isn't without strings." Her hand goes to her hip.

Lord, I love a woman full of sass. My dick just got harder. The corner of my mouth tugs up.

"Well?"

And suddenly we're playing let's make a deal. "All right. I show you how to shoot, you let me take your ride out for a spin." It's not what I really want, but it's a start.

She laughs. "You think you'll fit that long, tall body in this

35

seat?"

I chuckle, eying it and her body in it. "Sure would be worth a try."

"Look, I don't want to seem ungrateful for what you did, so thanks again for helping me that night. But you and me? That's not happening. Ever."

I grin and pull a pen from inside my cut. I grab her hand and scribble my number on her palm. "One thing I've learned, it's to never say never, Ashlynn."

I stand and walk away, hearing her call out.

"What is this seventh grade? I'm not calling you."

Damn, she's feisty. I yell back without turning. "Yeah, you will, babe. You don't, I'll come find you."

CHAPTER FIVE

Ashlynn—

I get my cup of coffee and head out the screen door onto the front porch of the old Southern farmhouse I rented. It's got this cute swing with a thick cushion and piles of pillows.

I have an afghan from the bed wrapped around my shoulders, and I snuggle up on the swing. It's cool and breezy this morning. It feels wonderful. I take a sip of my coffee and set it down. My new landlord is an older man whose niece worked the front desk of the hotel I'd stopped at.

When I asked for recommendations on a safe side of Atlanta to stay in and told her that I was looking to rent a place, she mentioned her uncle had a house in the country available immediately.

She called him, and he came right over to show it to me. Something about the place drew me in the minute I stepped out of the car.

It's about as different from a Vegas hotel as I can get, but it's really growing on me. I've found that I like the solitude and the quiet, not to mention the fresh country air, and I love having a front porch.

There's a honeysuckle vine that grows nearby, and it fills the yard with the most amazing scent. I'd love to find a perfume with that fragrance. I'll have to look for one. But that isn't the problem at hand—literally. I stare down at the number I transferred from my palm to a scrap of paper.

Last night I picked up the pistol and several boxes of ammunition, so I can practice. Now I just have to figure out if I try my luck by myself or take Rusty up on his offer. Right now he's the only person I know around here other than my landlord.

Oh, what the hell. I pull out my phone and dial Rusty up before I lose my nerve.

He answers on the second ring. "Yeah? Who is this?"

"Ashlynn," I say softly. I can hear the smile in his voice as his tone smooths the bark from a moment ago.

"Hey, babe. What time is it?" He sounds a little groggy, like I just woke him up.

"Oh God, it's early. I'm sorry. I wasn't thinking."

"No, that's fine. I'm up now. So, did you pick it up yet?"

"Yes. Last night."

"You want me to meet you at your place in about an hour? Give you a lesson?"

"If it's not too much trouble, and you don't have other plans, that would be great."

"Nothing planned I can't change. Just let me grab a quick shower first."

"Okay, do you have a piece of paper? I'll give you the address."

"Already got it."

"What? How?"

"Memorized it when you filled out the paperwork."

"You snoop!"

He chuckles. "I'm not a stupid man, Ashlynn. See you soon."

Before I can reply, he disconnects. My mouth drops open, and I pull my phone from my ear, staring at it. "What the hell!"

I smile and shake my head. No, the man is not stupid. I sip my coffee, set the mug down, and pick up the laptop I bought. I open it and pull up the Internet. I spend the next hour checking all the news outlets in Vegas, searching for the murders at Peerless Tower, but there's nothing. It's like it never happened. I can understand if they disposed of the bodies and cleaned up the place, that maybe no one has missed Ricardo Leona yet, but surely someone would miss Thomas, that sweet butler. I bite my lip and rack my brain.

Okay, maybe he was a bachelor or widow who lived alone. But wouldn't Axle notice he's gone missing? I pull up news about Axle and see he's still on tour. He might not be home for weeks.

My God, what did they do with the bodies? Poor Thomas. He didn't deserve to die like that.

I call Devon, just to check in.

The phone rings a few times. "Hello."

"Hi Devon. It's Ashlynn."

"Hey, girl. How are you? Everything okay?"

"Yes. I'm fine. I'm settled somewhere far away."

"Good. You haven't had any trouble have you?"

"No, none here. What about there?"

"Nope, no trouble, and no one's been snooping around. Gotta say, though, the hotel is all a buzz with your sudden departure."

Shit. I know if anything ever comes of it all and an investigation is opened, Axle will send the police straight to the Del Sol to interview me. When they find I'm gone, I'll be wanted for questioning. I take a deep, slow breath. *Don't get ahead of yourself, Ashlynn. That hasn't happened yet.* "I'm sorry I had to leave that way."

"You don't have to apologize to me, honey. I'm just glad you're safe."

"So… no one else has come around with questions?"

"Nope. It's been business as usual."

"Okay. Good. That's good."

The rumble of a motorcycle coming down the highway breaks into my thoughts, and I close the laptop. "I've got to go, Devon.

Thank you."

"Keep in touch, Ashlynn, and take care of yourself."

"I will. Bye."

The bike slows and turns down my gravel and dirt drive. It's Rusty.

I get up and move through the house to the back door. I skip down the few steps to the yard and over to the gravel drive to watch him roll up.

He looks good on the bike. He handles it like it's an extension of his body, rolling easily over the bumpy drive and stopping a way back from my car that's parked in front of the detached garage.

He drops the kickstand, swings off, pulls his helmet from his head, and smooths a palm over his hair.

He walks toward me, and damn, the man has the sexiest walk ever. His eyes sweep over me, and the things that does to me.

"Hi," I say lamely.

"Hey, sweetheart." He looks around the property. "Nice place. You like it out here, Vegas?"

I roll my eyes. "Don't call me that if you expect me to answer."

He chuckles, his eyes lingering on my face.

To fill the silence, I finally do answer him. "Yes, I like it out here. Surprising, I know. It's a big change, but maybe it's just what I needed. I like the peacefulness. I can't tell you the last time I heard birds chirping; now I sit on the porch with my morning coffee and listen to them chatter."

"Didn't figure you for a morning person."

"I'm not. I mean, I didn't use to be. But lately, I've been waking up with the sun. Strange, huh? Maybe it's all this fresh air." I slide my hair to the front over one shoulder hoping my hand doesn't shake with my sudden nerves.

"Life I lead, I'm more of a night owl."

DIRTY DEALS

I nod. It makes sense. "You probably don't roll out of bed until mid-afternoon. That used to be me, too."

"You got the gun?"

"Yes, and two boxes of ammunition for it."

"Should be enough."

I walk to my car and retrieve it off the seat.

"First lesson. Never leave your weapon in your car. It's gonna do you no good out here if you're in the house. Besides, some kid could find it." He scans the surrounding land. "Probably not an issue out here, but you never know."

"Right."

He takes it and lays it on the picnic table that sits in the yard. Then proceeds to demonstrate how to load and unload the weapon, and once he's satisfied I've got that part down, he glances around. I wonder what he's doing when he walks to the garbage can to pull a discarded pizza box out. He trudges across the yard with it to a tree near the property line. Beyond is a wide field and a tree line about two acres away.

He draws a long Bowie knife that I hadn't noticed from a sheath on his belt, tucked under his leather vest. He holds the box up to the tree and stabs the knife in the top, pinning it to the trunk. Then he walks back.

"Think you can hit that?"

I judge the distance. "I don't know. It's pretty far."

He takes my hand and leads me closer. I can't deny the jolt that zings through me at his touch. I like the way his big palm closes around my smaller hand. I almost hate it when he releases me.

"Always keep the safety on until you're ready to shoot."

I nod.

"This your strong hand?" He takes my right.

"Yes."

He puts the gun in my hand, positioning my fingers just so, curling them around the grip and pushing my index finger to an extended position along the side of the gun and off the trigger. "Always keep your finger off the trigger until you're prepared to pull it.

"Okay. Got it."

"Feel good?"

"Yes. It's heavier than I remembered."

"Get used to the weight of it in your hand. You need to be comfortable with it."

"Okay."

He steps behind me and lifts my arm. "Put your weak hand around and under your right hand to steady the shot."

I do as he says.

"The slide is pushed back by recoil, so keep your thumbs clear of it."

"Okay."

"The recoil can be wicked, so always fire it at arm's length."

He drops his hands to my hips and puts me into position.

"Comfortable?"

"Yes."

"Good. Now look down the sight. Line up the shot. Keep your focus on the front sight. Aim dead center. Aim small, miss small."

"Okay."

"Use your dominant eye, but keep both eyes open. That'll give you better depth perception."

"All right."

"You're not gonna be able to hold the gun completely still while aiming, that's just a fact. But don't grip it too tightly, that'll help with your aim."

"Got it."

"Ready to try a shot?"

Am I? I'm not sure, but I'm not going to admit that. "Yes, I guess so."

He steps away. "Okay, place the pad of your index finger on the trigger. To shoot, you're going to apply slow, steady pressure until the gun fires. Your breathing can move the handgun just enough to throw off your shot. So take a deep breath, exhale slowly out your mouth, and squeeze the trigger. Go ahead."

I squeeze the trigger.

Bam.

Not even close.

He grins. "This time try relaxing."

I breathe in and exhale.

Bam. I miss again.

"Okay, let's try some follow through."

"What's that?"

"Prevents you from jerking the gun before the bullet has left the barrel. Improves your accuracy."

"What do I do?"

"After you fire, don't lower the gun immediately. Instead follow through on the shot for a couple seconds. Keep squeezing the trigger and hold the target in your sight."

Moving to stand behind me again, he puts his hands over mine to steady them and holds them there. His arms around me feel so protective and comforting, and for a moment I'm lost in the feeling. The scent of his leather vest surrounds me, and I breathe it in.

"Ready?" he asks when I do nothing.

"Right. Yes."

I take a breath, exhale, and pull the trigger. This time I actually hit the box. I squeal.

He keeps my arms in position. "Again."

Bam.

"Again."

Bam.

"Again."

Bam.

I hit it with every shot.

He pulls the gun from my shaking hands. "Good shootin', Vegas."

I jump up and down, laughing, so excited that I mastered it. Well, mastered may be a strong word, but it feels so good to get it right.

He's smiling, obviously enjoying my excitement.

"Are you a good shot?" I can't help the question that bubbles out.

He arcs a brow. "You want a demonstration?"

"I do, actually."

He pulls his own pistol from a shoulder holster under his vest, tucked low under his armpit and against his ribs. The gun is way bigger than mine. I can only imagine how heavy it is, but he handles it like it weighs nothing.

He aims at the target, holding the gun up for barely a second before he pulls the trigger.

Bam. Bam. Bam. Bam.

All perfect bull's-eyes. I expected him to be good, but wow.

"Impressive," I say.

He grins. "I've had a little more practice than you."

"You want a beer?" I offer.

"I thought you'd never ask."

"Wait here. I'll get us both one." I walk in the kitchen, pull two cold bottles from the fridge, and head back outside. He's got one hip resting on top of the picnic table, his leg swinging. I hold out the beer. "Thanks for the lesson."

He takes it and clinks his to mine. "You're welcome."

We both drink, our eyes on each other. When he drops the bottle from his lips, he slides his hand around my waist and tugs me to him until our body's touch. I feel so petite next to him, but as he sits against the table, my head is close to his height. I still have to tip my head to look at him.

"I'm glad you decided to stick around town, Ashlynn."

"I am, too. I've never been in the South before. I like all the yes, ma'am, no, ma'am. Everyone has such good manners."

"Men don't open doors for women where you were raised?"

"Not like here." I push out of his arms, afraid of the questions that might follow about where I'm from. It's bad enough he knows as much as he does. "So, you ride everywhere you go?"

It's a stupid question but the first thing that pops out of my mouth as I attempt to change the subject.

"Most places. I've got a pickup for when I can't take the bike. You ever ridden on a motorcycle?"

I shake my head. "Not like yours. Once on Spring Break I rode on the back of one of those… What do you call them, ninja bikes?"

"Really? How'd you like it?"

"It was okay. Not my cup of tea."

He points toward his bike with the neck of the bottle. "Harley's a little different than a crotch rocket. The ride is unlike anything else, rumbling down the road. We'll have to take a ride sometime."

"That reminds me. I haven't kept up my end of the deal." I pull the Porsche fob from my back pocket, and it dangles from the ring on my finger.

He grins, snags it and stands. "You sure?"

I shrug. "I keep my word. Let's go."

He chugs his beer, and I can see the excitement of a little boy on Christmas morning in his eyes. We move to my baby and climb in.

He adjusts the seat back as far as he can and then starts the engine. "Goddamn, listen to it purr."

He backs up, maneuvering around his bike and turns in a circle, heading out the driveway onto the highway. When those wide performance tires grip the pavement, the car zooms forward. He shifts through the gears, quickly getting up to speed.

"Fuck, I want to take this up on the Interstate and see what she can do."

"Let's go."

"This gearbox is slick. It's got a much lighter clutch than anything I've ever driven. Goddamn it's smooth." He chuckles. "It's fucking amazing; you flick the gearlever with a couple of fingers."

I laugh out loud at his enthusiasm. "You're such a guy."

He glances over at me, grinning big. "Fast cars and fast women, gotta love 'em both."

What I'm loving right now is how happy he is just driving. He takes us up onto the interstate where he lets it off the leash and opens it up. My baby responds, as I knew she would.

Several miles down, he exits and takes some curvy back roads.

Finally, he heads toward my place and the road straightens out.

"Holy fuck, what an awesome sports car."

I burst out laughing.

"Not kidding, babe. Fucking phenomenal control, fantastic steering precision, gorgeous suspension – you can tell it's expensively engineered. The ride control, the stability, the way it tackles tight corners is just amazing."

"Porsche is proud of it, that's for sure," I say. "It cost enough."

"Yeah, babe, but having an engine do exactly what you want, when you want, and sound enthusiastic about it while doing it is fucking fantastic. It's worth every penny you forked over."

"Well, I'm glad you like it. That was pretty much how I felt the first time I test-drove one. It was like an instant high. Of course, I didn't describe it so technically, like you did. I think my reaction was more like, 'Oh my God, I want this car!'"

His laughter is deep and throaty, and I'm suddenly finding I'm just as addicted to it as I am my baby.

We pull back up the drive. Rusty parks and looks over at me. "Only one thing wrong with it."

I'm shocked he can find anything wrong with my baby. My face falls in unexpected disappointment. "What?"

"The fucking yellow color." He shakes his head. "I could never own a yellow car."

"Well, you don't. This is my baby, and I love the color."

"For you, yeah. It suits you. Flashy and fast."

I grin. "You give good compliments."

"That's not the only thing I do well. C'mere." He leans over, cups my jaw, and pulls me in for a kiss. There's something about a first kiss, and I'm glad ours is happening in my favorite place—my sexy car.

He's no slouch at kissing, and soon I'm completely oblivious of everything around me. There's just his mouth on mine as his tongue sweeps inside. His beard against my skin is erotic as hell, and the scruff is much softer than I'd expected. I lift a hand to cup his jaw, running my thumb over it.

Those soft strokes ratchet up his enthusiasm, and he leans farther into my space. Finally, he pulls back to breathe, but only an inch. He stares down at me and runs the pad of his thumb across my plump bottom lip that feels swollen from his kisses.

"Been wantin' to do that since I laid eyes on you, Ashlynn."

I don't want to talk, so I reach up and pull his head down for more.

He gives me what I want, one hand running over the curves of my body from thigh to waist.

The sudden pelting of rain on the roof and windshield startles us.

He pulls back to look. Big fat raindrops hit the glass. "Fuck, it's about to be a downpour." He glances up and sees the garage door opener the landlord gave me, and he hits it. The door rises, and he fires the car up and rolls us in.

"You should pull your bike in," I say.

We scramble out, and he dashes to it, taking the grips in his hands, kicking up the stand, and pushing it inside.

I glance across the yard to the back steps. The rain is bombarding the ground, but the drops are spaced out far apart.

"Make a dash for it?" he asks, grinning.

I smile and nod and off we go. We dash up the steps and into the door, laughing as we shake the water from us.

"Oo-wee," he says, running a hand over his hair.

We're both breathing hard, and suddenly we just stare at each other, neither one saying a word. It's magical, and I feel a jolt of desire skitter up my spine. He takes a step toward me, then another. I can't look away from the heat in his eyes. It's burning me up, and I feel my body's response. My nipples tighten under my damp shirt, and I know I'm wet in other places, as well.

He's standing close now, so close the air between us is electrified. He lifts a hand and brushes a lock of hair from my face, and then without warning he dips down and scoops me up in his arms, his hands on my ass. My legs go naturally around his hips as I gasp in a breath. He pushes me to the wall, and his mouth comes down on mine; hungry, starving, ravenous kisses convey exactly what he wants.

I cup his face and return his kisses with ones of my own, just as hot and heavy and needy as his.

This time when he breaks away, he's breathing hard as he stares down at me and growls, "Where's your bed?"

CHAPTER SIX

Rusty—

Ashlynn points to a door through the next room, and I carry her there, taking her to her back on the mattress of the wrought iron bed.

She lets out a needy mewl and pulls my head to hers. I cover her mouth with mine, pushing inside with my tongue. Her lips are soft, and I feel the moan vibrate up from her throat.

She cups my face, and her touch drives me wild. Her gentle fingers stroke my beard and my neck. I groan and pull back to stare into her eyes. Her chocolate brown pupils dilate, heavy with desire, her lids half shuttered. I kiss the tip of her nose, her eyelids, her chin, brushing softly over the skin of her cheekbones and jaw. I make my way to her ear and bite the lobe.

She arches, her head going back, offering her throat to me. I drop kisses along the soft underside of her jaw and wet open-mouthed kisses to the dip between her collarbones where I suck and lave my tongue.

I slip my arms under her ribcage, lifting her chest, arching her farther and bringing that fabulous cleavage thrusting up for me. My mouth travels to the valley between those lush globes, then climbs along the edge of her neckline.

I want her naked, want every barrier between us removed. I want to see her body, want it laid out bare for me.

My hand moves to the buttons along the front of her thin sleeveless blouse and work them with practiced ease that comes from years of expertise in undressing women. I silently count them in my head as I make my way patiently to the hem. As I do, I keep pressing open-mouthed kisses to her skin.

Her scent is light and floral, and I can't get enough of it. I breathe it in deeply and pull her shirt open to take in the pretty lace bra. It's see-through, and her dusky rose nipples press eagerly against the sheer fabric. They're erect little bumps so close to the low-cut edge, they tease. I skate my big palm over one breast, tuck my thumb inside, and pull the fabric down until that glorious nipple pops free. I run the fabric under her breast, and it pushes the plump globe toward my eager lips.

I close them over that sweet nub, sucking hard and grazing my teeth along it.

Ashlynn's fingers thread through my hair, holding me to her breast. Every breath she takes lifts her chest to me. I lave the nipple in a long stroke then continue sucking. I want her nipples sore tomorrow. I want her to think of me every time these beauties brush against fabric.

She moans deeply, and I yank down the other side and give that nipple the same treatment until she's thrashing and needy.

My palm strokes over her ribcage to the dip in her waist until my fingers find the button to her shorts. I pop it free and work the zipper.

Finally I release her nipple and rise above her to jerk her shorts down her hips and off her body.

She lifts and tosses off the blouse and her bra.

I move off the bed to stand at the foot. I pull off my cut and lay it on a chair, then tug my t-shirt over my head.

Ashlynn reclines on the bed, nude except for the matching lace panties. She takes in my chest, and her eyes drop to my hands as I unbuckle my belt. She licks her lips, and my dick throbs. I strip off everything until I'm standing there, letting her look her fill. I take my dick in my hand and stroke from root to tip, twisting the end. She lifts a leg, bending at the knee and rubbing the sole of her foot along the coverlet, enticing me.

I take a step toward her and grab her ankles, dragging her to the end of the bed, and she gasps. I lock eyes with her as I pull her panties down her legs, then drop to my knees and press her knees wide, my palms gliding up her inner thighs, my eyes on that beautiful pussy.

I dip my head and inhale her addicting scent, that arousing musk that's designed to drive the male species heady with erotic hunger. My dick jerks in response, eager to be inside her.

The need to taste her is overpowering. I reach the apex of her thighs and brush my thumbs over those pouty lips. She jerks in reaction at my first touch, her hips lifting.

"So pretty," I murmur, glancing up to meet her eyes. My thumbs stroke and then circle, parting her and seeking out that shy little clit that hides from me. I intend to give it all my attention. I dip my head and lave in a long lick. I peer at her as I do and watch her body arch, her breasts thrust up so pretty.

I tickle her clit with the tip of my tongue, and her hands fist the coverlet at her hips. Her knuckles are white with her grip. I pin her thighs wider and continue stroke after stroke, not letting up until she's so wet it's running down her ass cheeks. Then I thrust two fingers inside, and she moans my name.

"Oh God, Rusty. Yes. More. Please," she begs so sweetly.

I give her what she wants, thrusting deep and curling my fingers, the pads finding her g-spot, and she sucks in a breath, throwing her head back, grinding her hips against my hand.

I rub my thumb in circles around that pretty nub standing so pert, then dip my head and suck it hard, and she orgasms powerfully against my mouth, thrashing and panting, her breasts jiggling with her movements.

I lap up every drop of her honey release as she pants, her breathing slowly returning to normal. Then I slide my big body up over hers, dragging along her heated, sensitized skin. She's got a diamond dangling from a piercing at her belly button. It sparkles, and I toy with it, dipping my tongue inside. Her belly jerks in response. I smooth my palms along the curves of her hips and the indent of her waist, skating up over her ribs to cover and squeeze those lush breasts. I suck each nipple and then press my mouth to the tender skin under her jaw and suck hard. I want to mark her. I suck several more spots along her neck, knowing she'll look bruised with a necklace of love bites. She'll remember our first time. I don't want her to forget it.

My dick is throbbing with need, and I know I can't delay much longer. I twist and reach over the edge of the bed, digging a hand in the pocket of my jeans and pulling out a condom. I rip the foil packet open and go up on my knees to roll it on. Then I spread her wide and circle the head of my dick in her drenched opening. She moans and lifts her hips, eager for me.

"You want my dick?" I growl.

"Yes, so bad. Please."

She writhes, and I line up and surge inside her, pinning her down as I support myself on my palms. I settle into the cradle of her hips, and I know I never want to leave. I want to stay inside her, thrust deep, our bodies one. Fuck, I've never felt the way this woman makes me feel. I go back up on my knees, grab her thighs, and drag her body up, lifting her hips off the bed, bringing her pussy tight against my hips as I plow into her, slamming deep with every thrust.

DIRTY DEALS

With this angle I know I'm hitting that trigger spot deep inside her.

I know it's sensitive from all the attention my fingers gave it, and she ramps up again quickly, racing toward another orgasm.

"Yes, yes, yes," she pants.

I pound into her, watching those pretty tits bounce with every stroke.

"Put your arms over your head," I order.

She obeys immediately, and my dick throbs inside her.

"Grab the headboard."

She wraps her hands around the iron bars.

"Keep them there."

She nods.

"I love watching your tits bounce like that. So pretty. Are those nipples hard for me?"

"Yes. Touch them. Please."

I grip the back of her knees and press her forward, readjusting our position, and then lean over her to do as she asks. I tease the tip of my tongue over one then the other, just barely touching them. It drives her wild, and she eagerly thrusts them up at me.

The look on her face, I know she wants to release her hold on the bars and pull me to her. She needs her nipples sucked, and it's driving her crazy that I'm denying her, teasing her, making her wait.

I lock eyes with her. "Don't you dare let go."

Her lids drop, and her head falls back as she moans in torment. I reward her with one long suck, and she whimpers. I give the other the same, and she wiggles.

"Yes, God, yes."

"Gonna flip you over. Keep a hold of the headboard. Understand?"

She nods.

I pull free of her, flip her over and jerk her hips up high, stretching her out across the bed until her arms are stretched tight over her head.

I smooth my hands over her gorgeous ass and down her spine. She arches like a cat and begs me to take her.

"Fuck me. Please."

I pop one round globe of her ass with a smack and watch it jiggle. I dip my fingers to her pussy, circling and dragging the wetness up to her clit. I massage circles around it again and again.

"This what you want?"

"Yes, don't stop. Please."

"You close, baby?" I ask.

She nods, beyond words, her face buried in the mattress.

"I want you to come around my dick this time. Tell me you want that."

She nods again.

I smack her ass again. "Say it."

"Yes, please. Fuck me. Make me come."

I continue to play with her until she's panting and trembling. Then I take my dick and circle her clit and her opening. I'm so hard for her I can't delay much longer.

"Oh God," she moans. "Please."

I plunge inside her. It only takes a few strokes, and she's coming around my dick, squeezing down hard around me like a velvet glove. I'm so ready for release, and I feel it crawling up from the base of my spine, tingling, my balls tightening until I can't hold back. I explode in one of the best orgasms of my life, locking my arms around her hips and coming hard. I groan, falling to one palm on the bed near her ribs and stroking her ass with the other. "Fuck, baby. So good," I murmur, dipping to press a kiss between her shoulder blades. I feel her walls flutter around me, milking every last drop from me. Finally, I pull free.

"Don't move," I order and pad to the adjacent bathroom to deal with the condom. I return with a washcloth. She's still in the same position, her knees tucked under her, her ass in the air, hands on the headboard.

"Lay down, sweetheart."

She straightens her legs and sinks into the mattress. I wipe her clean, then slide next to her, gathering her in my arms. She's limp and relaxed. I bring her head to my chest and press kisses along her forehead.

"You good?"

"So good," she whispers in response and cuddles closer.

We drift off to sleep in a matter of minutes.

CHAPTER SEVEN

Rusty—

After waking and enjoying another rousing bout of sex in Ashlynn's bed, we move to the front porch and curl up on her big swing and watch the rain. She dozes in my arms, and I love how she's finally relaxed enough in my presence to do that. I kiss the top of her head and breathe in her scent. It's like warm peaches and spice, and I'm already fucking hooked.

The lower half of my leg hangs over the edge and every so often I give a nudge with my toe to keep the swing moving. I look at the big ropes that hold it up, wondering if I can make one of these.

Ashlynn stirs, and my palm strokes the soft warm skin of her naked back. I thread my fingers into her hair and let the silky strands cascade over my hand.

She moves and dips her head, pressing a kiss to my chest.

I don't want to ruin the mood, but I've got some questions, and it's time she gave me some answers. "You awake, Vegas?"

I feel her smile against my skin. "Told you, I'm not answering to that nickname."

I chuckle. "You don't get a say in your nickname, darlin'. That's not how it works."

She turns her head and nips at me.

I tighten my hold on her hair and gently pull her head enough to smile down into her face. "Careful, baby. I bite back."

She grins. "I know."

I dip my head and kiss her lips. "Wanna ask you something."

I immediately feel her body tense.

"Rusty, I—"

"Relax," I order. "No need for you to get all worked up."

"That depends, doesn't it? What do you want to know?"

She tries to sound nonchalant, but there's an edge to her tone.

"I think you know I'm not a stupid man, and I can add two and two. So tell me what you're runnin' from." My voice is calm, but it's the no-nonsense tone I use with the club.

She turns, twisting until the front of her body is no longer pressed to my side. She covers herself with the blanket. I've got her pinned on the inside of the swing, and she's not going anywhere unless I let her, and I'm not about to let her.

She's quiet a long while and I wonder if she's going to give me a hard time. "Ashlynn?"

"I hardly know you," she whispers.

I huff out a laugh. "Babe, I just spent the last two hours inside you."

"That doesn't count."

"I'm tryin' real hard to get to know you, Ash. You need to open up and let me in. Maybe I can help, ever think of that?"

Still, she stays quiet.

"Babe, I'm the last one whose ever gonna rat you out for something. So tell me the truth, you steal that money? You runnin' from the law?"

She snaps her head around to look at me. "Of course not!" Her voice is indignant, and if it's an act, it's a good one.

"So, what then? Something's got you runnin'. You drove across the country with nothing but a carryon bag of clothes and then you rent a house out in the middle of nowhere."

"It's not nowhere. Atlanta's less than an hour away."

"Ashlynn, be straight with me. Like I told you, not gonna tell anyone."

She bites her lip. "I just… There's this guy, and he won't leave me alone."

"Like a husband? Boyfriend?" I ask, and suddenly an uncomfortable feeling edges up my spine. I was just inside her, and I'm already wanting back in there again; last thing I want is to find out she's married or engaged or some shit.

She shakes her head.

"Ex?" I press her.

"Just this guy I met."

"That his money? His car?"

"No, I swear. It's all mine."

"That's an expensive car and a lot of cash, babe."

"I…"

"What?" I can tell she's trying to decide how much to share.

She takes a slow breath. "It's a long story."

"I've got time."

When she stays quiet, I pull her on top of me until we're eye to eye. "I'm not going anyplace, Ashlynn. I like you. A lot. You and me, we could be something if you let it happen. If you're in trouble, I can help you. Now, you bought a gun for some reason, and you wanted to know how to shoot it. Girl like you, that shit doesn't just happen out of the blue. Something's got you scared. Now what is it?"

"Okay. You're right. There's this guy, and he won't leave me alone. I left town to get away from him. It was all I could think to do—just go into hiding. He's violent, and he scares me."

"He hurt you?" My blood begins to boil at the thought.

She shakes her head. "No, but he could. I'm afraid of what he might do if he ever finds me."

"Who is he?"

She shrugs. "Just a stalker, I guess. I worked in a job where I met a lot of people."

"What exactly did you do?"

"I was a casino hostess, a luxury concierge."

"What the fuck is that?"

"For big time players. When the hotel had a particularly important high-roller coming into town, I took care of him, kept him happy and gambling."

"That pays well, does it? It must, judging by the car you drive."

She nods. "I make quite a bit, yes."

"And you haul it all around in cash?" I know my voice has an edge, but this doesn't add up, and I'm no one's fool.

"I get tips. Right before I realized I had to leave town I was given a poker chip as a tip. It was a large one. When I knew I had to run, I cashed it in and left."

I run my thumb across her cheek as a tear slips down. "Babe."

She dips her head, trying to hide from me, not wanting me to see the emotions that play across her face.

I kiss the top of her head, giving her that space.

"This guy… He got a name?"

She lifts a shoulder.

I slide my fingers in the hair at her nape. "It's gonna be okay, Vegas. Nobody's gonna find you out here."

She looks at me. "You think that's true?"

"You know anybody here? Got any connection to this place? This state?"

"No."

"There you go. The country's a big place."

She doesn't look so convinced.

"What's got you worried?" I press.

"I'm afraid I'm forgetting something, leaving some trail he'll find."

"Babe, unless the guy's hired a PI, there are only a few ways to track a person. Your cell phone, social media, your IP address, GPS tracker on your car or credit card usage. You been careful with all that?"

She frowns, and I'm not sure she has.

"You dump your phone?"

"Yes."

"Been on social media?"

"No. Not at all."

"Could he have a tracker on your car?"

She shakes her head. "I doubt it. I don't think he knew my car."

"Used your credit cards? I'm guessing no, but you stayed in a hotel, you've been getting gas, so…?"

"I've been careful."

"And now you've got a gun, and you registered it. That's a paper trail, but unless he's hired someone to check into you, I doubt he'll find it. I might be able to do something about it. If I'd known your problem the other day I could have gotten a gun for you off the books."

"Shit, I didn't think of that."

She looks worried. I slide my hand to her face and tilt her chin up with my thumb. "Hey, you see him around or you even get a weird feeling that something's not right, you call me. Day or night. I'll be here. If I can't get to you one of the prospects will. Understand?"

She nods, her eyes filling with tears. "I got lucky when I broke down."

I huff out a laugh. "Yeah, you did. I've been tryin' to make you understand that."

I pull the blanket from us and carry her naked body back inside, through the house, and to her bed. And then I lay her down and slide inside her. She's wet and ready, and fuck if it doesn't feel like coming home.

CHAPTER EIGHT

Ashlynn—

I stretch and reach out a hand, but the bed is empty. My eyes fly open. Did Rusty leave? Surely I would have heard the motorcycle start up. I fling the sheets back and crawl from bed. I breathe a sigh of relief when I see his shirt and leather cut hung over the chair.

I smile, slip his denim shirt on, and fasten one snap between my breasts, and then I slip my panties on and pad from the room. I see him through the lace curtains of the living room windows. He's out on the porch, sitting in one of the wicker chairs with a cup of coffee raised to his mouth.

The screen door creaks as I push through, and his gaze swings to me. He smiles, his eyes sweeping down and taking in his shirt and my bare legs. He lifts his arm for me to crawl onto his lap.

I curl up on him, wrapping an arm around his neck and stealing his steaming mug for a sip.

"Hmm," I breathe, taking in the rich aroma and flavor. "You make good coffee."

"It's your blend," he replies, his warm palm stroking up my thigh until he hits the edge of my panties. "Aw, I was hoping you had nothing on under here."

I grin. "Didn't think a scrap of lace would stop you."

He slips his fingers under the edging, accepting the challenge. "You thought right."

My hand trembles with reaction to his stroking fingers.

"Don't spill, Vegas."

He keeps up his feather-light touches until I set the mug down on the small table and shift, giving him better access. His muscled chest is bare, and his tattooed skin is warm as I cuddle to him, writhing under his touch.

I'm soon teetering on the edge of an orgasm when he presses his mouth to my ear and whispers, "My baby's so wet and ready this morning."

"Yes," I pant.

"What do you want?"

"I want you to make me come."

"Open the shirt," he murmurs. "Let me see those pretty tits."

It's early morning, and we're out in the country, still I've never been one for exposing myself in public. Never even flashed anyone. I've always been such a prude that way. Not that I'm ashamed of my body, I just have never had any exhibitionist tendencies. But his words are like silky smoke curling around me and urging me on. I want to please him. I want to obey him. Dare I?

I writhe, my back bowing against his hard chest, and my head falling on his shoulder.

"Pop that snap, Vegas." This time there's a deeper thread to his voice, a little more forceful and urgent.

I comply, closing my hands over the placket and pulling the shirt wide open with a pop of the snap.

"Shrug it down your shoulders a bit."

I do as he orders.

His lips press to my bare shoulder with the softest of kisses, then he works his way up to nuzzle my neck, behind my ear, and then nips at my lobe.

He spreads my legs wide as I lean against him, and two fingers slip inside me. My hips lift, my body wanting more.

My head rolls on his shoulder. "Yes, oh God, yes."

His free hand closes over one breast, squeezing, his thumb strumming across my hard nipple. With each brush, a zing shoots through me, straight to my core. My passage clamps down on his fingers, and he groans in my ear.

"Fuck, yeah, baby. Squeeze me tight, show me how much you want it."

"I do. Please."

He thrusts in and out, his fingertips finding that magic spot that has me panting. "Oh God. Yes. There. Right there."

"I know what my girl wants." His voice is thick with need, and he rotates a thumb around my clit.

I whimper, my hands clenching on the armrest. He keeps at me until I can't take anymore. When I'm so close I think I'm about to burst, he pinches down on my nipple, and an orgasm shoots through me hard and fast. I moan and thrash against his hand. He brings me down slowly until my rough breathing slows.

I melt all over him like puddled candle wax. His fingers slip from me, and my release coats them. He smears it across my nipples, and then lays me over his arm as he sucks them into his mouth, first one and then the other.

They're already super sensitized, tender and sore from all the attention he gave them last night. I moan, but it hurts so good that I can't help thrusting my chest up for more of his tender torment.

He groans, and I feel his hard erection pressing against my bottom. I know he needs relief, and with all the orgasms he's given me in the last twenty hours, I want to give back. I slip from his lap and kneel before him, my hands going to his zipper. His eyes are glittering as he stares down at me, letting me open his jeans and pull him out. His erection is long and hard for me, the tip glistening with pre-cum.

I lick my lips and smooth my thumb over it in tight circles. His hips lift off the chair as he thrusts into my tight hold.

He groans in need. "Fuck, baby, take it."

I dip my head and wrap my lips around him, taking him all the way down. The fingers of both hands thread into my hair, fisting and guiding my movements, soon locking me in place as he gently fucks my mouth, in and out.

"Fuck, yeah, Vegas. Give me that pretty mouth. Take it deep. Take it all."

I do. I take everything he has to give until he's ready to explode.

His growl is a guttural primal sound as he comes hard.

I take it all, every last drop.

I lap and lick and suck until he's floating back to earth, just as contented and blissful as he'd made me feel moments ago.

"Holy shit," he pants and drops his head. I lay my head on his thigh, and his palm strokes over my hair tenderly.

I realize I haven't felt this way about a man in so very long. Maybe never. But it's dangerous to let myself get attached. He'll never be mine and loving him could put him in danger as well.

Right now I don't want to care about any of that. I just want to relish the fact that I'm falling in love and how wonderful love is when it's fresh and new and we're both eager to please.

I smile, my eyes closed, just enjoying him caressing my hair.

"Ash, climb up here," he murmurs, his voice deep and thick. I look up to see his clear eyes staring down at me, something burning in their depths. Perhaps he's as affected by all this as I am. Dare I hope?

He fastens his jeans, and I curl up sideways in his lap, tucking my head under his jaw. I can hear his heart beating. It's a soothing sound. I could stay here all day, listening to that lulling rhythm.

One hand strokes the skin of my bare thigh while the other arm wraps me close, his fingers playing with my hair.

"Want to ask you something. I don't want you to get upset by the question, just tell me the answer."

Already my heart rate has increased. God, please don't ruin this wonderful moment with questions I can't answer.

"Your bag's still packed. What's that about, honey? You leavin' again?"

How do I explain? How do I tell him that I haven't felt safe anywhere since long before the murders?

"There's no reason for it. It's all in my head."

"What's that mean?"

"I don't know why I can't unpack. I don't know why I can't feel safe, even when my head tells me I am. It's irrational. I know that. I've tried before, and I freak out. Total meltdown, anxiety attack."

"When did this start?"

"When I was a teenager. We moved around a lot. My mom had a lot of boyfriends. She was never married to my father. She gave me a name once, but I've never met him. I'm not even sure she knew for certain it was him. I guess I've just never felt safe."

"These boyfriends of your mom's… They ever try anything with you?"

"Maybe. I think I've blocked some stuff out. I remember my mother packing us up and leaving in the middle of the night a couple times. I remember her telling me to hide in the closet a few times. But most of my memories don't start until I was in seventh grade. That's when I spent the summer with my grandparents. My mom left me there and didn't come back until Halloween.

"Then we moved into one apartment after another. But there were never any boyfriends after that. If she saw anyone, she never brought them home."

"You ever talk to anyone about all this?"

His hand strokes my head, fingertips massaging my scalp.

"I saw a therapist once a few years ago. One session. I never went back. I remember her saying someday when I truly feel safe, I'll stop keeping that packed bag in my closet. One day my mind would just know, and I wouldn't need it anymore."

"So, it's like an emotional crutch, a safety net?"

I shrug. "I guess so."

He kisses the top of my head, his hand squeezing my knee. "I want to make you feel safe like that, Vegas. You let me, I'll give it my best shot."

I smile. "I'm not sure that's how it works. I can't promise you anything, Rusty."

He nods. "I get that."

"Do you? I can't even promise from one day to the next I won't wake up and the urge to run will overwhelm me and I'll disappear."

"Okay."

"Okay? You sure?"

"I'll take whatever you give me."

I look at him in wonder. "Why?"

"Because with you I think I've found something. Never felt like this, Vegas. Not in all these years. It scares the crap outta me, not gonna lie. But I want to see where it goes. You in?"

"I'm not ready for a big relationship. I need to take this one day at a time."

"Fair enough. Got something else I want to talk to you about. I get you like it out here, the peacefulness and all that, but I'm wondering if it'll wear thin after a while."

"What do you mean?"

"You're isolated out here. Not that I don't mind ridin' to see you. But I've got an idea for how we could make this a little easier, get to see each other more."

"How's that?"

"Look, maybe you don't need money, I get that, but if you get bored out here all alone, I've got a motorcycle shop that could use someone to do the paperwork. My girl just quit. Left me in a spot. So, if you're interested, it'd help me out."

"I guess I do owe you a favor, huh?" I smile.

"You don't owe me shit, babe. Not why I brought it up. Just got that spot open, and no one I'd rather walk in and see sittin' in the office than you right now. If it's too much, I get that. Not tryin' to smother you. I'm just fuckin' enthralled with you, that's the God's truth. I see something I want, I go after it, in case you hadn't noticed."

I give a tinkle of laughter. "I got that about you."

"So?"

I suck my lips in my mouth and think about the offer, the pros and cons. I would get to see more of Rusty, and that's certainly not a bad thing, but I'm not sure about how controlling he could get. But one thing he's right about. I'm a people person, always have been, and staying out here alone day after day will drive me bat-shit-crazy. "Okay. I'd love to give it a try on one condition."

"What's that?"

"We pump the brakes on the sex thing and get to know each other."

"Are you puttin' me in the friend zone?"

"Just temporarily."

"You drive a hard bargain."

"Yeah, I get that a lot."

He chuckles. "I'll take your deal but reserve the right to change the deal at a later time."

"Fine. But I'm warning you, not sure how much help I'm gonna be to your business. I've never worked in an office before."

"Vegas, just having you in the building is going to bring in a shit-ton of business."

"Ah ha! So I'm just window decoration, there to lure sales?"

"Told you I wasn't a stupid man. I know an asset when I see one."

He laughs, and then pulls me down for a kiss. One leads to another and soon we're finishing in the shower, with me bent over with my hands on the tile and him driving into my soap slick body as hot water sprays over us and the room fills with steam.

CHAPTER NINE

Ashlynn—

I follow behind Rusty as he leads me to his motorcycle shop. It's in a town just west of Atlanta called Doraville. We turn in the lot. There are two sides to the business. One side is a retail storefront, and the other side is a garage with several bay doors. There's a sign on the wall that reads Rusty's Custom Chop Shop. Lettering on the plate glass windows states, *Full Service, Performance Engine Building, Custom Builds, Financing Available.*

There are several bikes parked out front. I'm not sure if they're ones he's built or just customers'.

He parks near the door, and I take the spot next to him and climb out. He pulls off his helmet, drops it on the seat, and grabs my hand, leading me in. I'm impressed with the place, and I can tell by his face, he's proud of it.

There are about half a dozen shiny bikes parked inside the store, all with beautiful lines and all custom as hell.

"So, Chop Shop… What does that mean?" I ask.

"Means I build custom chopper style motorcycles."

"They're beautiful."

There are a few racks with shirts and helmets and accessories and a full wall of parts hanging on pegboard. A counter in the back is set up with a register. The guy behind it is on the phone, but lifts a hand and waves hello.

Through an arched doorway on the right is another room. Rusty leads me into it. It's got more merchandise and some chairs for waiting. Beyond it is an office with a small glass window.

I follow Rusty into the office. It's a good size and air conditioned, thankfully, with a desk on one side. It's what's on the other side that catches my eye. A custom bike is parked like a showpiece. There's also an armless leather couch and a round glass coffee table with a funky tripod stand made out of chrome springs. The walls are lined horizontally in what looks like scrap wood, with assorted sizes of planks of varying ages and stains that look cool as hell. Framed prints of the business and some magazine and newspaper write-ups decorate it.

There's another metal door opposite the waiting area. When Rusty opens the door, I see it's the garage. Noise and hot air roll in. We walk through, and I see three guys working on bikes in various stages of repair or build. There are several ordinary stock bikes being worked on in the first two bays. Beyond that I can see several custom works of art.

The men look up and stare at me. One gives a whistle until Rusty cuts him off with a slashing motion across his throat.

"Listen up. This is Ashlynn. She's takin' over for Flo, so cut her some slack while she gets the hang of things around here. I expect you to show her the utmost respect, understand?"

They nod.

"One more thing. She's got a sweet ride that's gonna be parked out front when she's here. Anybody touches it, I'll cut off his dick."

With that, he leads me inside the office without even giving me their names. I'm still a little opened-mouthed over that last comment, but he carries on like he didn't just threaten all his employees with bodily harm.

"So this is where you'll hang. I need you to do the invoicing mostly and pay the bills. Things like utilities, parts suppliers and such. The guys up front will order the parts, so you don't have to worry about any of that end. I'll also need you to submit payroll and make sure it's done on time. The guys get a little pissy if their paychecks are late."

"I'm sure."

"Things might be a little cluttered. Flo was crap at filing. Never could find anything."

I take in the cluttered desk. "Why'd she leave?"

"Probably because she knew I was about to fire her ass. She started seein' some guy, and I'm pretty sure she started using. Crystal meth would be my guess. He was a shitty influence. I tried to warn her, but the heart wants what the heart wants. She wouldn't listen."

"That's so sad. What was the final straw that made you want to let her go?"

"Payroll started to get fucked up. I can't keep top mechanics if I'm gonna treat 'em like that. They can pick up their shit and go anywhere. The first time it happened, she managed to get their money direct deposited the next Monday. Still, their money wasn't available to them until Tuesday. That sucks when you're livin' paycheck to paycheck, and you expect that money to be in your account Friday morning. The second time I had to pay them out of my pocket to prevent a fucking riot. That was the last straw. She must have known she'd fucked up because she never came in that Friday. I called her, and her boyfriend answered, said she was done working for me. That was fine with me. It was too bad, though, because before she met that drugged-out shit for brains, she was actually pretty good at her job, bar the clutter."

"Okay, so stay on top of payroll, got it. Anything else?"

He grins and steps forward, backing me up until my ass hits the desk. "Keep your boss happy. That's number one."

I smile. "And how do I do that?"

"I'm sure you'll think of something." He glances to the window into the waiting area and the window in the door to the garage. "I'm gonna have to get some blinds put up."

I roll my eyes. "Is that why there's a couch in here?"

He chuckles. "You think I need a couch? I can fuck you bent over this desk just fine."

I glance to the couch thinking of Flo. "You didn't, you know…with Flo?"

"Fuck no."

I stare into his eyes. He doesn't look away.

"Not gonna lie. There've been women. A lot, but I usually don't piss where I eat."

"Good to know."

"Until now."

"I thought we had a deal?"

"Deals change, sweetheart." He lifts me and sets me on the desk.

"Rusty!"

"Never said I wouldn't try and change your mind." He takes my head in his hands, tilts it back, and kisses me, reminding me all over again how good he is at it.

We're interrupted when the door to the garage opens, and the man who was with Rusty at the gun counter walks in, talking before he sees me. "Hey, whose little yellow hot rod's parked out front?"

Rusty breaks the kiss and swivels his head toward the door. "Get lost, Reno."

"Aren't you gonna introduce us, Prez?"

Rusty lets out an impatient sigh. "Fine. VP, this is Ashlynn or as I call her, Vegas. Ashlynn, this is my VP, Reno."

"Pleased to meet you, Vegas."

"Now see what you've started?" I snap at Rusty's grinning face. "It's not funny. I don't like that nickname."

"Too bad," Rusty says with a chuckle.

"Don't worry, Ashlynn. I won't call you Vegas."

"Thank you. See, *he* has manners." I fling a hand in Reno's direction.

"Naw, I think Hot Rod suits you better," Reno replies, and Rusty snorts with laughter.

My mouth drops open.

Rusty lifts a finger under my jaw, shutting it. "Hot Rod's gonna be takin' Flo's place in the office."

Reno folds his arms and rocks back on his heels. "Oh, she is, is she? That should be interesting."

"How so?" Rusty asks.

"You know as well as I do, you ain't gonna keep the guys out of here. They're gonna be comin' in here every five minutes wanting to ask some stupid question about a customer's invoice or their paycheck. Hell, they'll make shit up."

"Oh hell no, they won't."

Reno's shoulders shake in silent laughter. "Yeah, good luck with that one, Prez."

He turns to the door and stops with one hand on the knob. "Welcome aboard, Hot Rod."

After he leaves, I glare up at Rusty. "What's with you guys and nicknames?"

He grins, takes my head in his hands again and pulls me to him. "Shut up and kiss me."

After a long kiss, he finally pulls back. "I've gotta go check on some shit with the boys. I know the desk's a mess, but maybe you can try to sort it out to something you can work with." He jerks his chin at the computer. "Password's Twizzlers. I'll be back in an hour or so to show you the programs."

I arch a brow. "Twizzlers?"

He gives me a boyish grin. "The red ones are the best. Those black liquorish ones suck donkey balls."

I burst out in laughter. "I'll remember that. Strawberry Twizzlers are the way to your heart."

CHAPTER TEN

Ashlynn—

At six p.m. with the shop closed up, I'm standing by my car, Rusty holding my hands.

"How was your first day?" he asks with a grin.

"Fine. I think I got a lot done. I organized the accounts payable. Tomorrow I'll tackle receivables."

"So, you're comin' back then? I was afraid Gully would run you off."

Ah yes, Gully. The man could talk a cornstalk's ears off. Twice Rusty had to run him out of the office. He's old as dirt, grizzled in the way that old bikers are and knows something about almost everything. Not in a bad way… in a been-around-the-block-way. He seems lovable and harmless, but he did suck the efficiency out of my day today. It was fun listening to all his stories, but I didn't get much done when he was parked on the couch in my office.

I call it *my* office, but it feels more like Rusty's office. I'm just using it. Which I guess is what happened with Flo. I'd asked him about it, and he'd said he wasn't one for sitting anywhere for long periods. He had to get up and move.

I'd asked him why he had such a nice office if he didn't ever use it. He'd said it was all about setting the right impression for customers. Some lay down tens of thousands of dollars for his custom bikes. He needed to have a place to talk with them and nail down the deal. That wasn't over the sales counter, and it wasn't in the noisy garage.

"I'll be back. I actually enjoyed it. It was fun to organize the files." I tilt my head to the side and frown. "That sounds crazy, right?"

"Yep. I'm glad you enjoyed it, though. I was afraid you'd hate everything about this place."

At one point during the afternoon, I'd sat there at his desk, wondering how I'd gone from the lights of Vegas and the world of high rollers to a motorcycle garage run by a dangerous MC. I assumed they were dangerous; I really had no proof of it at the moment. But here I was, oddly comfortable where I'd landed.

I stare up at him. "It's a world apart from where I came, I can't deny that, but"—I shrug—"I don't know, something about it feels right, feels comfortable, you know?"

He chuckles. "Hot Rod, I know exactly that feeling. Just surprised as hell you feel it, too. Pleased, but surprised."

"Who'd have thought, huh?"

He backs me against the car door. "So, you want the job then? You'll stick around?"

I suck my lips into my mouth. I'm almost afraid to make any promises. If I say yes, I need to keep my word. I don't want to be the type to let him down, like Flo. "How about a trial run? Say a month, see where we are at the end?"

He searches my eyes. "I can give you that. A month, then."

"Um, we never talked about salary."

"I guess we didn't. Job pays five bucks over minimum. I know it's not much, but you also get a bonus at the end of the year tied to profits, if you stick around that long."

"I see." It was nothing compared to what I've been earning. But I hadn't really taken the job for the pay, more for something to keep me from climbing the walls with boredom, plus it meant I'd get to

DIRTY DEALS

see more of Rusty. Win, win. Besides, I had plenty of money to tide me over until I decided what to do. Hiding out from the Rialtos brothers was my main objective, and this was probably as good a place as any. Besides, at least I'd have an ally in Rusty, and who knew if I'd need it. I doubted they could find me, but I really had no idea how motivated they were or what resources they had at their disposal.

"That amount gonna work for you?"

"Yes, for now."

He grins at my response. "For now, huh? You gonna try to renegotiate this later?"

"I'd be stupid not to at least try, wouldn't I? After all, every woman should know her own value."

"I got a feelin' you're worth more than I can ever afford."

I shrug. "Maybe we can work the balance out in trade."

He bursts out laughing. "Babe, you are one firecracker." He takes my face in his hands and gives me a kiss that curls my toes. I'm breathless when he releases me and opens my car door. "Be safe. Text me when you get home, okay?"

"Sure."

"I've got some stuff to take care of with the club tonight, but I'll call you when I get free, okay?"

"Okay." I climb inside, and he leans in the door for one last kiss before closing it.

I fire up my baby and back out, content to see him standing there watching until I'm pulling from the lot. Only then does he move to his bike.

***

The drive home is slow with traffic until I get into the country. I stop and pick up a bottle of wine and a microwave dinner. It's dusk and the horizon is turning a pretty purple blue as I park in the garage and go inside the back door. It's eerily quiet and dark. I turn on some lights, feeling better knowing I have the gun in my purse. Rusty made me bring it with so I'd have it when I arrived home.

I move through the house, turning on lamps, feeling silly for being scared like a child. I'm a grown woman. I walk into the kitchen and heat up my dinner, then take it and a glass of wine to the porch to watch the last streaks of the sunset.

The birds are chirping with their last chatter of the evening before settling in for the night. It's that perfect time between day and night. There's a breeze that keeps the bugs away, and I enjoy my wine and not half bad dinner.

I check the time and calculate the difference to Vegas time. I drain the last of my glass and go inside as it starts to get dark.

I move to the dining room table and open my laptop to check for any news of the murder. I can find nothing.

I close it, move to the couch and turn on the TV. I flip through the channels and stop on an entertainment news show. Suddenly what's on the screen has me straightening in my seat as a chill runs down my spine.

Axel Crow is at a podium with a group of people behind him, some in tears.

There's a news anchor speaking over the scene.

"Today country singer, Axel Crow offered a fifty thousand dollar reward for information in the disappearance of his personal butler from his Las Vegas residence. The man hasn't been seen since last Saturday night, and his family is distraught. Mr. Crow is close to his employee and told our Sandy McKay that he'll do whatever is in his power to locate the missing man and feels for his devastated family."

They switch to another story, and I turn it off. Oh my God.

I scramble back to the dining table and snatch up my phone. I can't punch the buttons fast enough. Shit. Shit. Shit.

A moment later Devon picks up.

"Hey, Ashlynn."

"I just saw on the news that Axle Crow is offering a reward for his missing employee."

His voice is low and hushed. "I'm driving a guest. Divider's up, but let me call you back in a few."

"Okay. Thanks." I disconnect and wait. I pace nervously, trying to run through all the ramifications. It's half an hour before he calls back. I answer on the first ring.

"Devon?"

"Yeah. I'm alone and can talk. You want to tell me the whole story now?"

"Have, um, the police been by?"

"Yup."

"Oh, shit."

"Honey, you can trust me, I didn't say a word, but they're pullin' video from the hotel right now. They already got me on camera waiting outside Peerless Tower that night."

"Oh, my God." I put my head in my hand. "Did they grill you?"

"Yeah. They already knew I picked you up. They haven't found out I loaded you into a car with your suitcase yet, but once the hotel pulls that footage and turns it over they will. Right now, Management's telling them you're on vacation."

"Shit."

"Ashlynn, what's going on? What happened that night? They're looking into a missing persons case. Axle Crow's butler."

"They killed him, Devon."

"Who did?"

"The Rialto brothers. They killed Ricardo Leona and then Thomas, Axle's butler. I was in the bathroom. They must have thought I'd already left. I tried to sneak out and they saw me. I ran out and made it to the elevator before they got to me."

He whistles. "So that's why you were so frantic when you came out of the building."

"Yes."

"But the police aren't lookin' into a murder. They didn't say shit about that."

"The Rialto's must have cleaned it all up and gotten rid of the bodies… I don't know. It doesn't make any sense."

"Fuck."

"I'm so sorry, Devon. I never meant for you to be involved in any of this."

"Don't worry about me. You just take care of you. You're wanted for questioning now, Ashlynn."

I nod, even though I know he can't see. "I figured as much. I'll be careful. Thank you, Devon. If you… If you hear anything, will you let me know?"

"Yeah, sure. Look, I'm pretty sure they're gonna pull my phone records. Maybe they can't trace that phone you bought, but if they can figure out where the call that I received came from, in regards to what cell tower it pinged off, they might get a location on you. Maybe not pinpoint it, but they might get some kind of radius."

"Oh, God."

"You better not call again, Ashlynn."

"Okay." My voice cracks. "Take care of yourself, Devon."

"You, too, babe."

We disconnect, and I stare at the wall.

I want to stay alive, but I feel so badly for that grieving family that has no idea where their loved one is or what happened to him. Thomas was such a sweet old man. The group with Axle looked like possibly Thomas's wife, now his widow, though she has no idea of that yet. Some were probably his children and some his grandchildren.

Guilt swallows me, and I can't breathe. I should have gone straight to the police. I should have come forward. At minimum I should come forward *now* and tell what I know, and give Thomas's grieving family some peace. It's the right thing to do, I know it is, but I'm so afraid of the Rialto brothers, and I don't want to die.

CHAPTER ELEVEN

Rusty—

From my seat at the bar I glance around the clubhouse. Not a whole lot of brothers stuck around after church tonight. The meeting didn't last too long, and I don't blame 'em for taking off. It's a good night for riding—the perfect temperature.

Pool balls clack together and draw my attention. Jammer and Bandit loiter around watching Quick make a shot.

Reno strolls over to me, and I lift my bottle to the prospect behind the bar, signaling to get me another one.

He pulls a cold one from the ice, twists the top and sets it before me. "Need anything else, Prez?"

I shake my head as Reno takes the stool next to me.

"VP, what can I get you?" the prospect asks.

"Whiskey." Reno turns to me.

"How's Butterfly? Why didn't you take off to go be with your new bride?" I ask.

"Now that her morning sickness is finally over, she's doing a spa night at a friend's house."

I nod. "Good of you to let the girl up for air now and then."

He grins. "I'm a nice guy that way."

I chuckle. "Right."

"So, how's you're new little hottie?"

"You mean Hot Rod? And by the way, thanks for that. I think

it'll stick."

"You're welcome."

My eyes stray to the pool table again, and Reno twists to look over his shoulder. "What do you think of Quick? Were we right to give him another shot?" I ask.

Reno continues studying the man. "Hard tellin' yet. So far, so good. I really want to know if he's gonna have our backs when shit hits the fan."

"Well, hopefully that won't be happening anytime soon. Things with the Evil Dead are good now that we have that alliance made. Death Heads have been staying out of our fucking business and keeping to the other side of the Florida border. So all's well for the moment."

Reno huffs out a silent laugh. "Unfortunately, you and I have been around long enough to know those moments never last."

I take a hit off my beer, and he knocks back a shot, then asks, "You driven that sweet ride of your girl's yet?"

I grin. "Yep. That thing corners like it's on rails. Fucking amazing."

He chuckles. "You get a hard-on drivin' it?"

"Almost. No fucking lie, it's sweet."

"Take your word for it."

"You'll have to because Hot Rod's never gonna let you drive it."

"That comin' from you or her?"

"Both."

"You suck the fun out of everything."

"I'm president. That's my job now."

He rolls his eyes. "Speakin' of that patch you're wearin', heard from Leroy. You remember him?"

"Yeah. Been in Rutledge, what now, ten years?"

"Yep. Guess who his new cellblock mate is?"

DIRTY DEALS

"You're shittin' me."

"Nope. Ol' prez."

"Thought he was goin' to Walker State Prison in Rock Springs."

Reno shrugs. "Maybe they're overcrowded. All I know is that's what Leroy said. Any word from the old man? He try and contact you?"

"Not since before he was transferred. I talked to him on the phone and told him about Rat. Let him know we killed the son-of-a-bitch, but that wasn't any consolation for the decades he'll do in prison. He wanted to put a hit out on the judge. I convinced him otherwise. Told him he doesn't run things around here anymore. Told him any effort to expose the way Rat rigged his sentence would expose the entire club to charges.

"Fuck."

"Yeah, he doesn't want to turn his back on the club, so he'll keep his mouth shut. With any luck, he might get out on parole."

"You believe that?"

"Fuck no. But I had to throw the man a bone. Can't have him losing all hope. Who knows with overcrowding… His crime wasn't violent after all, just drug charges."

"Guess so." Reno is quiet for a minute. "Glad I'm not him. Can you imagine facing decades in that shithole?"

"Don't even want to think about it."

"Leroy says that place is next to a landfill. On a hot day it stinks like a million dirty diapers and rotten eggs."

"You tryin' to make me puke?"

He grins. "Sorry."

"So, I take it you're not itching to make a run down to Columbus and visit your former president?"

"Nope. No itch." He rubs my head. "I'm too busy keeping my current president happy."

"What's the deal with Gypsy?" I ask.

He takes a sip of his whiskey. "What do you mean?"

"Showin' up late for Church. Tryin' to sneak his cell phone in. What the fuck is that shit about?"

"No clue."

"He hasn't said anything to you?"

"Nope."

"He's been acting strange, disappearing without a word, and now startin' to show up late for meetings. This shit's getting more and more regular. Time to nip it in the bud."

"You try talkin' to him?" Reno asks.

"Yeah, says everything's fine. Whatever's up, he won't talk about it. Have Jammer or Bandit keep an eye on him."

"Done."

I drain my second beer.

I smell her perfume before her arms slip around my neck. I twist my head. Vee. Her name's Victoria, but she's been Vee since the first night she attended a club party. She's kind of a stuck up bitch, never smiles, always a cutting glance for the other girls. But the boys like her because she can suck the chrome off a trailer hitch.

Myself, I haven't been too impressed. First, I can't stand a girl who thinks she's got some kind of sexual expertise that'll have me falling at her feet. I've never found one who wasn't over rating herself. Vee's no different.

Second, I like my women without a shit ton of attitude, thinkin' she's doin' me a fucking favor. Especially when I know she's dying to be in my bed.

I don't fucking play games. Not those kind anyway.

"Hey, baby. You feelin' all right tonight?" she purrs.

"Yup."

"You wanna go somewhere private? I could make you feel even

better."

"Nope."

Reno snorts, his shoulders shaking quietly.

She throws a glare his way, then returns her attention to me. "You sure? I know what you like."

I turn my head. "Beat it, Vee."

"Come on, baby."

I turn and pin her with a look. "Did I fuckin' stutter?"

Her eyes glitter like ice chips, and her chin lifts, but she wisely withdraws her touch and stalks across the room to the guys playing pool.

Reno lets out the chuckle he's been holding in.

"She keeps that shit up, she's gonna have to go," I grunt.

He twists to look over his shoulder. "She's botherin' Bandit now. You're safe."

"She gets on my nerves. You?"

"I never could stand her. She was only good for a fast blow, then I always pushed her out the fuckin' door," Reno mutters.

"You never hit that?" I ask.

"Nope. You?"

"Once. It wasn't anything special," I admit.

"Neither was the blow job." He chuckles, and adds, "I hope you wrapped your shit. No tellin' where that bitch has been."

"Always."

We're quiet for a moment.

I ask, "Any of the boys holdin' lingering resentment about what went down with Rat?"

"There were some grumbles at first about leavin' Growler hangin' out to dry like that, the whole loyalty thing, but when they were set straight on the cost to the club if we tried to get the sentence overturned, they shut up quick enough."

"Self preservation. It's a reliable reaction, unfortunately."

"It sucks it had to go down that way, but here we are."

"It wasn't by my making. Long as they understand that," I mutter.

"They do."

"So, how long you gonna let Butterfly out of the cage tonight before you track her down and haul her ass home?" I tease, trying to lighten the mood.

He glances at the time on his phone. "About another fifteen minutes."

I slap him on the back, and we both chuckle.

CHAPTER TWELVE

Ashlynn—

I park my car in the same spot as yesterday when I pull up to the garage. I climb out, grab my cup of coffee and purse, and enter through the storefront. The guy behind the counter glances up but doesn't say anything. My heels click across the linoleum as I move through to the office and set my purse on the desk, along with the cappuccino I picked up on the way in.

There's a cute little coffee shop with a drive-thru just a block down the street that I discovered while waiting in traffic this morning. I hope it lives up to the amazing coffee the casino hotel in Vegas used to serve.

I move to the metal door leading to the garage and peer through the small window inset. I don't see Rusty anywhere and hadn't noticed his bike, so I sit down and sip my coffee.

It's been on my mind all night and on the drive in this morning whether or not I should come clean with him about why I really fled Vegas. I don't know if anyone can track me here, but now that I know the authorities are tracking down video from that night, it makes it all that much more real.

Seeing those scared and worried family members on television last night really got to me. I feel so guilty for not going straight to the police. I also feel like such a coward. I only thought of myself and the threat to me. A better person would have done the right thing and reported what happened; they wouldn't have run like a scared little rabbit.

I can bullshit with the best of them—and stroke an ego—promising all kinds of things when it comes to schmoozing my high roller clients, but outright lies have never been easy for me. I get nervous, I get anxious, and I almost certainly give tells.

I don't want to lie to Rusty; he's a smart guy, and I'm sure he didn't climb to the rank of president of an MC without being able to read people. I already think he's suspicious of the reason I gave him for buying that gun. Most likely this relationship is too new for him to call me on it. But it's there—that doubt. I see it in his eyes.

I'm surprised he's let it go. Perhaps because I'm just not that important to him. Maybe I'm just a temporary diversion, one he'll cut loose at the first sign of bullshit or baggage.

If I tell him the truth, is that exactly what he'll do?

For reasons I don't want to examine too closely, I don't want to lose him from my life. Not yet. And maybe if I'm being honest, I'm using him for protection. But the time I spend with him has made me happier than I've been in a long time. It's been forever since I've felt the connection I feel with him. All he has to do is walk into the room and the air changes. I feel it. It pulses between us like a living breathing thing. Desire, that's what it is, a pull so strong it's palpable. But it's more than that. I get him and he gets me on some invisible wavelength, some emotional current that sparks between us.

When he stares into my eyes, when he smiles… good God, I can't look away. It's like I'm under his spell. What is wrong with me? I'm behaving like a damn teenager.

I fan my suddenly overheated skin with a file folder, pulling my hair off my neck.

Of course he picks that exact moment to stride through the door.

He pauses with his hand on the knob. "The A/C go out?"

I release my hair and drop the file to the desktop like it's suddenly turned into a snake. "What? No, its fine." I swivel to the computer and begin tapping away on the keyboard, punching in the password he gave me yesterday.

He moves to stand in front of the desk, staring down at me. "You okay?"

"Sure. Fine. Why?"

"You seem... flustered."

"Nope. I'm good."

He drops his head to the side, studying me a moment before dipping his eyes to my beverage. "Island Coffee. Didn't take you long to find them."

"It's pretty good."

He arcs a brow. "Where's mine?"

I stare up at him. He looks serious. "Um. I didn't know how you take yours."

"Usually Americano, once in a while a double shot espresso, and if I'm feeling relaxed, a café au lait." He winks.

"I'll be sure to pick you up one tomorrow."

"Cool. What are you drinking?"

"Cappuccino."

He nods. "Okay. Make you a deal. I'll get Monday, Wednesday, and Friday. You get Tuesday and Thursday."

I smile. "Deal."

"You got the program down?" He nods to the computer.

"Yes, I think so."

"Good. Let me know if you have any issues."

He puts his knuckles to the desk, leans forward, and gives me a kiss. It makes me want more, and I have to refrain from taking his face in my hands and pulling him closer.

He pulls back, breaking our contact, and his eyes drop to my mouth. "Have lunch with me later?"

"Sure."

He straightens and walks out.

I slump back in my chair. Good God the way he makes me feel.

***

Three hours later, Rusty walks in and sits on the corner of the desk. I'm on a call with a customer whose bike is ready, giving him the total amount of his invoice.

Rusty's leg swings back and forth as he waits for me to hang up. He picks a pencil off the desk and taps me on the nose with the eraser end. I smile and bat his hand away. "Yes, thank you, Mr. Evans. We open at nine."

I hang up just as Rusty's attention is drawn to something through the waiting room window, and he stands. I twist to look and see two uniformed officers approaching the counter.

"Wonder what they want?" he asks.

The blood drains from my body, and my skin goes pebbly with goosebumps. "Oh, God," I whisper.

Rusty's head jerks around, and his eyes sweep over me.

My heart pounds, and I'm mentally judging the distance to the garage door.

"You okay, Hot Rod?"

My eyes are locked on the two men, but his voice draws my gaze. "What?"

"I asked if you're okay? You look like you've seen a ghost." His head swivels back to the men, then me. "You in trouble?"

"I… Why are they here?"

He lifts his chin, his eyes studying me. "Wait here. I'll find out." As if reading my mind, his gaze moves to the back door, and he points a finger at me. "Do not go anywhere, you hear me, Ashlynn?"

I nod, his words cutting through the choking fog that's swirling around my mind. *Oh, shit. Oh, shit. Oh, shit. Shit. Shit.*

My mouth goes dry as Rusty opens the door and steps out. He's visible through the window, moving to stand behind the counter, his arms folded, rocking on his heels. They converse a minute, but I can't hear any of it. He smiles, and the tone changes. They're joking about something. Rusty nods.

One of them is middle-aged and bald, while the other is younger with wraparound shades pushed up on his head. The older one leans a fist to the counter, his other hand on his hip, and that's when I see the gloves he's wearing. He steps back to look at a photo on the wall, and I see the knee high black boots he wears.

Fucking hell, they're motorcycle cops.

I feel the steel band around my chest loosen, and I can finally breathe again. I put a hand to my chest and suck in air. *Thank you, God.*

Rusty leans his elbows on the counter and chats with them a while. They're obviously joking and shooting the shit.

One officer points toward the entrance, and Rusty moves around the counter to follow them out.

I relax in my chair and stare at the desk top, relieved for the moment, but my mind is still racing. What if they had been here for me? Isn't it only a matter of time before I'm suspected in Thomas's disappearance? Surely they'll put me at the scene, if they haven't already. They'll want to talk to me; hell, they may even suspect me.

I'm sure the Rialto brothers have considered all these possibilities as well and want to find me before the police do. I have to face the fact that this isn't going to go away. I may be running for the rest of my life.

I've got two options. I live my life in hiding, always fearful of who might walk through the door, or I face the music, go back, and tell what I know. Am I ready to risk everything, including my life to do that? I don't want to be a coward, but I'm scared. I'm not a fool, and I really don't think the police can protect me once the Rialto's know where I am.

The door opens, startling me from my thoughts, and Rusty strolls in. "Grab your purse and come on."

"Where are we going?"

"Takin' you to lunch." His eyes sweep down me as I stand. "You're in jeans. You want to take the bike?"

"Okay."

"Relax, Hot Rod, they're gone."

"I'm relaxed." I'm such a big fat liar.

"Right." He grins and holds the door for me.

I follow him outside, and he moves to his badass bike. Its sleek and low and a work of art. He pulls a helmet from the saddlebag and passes it to me.

"Here put this on."

I set it on my head and buckle the strap as he throws a leg over his motorcycle, lifts it off its kickstand, and fires it up.

"Climb on."

I scramble behind him and put my feet on the pegs.

"Hold on, babe."

I wrap my arms around him, and he takes off across the parking lot. He roars out onto the street and shoots down the highway.

The wind blasts over me, and it's exhilarating. I marvel at how completely different this is from riding in a car. I feel entirely immersed in my surroundings, a part of it as the bike moves through town. He rides surprisingly far before stopping, but I'm enjoying the ride so much that I'm almost sorry when he turns into the parking lot of a restaurant.

It's a small barbeque place with some outdoor picnic tables set up under a vine covered pergola. He orders for us both, and we take our drinks and wait at a table outside for our food to be served. It's not crowded, and we're the only ones out here.

"So, let's talk about what happened back at the shop," he says, cutting to the chase.

I exhale and hedge. "What do you mean?"

"Babe. Come on. You looked like you thought you were about to be put in handcuffs. Tell me what's going on."

"Nothing. Cops just make me nervous."

"Why's that?"

I shrug. "Do I have to have a reason?"

"Hot Rod, you show up in town, obviously running from something, with a bagful of cash. First stop you make you buy a gun, one you don't know how to use. Now you tell me, that doesn't seem suspicious?"

"I told you why I wanted the gun. And where the cash came from."

"Yeah, you did. But there's a lot you're not tellin' me, Ashlynn. I get we just met, and maybe you don't trust me. I get that, babe. But if you need help, all you gotta do is ask. Understand?"

I nod but stay quiet. I can't meet his gaze, so I stab my straw at the crushed ice in my cup.

"You don't want to talk, that's fine. But I know there's more to this story. You decide you're ready to share, I'm here, okay?"

I nod again.

"Babe, look at me."

It takes me a moment, because I'm afraid I'll fall apart when I meet those penetrating eyes of his, and I've got to pull it together. I blink and look up, hoping he can't read everything in my eyes.

"Ashlynn, babe." He closes his hand over one of mine. It's big and warm and comforting. I look down at our joined hands. He wears a big silver ring with crossed pitchforks. It must represent his MC, the Devil Kings. It reminds me of the kind of man I'm dealing with, but his tender gesture, reaching out to take my hand, is in such contradiction to the position he bears.

"I'm fine, Rusty."

A smile tugs at the corner of his mouth. "Yeah, you are. Finest woman I've met in ages. But are you okay?"

My heart lightens at his compliment. "Yes, of course."

"Don't bullshit me, babe. If you're in trouble—"

I shake my head.

"You're a stubborn one aren't you?"

I smile. "Maybe."

The waitress brings our food, setting two red plastic baskets lined with wax paper down in front of us. The aroma hits my nose, and I inhale.

"Oh, my God, that's smells so good."

"Enjoy," she says, bouncing off.

I dig in, partly because I'm starved and partly because I want to end Rusty's questions.

He watches me for a moment, and then, apparently content to let it go, he digs into his own food.

"Tell me about your club," I say around a mouthful of food, licking my fingers.

"DKs? What do you want to know?"

I shrug. "How long have you been a member?"

He huffs out a laugh. "Seems like a lifetime. Joined up a dozen years ago."

"And how long have you been president?"

"That's a recent turn of events. Wasn't really in my plans, but shit went down, our old president got sent to prison, turned out our VP was a fucking rat, and I ended up in the chair."

"I'm sure that's not something you just "end up" in, right? Seems like there would be a little more internal politics than that."

"Some things I can't really talk about, babe."

I hesitate, a forkful of food halfway to my mouth. "Okay. So, how does it feel to be in that position? Can you tell me that?"

He shrugs. "It's new. Still breakin' it in. Coming to terms with the fact I've got to understand that my choices and actions will not always be painless or popular. I've always been a big-picture kind of guy, always lookin' to the end-game."

"That's a good quality for a leader to have, I imagine. Right?"

"Guess so. Club's goin' through an adjustment period. Change, whether it's for the good or not is never easy. Some people go their whole lives avoiding it."

"True. Change can be scary." I raise my hand. "I can testify to that."

He chuckles. "Bet you can." He nods to my plate. "How's your food?"

"Delicious. Thank you."

"So, work… You settlin' in? Guys givin' you any problems?"

"No, they've been fine. Why?"

He shrugs. "There's a beautiful woman in the shop. That's a major distraction for them, I get that; don't mean I'm gonna stand for 'em to be goofin' off, hangin' out in your office all day."

My fork slows, and I search his eyes. "I don't want to be a problem for you."

"No problem, Hot Rod. Just need you to tell me they start hangin' in your office. I'll set 'em straight. Okay?"

"Okay. I can do that." I study him for a moment. "Can I ask you something?"

"Sure. What do you want to know?"

"You ever been in a serious relationship?"

He huffs out a laugh. "Define serious."

"You know what I mean. Someone special, someone who meant something to you."

"The one that got away, you mean?"

I shrug. "Maybe. Did one get away?"

He hesitates, draining his cup and munching on the ice. He looks off toward the traffic out on the highway, and I think he's not going to answer. But then he starts to talk. "Few years back… there was someone. Thought we had something. But things went to shit real fast. Club blamed her for something that wasn't her fault. She fled. She thought I'd been killed." He shakes his head. "It's a long story, but bottom line, she's with another guy in another state now. They've got a kid. She's happy. I'm happy for her."

"Did you love her?"

He's quiet again, and I think I've overstepped.

"Thought I did." He shrugs. "Maybe… maybe if things hadn't gone down the way they did, who knows, maybe we'd still be together. And maybe her baby would be mine, not some other man's child. But that's all water under the bridge. Past is the past. Can't go back, can't change it. Best to just let it go and move on. I've had to learn that."

"That's a big thing to learn. Most men I've found don't let things go."

"You sayin' we men aren't an evolved species?" He grins when he asks and digs a piece of ice out of his cup and throws it at me.

CHAPTER THIRTEEN

Ashlynn—

The week flies by, and before I know it, it's Saturday. I'm sitting on the front porch, sipping on a lemonade and enjoying the day when the rumble of a couple of motorcycles carries to me. I look up and spot two bikes coming down the highway. They slow to make the turn into my driveway. I stand and take the steps to meet them in the yard.

Rusty's on one bike, and Reno's on the other with a girl on the back.

They climb off and remove their helmets. The girl is pretty with dark hair like mine in a braid down her back. She's got on a pair of high black boots that I'd kill for over her jeans. They've got buckles going all the way up on the side.

Reno throws his arm around her shoulders, and they follow Rusty, who cups my cheek and kisses me.

"How's my girl?" he asks.

"Good. What's going on?"

"You up for a ride?"

My face lights at his suggestion and the thrill moves over me, filling me with excitement. "Seriously?"

"Yeah. Get your shoes on, woman. Let's go."

"Okay."

"Oh, by the way, this is Reno's ol' lady, Kara."

"Kara. Nice to meet you. I'm Ashlynn." We shake hands.

"Come on inside, everyone. Would you like something to drink?"

They follow me inside and wait while I throw on a pair of shoes and braid my hair like Kara's. I walk into the living room, wrapping an elastic band around the end, my sunglasses hanging from my mouth.

"You ready, babe?" Rusty asks.

We move outside, and he passes me a helmet from his saddlebag. I put it on and climb on behind him. He pats my leg.

"Hang on."

I do as he says, and we roar out onto the highway.

We ride for miles and miles through the countryside, finally stopping at a diner for lunch.

We talk and laugh, and I realize how funny the guys are. They cut up with each other constantly.

Kara is a sweet girl, although years younger than me. Still, she's got a maturity rare for her age.

It's a glorious day, and I enjoy myself immensely, letting go of my problems and just having fun living in the moment.

Mid-afternoon, Rusty pulls back in my drive, and we climb off the bikes.

"I had fun."

"Babe, Reno and I have some shit to take care of. Think Kara could hang out here with you for the rest of the day? It may be later tonight before we get back."

"Sure, if she'd like to."

Reno looks at her questioningly.

"Thanks. I'd like that," she murmurs.

The boys head out, and Kara follows me inside. I offer her a lemonade, and we sit in the dining room.

"I need to pee. Where's your bathroom?"

I laugh and point through the bedroom. "That door there."

She moves off, then when she returns she pauses in the doorway, looking down at my suitcase open on the floor.

"You haven't unpacked yet?"

"I've been busy, and the closet's small."

"I could help you."

"No, that's okay."

She holds the sparkly dress that hangs out of it. It's the silver one I had on the night I worked the poker game—the night I fled Vegas. She holds it up to herself and looks in the mirror. "Wow. I'd kill for a dress like this."

"Keep it. I was going to get rid of it anyway."

"Why? It's beautiful."

"Bad memories." I nod to the bathroom. "Try it on."

She comes back out in it and twirls. "Oh, my gosh, I love it. But does my bump show?"

I frown. "Are you pregnant?"

She nods. "Only a little over three months. I just got over having morning sickness. Thank God." She turns to the side and looks in the mirror, running her hand over her stomach. "You really can't tell?"

"Nope. Not at all."

She whirls on me. "We have to go out tonight. I know this amazing club that just opened. I haven't been yet, but they say it's super exclusive, but they let pretty girls in."

"But you're pregnant."

"I won't drink. I just want to feel pretty and dance. And you said I didn't show yet. After the baby, I may never fit in this dress again."

"Kara, I'm really not up for clubbing. But if you want to go with your girlfriends, go ahead."

"No. Reno wanted me to stay with you."

"Why?"

She shrugs. "I don't know. I'm new to this MC stuff. Maybe it's a thing. Maybe they do this when they leave town."

"What are the other women in the club like?"

"I haven't met any yet. Reno wants me to steer clear of them. Says they'd be a bad influence."

I can't stop the burst of laughter and slam my hand over my mouth. "Sorry."

"That's okay. He's so overprotective of me. I guess it's my age."

"How old are you?"

"I turned twenty-one a few months ago."

"And how long have you been with Reno?"

"About four months."

"So it's new."

"Um hmm."

I cock my head to the side. This poor girl barely had a chance to experience life as an attractive single girl. Reno nabbed her up before she had a shot at it. Maybe I can do something to correct that. "Kara, I changed my mind. Let's go check this place out tonight."

Her face lights up. "Are you serious?"

I nod. "As long as you promise not to drink."

"I swear. I'd never do anything to hurt the baby."

"Okay, then, but first, we're going to need a shopping trip. I need a new outfit. You're welcome to have that dress, but if you want to buy something new, that's cool, too."

"Let's go."

An hour later we're in the dressing room of an exclusive shop. I slip on the dress I'd picked and step out.

"Oh, Ashlynn. That is hot!"

"Really?" I look in the mirror and turn, checking all sides.

"Yes. You have to get it. It's perfect. I'll be in silver, and you'll be in gold."

***

I raise my cocktail, a glass of Jameson Irish Whiskey on the rocks. "To girls night."

Kara lifts her virgin cocktail in the pretty sugar-rimmed martini glass and clinks the edge to mine. "Girls night."

I take a sip and look around. From our seats at a high-top table up on an elevated section against the wall we have a good view. The place is not as obnoxiously loud as I expected, and I'm pleasantly surprised, though there is a packed dance floor.

We've already danced to quite a few songs. Men keep coming around, but we've managed to politely tell them no. Kara's flashes her sparkly ring at them, and it works like a charm.

Another guy approaches to ask Kara if she'd like to dance. Again she holds up her hand with the sparkling diamond. He nods and walks away.

I smile at her. "That thing's like flashing a cross at a vampire." We both giggle.

"It's my personal kryptonite against men," she adds. "I really appreciate you coming out with me tonight. I needed this."

"I'm glad you're having a good time."

"Aren't you having a good time?"

"Sure. So, tell me, how did you and Reno meet?"

"Oh, God, that's a long story. You wouldn't even believe it."

I chuckle and lean forward, dying to know. "Tell me."

"Let's just say it involved him doing some crap the old club ordered him to do, back before he and Rusty took over."

I frown. "When was that?"

"Not long ago."

"So, tell me about the first time you laid eyes on him." I put an elbow on the table and my chin in my hand, eager to hear some romance.

She runs her fingertip down the stem of her glass, smiling dreamily. "I bumped into him in a bar, literally. I'd never met someone like him, and when he looked at me I felt it clear down to my bones. We had an instant connection, that's for sure."

"And he snapped you up quick enough, huh?"

"It was quite the whirlwind with a lot of drama that I won't go into, but we made it to the other side, and I'm so grateful to have him. I know I can trust him with my life, and maybe more importantly, with my happiness."

"That's sweet."

"Oh, I know he plays the gruff badass, and he is one, definitely. But he's also got a sensitivity about him, ya know? It's like he picks up on my feelings and can read me like a book. I don't know if that's good or bad." She pauses to laugh. "But I've never felt more connected to anyone in my life."

"You seem very happy."

"I am." She tilts her head to the side. "What about you and Rusty?"

I pull back a little. I'm completely comfortable probing her private life, but not so open when it comes to my own. "Um, he's a really nice guy."

"A nice guy?" She giggles. "Don't let the president of the Devil Kings MC hear you refer to him as that."

I grin. "Right. But I mean, the side I've seen so far is that of a good guy. I'm sure that's not all he's been in his life. I'm not naïve. But he's been really good to me. I feel like…" My voice drifts off as I wonder if I'm revealing too much.

"Like what?" she prods.

"I know its silly, but I really feel like I hit the jackpot when I met him."

She searches my eyes. "You two seem really right for each other. You're really similar in a lot of ways."

My eyes widen, and I huff out a laugh. "Really? How so?"

"Well, you're both social; you're both good at talking to people and making them feel comfortable around you."

"I guess that's true."

She studies me a moment, like she's reconsidering. "But you'll probably bump heads on things, because he's a take-charge kind of guy, and you seem really independent. Hard for you both to win in a situation like that."

There's definitely some truth to her analysis. I can't help but take exception to some of it, though. "It's not that I don't like a guy that takes charge, I do, but—"

"Wait. You do?"

I shrug. "I mean in some situations." I smile.

She grins big behind her glass and murmurs. "The bedroom?"

I turn pink. "Yes, and other times. I like a man who acts like a man. I just don't want one who's going to tell me what I can and can't do and how to live my life."

Her brows knit together. "You think Rusty would tell you how to live your life?"

"Maybe I'm not saying it right. I just haven't had someone in my life for a while, and I'm not sure if we're going to mesh that way. Compromises and concessions and giving up things…that's not easy for me. Besides, I never seem to stay in one place very long."

"Relationships aren't easy, but I guess you just have to weigh whether you'd be happier without that person around. Me, I couldn't bear to think of my life without Reno in it. And it almost came to that. He thought it best if he was out of my life, thought he'd bring me nothing but trouble. I had to fight hard to get him to see that I couldn't bear to be apart, that he'd become my world, my everything." She chuckles. "Men can be stubborn asses sometimes."

"True that."

We both giggle.

Her phone lights up on the table, and she leans to read the screen.

"It's a text from Reno. He says they're on their way back." She looks at me with wide eyes. "We need to get back to your place, quick."

I take a sip of my drink, teasing, "Maybe now's a good time to test all that understanding you were talking about."

"I never said he was understanding."

I chuckle. "You have just as much right to have a life as he does. He can't keep you locked in a cage."

"He doesn't. I went out the other night with my friends."

"What? You had me believing you were never allowed to go out like other young people."

She makes an oops face. "Sorry. I just wanted to get you to come out tonight."

I roll my eyes. "See if I trust you again."

"Oh, come on, you had fun."

"I did. And it was nice getting to know you." I take a sip of my drink and tease, "Too bad Reno's going to kill you."

"Are you seriously not going to drive me back, so we can beat them home?"

"Are you seriously going to lie to him about going out tonight?"

"Not lie exactly, but what he doesn't know won't hurt him."

"How about you find out? Maybe he won't care. After all, what was all that talk about him just wanting you to be happy?"

She gives me a death look.

I smile back. "Tell him we're up here. I dare you."

She lifts her chin. "Fine, I will."

I lift a brow.

Her shoulders deflate. "Come on, don't make me."

I pick up my phone. "I'll just tell Rusty where we are."

"You wouldn't dare!"

"Kara, where's your backbone? What's the worst that can happen? You have angry makeup sex? Believe me, when he takes one look at you in that dress, he's gonna forget every thought in his head."

She bites her lip. "Well, the angry makeup sex does sound kind of appealing."

I giggle. "So? You want to tell him or you want me to?"

CHAPTER FOURTEEN

Rusty—

Reno sits astride his bike, his head bent, his thumbs moving over his phone.

"Who you texting?" I ask.

"Kara. Lettin' her know we're headed back."

I sit on my bike at the rest stop outside of Atlanta, parked in the spot next to him, and wait.

"What the fuck?"

I jerk my head toward him. "What's wrong?"

"She's at some club."

I frown. "What the hell do you mean? Did she leave Ashlynn's to go out clubbing?"

"She can't go out clubbing, she's pregnant!"

"I'll call Ashlynn and find out what's going on."

"Ashlynn is with her."

"Where?" I'm already lifting my bike off the kickstand.

"Club Apex. New place."

"Wait a minute, I know that place. Guy named Evans just opened it. I just did a custom bike for him. Let's go."

Both bikes thunder to life, and we take off.

Thirty minutes later we're standing in front of the bouncers.

"Is Todd Evans here tonight?" I ask.

"Who's asking?" the thick-necked guy on the right asks, his eyes dropping to my cut.

"The guy who built his custom chopper."

He doesn't say anything, but puts his hand to his earpiece and talks into his headset.

A minute later, he's moving the velvet rope aside and waving us through. We walk in the doors, and I already see Todd cutting a path through the crowd to us.

He extends his hand. "Rusty, how are you, man?"

"Good. Our girls are up here tonight. Just came by to pick them up."

"Sure. Stay as long as you like." He motions over a waitress. "Felicity will get you whatever you want."

"Thanks, man. But we can't stay."

Reno taps me on the chest with the back of his hand, then points to a section against the wall. "There."

I turn to look and spot the girls immediately. They're like matching bookends. Both dark haired in sparkly short dresses, Kara in silver and Ashlynn in gold.

My eyes sweep over my little Hot Rod. Sitting up on the dais, she's on display for half the club. Her short dress shows off her sexy legs and fuck-me shoes. There's no other way to put it, they're strappy little stilettos that every guy in here probably fantasizes having wrapped around his waist. From this angle I can see that the back of the dress dips so low I can see the dimples above her ass. And what a phenomenal ass it is.

"There better not be alcohol in that glass," Reno growls and heads for their table.

The crowd parts like the Red Sea when they turn and spot us. The only ones who don't see us coming are Ashlynn and Kara. They're too busy giggling over something.

We're almost to their table when Kara's eyes get big as she spots Reno. In response to Kara's reaction, Ashlynn twists to look over her shoulder and spots me. She smiles and drawls out is a sexy tone, "Hey, stranger."

I lay a palm on the warm skin at the small of her back and dip down to her ear to murmur, "Hey, Hot Rod."

Reno pulls Kara's glass from her hand and takes a sip. Then sets it down. "You're lucky."

She giggles and runs a fingertip slowly down his vest. "I am."

He cups her neck and hauls her to him, kissing her mouth, then pulls back to murmur against it, "Can't leave you for a minute, can I?"

"Nope."

I take Ashlynn's glass and lift it to my nose. "Whiskey?"

"Jameson on the rocks. It's my drink."

"It's not for the faint of heart. You don't half-ass anything, do you, babe?"

"Nope."

I set it back down. "A brown-eyed girl who likes whiskey. I'm done for."

She giggles and lifts a brow. "You are."

"You know what they say about women who drink whiskey, don't you?" Reno asks.

"What's that?" I say, not taking my eyes from hers.

"They're the best kind of complicated."

"I couldn't agree more."

Reno pins Kara with a hard look. "Since you're in such a partying mood, there's one at the clubhouse. You want to go?"

"You want me to go to a clubhouse party?" she asks, her voice sounding stunned.

"No, but at least there I know every guy in the place is not trying to hit on you."

"Well, what fun is that?" she teases.

He takes her face in his hands. "You want fun, I'll give you all you can handle tonight." He glances down at her legs. "Are you wearing stockings?"

She nods, grinning.

"Fucking hell, woman." He runs his hand up her thigh until he feels the garter-belt and snaps it. "You know what those do to me, don't you?"

She nods again.

He turns to me. "Let's go. I'm suddenly in a hurry to get out of here."

I drop my eyes to Ashlynn's legs. "You too?"

She shrugs. "That's for me to know and you to find out."

I go to reach for her leg, but she pushes my hand aside. "*If* you play your cards right."

"I always play my cards right. I got a feelin' tonight's my lucky night," he says.

Her smile falters.

I frown at her reaction. "What?"

She shakes her head. "What you just said, that's what we used to say at the casino if we needed one of the other hostesses to rescue us, usually from a client who couldn't keep his hands to himself. We'd say that phrase—*tonight's my lucky night*—and they knew we needed help." She smiles. "Sorry, it just took me back there for a second."

"That happen often?" I ask while Reno motions the waitress over and pays the bill.

"About once a week." She smiles and shrugs. "All part of the job."

"Let's go," Reno says.

We escort the girls out to Ashlynn's car, and they follow us to the clubhouse.

I'm not too thrilled with having every brother in the place see my little Hot Rod in this sexy dress, but on the other hand, I love the idea of rubbing their noses in how fucking hot this woman is and knowing she's with me.

We walk in, and the place is packed with brothers, hang-arounds, and even some of the strippers from the Cadillac Club. Loud music blasts through the big warehouse. Jammer, Bandit, and Quick have their arms around each other and are swaying back and forth singing along with Creedence Clearwater Revival's Run Through the Jungle. Gypsy is over at the bar with Vee hanging on his neck; I'm not sure which one looks more bored.

"Prez!" Bandit calls out and breaks from the three to stagger toward us. "You need a beer." He hollers over his shoulder at the prospect behind the bar. "Get Prez a beer."

I grin at the silly, happy look on his face. "You havin' a good time, you drunken fool?"

He grins stupidly, and his glassy eyes move to Ashlynn. "Well, hello, doll. Where have you been all my life?"

She cuddles closer to my side, and I throw an arm around her. "Relax, Hot Rod."

"Who's the babe?" Quick asks with a sloppy grin. He can barely keep his eyes open and looks like he's about to pass out. "You a friend of Butterfly's?"

"She's with me," I tell him, then turn and shout over the music to the room in general. "There's a yellow Porsche parked outside. You touch it, you're dead."

Ashlynn whispers in my ear, "Who's Butterfly?"

I grin down at her. "That's what we call Kara."

"Oh."

"You want another whiskey, babe?" I ask her.

She shrugs. "Sure. Are you having one?"

"Yeah, I'll have one with you." I pull her behind me through the crowd toward the bar. She scoots up on a barstool, and I can't help checking out her legs. I slide one hand to her thigh and squeeze as I lean across the bar. "Prospect, bring me a bottle of Jameson and a couple of glasses. The lady wants hers on the rocks."

He moves off to grab a bottle off a shelf, then sets a glass in front of me and scoops ice in the other for Ashlynn. From somewhere behind the bar he comes up with a couple of coasters that I didn't even know we had.

"Would you like a water chaser, ma'am?" he asks, leaning to be heard over the noise. She nods, and he sets her up.

I grin at his eagerness to please her and am proud he's treating her with the respect she's due just for having walked in the door with me. I pick up the bottle and pour an inch in her rocks glass, then do the same for mine. I set the bottle down and lift my glass. "Here's to brown-eyed girls who drink whiskey."

She smiles and comes back with a toast of her own. "To men who stop and help damsels in distress."

We clink glasses, and I watch her take a sip as I down half of mine.

She glances around. "I like what you've done with the place. Concrete, brick, and steel beams. Good decorating choices."

"Is that sarcasm?"

"Maybe." She lets out a tinkling laugh that I could listen to all night. "So, your clubhouse is a converted old warehouse. Interesting. Who's idea was that?"

I shrug. "Hell if I know. This has been the Devil Kings clubhouse since long before I joined."

"You've certainly got room, but it's kind of bleak."

"You should have seen it a few months ago. This is the new improved version."

She cocks a brow. "Really. What were the improvements?"

I chuckle. "We cleaned, for one."

Her gaze drifts around the twenty-foot ceilings. "Like what, the cobwebs?"

"You're a laugh a minute, kid."

She smiles. "Sorry, it's a long way from the Del Sol where I spent most of my days."

"I'll bet it is." I lift my chin. "Finish your drink, and I'll show you where some major improvements were made." I see the curiosity behind those dark eyes, and she lifts her glass and takes another slow sip.

My hands on her knees, I pull her around to face me, and hold her gaze as I run a palm up her leg until I find the bare skin at the top of her stockings. I quirk a brow, and she smiles. I skate my fingertips along the edge until I locate that garter strap.

At that point she bops my hand with a popping smack. "Hands to yourself, mister."

I slide my hand free and cup the back of her neck, hauling her close to plant my mouth over those soft plump lips. She tastes like the smooth whiskey she drinks with its honey and spice notes. I glide my tongue over hers, and she goes soft and compliant, letting me take the kiss as deep as I want.

It only drives my need higher.

I break free and stare at her, bumping my nose to hers. Then I put her glass in her hand. She gets the message and finishes it.

"Come on." I take her hand and pull her off the barstool and lead her toward the back. It's dark, but there are some lights every so often in the low ceiling. I stop and key one of the doors on the right.

"What's in here?" she asks.

I just smile, open the door, and pull her in.

CHAPTER FIFTEEN

Ashlynn—

I walk in behind Rusty and look around.

The room is big, with a king-size platform bed, a couple of nightstands, a highboy dresser, and a chair. The furniture looks new. It's black, sleek, and modern. Befitting a president, I suppose. There's a rug covering the polished concrete floor around the bed, giving a little softness to the room.

I turn and look back at Rusty. He locks the door and prowls toward me.

"That's a real pretty dress, Hot Rod."

"Thank you."

"Is it new?"

"Got it today."

His eyes sweep over me. "You want to keep it in one piece, you better take it off quickly. If I do it, it's gonna be in tattered shreds on the floor. That's how badly I want you."

His eyes promise all kinds of things—dark things, dangerous things. He's seducing me, and he hasn't even touched me yet.

I take a step back, then another, enjoying the hunt, disobeying his demand. His eyes fall on the pulse I can feel beating in my throat. He stalks me across the room until I come up against the dresser. He stops two feet away. He reaches out, and his callused fingertips glide along my collarbone. My skin tingles in response, heat flames through my body like wildfire, and I tremble.

"I really want to see what's under this dress," he murmurs, his voice a seductive lure as he dips his head closer to mine.

"Does every girl you bring in here fall at your feet?" I whisper, wondering just how special I am.

Those hypnotic eyes of his drift along my throat, and his finger brushes where my rapid pulse beats. He moves closer, inching forward, crowding my space as his head inclines toward mine. He dips down, his nose brushing along mine and his voice goes rough. "Want to know what I think?"

"What?" I breathe.

"I think you look beautiful at my feet, staring up at me with those dark eyes I could drown in. Makes my dick hard thinking of the last time you were on your knees, taking me deep down your pretty throat." He skates his hand up my neck, encircling it, cuffing it, bringing my jaw up until our mouths are a breath apart. "And I think you're absolutely dying for another taste."

I lick my lips. I can't deny it, any of it.

"Let me see what's under that dress, beautiful." He drags his fingertip along the neckline, and I'm powerless to resist. I pull the dress off my shoulders, and it flutters over my body to pool on the floor.

His eyes drag over every inch of me, and they light up with liquid desire. He sucks in a breath and steps back to take it all in.

My breasts are bare, my nipples tight with arousal. I'm wearing a tiny G-string panty under the garter belt and lace-topped stockings, all in a golden glimmer.

The gold stiletto heels with their sexy straps finish it off.

"Fucking hell, woman. You're a walking wet dream. Every man's fantasy."

I stand, slightly at a disadvantage, as he's still fully clothed. It tilts the power balance in his favor. Although, seeing the need in his eyes, I may have the power over him right now. He wants me, badly. I up the ante and whisper in a throaty seductive voice, "I bought it for you, baby."

His eyes flare at my words, and he reaches for me.

He threads his fingers into my hair, fisting it, and tugs, tilting my head until I have no choice but to meet his eyes. His fingers curl around the back of my neck, commanding and possessive, and my insides melt.

He kisses me, long and deeply until I'm breathless and so wet for him. He reaches for my breast, but I plant my hand in his chest and push him back. I raise my finger. "Uh uh uh. Your turn to strip for me."

He arches a brow but shrugs out of his cut and strips down for me. His glorious ink is displayed across his rippling muscles, and I have an intense need to trace every line with the tip of my tongue. I want to push him down on the bed and tease and torment him like he did me our first time together. Will he let me?

I move aside and step away, and we circle each other. I can see he likes that I'm playing coy, and the tease in me comes out to play.

He's lean and strong—badass written across him, like the ink covering his skin. His cocky grin is lethal. Excitement shivers down my spine as he stalks me across the room, loving this game as much as I do. The hunter in his eye makes my belly flip with the thrill.

My God, this man is so absurdly hot, so damned gorgeous. I know as president of this MC, all he has to do is reach out and take whatever he wants. No doubt he's accustomed to having it thrown at him at every turn.

His gaze wanders down my body, then slowly drags back up again and desire slicks warm and slow through my veins. That fluttery feeling that only a man can induce thrums through my senses. He makes me feel things I haven't felt in longer than I care to remember.

Dangerous things.

He lifts his chin to my panties. "Take off the G-string. Let me see that gorgeous pussy framed by that garter. That's how I want to fuck you—with those stockings and heels on and nothing else."

My pulse kicks up a notch, and I feel my body flush. I suddenly feel light headed and breathless. A moment later, his strong arms catch me around the waist, taking my weight.

"I've got you, angel." He lays me down on the bed, and the room rights itself. I clutch at his neck and drag his face down to mine, taking his mouth with a desperate kiss. He complies, kissing me like he'll never stop.

He cups my breast with his big palm and squeezes, then brushes his thumb back and forth across my nipple faster and faster until I had to have his mouth there. I pull his head to my breast, and he latches onto my nipple, sucking hard.

I almost detonate right then and there, arching up, my mouth falling open. "Yes. Yes. Oh, God what you do to me."

He plays and toys with both, giving them equal attention until I'm writhing. I know I'm drenched when he reaches for the little bow ties at my hips and slowly pulls them free.

He whistles. "So goddamn beautiful."

He hooks a finger under one garter strap and snaps it, and I jump... then giggle. He smiles at me and glides down my body, his mouth on my pussy at last. The man has a magic tongue, and I lay back and enjoy all the ways he uses it, driving me higher and higher. He adds his fingers, driving inside me, while his thumb takes up its ministrations on my clit.

"Play with your nipples," he orders, and I'm helpless to refuse him anything. I do it, pinching and twisting, moaning in need.

"Don't stop," he growls as he torments my clit and that spot deep inside me with his skilled fingers.

"Make me come, Rusty. Please."

"Been waitin' for you to ask, Hot Rod."

He amps up his strokes, and I explode, crying out.

When I float back to reality, he pulls his fingers free, and I feel empty. I want him to fill me. I grab his face in my hands.

"Take me. Hard. Please."

He rises and flips me over, yanking and moving me around the bed with ease until he has me how he wants me. My arms outstretched, up on my knees, with my ass in the air.

I wait like that, desperate for his touch, anticipation stringing my nerves tight. I bury my face in the mattress, eager and impatient.

I feel his finger slide under the garter strap that runs down my ass cheek. He pulls and snaps it, making me jump. I'm so wet, but at that sting another gush of wetness flows from me. He slides his fingers in the wetness.

"That's my good girl. So fucking wet and ready for me. I love how your body trembles with need. Maybe I'll keep you like this all night."

"Baby, please."

"You do beg so sweetly, though." His face brushes against me, and I feel his tongue plunge deep in my pussy.

I stutter in a breath and push against him, wanting more, always more. He's got me strung so tight I don't know how much I can take.

"Don't move," he orders, and I'm helpless at his command.

He licks and laps and takes his fill, toying with me, knowing he's drawing out my desire until I'm so hungry for him I'm quivering. I feel my legs shaking, and with every movement of my body, my sensitive nipples drag across the coverlet, sending another zing of excitement through my body.

Finally, I hear the foil pouch crinkle, and I know I won't have much longer to wait. His warm hand cups my hipbone, and the head of his dick slides through my wetness, circling my clit. I practically hump it, thrusting my hips back and forth until the sensation brings me right to the edge.

"Oh God, Rusty. Take me, quick. I'm going to come."

He plunges inside me so deep I gasp. He reaches around and fingers my clit, rolling it between his thumb and finger, and then he takes up an intense stroke sweeping up and down until my orgasm hits me, long and intense, and sparkly fireworks dance behind my eyelids. I groan as ecstasy washes over me.

Rusty pounds into me, taking me fast and fierce, gripping my hips as he jackhammers into me, then shouts and goes solid, jerking me against him and holding me trapped as he comes hard.

Lord, this man can fuck.

He collapses on top of me, taking me down to the bed. He's breathing hard, his breath sawing in and out, his skin slick with sweat. After a moment, he goes to deal with the condom then returns and slips my shoes and stockings and garter off. He crawls in bed and gathers my sweaty body to his.

I don't want to move, my limbs too heavy. I tuck against him and put my ear to his chest, letting his heartbeat lull me to sleep.

Just as I'm drifting off, he reaches for my hand and brings it to his lips, kissing the inside of my wrist. I smile and kiss the warm skin under my cheek.

CHAPTER SIXTEEN

Ashlynn—

Monday afternoon, I'm standing in the office, digging in my purse when the door behind me opens. I look over my shoulder to see Rusty come in.

His hands slip up my hips. I feel his lips on the back of my neck before he breathes in my ear, "Hey, sexy girl."

I grin. "Hey, sexy man."

"I've got a meeting tonight with the club. You getting ready to leave for the day?"

"Um hmm." I find my keys and twist in his arms. "Call me later?"

He settles his hands on my waist and presses a kiss to my forehead. "Absolutely." His eyes drop to the desk. "Did Gully bring in the paperwork on that street glide with the transmission rebuild?"

"Umm, what was the name?"

"Abernathy."

"Right, here it is." I grab the yellow copy off the desk.

"Thanks."

"You're welcome."

"Drive safe, Hot Rod."

He moves off through the door to the garage, and I can't keep my eyes from dropping to his cute ass in those jeans he's wearing.

I grab my purse, hit the lights, and head out through the front doors. I'm parked on the side of the building today, because I've learned it's shady in the late afternoon.

I beep the locks open and have my hand on the door when I spot something sitting on the roof. I frown, staring at it. It's a poker chip keychain with the famous Las Vegas sign emblazoned on it—a common enough souvenir sold on the strip. I've seen a million of them. But the fact it's laying on my car raises the hair on the back of my neck.

I glance around the parking lot, my eyes darting everywhere. It's giving me the creeps. Did they find me? Is this some sick game of cat and mouse? Or am I overreacting? Is it possible Rusty or someone else in the club left it as a gag gift? I grab it and quickly slip in the driver's seat, fire the car up, and take off. I'm three stoplights down and constantly checking my mirrors before I feel comfortable enough to relax.

I'm being silly, but I can't stop the intuition that tells me different.

By the time I've made the drive out to the house, I've relaxed a bit. No one's been in my rearview mirror for miles. I slow and pull in the drive. I study the land as I roll in, the gravel crunching under my tires. Nothing seems strange.

I park in the garage, reach in my purse, and pull the gun out, taking the safety off, then I climb from the car.

I'm quick as I move to the door, unlock it, and go inside. It's not till I flip the deadbolt that I can breathe again.

I toss my purse on the kitchen table and set the gun beside it. I'm being ridiculous. No one knows where I've gone. I move to the fridge, pull out the bottle of wine I bought the other day, and pour myself a glass.

Then I stroll through the house to the front porch and sit. I take the gun with me, because even if I'm being silly and overreacting, better safe than sorry. I sit in one of the wicker rocking chairs and watch the sky turn orange with streaks of pink as the sun sinks into the horizon.

I breathe in the honeysuckle and tell myself everything's okay. The distant call of a whippoorwill carries to me.

A lone car drives past on the highway. I sit and rock and eventually relax enough to think about the weekend. Rusty is worming his way further and further into my heart. I'm afraid that when the time comes I'm not going to be able to leave him, and that scares me.

I take another sip of wine and think about the things he told me. I know it wasn't easy for him to confide those things. It's never easy to talk about past relationships, whether they end good or bad. I think it must be especially hard for men to open up. I appreciate that he did that. In a way I think he was trying to make it easier for me to open up to him about the things he asked about.

I'm just not ready to go there yet. I may never be ready. I'm terrified to tell him the truth. Before it was because I didn't know who I could trust; now I'm afraid I'll either drag him into my mess or drive him away. I don't know which is scarier.

I never want Rusty to pay a price for having helped me. And so I stay quiet about the truth and feed him a story about a stalker I don't have. It's better this way. The less he knows the better.

But I'm not sure I even believe that.

A big shiny tanker truck rumbles down the highway, and I wonder if it's carrying milk from the dairy farm down the road that I've seen signs for. Behind it is a car, stuck behind the slow moving vehicle.

My eyes focus in on it, and my head straightens. I frown. It's that same blue sedan I saw earlier. Maybe not. Maybe I'm just being paranoid. They disappear down the road.

The light disappears from the sky, and the crickets begin their nightly song. I pick up my wine glass and the gun and move inside.

I stroll through the living room, the dining room, and past the open door to my bedroom on my way to the kitchen to get another glass.

Something out of the corner of my eye catches my attention, and I back track two steps. I glance into the bedroom. My suitcase is open on the floor, my belongings looking disturbed as if someone had riffled through it.

I think hard, trying to be sure, but I'm almost positive the bag was closed. Not only closed but shoved by the closet door.

I bite my lip. Did I open it for something I'm not remembering? I step into the room and flick the light. Everything looks as I'd left it, except the pillows look tossed. I'm sure they were up by the headboard. Now one is cockeyed on its side in the middle of the bed and another is at a strange angle. I scan the room. The closet door is wide open, and I thought I closed it.

The hairs on the back of my neck stand up again. I set my wine glass down and tighten my hold on the gun. I step toward the closet, staring hard at the clothing. If someone were hiding inside, the clothing would be swaying, but it doesn't move. I back up a step and stand perfectly still, straining to hear any noise that would give away the presence of another person inside the house. I hear nothing.

I move from room to room, flicking on all the lights and making sure all the doors and windows are locked. After twenty minutes of nothing, I convince myself I've imagined all of it and that everything is exactly how it must have been.

I pull all the shades and put the television on, the volume down low, and I keep the gun at my side.

After a few hours of this, the muscles in my neck and shoulder are stiff and sore from the tension.

My phone rings and scares me half to death. I look at the

readout. Rusty.

I've never been so happy to hear from someone. I grab it up and answer it.

"Hello."

"Hey, babe. You still up?"

"Yes. How was your meeting?"

"Fine. Just having a drink with the boys before I head home."

"Oh," I say softly. He must hear the disappointment in my voice.

"You okay, babe?"

"Sure. Just kind of lonely out here tonight. It's so quiet in the country; it's kind of freaking me out."

He chuckles. "You want some company?"

"Sure," the word vaults out of my mouth practically before he finishes the question.

"All right. I'll be there soon."

"Okay. Ride safe."

***

Half an hour later, I hear his bike come up the road and slow to make the turn in the driveway. I peer out the window to watch the single headlight bump along the gravel and pull to the back of the house.

I set the gun down on the kitchen table and meet him in the yard.

He looks tired as he climbs off the bike.

I jam my hands in the back pockets of my shorts and smile. "Hey."

He strides to me, looking so good my heart flutters. He hooks an arm around my waist and hauls me against him for a long kiss. I wrap my arms around his shoulders, and when he breaks the kiss, I bury my face in his neck, clutching him tight.

He holds me a long minute, as if he somehow knows I just need to be held. His hand strokes over my hair, and he murmurs, "You okay, Hot Rod?"

I pull back, pasting a bright smile on my face. He's frowning, his penetrating eyes searching mine.

"I'm fine." I tuck my arm in his and pull him toward the back door. "Are you hungry? I could make you something to eat."

He pulls me into the bedroom, and we do what we do best. He strips my clothes and then his. This time he bends me over with my hands on the bed, and he takes me fast and hard from behind with no foreplay. It's exactly what I need, and I wonder if he could somehow read it in my face, in my voice, in my nerves. However he knew, his command and control of my body takes me right out of my head and breaks that energy that's had me strung up all evening. I give myself over to him, and he releases me from my problems.

He makes sure I come, bringing his hand around and strumming my clit as his thrusting escalates. He leans over me, bites my earlobe, and orders me to come, growling the command in my ear. My body submits, obeying him immediately before I can even process the thought in my head.

He follows me in four strokes, grabbing my hips and plowing hard, shouting as he explodes in orgasm.

"Fuck, I needed that," he groans, dropping us both to the bed.

When both our breathing settles, I whisper, "We can't keep doing this."

He turns his head to me. "Why?"

"I work for you now."

"So."

"I keep telling myself I need space, but then you look at me and I'm done for."

"Not gonna stop lookin' at you, Ashlynn."

"Rusty, I don't know if I can be what you want."

"Now you know what I want?"

"You're right, I don't."

I go up on an elbow, my head in my hand, and study his face while my fingertips lightly move down the scar on his chest. It's camouflaged by a tattoo, but I've felt its puckered ridge. It's a straight line about two inches long. I've been hesitant to prod him about it, but I think we've been together long enough that I can ask.

"What happened here?"

His hand comes up to cover mine, and I fear I've overstepped. The mood was nice, and now I worry I've ruined it. When he doesn't say anything I feel the need to apologize. "I'm sorry, I shouldn't have asked."

"No. It's okay. Just not something I like reliving." He turns his head and meets my gaze. "Happened years ago. I was stabbed with a dagger."

I frown. "A dagger?"

He nods. "Strange, I know. I'd bought it for that girl I'd been involved with—"

I straighten, dropping my hand from my head. "She stabbed you?"

He shakes his head. "No, but she got blamed for it by my club. Turned out she was innocent, but they saw her running from the apartment, assumed she'd done it. Especially when they realized some cash that belonged to the club was missing."

"Running from your apartment?"

"Yeah. I was passed out drunk. Some street gang broke in while Skylar was out getting morning coffee. They stabbed me and took the money. She walked in and found me like that, called the paramedics, then saw the club rolling up. She thought I was dead and that they'd never believe she was innocent, so she ran.

"Took months before the club tracked her down and brought her back. She was shocked to discover I was very much alive. I spent a long time recovering, but I made it."

"Oh, my God."

He brings my hand to his mouth and kisses my wrist. "That was a long time ago. When I told you about her before, didn't see the need to go into all this, so I skated over most of it."

"What happened to the girl? You said the club found her and brought her back."

"She vowed she was innocent. By then she'd hooked up with a member of the Evil Dead MC in Alabama. He came and offered evidence she wasn't involved. It was a mess, but I saw the truth. I let her go. She's with that guy now, and they have a kid." He shrugs. "She's happy. I've moved on. Some shit just isn't meant to be, ya know?"

I nod, because I don't know what else to do. I can tell she meant something to him, and it bothers me more than I want to admit. I feel the cold fingers of jealousy wrapping around my heart, and I hate that. I don't want to feel jealous, because that means I'm starting to let my heart get involved.

I reach up and brush the pad of my thumb over his lower lip. He looks vulnerable, and I know it's strange to describe this man in those terms, but he does. I lean over him and kiss his lips. He seems uncertain for a moment, before his hand cups the back of my head and his fingers lace through my hair. He takes my kiss and before long it's not enough. He rolls me to my back, moving over me.

It's several more orgasms before he lets me sleep.

CHAPTER SEVENTEEN

Rusty—

I must have dozed off, because something makes me jerk awake. I curl at the spine, lifting my head off the pillow. Moonlight streams in through the lace curtains. Ashlynn lies on her side, turned away from me, the sheet draped over both of us. I'm not sure what woke me, but I swear it was a sound. I grab my phone off the nightstand and peer at the time. One a.m. I swing my legs over the edge of the bed and sit, running a hand through my hair. I yawn and realize I could go for a smoke. I pull my jeans on and grab my cigarettes. I pad to the kitchen and flick the light switch. Nothing happens. I flip it on and off. I glance to the microwave, but it's dark. I pull the fridge and its dark too. Fuck. The power's out. I pull my phone from my pocket and flip on the flashlight app. I locate the fuse box just inside the back door. I flip the breakers off and on but still no power.

I frown. We didn't have a storm.

I pad through the house and out onto the front porch. It's warm outside, and I know without the a/c the house will soon heat up, too. I shake out a cigarette and dip my head to light it. When I lift my head to exhale, I notice the house down the road has a porch light on. I glance the other way. I can see a garage up on the rise, and it's got a light shining above the door as well.

I take a drag, wondering why we've lost power here. I move to the driveway side and see the utility light up on the pole is lit. So, it must be just the house, because the wire from the road to that light still works. Odd.

I take a drag and sit in a rocker. It's quiet as hell out here. I check my phone and see that Jammer texted about ten minutes ago. I frown, at first thinking maybe that's what woke me, but it hasn't been ten minutes. Whatever woke me was not that long ago.

I read his text. He, Quick, Bandit, and Gypsy are at the Cadillac Club. Wants to know if I'm coming out.

I grin and exhale a stream of smoke at the sky.

Standing, I slip the phone in my pocket and move to the side of the porch to pitch my cigarette butt into the driveway. As I do, the post near my head explodes as a bullet hits it. I duck and see a dark shadow dash around the corner toward the back door.

Out of reflex, my hand lifts toward my shoulder for the gun that isn't there, because it's in my shoulder holster hanging over a chair in Ashlynn's bedroom. I stay low and charge across the porch, through the screen, and to the bedroom. I find my holster and slip my gun free. Ashlynn's still asleep. I shake her shoulder. "Babe. Wake up."

She sits with a start.

"Someone's outside creeping around. Where's your gun?"

"What?" She's still drowsy.

"Where's your gun?" I snap, and she's suddenly wide-awake. She pulls the drawer on the nightstand and takes it out.

"Get down on the floor."

She slips off the bed to the opposite side from the door.

"Do not come out. Shoot anything that comes through this door, understand?"

She nods, her arms trembling as she holds the gun.

"Remember what I taught you. Safety off. Finger off the trigger until you're ready to shoot. Take a breath and fire."

She nods.

DIRTY DEALS

"You shoot, you don't stop until you empty that clip, understand?"

She nods again.

I move through the door, closing it behind me, then run bent over to the back of the house. I can hear someone out on the steps, jimmying with the door. I contemplate whether to shoot them through the door or let them walk inside before I kill them. I slide closer to the kitchen window near the table and rise up just enough to peer out. All I can make out is a dark shadow, but then I catch a glimpse of moonlight on his face. He's got on a ski mask, so I know it's not her landlord or some neighbor kids goofing around.

I'm wondering if this guy somehow cut the power to the house. That'd take some skill and gives me a hint to the level of criminal I'm dealing with here.

If I wait until he's inside the house, I've got the legal right to kill him. But I don't give a damn about that. I pull out my phone, text Reno, and tell him to get the guys to Ashlynn's ASAP. I know he'll pick up, and I know he knows the address.

I slip the phone in my pocket and aim my gun at the glass in the top of the door. I fire three rounds through it. Feet pound down the steps, and I scramble to the window in time to see him dashing around the garage. I got a better look at him this time. He's tall, at least 6'2", and slender. I'm sure I didn't hit him; he was running just fine.

I scurry to the bedroom, staying low in case that asshole has a rifle with a scope stashed out there somewhere.

I lean against the wall and tap on the door. "Babe, it's me. Don't shoot."

"Okay." Her voice is soft and on the verge of tears.

I turn the knob and shove the door open. "You okay, Hot Rod?"

"Yes, is he gone? Did you get shot?"

"No. That was me. I scared him off for now." I move into the room and around the bed to her. She starts to stand, but I yank her back down, sitting on the floor next to her. "Stay down. Cavalry's comin'. Be here soon. I don't want to risk you getting shot. He's still out there."

"I should call the police."

"Help's already on the way. Be here in about five minutes."

"They're that close?"

"No, but you're not that far from the interstate. Won't take 'em long; they do a hundred miles an hour, and they will, I promise you." I watch her reaction. She's terrified, but I'm connecting all the dots. "Who's out there, babe? You bought that gun worried about someone."

"My stalker, maybe, I don't know."

"Enough to follow you across the fucking country?" I'm not buying it. "Somebody wants you dead, Ashlynn."

"I figured that out."

"Is there something you're not telling me?"

"When I walked to my car after work tonight there was a Las Vegas keychain on the roof of my car. Did you put it there?"

"Fuck no."

"A while after I got home, I noticed some things. I think maybe someone had been in the house earlier."

"Why?"

"Things in my bedroom looked out of place. Not like it had been ransacked or anything, just not quite in the same way I left them. I half convinced myself I was imagining it."

"So that's why you acted like you did when I pulled up? You were scared?"

She nods.

"This stalker—I want a name." She licks her lips, like she's contemplating whether or not to give it to me. I'm checking my clip, but my hands still at her reaction. "Babe, give me his name." My tone gets through to her.

"Everett John Malachi."

"He from Las Vegas?" I ask. She nods as I move to my holster, grabbing another clip and shoving it in my back pocket.

"What are you doing?"

"Gonna check the back again. Stay here."

"Rusty."

"Don't move." I slip out and move to the kitchen. I don't see anything. I prowl through the house, looking out the windows as I move. I don't see any movement. It's not long before I hear the distant roar of five motorcycles at full throttle. They rumble around the curve and over the rise. I see their headlights through the front windows coming up fast on the highway. They make the turn, one of them fishtailing before righting his bike. They roll across the front of the yard and dismount.

I shout from the front door, "Fan out. He was near the garage. No idea where he is now." I see Jammer and Gypsy take the left while Quick and Bandit head along the driveway. Reno bounds up the stairs.

"You okay?"

"Yeah. Shot off a couple of rounds, and he took off. Guy in a ski mask trying to break in the back door. He cut the power to the house."

"Fuck. That doesn't sound like some random break in."

We move inside. I watch the back, and Reno keeps an eye on the front.

"Babe? Stay put. Put the safety on the gun. Reno's in the house. Don't want you shootin' him by mistake. Okay?"

"Okay."

Reno moves to the kitchen, keeping an eye on the front but stays close enough to talk softly to me. "You know what you stepped into with this one?"

I shake my head. "Not a clue."

"Rusty, she was buying a gun. She's runnin' scared from something. I think whatever it is, it found her."

I lock my jaw. Every word he says is true.

"Just know what you're getting into, bro. You don't need to end up collateral damage in God knows what fucking shit she's messed up in."

"I don't have a fucking clue what I'm getting into. But I know I'm not walkin' away."

"You can't be with her out here all the time."

"I know."

"So what are you gonna do if we don't catch this guy?"

"Only one place I can protect her then, isn't there?"

"Fuck, man, have you really thought this through?"

"No. But when has that ever stopped me?"

The guys return.

Quick enters, and shakes his head. "No sign of him. Saw some tracks through the mud leading across the field toward that distant tree line. It's dark as hell, though. I think he's long gone."

I nod. "Thanks. Give me a minute." They go outside, and I walk into the bedroom. I push the curtains aside to give us more moonlight and sit on the bed.

"Did you find him?" she whispers.

I pull her up from the floor to sit next to me. "No. The boys found some tracks leading off across the field to the trees."

"Oh."

"You got anything more you want to tell me?"

"What do you mean?"

"I need to know what I'm dealing with, Hot Rod."

"I don't know who that was, Rusty."

I blow out a frustrated breath. I know she knows more than she's telling me, and it's pissing me off. "Okay, that's the way you want to play this, until we find this guy, you're coming back to the clubhouse with me. Pack a bag. It might be a few days." I stand.

She shakes her head, not meeting my eyes. "I can't do that, Rusty."

I grab her chin and yank her gaze to mine. "Yeah, you can, and you will. You want me to protect you, I got no problem doing that, but I drag my club into this, we're doing this my way. You're moving into the clubhouse until this is over."

"What?"

I drop my hand. "Did I stutter?"

She surges to her feet. "You don't run my life."

"Babe, I do tonight. Now move."

She turns away. "Maybe I should pack up and leave town. Find someplace else."

"Your choice, Ashlynn." I've been shot at, and I've about had it. I yank her around to face me, my hands on her arms. "That what you want?"

She stares into my eyes, and I'm wondering if what we have is just that easy for her to walk away from. For me, it's not. Finally, she shakes her head ever so slightly. "No."

While I've got her yielding, I push it a step further. "You're also gonna be in my bed and willing, understand? If I'm gonna involve my club in this shit for you, then that's the deal. Take it or leave it. You either stay and put some trust in me or pack your little yellow sports car and get the fuck outta my town. What's it gonna be?" I'm pissed. I'm pissed I didn't blast an entire clip through the wood of the back door and kill that guy. I'm pissed he got away, and I'm pissed my guys couldn't track him down. Maybe I'm taking it all out on her, but there's a boiling point, and I've reached it.

She yanks free, huffs, and throws attitude, but underneath she's scared shitless and not about to disobey me in this. She needs my help. She'll never admit it, but she's terrified.

"All right." Her voice is soft, but it's a concession nonetheless, and I'll take it.

"Pack what you need and meet me outside." I stalk from the room.

The boys are out in the backyard. I stomp down the stairs through the shattered glass shards and snap at Reno. "Have a prospect come board this up tomorrow."

Bandit is bent down near an outside power box. His phone's flashlight app lighting it up. "Looks like there's a main breaker out here that was thrown." He hits it, and the outside light comes on and the a/c unit whirls to life. He looks up at me. "Who the fuck are we dealing with here?"

"No clue." I look over at Quick. "See more than one set of footprints?"

He shakes his head.

I glance to the others; they all respond in the negative. My eyes land on Gypsy. He's busy texting on his phone, and I snap, "We keepin' you from something?"

He looks up, shoves the phone in his pocket, and has the brains to look contrite. "No, boss."

Reno shoves his shoulder and glares at him like he's an idiot. "The fuck, bro."

"Sorry," Gypsy grunts.

I huff out a breath. "Go on home, all of you. I got this."

"Not a fucking chance, prez," Reno snaps. "Club's not leavin' you out here unprotected. We'll escort you back. We already lost one president this year; don't plan on losing another one to some madman with a gun who could still be out there. We watch your back until we put this guy in the ground."

I want to argue with him, but I know he's lookin' out for his president, and that's his fucking job, so I shut up. The door creaks, and I look up. Ashlynn's standing there with her suitcase.

"You ready?" I snap.

She nods and looks at the broken window.

"Careful of the glass," Reno says, moving toward the stairs and offering his hand to help her down across the broken shards.

I move to her and take the bag from her hand. I stalk across the yard and pull up the garage door. I glance around, but I know my guys are smart enough to have already cleared it.

Ashlynn pops the trunk, and I shove her bag inside and slam the lid.

I open the door for her, but grab her around the waist before she climbs in and tug her against me. "I just want you safe. I can be a dick, I know. Get used to it."

It's a sucky apology, but she nods.

I press a kiss to her forehead. "Reno and I will lead you out. Just keep your distance back a few car lengths. Rest of the boys will ride behind you."

"Thank you."

I swipe my thumb down her cheek, and she climbs in. I shut the door and move to my bike. The boys all mount up, and we roll out.

CHAPTER EIGHTEEN

Rusty—

An hour later, I'm tossing Ashlynn's bag on the bed in my room at the clubhouse. She acts put out until I strip off my clothes and get in bed. I lean against the headboard and watch her. She stares, then huffs off into the bathroom and reemerges wearing a tight racer back t-shirt sans bra and boy short panties. On a body like hers, it's sexy as hell.

I pull the sheet back, and she climbs in next to me. She cuddles against my side and murmurs, "I'm not ungrateful. I appreciate everything you've done for me."

"I'd have a hard time knowin' that, way you're actin'."

"I need you, I know that, I just hate needing anyone."

"I get that, Hot Rod, I do."

"I hate being afraid. I don't play the victim well."

"You're a confident woman. You are no one's victim." I tilt her face up and peer down at her. "Hey, club's gonna find this asshole, and I'm gonna keep you safe until we do. That's a promise."

She shifts and presses her lips to mine, then puts an inch of space between our mouths. "Thank you."

I roll her to her back and move over her. "You want to thank me, I can think of a few ways."

She finally gives me the smile I've been waiting for, the first one I've seen in hours, and something inside me settles. Her happiness, I realize, is enough to keep me content, but keeping her that way may be a lot of work.

I make love to her this time, and that's what it is—love, not sex. I'm not ready to admit that to her or myself, but deep inside I know that's what this is.

She senses the difference, too. I can read it in those expressive brown eyes of hers. And if I have my guess, I'd say it scares the crap out of her, just like it does me. We don't talk, not a word. We just give and take until we're both exhausted and satisfied.

After she falls asleep, I reach for my phone on the nightstand and tap out a text to Reno. I tell him to have someone look into the name Ashlynn gave me.

I know he'll do a thorough job, leaving no stone unturned until he tracks down this guy. Everett John Malachi of Las Vegas, Nevada.

I get an affirmative answer and set the phone aside, curling around this woman that's becoming everything to me.

CHAPTER NINETEEN

Ashlynn—

The phone on the desk rings, so I answer it. "Rusty's Customs. Can I help you?"

"Hey, it's Bill up at the counter. Is Rusty in there?"

"Yes. Just a minute." I hold the receiver out. "It's for you."

He takes it from my hand, resting a hip on the desk. "Yeah?" He listens a moment, his smile disappears, and his gaze drills into mine. "He say what he wanted?"

I frown, wondering at his reaction, hoping it's not an irate customer.

"Send him back." He stands and quietly hangs the receiver in the cradle. He plants both palms on the desk and stares at me. "You know a guy by the name of Canfield? Warren Canfield?"

"Should I?"

"You tell me; he's asking to see me about the yellow Porsche out front."

I frown. "Maybe he thinks it's for sale?"

He straightens as the man walks up to the counter in the waiting area. He's visible through the window. We both turn to stare. He's an overweight man in his fifties, I'd guess, with gray hair and a mustache. He doesn't look like some connected mafia guy, but suddenly that's the thought that sends a jolt of fear skittering down my spine. I feel the blood drain from my face, and I grip the edge of the desk.

Rusty swivels his head to look at me. He must see my reaction. "You know him?"

I shake my head.

"Then why are you gripping the desk like you're ready to jump and bolt out the back door?"

I just shake my head again and remain mute.

Rusty glances at the man. "He's got retired cop written all over him. You in trouble, Hot Rod?"

"Maybe."

His sharp eyes cut to mine. "Let me do the talking."

I nod.

He moves to the door and opens it. "Mr. Canfield, please come in."

The man steps inside, his brusque stride slowing when he sees me.

"Are you Ashlynn Fox?" He looks like he already knows I am.

Rusty, God love him, steps between us, his arms crossed. "Who's asking?"

"I'm sorry." He extends a business card to Rusty. "Warren Canfield."

Rusty holds it up, reading it. "Private Investigator, Las Vegas, Nevada." He doesn't look back at me; instead he moves a step forward, backing Canfield up. "What brings you to Georgia, Warren?"

He reaches in his suit jacket pocket and holds up a piece of copy paper with a picture of me. I recognize it immediately as one from the Casino's website.

He turns and looks at the picture, reading the copy. "*The girl that can make your every dream a reality. Luxury Concierge, Ashlynn Fox.*" His eyes cut to me, although he has to peer around Rusty to do it. "That's you, correct?"

It's obviously me, and there's no sense in denying it. I'm just terrified of who hired him. My gaze darts to the window overlooking the waiting area. Are the Rialto Brothers here?

"Who you workin' for?" Rusty growls.

"Axle Crow. He hired me to try to find an employee of his who has gone missing. The trail leads to Miss Fox as being one of the last people in Mr. Crow's penthouse that night."

He makes it sound torrid, and Rusty cranes his neck to pierce me with his eyes. I'm sure he's suddenly got a million questions for me, but he refrains. Instead he asks, "You want to talk to this guy?"

My heart is pounding, and I'm not sure I want to tell this man anything, but I do have one question, and I can't stop it from bursting forth. "How did you find me?"

If he can find me, so can the Rialtos. In my mind I'm already leaving town, my car climbing the entrance ramp to the nearest interstate, my foot pressing the gas pedal to the floor. My mind is reeling a thousand times faster than reality, where I sit here waiting for him to answer.

"You lease your car. I pulled a few strings with the leasing company, got them to track the GPS. Didn't take much, really—a few backstage passes and a meet and greet with Axle, and they looked the other way on their privacy rules."

"Oh, my God," I whisper. My baby led him right to me. How long before Las Vegas Detectives show up? Or the Rialtos' own PI? I'll have to ditch my pride and joy, get some junker from a used car lot, and start running again.

My eyes lift to Rusty. I'll have to leave him, too. I'll have to leave everything here behind. I'm not even sure if it's safe to go home.

"Babe, take a breath," Rusty murmurs low. He turns back to Canfield and jerks his chin to the couch. "Sit down. Tell me everything."

And he does.

And while he does, Rusty moves behind my chair and rests his big hands on my shoulders, squeezing. I'm not entirely sure if he's doing it to offer me comfort or if he's doing it to keep be from bolting for the exit, jumping in my car, and disappearing from his life.

Yes, that's exactly what I'm thinking. I'm trembling in my seat, my leg bouncing a mile a minute like I'm suddenly jacked up on one of those double shot espressos Rusty loves. Only it's not caffeine; it's pure liquid adrenaline coursing through my veins. The fight or flight instinct has kicked in, and flight has fully engaged. Again.

A small weak voice dares to speak inside my head. *You can't keep running.*

Oh, hell yes I can. Watch me.

"What is it you want, Warren?"

"I want whatever information Miss Fox can give me about the night Thomas Reilly disappeared. He's been Mr. Crow's employee for ten years. The family is very worried."

Rusty squeezes my shoulders again.

I stay mute.

"You got a motel here in town?" Rusty asks.

The man's eyes move from mine to the man standing behind me. I think he realizes he's not going to get anything out of me now, and if he pushes it with Rusty, he'll get nowhere. "I'm at the Garden Inn on Hillcrest. Room 120."

Rusty moves out from behind my chair. "I've got your card. We'll call you."

Canfield stands, his eyes moving to mine. "The family just wants to know where he's at. He's diabetic you see; he doesn't have his medication, and they're very worried."

My eyes glaze, knowing no medication can help Thomas now.

"We'll be in touch." Rusty's tone brooks no further discussion. He holds the door open.

"I'll be waiting for your call." Canfield looks from Rusty to me, and then walks out.

Rusty moves to the window and waits until Canfield is out of sight and gone. Then he locks both doors, and moves to stand over me.

"I want the truth, Ashlynn, all of it."

"I told you, I—"

He cuts me off, cupping my chin and pulling my face up to meet his sharp eyes. "Don't. Don't even go there. I checked into the name you gave me. There is no Everett John Malachi in Vegas. Can't find any trace of the man. The jig is up, babe. If you're ever going to trust me, if you're ever going to tell me the truth, now's the time."

CHAPTER TWENTY

Ashlynn—

I stare up at Rusty—this man who in such a short time has come to mean so much to me. I'd do anything for him; I'd do anything for his love, but trusting someone to do right by me without having an exit plan is more than I can fathom. If the going gets tough, I leave. It's what I do; it's the way I've lived for so long that I can't grasp doing anything else. I don't give up control. I'm no one's victim. Opening myself up and being vulnerable is scary, but the feelings I have for Rusty are strong, and I'm so conflicted.

I'm quiet too long, and he takes a long deep breath and shakes his head.

"Babe, you pretend to be afraid of nothing, but you're so afraid of trusting me. Why?"

"I've been taken advantage of too many times. I swore to myself those days were done and that I could only count on myself. It's hard for me to be any other way."

"That's what you think I'm doing, taking advantage of you? 'Cause I thought we had a hell of a lot more."

I shake my head. "We do. I'm sorry. It's just… hard for me to trust."

"Hot Rod, I'll do anything for you, just don't ask me to stand by and do nothing; that's not who I am. I take control. I take charge. I fight, and I sure as hell don't run."

"I know that's who you are, and I wouldn't want you to be any different."

"*Do* you know that? Because I'm not so sure that you do."

I've pissed him off, and I know he has a right to be angry.

"Ashlynn, there was a day not so long ago in my MC that I did what I was told—I followed orders. Those days are done. I'm a leader now. I'm the president of an MC with a club full of men who look to me now to lead them. They trust me not to risk their lives, uncaring about the danger I put them in."

"I know you do, Rusty."

"I'm willing to go to the mat for you, Ashlynn, and to ask my club to do the same—for something that has nothing to do with them except for the fact their president has fallen for a woman in trouble and in need of protection. Maybe you don't get the gravity of that, but if I'm going to be that man, I need to know that you trust me with all of it. If not, we've got a problem. Hell, if not, we've got nothing."

I nod, tears falling down my cheeks. I dip my head to wipe at them. "Okay."

"Tell me what happened to you, baby. Sometimes telling someone makes it easier to bear."

I squeeze my eyes tight. "It was bad, Rusty."

He moves to a low cabinet across the room and pulls out a bottle of Jameson and a shot glass. I frown. I didn't even know he had liquor in here. He brings it to me and pours some.

"Here, babe. This'll help."

I down it in one gulp. He takes the glass and refills it, but I wave it away. He sets it on the desk.

I tell him the story, starting with my arrival at the penthouse right up until Devon loaded me into my car with my suitcase. He stays quiet throughout, letting me get through it without interruption. Then he picks up the shot, drains it, and slams it down on the desk.

DIRTY DEALS

I jump. My nerves are shot, and I'm not sure what he's most angry about: what happened to me, or the fact I've drug his whole club into this.

He stands and paces, running both hands down his face. "Mafia. Jesus Christ, babe. I had no fucking clue."

"And now that you do?"

He shakes his head. "What a fucking mess." He pauses his pacing and looks at me like my question just now sinks in. He blinks, almost like I've asked a stupid question, like there's only one solution. "Now we find those bastards and put 'em in the ground."

I let out a breath, and my shoulders slump. He's at my side in a split-second, kneeling before my chair and lifting my chin again. "You really thought even for a second I was gonna hang you out to dry on this, babe?"

I shake my head, my eyes on my lap. "I don't know what I thought. I've been terrified to tell you." I look up at him. "I have no right to involve you in any of this. I know that. It's not your problem. *None of this* is your problem, Rusty."

"All of this is my problem now. And I'll take that weight gladly, if for no other reason than it's not on your shoulders anymore. You can rest easy; let me worry about it from here on out, understand?"

"But Rusty—"

"No buts. A man who puts a hand on what's mine, never puts a hand on anything again."

"Am I yours?"

"Aren't you?"

I stand and so does he. I hug him tight. It's answer enough, and his arms wrap around me. I feel his murmured words into the crown of my head. "I've got this, Hot Rod. Don't want you worryin' another second about it."

CHAPTER TWENTY-ONE

Rusty—

I stand at the head of the table and slam the gavel down, calling the room to order. My brothers stop talking, and some lean forward to stub out their cigarettes, their chairs creaking. A stack of sheets off the printer makes its way around the room, each brother taking one. I hold up my copy with two faces on it. "The Rialto brothers, Nick and Luca. Read up on them because we're going hunting tonight. I want you to put the word out on the street, anyone connected to the club, supporters, hang-arounds, anyone, understand? I want every person we know looking for these guys. We're going to hit every hotel and motel. Check with the employees. That includes the front desk, cleaning people, whoever you can find, day staff and night staff. I don't care how much money you gotta promise for a tip that leads to getting our hands on them. They're dangerous—murdered two people in front of my girl, so be careful." I turn to Reno. "VP got anything to add?"

"Watch your backs. Be diligent about anybody coming around the clubhouse. They want Hot Rod, and they'll do anything to get to her. Jammer, you organize a perimeter watch." He unrolls a map on the table. "I've broken it down into quadrants. Gypsy, you take the Northeast. Bandit, the Southeast, Quick, you take the Southwest. Prez and I will take the Northwest. Each of you grab a couple of brothers to take with you. Questions?"

"This club related?" someone in the back of the room calls out.

I look around the table as well as the men standing against the wall. "This is personal to me. If you got a problem helping me out here, I understand and you can go play pool, get your dick sucked, or however the fuck you want to waste your day. The rest of you, I'd be grateful for your help. And know, you ever have a problem, the favor will be returned."

There's not a word.

I slam the gavel down. "Meeting adjourned."

They file out, some already texting their contacts as they shuffle through the door. Soon it's just the six of us—me, Reno, Jammer, Gypsy, Bandit, and Quick. The men I rely on most, the ones who stood by my takeover of the club and the ones who came to my aid that night at Ashlynn's.

"How many you think are gonna bail?" I ask Reno.

He looks at me with a grin. "After that little speech, I doubt there'll be a soul at the bar or pool table. I see anyone I'll beat their ass."

I shake my head. "No. This isn't club related. That's a fair fucking point to be made. I can't expect them to put their asses on the line for this; I shouldn't have asked, but I did anyway. I hope they understand."

"They're loyal to you. If they weren't, they'd have walked out the fucking door the day you took control," Jammer murmurs.

I meet his eyes. He's always been a straight shooter. Never hesitated to tell me when I've fucked up, so I trust him now. I give a slight nod. "Thanks. All of you. Means a fucking lot."

Quick grabs my shoulder and gives it a shake. "Let's go find these two motherfuckers."

***

It's a long fucking day of riding in the hot sun. I love a good ride, but all this stopping and sitting in traffic has my nerves on edge. Place after place, the answer's the same—no one recognizes the photos, no one has seen them.

Finally, I've had enough, and I need a break and a cold beer. I motion for Reno to follow, and I head back to the clubhouse. We climb from our bikes, stiff and tired, and trudge inside. One thing about having a clubhouse in a big warehouse, it's always cool inside.

Ashlynn's sitting at the bar, flipping through a magazine. When she spots me, she slides off her barstool and moves to me.

I cup her face and kiss her mouth, then press a soft kiss to her forehead as her arms wrap around my waist. She tucks against my side as I walk to the bar and signal the prospect. "Give me a cold one."

"Any luck?" she asks.

I shake my head and chug down half the bottle of beer. She deflates at my response and lines form between her brows. I hate to see her anxious. "Don't worry. We'll find them. It's just a matter of time."

"Okay."

"You hungry, Prez?" the prospect asks. "Ruby's got a big pot of shredded barbeque pork on the stove and some fixings. The men have been helping themselves to sandwiches as they come in and out. I could get you a plate."

I nod. "Thanks, prospect."

Ashlynn stands. "I'll get it." She looks to Reno. "I'll get you one, too."

"Thanks, doll. That'd be great." He winks at her, and she moves off.

I drain the rest of the bottle, and the prospect brings me a fresh one.

"She's finding her way, huh?" Reno asks.

"Yeah. It's not an easy life to blend into, though. I'm sure it'll take some getting used to."

"She stickin' around?" he asks.

It's a fair question, but I don't have an answer. "If I have my way, she is. But that'll be for her to decide."

"Kara likes her. Said they had a great time the other night."

"Good. We don't find these guys tonight, maybe she could come and spend some time with Ashlynn tomorrow, just so she's not so lonely hanging around here all day with nothing to do but worry."

"Sure. I can ask her to do that." His phone lights up with a text, and he picks it up off the bar. "Bandit says they've had no luck. Hit every motel in his quadrant."

I nod. "If he hasn't had a break, tell him to come on back."

It's near sunset, and the worst of rush hour traffic is over.

I pick up my phone and look at the time, thinking I should have called and checked on the shop, but I realize the garage closed an hour ago. I've got a special build the boys are working on, and I promised it'd be finished Monday. Not sure that's gonna happen if I'm not there to work on it. My crew is experienced, and every one of them is a good mechanic, but they sometimes lack the motivation to stay on schedule if I'm not there to crack the whip.

Reno looks over at me. "Sturgis is coming up quick, and we've got plans to make for the trip out. I talked with Shank at the St. Louis clubhouse. He wants to know how many to expect and what time. And we need to decide if we're stopping in Sioux City or Sioux Falls this year."

I nod and run my hands down my face, too distracted and exhausted to make any plans or decisions now. I need to get things settled with Ashlynn before I can even think about anything else, but the fact is what Reno is talking about is club business—what I'm actually supposed to be concerned with. Hell, I don't want to let my

DIRTY DEALS

chapter down. Especially not when my leadership is still so new. I fuck things up this early in, I'll have a mountain to climb to get that trust and respect back. I know that. I know all of it. But yet, I can't change the driving need inside me to protect Ashlynn. My hand on the beer bottle tightens.

Reno's eyes are on me. I can see him out of the corner of my eye. He knows the spot I'm in. He can read me like a book.

"We got time, brother. I'll tell him we'll get with him next week."

"Thanks."

We eat and then go back out for a few more hours, hitting all the same places, talking to the night shift this time around.

We're walking out of a crappy budget inn off Buford Highway when my phone goes off. I answer it as we approach our bikes. I glance down at the screen. It's Gully. I frown, finding it odd he'd be calling me this late. "Yeah?"

"The garage is on fire. I was driving by and saw smoke coming out of it. Hurry."

I shove the phone in my pocket and jump on my bike, shouting to Reno, "Garage is burning. Let's go."

We race across town, pulling up as the fire department is just finishing spraying it down. The building is still standing, but the store is torched. It looks like it took the worst of it. The garage looks like it is mostly untouched. I jump off my bike and find a Fire Marshal, telling him I own the place.

"Anybody stay here at night? Any chance someone's inside?" he asks.

I shake my head. "No. No one should be here."

"Looks like the store front took most of the damage. We caught it pretty quick."

"Can I get inside to look around?"

"Not yet. My men need to make sure the roof isn't damaged. Can't have it falling on anyone."

"Could you tell how it started?"

"Appeared some kind of incendiary device was thrown through the front window. There's a lot of flammable stuff in the store, T-shirts, carpeting, and such."

"How about the garage? Can I get in there?"

He shakes his head. "Just let us do our jobs, okay. I'll let you know as soon as you can check the damage."

I nod, because arguing will get me nowhere. I spot Gully and motion him over. "Soon as we can get access I need you to try to pull up the security footage. Hopefully, they aren't destroyed. I want the motherfucker that did this."

"You got it, boss."

Reno stands next to me. "Your girl's involved with a mafia hit, you give her protection, and now your garage burns. You think this is a coincidence?"

"Nope."

"Fucking hell."

"That's exactly what I'm going to rain down on the Rialtos."

I straighten, fear chasing down my spine at the thought of Ashlynn. I dig my phone out and call her. She picks up on the second ring. Thank God.

"Hey, babe." She sounds sleepy, like I woke her.

"You okay?" I ask, my voice gruff with the emotion constricting my chest.

She's sounds more awake now. "Yes. Why? What's wrong?"

"The shop was set on fire tonight."

"Oh my God. Is everyone okay? Is it all gone?"

"No one was inside. It's still standing. I'll find out how bad it is when the firemen finish. Garage side looks in one piece."

DIRTY DEALS

"How did it start?"

I almost tell her, but I'm suddenly struck by the thought that she'll immediately jump to the conclusion it's because of her. She does that, I'm afraid she'll run. And I sure don't want to give her a head start. Suddenly I need to get to her.

"Might have been electrical," I lie. "I'll be there in a few minutes. Reno's gonna stick around and see what they say."

"Okay. Be careful."

"See you soon, babe."

I disconnect. Reno must have heard what I told her. He pats my shoulder. "I got this prez. Go. You and I both know this might just be a distraction so they can get to her."

I nod. "Call the boys. Pull them all back to the clubhouse." I'm already throwing my leg over my bike and starting it up.

"Will do." He's got his phone in his hand, already making the call.

I race to the clubhouse, blasting through the gate the prospect opens for me. I almost fishtail stopping to shout at him. "They may be looking to hit us here. Nobody gets in without a patch."

He nods, and I roar off to the door. The old warehouse is big with a lot of concrete and loading docks, and thankfully eight-foot chain-link fencing and razor wire on top surround it. Thing about fences though, they're easy to cut through. Fortunately the warehouse itself only has a few access points.

I park my bike and stride inside. First patch I see I order him to secure all the doors with chains and padlocks and put a man on each. No one's getting in my fucking clubhouse. The fact that my enemies are capable of turning to arson doesn't escape my thoughts. They set the place on fire, padlocks may be the worst move I could make. I'm going to have to take the chance that my men can keep the place defended and keep anyone from getting close enough to set a fire.

I find Ashlynn in my room. She's pacing when I throw the door open, but flings her arms around my middle, burying her face in my cut. I cup the back of her head and press a kiss to her temple. "You okay?"

She nods and lifts her face. "You?"

"I'm good."

"Don't lie to me, Rusty. Was it arson?"

I nod. "Looks that way, Hot Rod."

"Do you think it's the Rialto brothers?"

"I don't know. Hoping I can get a shot of who did it when we get access to the security footage."

"Oh God. This is my fault. I brought this down on you, and now look. Your beautiful garage is destroyed."

"Babe, it's not burned to the ground. The store area took the worst. I can rebuild it."

"I should go back to the house."

"Told you, safest place is here."

"No, I can't stay here. I—"

"I can't protect you if you won't fucking listen and do what I tell you."

"I should go. I can't do this to you. I never meant for you to be hurt."

She pushes out of my arms, and it's then I notice her suitcase is zipped up and resting on the bed. What the actual fuck?

"You leavin' me, Ashlynn? Seriously?"

She whirls on me, her eyes glassy with tears, her voice damn near a shout. "It's my fault, Rusty. Can't you see that? I have to go before they do worse, before they destroy your clubhouse."

I grab her arm and yank her to me. "So that's it? Just pick up and leave? Walk out and don't look back? That your M.O?"

The tears spill over, and she shakes her head. "I don't want to leave you, but I have to, don't you see?"

"What I see is a coward."

She pulls her head back like I've slapped her. Then moves toward the bag.

"You touch that suitcase, we're done."

My words stop her. She hesitates, but she doesn't look at me. I step behind her and close my hands over her shoulders, dipping my head alongside hers. I murmur in her ear, "I love you, Ashlynn. Fucking fell hard for you a long time ago. I know I haven't said it. Been keepin' it to myself, but you need to know." I feel her body tremble, and she covers her face with both hands and bursts into sobs. Not exactly the reaction I was expecting, but an honest one at least. She turns and buries her face in my chest, clinging to me. She mumbles something, but between the sobs and her face against my leather, I can't hear her. "What, angel?"

"I love you, too," she whispers between breaths.

I clutch her to me, drawing strength from the feel of her in my arms.

"You can't keep running, baby. I'm not going to let you," I growl. "Trust I'm gonna handle this shit, babe."

"I'm tired, Rusty. So tired of running."

"Then stop. Whatever comes, we'll face it together. You with me?"

She nods, and I take her head in my hands and brush the wetness from her cheeks with my thumbs.

"You're safe with me. I swear it. Gonna spend the rest of my life makin' sure you stay that way."

CHAPTER TWENTY-TWO

Rusty—

I'm standing with my arms folded, watching the company I hired board up the storefront to my shop.

Reno tosses his cigarette and looks over at me. "You get any sleep last night?"

"Not much. Too worried about this shit."

He nods and looks at the sky. "Barely noon and it's already hot as hell."

"Yup."

He lifts his chin toward the garage bay doors. "You think it'll be safe there?"

"Yeah." I don't have to look to know he's referring to my prized motorcycle, the first I ever built. We were allowed in the building for a quick survey with a fireman escorting us. Got damn lucky that the office and that bike I kept there took no damage, although the place is going to reek of smoke for a long time. The security tapes revealed nothing, unfortunately.

"You want me to organize the club to start cleaning the place up?"

I shake my head. "We've got more important shit to do."

"Find these sons-of-bitches?"

"Exactly. Can't waste club manpower on this bullshit."

"Good point."

"I made some calls this morning. Hired a fire damage restoration company to clean up and remove the water and smoke damage. It's gonna cost a small fortune, but it needs to be done right."

"Well, at least we were able to get your bike moved."

"Yeah."

"How's Ashlynn doing?" he asks.

"I got her settled down. She wanted to run last night, but I talked her out of it. She feels guilty as hell about this." I turn to him. "Thanks for bringing Butterfly to be with her today. Means a lot."

"Absolutely. When Kara heard what happened, I couldn't have kept her away. Apparently, some of the other women felt the same way. Hell I even saw Vee pull up before we left."

I nod, distracted. I reach in the pocket of my cut for my smokes and lighter and feel a piece of paper. I pull it out and stare down at it. Warren's business card.

I light my cigarette and think.

Reno squats down, watching the workers.

I blow out a stream of smoke. "Feel like taking a ride?"

"Sure. Where you wanna go?" He stands, his knees cracking.

I hold the card up. I'd already told him about Warren's visit. We'd discussed him at length.

He eyes the card and smiles. "Let's go."

I drop the cigarette, grinding the butt under my boot, and we mount up.

Twenty minutes later we roll onto the lot of the Garden Inn on Hillcrest, park, and find his door.

I knock. "Warren?"

He opens the door about six inches. I'm tall enough to see over his shoulder to the suitcase on the bed. Looks like he's leaving town. "Hey pal, got a second?"

DIRTY DEALS

"I do not actually. I've got a plane to catch."

"I'm sorry, let me rephrase that." I pull my gun and aim it at his forehead. He backs up, and we enter. Reno closes the door behind us.

"Do you know who I work for?" Warren asks, an indignant expression on his face.

"Do you know how much I don't give a shit? But I'm betting it's not Axle Crow." That we're onto him takes him aback, but only for a moment.

"Your real bosses in town?" Reno asks.

His eyes shift between us. "Look, I was just hired to find her. I had no clue they were planning to kill her. I told 'em I'm not sticking around for that. I'm done."

"Oh, you're done, huh? People you know walk away from the mob often, do they?" I ask.

He has the good sense to look worried, which explains the suitcase. "I'm leaving. I want nothing to do with any of this. If you have any sense, you'll be careful of these guys. They're some scary dudes, and if I never lay eyes on them again, it'll be too soon."

I return my gun to my shoulder holster. "You're not going anywhere until you tell me where the fuck they are."

He shoves the last of his clothes in his bag and closes it. "I don't know. They contact me, not the other way around."

"Where are they staying?" Reno asks.

Warren looks over his shoulder at him. "They'd never trust me with that information."

"What are they driving?" I ask.

He shakes his head. "I'm sure it's a rental. They flew in."

"What's it look like?" I grab him by the shirt and yank him to me. I know he's got more information than he's sharing.

"Okay, okay. It was dark out, but I think it was a Lincoln

Navigator, big black SUV. Look that's all I know. If you're smart you'll get Ms. Fox the hell out of town before something happens to her. My advice, she tells the police what she knows, they lose their motivation for wanting her dead. Once her story's out, what's the point?"

"Except they'll want her to testify," Reno corrects him.

"Still, the police are her best bet now."

I let him go with a shove. His legs hit the back of the bed, and he almost falls over. I stand over him. "Bullshit. I'm her best bet. The only one she needs."

"Then I wish you well with that. I heard on the news your shop burned last night. I'd watch your back if I were you. Now, please, I've told you everything I know, and I really do have a plane to catch. I've got a family. I never should have gotten involved with this."

He turns my stomach, but he's of no more use to me. I step back and signal for Reno to let him go. He opens the door, and Warren grabs his bag and dashes out. We move to stand outside the room, watching him run like a scared rabbit.

Reno folds his arms. "Little shit. Why didn't we beat the crap outta him? He led 'em right to your shop and Hot Rod."

"He was just a pawn."

Warren throws his bag in the backseat and jumps behind the wheel. I hear the ignition turn over, and the car explodes in a fireball. Reno and I are thrown back against the motel door and the brick wall. We collapse to the concrete walkway.

I shake my head, but hear nothing but a strange roaring sound like I've got a big conch shell pressed to my ear. The heat of the explosion radiates over me like a blast furnace. I took a wallop to the back of the head.

Reno pushes to an upright position, running a hand over the back of his head. He's talking, but I can't hear a word of it.

I look at what used to be Warren's rental car. It's a smoldering heap with smoke billowing out. I don't think there's enough left of his body to scrape into a dustpan.

Holy hell. I think I mouth the words. If I said them out loud, I can't tell. I kneel in front of Reno and point to him then make the okay sign with my hand, asking if he's all right. He nods, still rubbing the back of his head.

I point at our bikes; thankfully they're still standing and unharmed. I help Reno to his feet. By the time we stagger across the parking lot, my hearing is beginning to return, but sounds are distorted and muffled as if they're coming through a long tunnel. I can hear the car alarms going off from the surrounding vehicles, most of which took heavy damage, some with their windows blown out. I can hear sirens in the distance, and I know we need to get the fuck out of here before we're connected to this bullshit.

Reno taps me on the arm, and I turn to him. I can actually hear his words this time.

"What the fuck did this chick get you and the club into? This is the fucking mob we're talking about, Rusty, whose hobbies are car bombs and dissolving people in acid in case I gotta remind you."

"I know exactly who we're dealing with, Reno, and I'm gonna rain hell down upon them."

He looks back at the devastation. "Guess they terminated his employment. That's a hell of a pink slip."

CHAPTER TWENTY-THREE

Ashlynn—

I'm sitting at the bar, Kara on the stool next to me, a mimosa in my hand. The clubhouse is relatively quiet, the mood somber. Everyone's on edge. Maybe I'm overreacting, but every time someone glances at me, I feel like they're blaming me. And they'd be right.

A woman I saw the first night I came here with Rusty walks over to us. She sticks her hand out. "Hey, I'm Vee. We haven't been properly introduced."

I shake her hand. "Ashlynn. Nice to meet you."

She looks between Kara and I. "You ladies doing okay?"

"Holding down the fort. How about you?" Kara asks.

"Just wanted to be here to do my part."

"And what would that be?" I ask.

She shrugs. "Oh, just whatever the boys need." She looks to Kara. "Rumor around the club is you're pregnant. Congratulations."

"Thanks," Kara says hesitantly. "I didn't know anyone knew."

"You know how these boys are. They gossip worse than women." She giggles, but it sounds forced. "You ladies bored?"

Kara looks around, pulls the stir stick from her Shirley Temple, and chews on it. "Not much to do, unless you're into pool."

Vee laughs. "Come on, I'll show you a part of the warehouse

you've never seen before."

"Where's that?" I frown.

She jerks her head. "This way. Come on."

I look at Kara, and she shrugs. We both climb off our stools and follow Vee down a hall. It's not the one that leads to Rusty's bedroom, nor the one that leads to the kitchen. I've never been in this part of the warehouse. We move through a set of double doors. There's a large cavernous space and even in broad daylight it's dark and gloomy. She leads us through another set of doors and another hallway.

"Where are we going exactly?" I ask, all kinds of silent warnings going off in my head. When Vee doesn't answer, I turn to look over and see her reach her hand to the small of her back, up under her shirt and come out with a gun. I gasp and take a step back. She points it at Kara's belly.

"Don't make a sound."

I raise my hands, placating her. "Please, don't hurt her. We'll do whatever you want."

"Good answer. Now move." Kara turns, and Vee pokes her in the back. "Get going to the end of the hall."

We walk silently. Panic surges through me, but I try to stay calm. A million thoughts fly through my head. Could I wrestle the gun from her hand? Could the two of us overpower her? Could we run? But I know I'll do none of that, because even if I'm willing to risk my own life, there's no way in hell I'll risk Kara and her unborn baby. I'll do whatever this bitch wants—give her anything, my car, money… and then it hits me. Does she know about the cash? Did Rusty tell Reno? Did she perhaps overhear?

"Stop," she orders and motions to a door. "Here."

I push it open. It leads to a set of loading docks. She moves to the doors, but they're all chained shut.

DIRTY DEALS

"Goddamn it," she snaps, holding the gun on us and moving to the overhead doors. The pulley system is chained as well, so she can't roll them up. "Fuck!"

"What are you doing, Vee?" I ask.

"Shut up." She glances around.

My eyes fall to the wavering gun in her hand. Dare I chance it? I look over at Kara and see the terror in her eyes. I reach out my hand and clutch hers, squeezing. "It's going to be all right."

Vee looks back at us and chuckles. "Of course it is, we're just going for a drive."

"A drive? Where?" Kara asks, and I can feel her trembling.

Maybe Vee thinks I've got a big bank account, and she's planning on making me go get her cash. If that's all this is about, I'll promise her all of it. "Vee, I've got money. Lots of it. Is that what you want?"

She stares at me, chewing on her lip as she thinks her way out of this plan of hers that's obviously not working. Then she waves the gun back the way we came. "Move. We're going to walk out the front doors, and you're going to play it cool. You're going to make every patch and prospect you see think we just need some air. Once we're outside, we're getting in my car and driving off the property. Anyone stops us at the gate, you're gonna tell them we're going to meet your guys." She glares at Kara. "You tell them you don't feel well, and Reno's meeting you at the clinic."

I have to give Vee credit; the girl can think on her feet.

Kara nods. "Okay. Whatever you say."

Fifteen minutes later, we're in Vee's car. I'm driving, Kara's in the passenger seat, and Vee's in the back, her gun on us both. I bullshit our way past the prospect at the gate, and we're soon headed down the road.

"Turn right here," Vee orders.

I make the turn and see several banks in the distance. I also see a sign for the interstate up ahead. "Get in the left lane and take the eastbound entrance." I do what she says, but this is completely dashing my 'going to the bank' theory. Now I'm not sure what Vee is really after. I glance over at Kara and meet her scared look. I smile, trying to reassure her.

"Where are we going?" I glance to the rearview, locking eyes with Vee.

"Just drive."

I do what she says for ten tense miles before she spots an exit.

"Get off here."

I swallow. This is my exit—the one that leads to the farmhouse I rented.

"Do it," she snaps.

I put the blinker on and check over my shoulder, moving into the right lane. When I do, I see Vee holding a phone in her other hand, her thumb moving over it like she's texting someone.

I slow the car and take the ramp. I already know she's going to tell me to make a left, and I get in that lane, putting on my blinker.

"Figured out where we're going, did you?" she purrs.

I want to throat-punch this girl. I know I've got about three miles before I come to my gravel driveway. I glance around the car, looking for a weapon, but I see nothing. My mind is whirling, trying to think what she's up to. Best I can figure is she's after the money. Maybe she thinks its stashed at the house, which it is. I stashed it in a pillowcase and shoved it in the dryer in the basement before I left with Rusty.

I pull down the drive and park in the back.

I'm hoping I can give her the money, and she'll take off. We climb from the car, and she motions us up the back steps, the gun still in her hand. The door's unlocked, the broken window boarded up. I lead the way inside, stopping in the kitchen. It's eerie being back.

She motions us on, and I walk into the dining room and stop short. There, sitting at the table, are Nick and Luca Rialto. I suck in a breath and real terror floods my body. Vee is nothing compared to the danger we're in now. God, how could I have been so stupid? I let her walk us right into a trap.

Nick leans forward, lifting a glass from next to the bottle of wine before him. "We meet again, Ms. Fox. You've given us quite the chase." He takes a sip. "You have excellent taste in Italian wines."

I swallow. A million sarcastic remarks on the tip of my tongue, but I've got more than myself to worry about. I step between them and Kara. "Well, you caught me, but Kara isn't involved in any of this. Let her go."

He cocks his head to the side. "Well, that's a pity. Too bad she's seen us."

A chill runs down my spine. I'm frantically coming up with and discarding a hundred different options to get out of this, but I can't find one where we don't end up dead.

My cell phone rings from the back pocket of my jeans, making me jump. I take a slow breath.

Vee pulls it out of my pocket and looks at the screen. "That's Rusty, president of the Devil Kings MC."

I stare at my phone then look at Nick. "If I don't answer, he's going to come find me. And this is one of the first places he'll look."

The brothers glance at each other, then Nick turns to me. "Fine," he stands and pulls a gun. He grabs Kara's hand and yanks her to him, putting the barrel to her head. "Say nothing that makes him suspicious or your friend dies."

She whimpers.

I grab the phone from Vee's hand, glaring at her. I can't believe she's a part of this. How the Rialto's got to her, I can't imagine. I tap the phone and take the call, frantically trying to think of a way to let Rusty know I'm in trouble without letting on to Nick.

***

Rusty—

I pull the phone from my ear, and stare down at it, frowning, thinking about what Hot Rod just said and what it means. *I ran out to buy lottery tickets. I feel like tonight's gonna be my lucky night.* What the fuck? I gave her explicit orders to stay at the clubhouse. And why the hell did she hang up on me? I try her back, but it goes straight to voicemail. Then it dawns on me. Her code phrase for help. The blood drains from my face and my stomach drops. "Fuck, something's wrong. She's in trouble. They've got her."

Reno calls the clubhouse while I pace back and forth at the gas station we've stopped at, a million worst-case scenarios running through my brain.

"They can't find her," he hisses. "Prospect thinks he saw them leave in Vee's car." He disconnects and pulls up an app on his phone.

"What are you doing?" I snap.

"I gave Kara a necklace the other day. After that stunt she pulled I wanted to make sure I knew where she was at all times. It's got a GPS tracker in it."

"Where the fuck you get that?"

"Jammer hooked me up with this place that sells them. They sell a bunch of spy shit." He pulls it up on his phone, and a pulsing circle on a map appears.

"Thank God for you and your possessive paranoia, Reno."

"I'm not paranoid. It's happening isn't it?"

The dot blinks. And I know exactly where they are. "The

farmhouse. Let's go. Call the club; tell them to meet us on the roadside just before the curve in the road. I want to make sure we're not walking into a trap."

CHAPTER TWENTY-FOUR

Ashlynn—

I hang up, and Nick releases Kara.

"Please, ladies. Sit. You must try this wine. It's exquisite."

"She can't have any; she's pregnant," I inform him.

"What a shame."

Vee puts her hand on her hip. "Screw the wine. Look, I did what you want, now where's my money?"

"Greedy bitch. I hate greedy bitches. Especially ones who turn on their own people. Got no loyalty, do you?"

"What are you talking about? This was all your idea. You followed me to that diner, sat in my booth, and made me that deal. Promised me if I brought her to you, you'd pay me a thousand dollars. Now where the fuck is it? I held up my end of the bargain, now I want to get the hell out of here."

"You sold us out for a thousand dollars?" I ask, stunned. "You stupid bitch, I could have given you a hundred times that."

Luca moves behind her and brings the butt of his gun down on her head. Vee drops like a bag of rocks, her body thudding on the wood floor.

Kara sucks in a breath, and I try not to react, although I'm trembling.

"Get rid of her," Nick snaps.

Luca aims the barrel of his gun at her head.

"Not in here, you fool. We don't need blood and brains everywhere. Take her out to the garage." He moves to the living room and grabs a throw pillow, tossing it at him. "Muffle the sound. And find something to wrap the body in. A tarp or something."

We stand quietly with Nick's gun on us as Luca throws her over his shoulder and carries her limp body outside. I want to stop him, but I don't know how.

"You don't have to kill her," I plead, turning to Nick.

"Don't waste your breath. She sold you out, knowing exactly what was going to happen. Bitch like that would betray her own mother. Women like her turn my stomach."

I agree with everything he says, but that doesn't mean I want her dead. A faint *pop, pop*, carries to us, and I jump at the sound. So does Kara. We both know its gunshots.

I glance to Kara. Tears stream down her face. I know she's terrified for her unborn baby. Guilt floods me at the thought that I might be the cause of anything happening to her or her child.

I need to get Nick talking and stall until Rusty can get here. "What did you do with Thomas?"

"Who the fuck is Thomas?" he grunts, motioning us both to sit at the table.

I take a seat, Kara beside me. "The man you killed at the penthouse. Axle Crow's butler."

"Oh, him. Don't worry about him." He lifts the bottle of wine and fills me a glass.

"Tell me. Did you clean up the mess, and what? Haul him down the freight elevator? Did you throw him in the dumpster?"

He pauses, the bottle over his own glass. "Dumpster? Really, my dear, you make us sound like animals… or amateurs. He's where they'll never find him."

"Not a whole lot of places to stash a body in Vegas. Can't

DIRTY DEALS

exactly dig a hole in the hard ground."

"No, but the funny thing about Sin City, there's this vast desert all around it. The buzzards probably disposed of him by now."

"Did you load him in your rental car, then?" Kara asks.

He looks uncomfortable, like she's on to him. "Shut up."

That doesn't stop her. "You know rental companies use GPS trackers. Hell, they can check everywhere you drove. Shouldn't be too hard for the detectives to find out exactly where you dumped him."

"You think you're so smart?"

"Shut up, Kara," I snap, and then give Nick my attention. "Look, I haven't gone to the police, and I don't plan on it. If I had, wouldn't I have done it by now?"

He shrugs. "Sorry, sweetheart. You're a loose end. I don't like loose ends."

"Maybe I could be of other use to you?" I smile at him, running my eyes over his expensive suit. It turns my stomach, but it might buy us some time.

He leans to me and strokes my cheek, then takes my jaw in his hand, lifting my face to his. "I like you, Ashlynn Fox. I liked you the moment you walked into the room that night… in that pretty silver dress. Where is it now? Do you still have it?"

I lick my lips, thinking, stalling, wondering how long it will take Rusty. "It's back at the clubhouse."

"What a shame. I would have liked to see you in it one more time."

"I have another dress. It's hanging in the closet here. Maybe you'd like it even better."

"You think so? What color is it?"

"Gold, like your pinkie ring," I reply. He smiles, and my stomach turns. Oh, God, can I really do this?

"I do like gold. Yeah, I'd like to see it on you. Go put it on."

I stand, and so does he; I turn but he jerks me back by the arm, his face inches from mine. "You try anything, I'll put a bullet in sweet Kara's head. Understand?"

I nod, and glance to her frightened eyes. Her hand splays over her belly, but I don't need the reminder. I'm already sure I'll do whatever I need to protect her. "Yes. I promise."

He releases me with a shove. "Hurry up. I want to see it before Luca comes back, although it should take him a few minutes to stash the body."

I move quickly into the bedroom and open the closet, wishing I'd left my gun here. I remove my jeans, shirt, and bra, then shrug the dress over my head. The last time I wore it, I'd felt so beautiful. Now I just feel cheap and demoralized. I slip on the matching shoes, fluff my hair, and look in the dresser mirror. I steel myself for whatever I'm about to do. I long for the sound of a pack of Harleys thundering up, but I know if they do, they could risk the life of Kara. I hope Rusty is smart enough to know to sneak up. I bend and glance out the bedroom window, but see nothing that looks like rescue is on the way.

I've got to convince Nick that we could be valuable. I just have to figure out a way to do that.

I walk out to find Nick standing near Kara's chair, the muzzle of his gun stroking down her cheek. My stomach drops when I see he's tied her arms to the chair.

The sunlight coming through the window flashes on the gold fabric of my dress, and the reflected rays dance across his face, drawing his eyes to me. I move toward him, swaying my hips and rolling my shoulders in the sexiest strut I can pull off. I smile as his eyes sweep down my body. I stop a few feet away and do a slow spin, lifting my hair up so he gets the full effect of the low back.

He whistles low and slow.

"You like to play poker, Nick?" I purr. "I could be your lucky charm. Wouldn't I look nice on your arm, walking through all the best places? We could go to Monte Carlo. Ever been there? How about the French Riviera? We could have so much fun."

He smiles. "Bet you could be a lot of fun, doll."

I bend forward and make a kissy face. "I could be whatever you want."

He doesn't miss the cleavage I flash him. He shifts his stance, and I'm sure he's getting a hard-on.

I put my hand gently on his chest. "Sit down. Let me dance for you."

He backs up and falls into a chair. But he's still got that gun in his hand. I move to an ancient stereo and flip it on, then dial it to some smooth jazz. The music floods the room, and I roll my hips and undulate my body, trying to remember every dance move I've ever seen a Vegas showgirl make.

I turn my back and look coquettishly over my shoulder at him. He's got the gun in one hand, and the other is adjusting his crotch to ease the pressure on his cock.

Perfect. I smile and wink at him.

CHAPTER TWENTY-FIVE

Rusty—

We leave our bikes on the side of the road and dash through the trees to the edge of the field adjacent to the farmhouse. I squat down, and Reno squats next to me.

I study the house. "There's a car."

Reno pulls a small scope out of his inside pocket and looks.

I frown. "More spy gear?"

"Be glad I'm a good customer."

"You're always prepared, VP. I'll give you that."

"That's Vee's car."

"Prospect said the girls left with her, so they're in there. And I'm betting the Rialto's are, too."

Reno's jaw ticks, and I can tell he wants to dash across that field to his pregnant ol' lady.

"I'm goin' in," he growls.

I feel for him. I know it's got to kill him to restrain. I put a hand on his arm. "We've got to be smart, brother. We've got to surprise them. They see us coming, the girls are dead."

He turns his face to me, and I can see the agony written there. "What if they already are? I can't fucking lose her, Rusty."

"Get that fucking thought out of your head, understand me? You know I'm right."

He gives me one quick nod.

"Let's go. The boys should be pulling up any minute."

We sprint to the road, but it's just our bikes sitting alone, and no Harley engines approaching in the distance.

I run a ragged hand through my hair, pacing again. I'm about to tell Reno we go it alone when they coast over the rise, as quiet as they can be. They're off their bikes and surrounding me in moments. Bandit pulls a sniper rifle from a long holster strapped to his bike, and not for the first time I'm grateful for his Marine Corp sniper skills. He lifts his chin at me and I know he'll do whatever's necessary. I nod at him, and then look around at all my brothers' faces. "Ain't gotta tell you what's hanging in the balance here. VP's about to lose his shit knowin' his ol' lady's in there, and she's pregnant with their first kid." I squat down, pick up a stick, and sketch out the property. "Spotted Vee's car. Not sure what the fuck that means. Maybe she's involved, maybe not. There's a garage here, a field here, the driveway here. On the other side more woods. We'll have to circle around to catch them by surprise."

"What's across the street?" Quick asks.

I glance up at him. "Woods."

"Then let's cut across this side and move in. Be faster than circling that field." He points to my crude drawing.

I nod. "You're right. We get just past the house, cut over and up the tree line on the other side of the house. Then we spread out and surround the place. Got it?"

They all nod. I notice Gypsy staring off.

I stand and Reno leads the men, thrashing off into the woods. I grab Gypsy by the shirt, stopping him. "Brother, I don't know what's the fuck's up with you, but when this is over, I'm gonna fucking find out. Every time I see you, you're distracted. You can't be fucking distracted today."

He nods. "I won't be, prez. I promise."

"Let's go."

***

Ashlynn—

I shake my ass, jiggling it in rhythm to the music, popping it right, then left. I bend over, stroke my legs from toe to hip, and glance back. Nick's got his eyes on my ass. I've got him practically hypnotized.

I dart my glance to Kara. She makes a subtle nod to the window. I cast a sly look outside, while I keep Nick's eyes on me. I see a couple of the guys dart up the driveway on the other side of the bushes. I know from his seated position, Nick can't see them.

I say a prayer of thanks and keep dancing. If they can take out Luca, then I just need to make sure to keep Nick distracted.

I notice him adjust himself again, and I glide toward him. Scooting onto his lap, I shove my chest in his face. His free hand skates up my bare thigh, and my skin crawls. I try to think of anything else, but the only other thing I can think of are the men outside risking their lives for us.

I'm terrified I'll hear gunshots. I know I shouldn't worry for the club; I'm sure the odds are in their favor, but there are two men outside Kara and I love, and in a situation like this, anything can happen. I wonder if this is what Rusty's life is like on a daily basis. If it is, I'll never be able to handle it, worrying every time he walks out the door that he might not come home.

Home. Look at me already picturing the white-picket fence and the whole nine-yards. Amazing. I know my thoughts are rambling. I think it must be a defense mechanism to protect me from what's really happening. Nick's still got that gun in his hand, and it's very close to my head.

I know I'll have to take this as far as necessary, and it's getting to the point of no backing out.

My distractions will only work for so long before Nick gets suspicious.

I wiggle on his lap and slide to the floor between his knees. Maybe if I can get his pants open it'll slow him down if he tries to jump up and shoot.

"Can I help you with this?" I purr, stroking my hands over the bulge in his pants.

He threads the fingers of his free hand into my hair, tightening his fist. "I think you can. Open my belt."

I busy with doing just that, then unfasten his pants and pull them wide. I take him out and circle my palm around his girth. Inside I feel like retching, but I don't let it show on my face. I paste a sexy smile on. "You and I could have a lot of fun, Nick. Take us with you. I'm sure Luca will enjoy Kara. The four of us could tear up Atlantic City. What do you think? I've always wanted a man like you—a real man. One who knows class when he sees it, one who knows how to treat a lady."

He doesn't say anything, so I keep talking.

"A high roller like you, I bet you get all the primo perks. Do you know Ricardo left me a hundred thousand dollar poker chip as a tip?"

His eyes light up at that, like he doesn't fucking know.

"I haven't cashed it yet," I lie. "I put it in a deposit box. We could cash it and have a grand old time." I chuckle. "Wouldn't that be funny? You and me drinking on Ricardo Leona's dime?"

He actually chuckles at that idea. "He was a dick. Do you know he stood my sister up at the altar six months ago? Guess he thought I had no honor. Thought I wouldn't kill him if I ever saw him again.

DIRTY DEALS

That poker game came up, saw my opportunity. Had no clue Axle Crow knew him. His fucking manager is into me for a fifty grand loan. Can you believe it? He don't pay, I'm gonna break his legs, just like in the movies. Won't that be funny?"

Hilarious. I nod. "I hate people like him. So full of themselves."

"Exactly."

"Why don't you put the gun down? You really don't need it anymore, do you? And you're scaring my girl, here. Do you know sometimes we do threesomes?" I only hope Kara doesn't look surprised and give me away for the liar I am.

He eyes Kara, as if considering it, as if he's picturing us both climbing all over his body. Kara, god-love-her gives him a little wink and a sexy smile, then says in a sultry whisper, "I like it rough. Are you the kind of man to give it to me rough, Nick?"

He grins.

The window behind him shatters, and Kara screams. Then everything registers in my brain in slow motion. I'm splattered with blood as he pitches forward; the gun he was holding clatters to the hardwood floor. There's a bullet hole in the back of his head and part of his face is blown off.

I shove him away and shuffle backward as fast as I can. The back door bursts open, and Reno and Rusty dash inside.

Reno rushes to Kara, taking her face in his hands and searching her for wounds. His eyes flare when he sees her restrained. "Butterfly, are you okay?"

His voice sounds distorted to me.

She nods and bursts into tears as he jerks a knife from his belt and slices through the zip ties.

It isn't until Rusty drops to his knees next to me, grabbing my upper arms, and taking in the blood splatter, that my mind rights itself back to reality.

"Are you hurt, Hot Rod?"

I look into his face. His skin is tight, his lips thin, his nose flared, and his eyes wide. I can only shake my head, too choked up to speak.

He grabs me tight in his arms, and I cling to him, breaking down with a sob. I was so terrified he wouldn't get here in time. Over his shoulder I see Reno press an open palm over Kara's belly, his glazed eyes on hers, silently asking the question he's afraid to voice.

She nods, her eyes brimming with tears. "I'm okay, honey."

He grabs her up in a hug, and I can finally breathe again, knowing she's safe. I pull back and meet Rusty's eyes. "Vee?"

He shakes his head, confirming what I already knew. "She's dead. So is the other Rialto brother. He was behind the garage diggin' her grave. Now it's gonna be his." He glances over as Reno leads Kara out of the house, then turns to me and asks, "Prospect said you'd left with Vee?"

"She had a gun on us. I was afraid she might hurt Kara and the baby, so I went along with her."

"Why would she do that? I don't get it."

I lift my chin to Nick's body. "They followed her, made her an offer. She sold us out for the grand they promised her."

"You're shittin' me?"

"Nope." But I don't want to talk about her. I search his eyes, thinking about everything he just did to save us. "I'm glad you figured out my message for help."

He huffs out a laugh, some of the tension leaving his face. "Took me a second, but, yeah. You were smart to do that." He looks down at my dress and frowns. "What's with the outfit?" His eyes move again to Nick, and he realizes the man's dick's hanging out of his pants. "Ashlynn—"

I pluck at the hem. "I was trying to think of any way I could to distract him."

"I see." He's quiet a moment, then asks the question burning in his brain. "He didn't—"

"No," I quickly assure him. "It never went that far. Thank God, you got here in time. I'm not sure how much longer he would have waited before he finished us off."

"Christ, baby. You damn near gave me a heart attack."

"I'm sorry I dragged you into all this."

"Shut up about that. Don't you ever apologize for any of this again. I'm the one who didn't keep you safe. I let you down." He drops his eyes.

I cup his face in my hands and make him look at me. "You didn't let me down. You risked your life for me, the lives of your men. You saved me. How can I ever repay you for everything you've done for me?" I shake my head. "I'll never be able to—"

This time he cuts me off with a kiss. Its urgent and demanding, then turns soft and tender. When he finally pulls back, he brushes the corners of my mouth with his thumbs. "One way you can repay me."

"What's that?"

"Stay with me. Build a life with me. What do you say, Hot Rod?"

I smile. "Just try and get rid of me, handsome."

CHAPTER TWENTY-SIX

Ashlynn—

I'm in Rusty's bed at the clubhouse, cuddled to his side.

I'd tried asking about what he'd done with the bodies at the farmhouse, but he refused to tell me anything more than that it was handled, and I wasn't to think about it ever again.

It's pouring rain outside, and I can hear it on the metal roof. Rusty's awake and staring at that ceiling, the tips of his fingers trailing up and down my spine.

"I'm no saint, Ashlynn," he murmurs quietly.

I lift my head to look at his face, and he turns to meet my gaze. "I don't want a saint."

"I'm serious, babe. I want you to know what you're getting. I've done shit I'm not proud of, I've done *a lot* of shit I'm not proud of, especially back before I took over the club."

"And now?"

"Now, I'm tryin' not to be that man. Used to be I did shit like that, I buried it deep, so deep it'd never see the light of day again. Funny thing, no matter how much booze and drugs you try to bury it under, that shit always finds its way to the surface. Ain't no escaping it. And someday I'll have to answer for it."

"Ask for forgiveness," I suggest.

He smiles. "Ain't that easy, baby."

"If you really mean to live a better life, to be a better man…"

"I want to be that guy for you, because you deserve that guy. But I can't promise you that's who I am or who I'll ever be. But you make me want to try."

"What are you trying to say?"

He looks at the ceiling again. "Guess I'm afraid you won't stick by me if I never become more than I am right now. I'm afraid I'll do something, and you'll up and leave."

"It's a hard promise for me to make, Rusty. Running's become so engrained in me, never staying in one place too long. But for you, I'll try."

"You have a problem, talk to me, we'll work through it. I promise I'll listen. I promise I'll hold you through the tears. I promise if it's in my power, I'll give you anything you want." He pauses and tilts my chin up to meet his eyes. "I can't promise I'll always do the right thing, but I'll never intentionally hurt you. I'll never be callous of your feelings. And I'll never give up on us. That gonna be enough for you?"

"Yes. Except for one thing."

"What's that?"

"You can't have your cake and eat it, too."

"What's that mean?"

"It means no other women. I can't bear to think of you with someone else. I know me, and I know I'd have to pay you back in kind. Then where would we be?"

"Feeling's mutual. The thought of you with another man guts me. So I'm not about to fuck up what we have by hurting you that way."

Rusty rolls on top of me and frames my face with his hands, his thumbs gently brushing along my cheekbones. His eyes move over my face like I'm the most precious thing in the world. He dips his head and softly brushes a kiss to my lips. Pulling back slightly, he searches my eyes and whispers, "I love you, Hot Rod. Not gonna fuck this up."

I smile as I hear those words I've waited to hear, and I watch his eyes crinkle with his responding smile. "I love you, too, Rusty."

He puts a knee between my thighs and spreads my legs, then sinks into me.

I run my hands up his chest and cup his corded neck as I wrap my legs around him, taking him deep. A hiss of pleasure escapes his lips.

"I don't want to ever be apart. I know you're afraid I'll run, but I'm terrified you'll be the one to walk away," I whisper.

"I'm right here, baby. I'm not going anywhere. Promise." He kisses the tip of my nose, then my forehead, and then my mouth as he thrusts slowly, his back arching with his movements.

He makes slow, sweet love to me, worshiping me, letting me know with his body how he feels about me, and I'm happier than I've ever been.

Afterwards, as I cuddle against him again, and as sated as I am, I can't help the niggling feeling that I won't live easy until I take care of one last thing. Rusty must sense my mood.

"What's wrong?" he asks. "You should be relaxed, but your body's still tense."

"I have to go back and tell them where to look for the body. I have to tell my story."

"You sure?" The hand stroking my back doesn't even slow its movement, and somehow that more than anything tells me we're in this together, completely, whatever comes.

"I have to face my fears head on and do the right thing. Will you go with me?" I whisper it because, even with all he's done for me, I'm afraid it's asking too much.

He's quiet a moment, and I listen to his heartbeat, my ear on his chest, then his words rumble up, vibrating beneath my cheek.

"Hot Rod, I think you ran from more than the Rialtos. I think you've been runnin' all your life. Maybe someday, when you believe in me enough, when you trust what we have enough, you'll feel safe like that therapist said you would. As for going back, I think it's up to you. If you've got any hesitation, I don't think it's anything that can't be shared in an anonymous tip.

"But if that's what it takes to show how much you mean to me, I'll gladly go with you and hold your hand and be there to lean on, 'cause that's what men do for the women they love."

And hearing his sweet words, I ugly cry, and he does what he promised; he holds me through the tears.

CHAPTER TWENTY-SEVEN

Ashlynn—

Rusty and I walk out of the Las Vegas airport hand-in-hand, me with my suitcase rolling behind me, him with a backpack over his shoulder. The desert heat blasts us like a furnace, but my face lights up when I see Devon waiting in the limo line, standing next to the big black car.

I drop the suitcase handle and run to him, my arms in the air, squealing with joy.

He catches me in a bear hug before pushing me back and eyeing the big man that joins me.

I look at Rusty, grinning. "Devon, this is Rusty. Rusty, Devon."

I've told each of them about the other, so they smile and shake hands.

Devon loads our bags in the trunk and off we go to the Del Sol.

I reach over and lace my fingers through Rusty's, smiling, happy to be showing him my town, even if it's only for a long weekend.

Devon slides the divider down. "Place hasn't been the same without you, Ashlynn. You sure you don't want to stick around, get your old job back?"

I squeeze Rusty's hand. "No way, Devon. I'm happy where I am."

Rusty brings my hand to his mouth and kisses the back of it.

Devon takes us to the hotel where I have a suite arranged, one of the best, because, hey, I've still got connections.

He drops us at the door and a valet takes my bag away. Rusty refuses to relinquish his. We check in, and John comps our room. I hug him and apologize for what happened and how I had to leave. He's already aware I'm back in town to give my story to the police.

I'm to arrive at three p.m. with my lawyer. Rusty made those arrangements with someone the local Devil Kings chapter uses. We've got an appointment with him in two hours. But right now I just want to relax in our room. Later I have plans to give Rusty a tour of the hotel and the town. Surprisingly he's never been here.

We ride the elevator up and key the door. The suite is modern with floor to ceiling windows and a sweeping view of the strip and the mountains in the distance.

We both move to stand in front of the glass. Rusty steps behind me and puts his hands on my shoulders, then dips to my ear. "Not a bad view, Hot Rod."

I chuckle, and he wraps his arms around me. I lean against him, rubbing my cheek along his beard, loving the feeling of it against my skin.

"When we get this business done tomorrow, want to take a ride?"

"A ride?"

"Made arrangements with the local DK chapter. They're loaning me a bike. Thought we could take a ride, see the sunrise or sunset from somewhere other than the strip."

"Sounds wonderful."

He kisses my temple.

"Now how about a shower before we go meet the club's attorney?"

I shriek as he bends and puts a shoulder to my stomach, hefting me up and carrying me like a sack of potatoes to the bathroom. He stops and sets me down, his gaze moving around the fabulous spa-like room, and he whistles. "This is livin', babe."

I push out of his reach and put my hands on my hips. "Strip for me."

He arcs a brow but complies, his hands moving to his t-shirt, exposing all that gorgeous inked skin. He keeps his eyes locked on mine as his hand moves to his belt. He kicks his boots off and soon he's standing there in all his naked glory.

"You're turn, Hot Rod."

I'm wearing shorts, a halter-top, and wedges. I slip off my shoes, then shimmy out of the shorts, and pull the top over my head. I'm down to just my panties, and his eyes move over my body. I watch his erection spring to life as I slip the scrap of lace down and move to him.

He leans in and turns on the water, adjusting the temperature, then pulls me under the spray. I glide my hands over his wet chest as he pours some of the exquisite smelling bath gel into his palm. He soaps my body, slicking his big hands over every inch of my skin until I'm quivering with need.

I return the favor, soaping his muscular body, and he watches me. We rinse, and he lathers my hair, and then tilts me under the spray. When he's finished, he drops his mouth to my breast, capturing my nipple between his teeth, and I gasp. He toys and sucks, and I thread my fingers through his hair, loving every second. His hand moves between my legs, his fingers stroking until I'm moaning, then he slides two long fingers inside me, and I clutch at him. He works me, finding that spot that has me stuttering.

"Yes, there."

His thumb rotates over my clit, and I'm soon desperate, balancing on that razor-thin edge. He sucks hard on my nipple, and I plummet over the edge, falling as he moves his mouth to my neck and sucks.

I groan deep in my throat when he pulls his fingers free and spins me to the wall. He lines his thick hard cock up with my opening and thrusts deep. I gasp, going up on my toes. His big hands grab my hips and cant my ass back as he plunges inside over and over. Every thrust strokes over that sensitive trigger, and I'm soon panting heavily.

My forearms are pressed to the marble tile, and my breasts are bouncing. He curves his body over mine, his arms anchoring me in place as he increases his speed. My breasts are cupped in his hands, and those fingers of his pinch my nipples, hard. I explode into another orgasm as he rams deep and goes still, coming inside me.

One hand glides down over my wet skin, long fingers finding my clit to massage it as I sink into oblivion, moaning.

He gathers me close, his mouth at my ear, and my head falls on his shoulder.

"So fucking beautiful," he whispers, then dips his head and bites the muscle between my shoulder and neck.

I gasp as another shudder moves through my body, zinging right to my sensitive clit. His fingers rub in another circle.

"You got another orgasm in you?" he asks.

"I...I can't," I stutter out, gasping. "No more..."

"You sure?"

I nod. He scoops me up, dries us off, and then carries me to the bed. He moves down my body, puts his mouth to my pussy, and proves me wrong.

CHAPTER TWENTY-EIGHT

Rusty—

I ride the elevator down and stroll through the hotel. This place has everything you can imagine for people with money to burn. People with more money than sense, no doubt. I pause in front of a display window for a jewelry store.

Sparkling diamonds flash back at me from under the pin lights shining down at them. I try to imagine Hot Rod in one of them. Her fingers are so small and delicate. I press my forehead to the window, feeling completely out of my depth. I don't have a clue which of these, if any, she'd like.

I wander inside and find the engagement rings. It's a big case with a wide selection. This is Vegas after all, the king of destination weddings.

A pretty sales woman approaches with a mega-watt smile. "May I show you something, sir?"

"Thinkin' about that one." I point to a simple round stone.

She pulls it from the case and holds it out to me. "This is a half carat princess cut. It has exquisite color and clarity."

I take it and study it. "How much?"

When she tells me the price I exhale. Even with the twenty grand I made off the custom job I just delivered to the owner of Club Apex, I know that amount will be a stretch for me. Especially with the cleanup and rebuild of the shop that's going to take a huge chunk of change.

Still, my baby deserves a decent ring. This hotel is probably not the best place to find a deal. I pass it to the sales woman. "It's nice. Let me think on it."

"Of course, sir. We're open until seven tonight."

"Thanks." I wander outside the hotel entrance and pause to light up a cigarette. Exhaling a stream of smoke toward the sky, I watch the valets loading and unloading guests.

I think about the meeting Ashlynn had with the police detectives. She was brave as hell, not holding anything back. They grilled her for hours until finally the club's attorney had enough and ended it. When that ordeal was over, she walked out and found two members of Thomas's family waiting. She didn't have to meet with them, but she did. One was the widow, an elderly woman, the other their daughter. It was heartbreaking to watch, even for a guy like me. The widow broke down in sobs when Ashlynn quietly sat next to her in a chair, took her hands, and told her what had happened to her husband. Hopefully, with the information Ashlynn gave the detectives, they're able to recover his body and give him a decent burial. The DK's attorney told me they were tracking down the rental car right now.

As for what happened to the Rialto Brothers, that piece of information she kept quiet about, saying they had disappeared after tracking her to Georgia and attempting to break in to her rental house. Said she'd fled and was able to get away.

They questioned why she hadn't reported it, but so far had been satisfied with the fact she'd been terrified. They tried to get her to stay in Las Vegas for further questioning, but the club's attorney had fought them on that one, assuring them that as Miss Fox had willingly come forward and told her story, she'd be happy to return at a later date if the Rialto Brothers were brought into custody. Until then, she would remain in hiding.

As we left the headquarters, I could tell Ashlynn had a weight lifted off her shoulders and could finally put it to rest. The family had been grateful to her as well.

I take another long drag off my cigarette, enjoying the cooler evening air outside the Del Sol. My gaze moves to the right, and I notice Devon parked a distance down, wiping a cloth over a shiny black limo. I stroll over. "Hey, man."

He turns. "Good evening, sir." His eyes slide past me. "You and Ashlynn need a car to go somewhere?"

I shake my head. "Not tonight. Just came out to have a smoke. We might need a ride tomorrow, though. You available?"

"Of course, sir. Just let me know what time. Are you enjoying your stay, sir?"

"Devon, enough with the sir shit; call me Rusty. And yeah, it's a gorgeous suite they gave us."

He nods. "It's a nice hotel. One of the best on the strip."

I take another drag off my cigarette. "You wouldn't happen to know a place I can buy a diamond ring, do you? One more reasonable than that joint in there." I hike my thumb over my shoulder.

He gives me a big grin. "You proposing to Miss Ashlynn?"

I just give him a wink.

He jerks his chin at the limo. "Climb in. I know a place that'll give you a good deal."

An hour later I'm back with a ring bigger than the last one and at less than half the price. I guess you could say Devon hooked me up.

I slide him a hundred dollar bill for his trouble and make arrangements for the car tomorrow.

When I get back to the suite, I find Ashlynn showered and dressed for dinner. I'd just as soon order room service, but I know she's excited to show me the hotel, and as gorgeous as she looks tonight, I kind of want to show her off.

She's sitting on the bed, slipping on those sexy heels that match the gold dress she wore the other night. I know what she has on underneath, and no matter how great dinner is, it's going to be torture waiting to get her back up here so I can undress her.

I stroll toward her and cup her face with one hand. She smiles, and I swear that smile is more beautiful than any glitzy gown or jewelry she could put on.

I stroke her cheek with my thumb, cock a brow, and tease, "Sure you want to go downstairs?"

She kisses my palm. "You're not getting out of this that easy, mister. Get dressed."

Again my eyes sweep over her. "You know I've only got jeans with me."

She gives me a mischievous look. "I had something sent up from one of the shops." She lifts her chin toward the bathroom, and I swivel to see a dark suit hanging on the door. It's a little out of my comfort zone, but if it makes her happy to see me dressed up this once, I can give her that.

My eyes return to her. "Give me ten minutes to shower."

"Hurry up, cowboy. We have reservations."

"Don't suppose you want to slip off that dress and scrub my back."

"Nope. You're on your own."

I shower and dress, somehow not surprised she got the fit of this monkey suit perfect. I look in the mirror as I adjust the cuffs under the jacket. It's a quality garment, and I wonder its cost. I study myself. The man in the mirror is unrecognizable. It's like a glimpse into an alternate universe where I took a different path in life. It's like seeing myself if I'd become a different man altogether.

I look good in the suit, I won't deny that, but I'm not that guy in the mirror. I exhale deeply, suddenly worried that perhaps Ashlynn won't be satisfied or content with the man I am, that she'll want to change me as easily as she's redressing me. Perhaps she'll want me to become someone different, someone more like the man in the reflection. I'll never be that guy, and it suddenly makes me nervous about the ring I bought and the question I plan to ask her.

While I let the hot water sluice over my body in the shower, I thought about her in that dress and me putting on this suit. Thought about going down to dinner with her on my arm and that maybe tonight would be the better time to give her that ring.

But now I know it's not—not when I'm dressed up like an imitation of someone else. When I ask her that question, I want to stand before her in my clothes, next to a motorcycle, out in the desert, watching the sunrise. Because that's the real man she's getting and that's the kind of life she'd be accepting.

I walk out of the bathroom. She looks up and does a double take; her eyes slowly drift over me.

"Wow," she whispers.

I shove a hand in my pocket. "Enjoy it, 'cause it's the only time I'm giving this to you."

She moves toward me and slips her arms around my waist, staring up into my face. "I appreciate the effort. And so will every woman who lays eyes on you."

"Will that bother you?"

"Nope. Because I'm the one who gets to come back here with you tonight."

"Hopefully sooner rather than later." I cup her face and press my lips to hers. Once, twice, three soft kisses. "You ready?"

She tucks her hand through my arm. "We're going to have a wonderful night."

This won't be my idea of fun, but my baby's happy, and that's all that matters. I smile down at her, and agree, "That we are, Hot Rod."

CHAPTER TWENTY-NINE

Ashlynn—

"Babe, wake up."

I crack an eye open to see Rusty standing at my side of the bed. He bends and flicks the bedside lamp on. I squint and blink. He's fully dressed in his jeans, boots, and a thermal shirt along with his cut over it. I hadn't realized he'd brought it. He must have had it in his pack.

I look toward the windows. It's still dark outside. "What time is it?"

"Four-thirty."

"In the morning?" I lift to an elbow. "Is something wrong?"

"Nope. Just want to take you somewhere."

"Now?" He's lost his damn mind.

"Yep. Go throw on jeans and a shirt. We're goin' ridin'."

"Riding? On what?"

"I made arrangements. Now hurry up. We got some people to meet."

"I haven't even had any coffee," I whine.

"Thought you told me you were turning into a morning person. All that fresh air, yadda, yadda."

"Four-thirty a.m. is not morning. The sun hasn't even come up yet."

"That's what I'm trying to beat here, so move it, woman."

With that, he rips the covers back.

I huff out a breath and stand. "Fine, but you better have a coffee for me by the time I finish putting on my makeup."

"No time for makeup. Just braid your hair and let's go. You've got five minutes."

"Five…? Have you lost your mind? For real?"

"Four minutes and forty-five seconds. You want to stand here and keep arguing with me?"

I give him my best eye-roll and stalk to the door, slamming it shut.

My gaze immediately falls on the stack of clothes on the vanity. He picked my outfit already. "What the?" I cock a brow. It's not a bad outfit. I like the shirt he picked, and it'll look cute with the jeans. When he told me to pack at least one pair of jeans I humored him, but I never thought I'd actually wear them.

He taps on the door. "Three minutes, Hot Rod."

I stick my tongue out at the door and scramble into the clothes, determined to prove I can meet his damn deadline. I walk out, wrapping the hair tie around the end of my braid just as he counts down from ten.

I glare at him. "I'm only being nice about this because you were so accommodating last night."

He grins. "I was accommodating several times last night, and you enjoyed every minute of it."

Damn this man, I can't hold back the smile at the reminder of the fabulous sex we had. "Fine. I did. But I was talking about you dressing up for me for dinner."

He wraps an arm around my waist and pulls me tight against his body. "Got no problem givin' you the things that make you happy when it's in my power. Just don't expect me to be a different man than the one you're looking at, Ashlynn."

Suddenly the vibe in the room has shifted. It'd been light and teasing, and now his words hold a deeper meaning than what I'd been expecting.

The words are gone from my throat, and all I can do is stare up into those penetrating eyes of his and nod.

His gaze roams my freshly washed face. "Like you better without all the makeup. You're beautiful just like this."

I melt inside. "Babe."

He grabs my hand. "Come on."

We ride the elevator downstairs, and I have to double-step through the lobby to keep up with Rusty's longer stride. He pulls me out the front doors, and there stands Devon next to his limo, smiling big. He opens the back door like he would for any guest.

"Miss Fox. Good morning."

"Do you know where he's taking me?" I ask him.

He runs his hand over his lips like he's closing a zipper.

I climb inside the big car, and Rusty passes Devon a slip of paper. I suppose it's the address, but who knows?

We pull away from the hotel and out onto the boulevard. Devon drives us for about fifteen minutes, finally stopping in an older section of town. He pulls to the curb in front of a two-story building. The sky is just beginning to lighten enough for me to see.

I crane my neck to check the place out. The front yard is a concrete parking area that's gated in a way the surrounding houses are not. The way he talked I thought maybe we were renting motorcycles from a dealership. This is no dealership obviously.

Devon looks in the rearview mirror. "This the place?"

Rusty glances out the window at the two motorcycles and an older black Chevy El Camino parked beyond the gate. "This is it," he confirms. "Thanks, man."

We climb out, and Rusty makes a call as Devon drives off.

The front door opens, and a man in a Devil Kings cut comes out and unchains the gate. He and Rusty shake hands. "Hey, Rusty, I'm Fish," the man says.

"This is Hot Rod," Rusty says, by way of introducing me.

The man nods at me. "Nice to meet you, Hot Rod." He jerks his head at both of us. "Come on. Got a soft tail for you to use."

We walk over to one of the parked bikes with two skullcap helmets sitting on it.

"Thanks, Fish. I appreciate you takin' the trouble. Means a lot."

"No problem, brother." He jerks his thumb over his shoulder. "I'm the only one here besides the prospect who rode the bike over for me. But if you want to come inside…"

"Naw," Rusty says. "Kind of on a time limit here."

Fish digs the keys out of his pocket and tosses them to Rusty. "Have fun."

Rusty snags them out of the air with a fist and passes me one of the helmets. I strap it on while he does the same, and we both climb on the bike.

We pull out on the road, and Rusty drives us west toward Red Rock Canyon. At a point he pulls to the side of the road, and we hike up a low hill just as the sunrise is splashing the sky in vibrant pinks and orange and gold.

The creosote bushes growing nearby give off the lovely scent of a fresh rain along with the citrusy smell of verbena.

I breathe it in deeply and listen to the quiet chirping of some distant desert bird. "It's beautiful." I turn to Rusty. "How did you know about this place?" I'm the local, yet I feel like he's showing me a part I've never taken the time to see or absorb.

"I asked Devon if he knew a good place to see the sunrise. He told me to head out 159 toward Red Rock Canyon. We ain't there yet, but this looked like a good place to take it in, and I didn't want to miss this light." He nods toward the beautiful show of colors painting the sky.

"Want to talk to you about something, babe." He takes both my hands in his and turns me to face him. My heart speeds up at the serious look in his eyes. I have no idea what he's about to say, but a shiver down my spine and a prickling of my skin tells me it's going to be life-altering.

The corner of his mouth pulls up, and I swear that little smile is enough to make my stomach flip with excitement. "When I met you, I knew I'd met my match. It was only a matter of time until we arrived at this moment. How it turns out is all in your hands."

Oh God. I swallow and take in a slow breath.

"Babe, you deserve the best, probably a better man than me—someone who will back you up without limits, let you grow without boundaries, and love you without end. I want to be that man if you'll let me.

"Before you decide if you want to take me on, I guess I better warn you. Our life's gonna be full of challenges, no doubt about it. Bein' president of an MC, I'm gonna have my hands full with all kinds of trials and tribulations. I'm not gonna sugar coat it. But, I know I can meet them if I've got you by my side."

My eyes sting with unshed tears. He looks down and huffs out a laugh, then squeezes my hand.

"Last thing I want to do is scare you off, but I want to lay it out for you, so you know what you're gettin' yourself into, girl. Not sayin' it'll all be bad; there'll be plenty of good times. I'll see to it."

I nod, my mind in a daze. This is happening. He's proposing to me.

"Ashlynn, I can't promise you every day will be sunshine and roses, but I can promise you that no one will work harder to make you happy or cherish you more than I will. I know my life is complicated and messy and won't be easy on you, but I also know I will never be complete without you beside me to share it."

My tears spill over, and he cups my cheek in one palm, brushing one drop away.

"When I think about you, I know that no one else will ever hold my heart the way you do. I guess what I'm saying is, I'm hoping the story of our love is only beginning."

He drops down on one knee. "I love you, Ashlynn, in a way I know I'll never love another soul on this earth." He digs in his pocket and holds out a beautiful emerald cut diamond. "So, what do you say, Hot Rod? You and me, together forever?"

At that moment the sun peeks over the horizon, sending its beams to us. I cover my face with both hands, staring down at the ring sparkling in that light. My eyes lift to his, and I take him in. This man, down on a knee, telling me I'm his everything. I try to suck it all in and store it up, wanting to remember every detail of this moment. I can't hold in the bubble of happy laughter that bursts from me as I nod frantically like a bobble head. "Yes, yes to all of that."

He takes my hand and slips the ring on, then bends and kisses my fingers.

I drop to my knees so we're on equal ground and throw my arms around him. "I love you, Rusty, with all my heart."

We kiss, and it's sweet and meaningful, and I know I'll never regret my answer. Finally, we climb to our feet, and he wraps his arm around me as we watch the sun rise. In this moment I feel like my life is truly starting, and I can't think of a better way than this, out in nature, away from everyone, just the two of us.

Eventually, he turns and looks down at me. "Come on, I need to get my girl some coffee."

I grin. "My man knows me so well already."

He turns his back, and I hop up on, and he carries me down the trail, laughing. I hug his neck tight and press my cheek to his, happier than I've ever been in my life.

EPILOGUE

Rusty—

"No, I think we should put it there." I point to a spot on the plans spread out on the table in the clubhouse.

Ashlynn leans close, her attention on the blueprint. She points to another spot. "What about this wall? We could make the cased opening larger."

Her ring sparkles on her finger, along with the wedding band next to it. She was insistent that we get a license and get married before we left Vegas, so that's what we did. A small intimate wedding with just the two of us suited me fine, and I even wore the suit for her. She looked amazing in the sleek backless dress she bought, and I couldn't have been more speechless when I saw her in it. The memory of it makes me smile.

I turn my head and look at her now. She's completely thrown herself into this partnership with gusto, always listening to my ideas, and never hesitating to toss her own out as well.

The rebuild of the motorcycle shop has been a labor of love for both of us. I've been impressed as hell with her ideas. I knew she was intelligent, but her quick grasp of the flow and organization of the shop has really been a wonderful surprise. I had my doubts about how easy it would be for her to take on the MC, I'll admit, but she's blown them all out of the water with her enthusiasm to blend into my world, making it her own, as well.

Reno approaches and taps me on the shoulder. I straighten and meet that gaze of his I know so well. The one he gives when shit's about to hit the fan.

"What is it?" I snap.

"You know how Gypsy's been so fuckin' distracted all the time and you wanted the guys to keep an eye on him?"

"Yeah, and…?"

"You ain't gonna believe where he's been goin'… and who been goin' with him."

To find out just what Gypsy's up to….
Preorder DIRTY DESIRES: A Devil Kings MC Story.

If you enjoyed DIRTY DEALS…please post a review here.

DIRTY DESIRES: A Devil Kings MC Story.

The final book in the trilogy will be available in September 30, 2020.

ALSO BY NICOLE JAMES

DEVIL KINGS MC:

Dirty Deeds
Dirty Deals
Dirty Desires

SLY: Kings of Carnage MC

EVIL DEAD MC:

Outlaw
Crash
Shades
Wolf
Ghost
Red Dog
Blood
Undertaker
Joker
Hammer

BROTHERS INK TATTOO:

Jameson
Maxwell
Liam
Rory

RUBY FALLS

Coming December 1st:

CLUB PRINCESS: Royal Bastards MC Durango, Colorado

ABOUT THE AUTHOR

Nicole James is a Wall Street Journal and USA Today bestselling author of passionate, dangerous, addicting romance where the badass hero will do anything for the woman he loves…

The Evil Dead MC Series, The Devil Kings MC Series, The Kings of Carnage MC Series and The Brothers Ink Tattoo Series.

She makes her home in Alabama.

Sign up for Nicole's newsletter: **http://eepurl.com/biN_p5**
Like Nicole James on Facebook:
https://www.facebook.com/Nicole-James-533220360061689
Join Nicole James' Clubhouse reader group:
https://www.facebook.com/groups/763490467147322/
Follow Nicole James on Instagram and Twitter:
https://www.instagram.com/authornicolejames
https://twitter.com/@Nicole_James1
Visit Nicole's website for her current books.
https://www.nicolejames.net

Made in United States
Troutdale, OR
09/12/2024